Mamluk

PAUL BRANDIS

DEDICATION

To Bette, always and forever.

MAMLUK

ACKNOWLEDGMENTS

Many thanks to Johnny Shumate for his brilliant cover, and to Billie
Mazzei for her fine editing

CONTENTS

MAMLUK

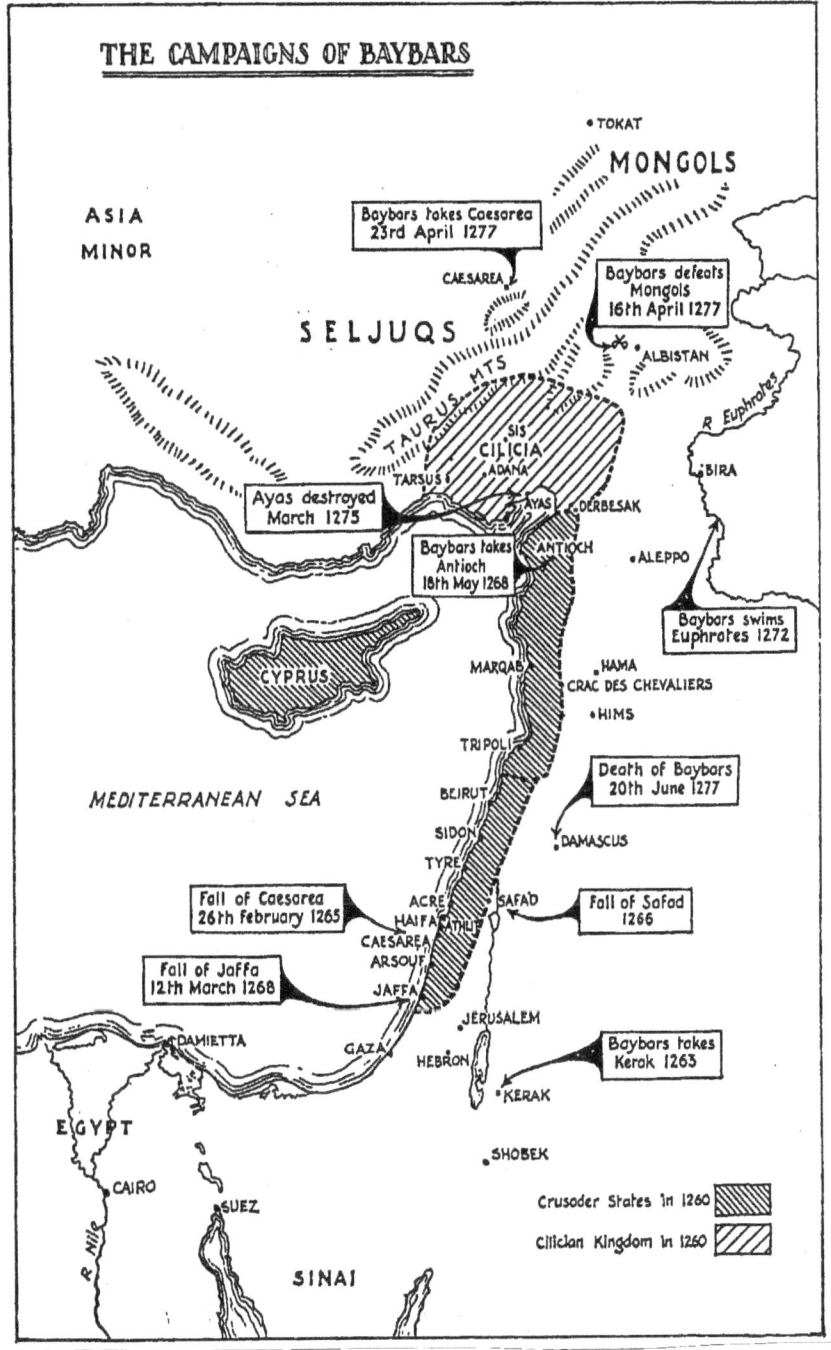

THE CAMPAIGNS OF BAYBARS

• TOKAT

MONGOLS

ASIA
MINOR

Baybars takes Caesarea
23rd April 1277

CAESAREA

Baybars defeats
Mongols
16th April 1277

SELJUQS

ALBISTAN

R. Euphrates

TAURUS MTS

SIS
CILICIA
TARSUS • ADANA

• BIRA

Ayas destroyed
March 1275

AYAS • DERBESAK

ANTIOCH

• ALEPPO

Baybars takes
Antioch
18th May 1268

Baybars swims
Euphrates 1272

CYPRUS

MARQAB

• HAMA
CRAC DES CHEVALIERS

• HIMS

TRIPOLI

MEDITERRANEAN SEA

BEIRUT

Death of Baybars
20th June 1277

SIDON

TYRE

• DAMASCUS

Fall of Caesarea
26th February 1265

ACRE
HAIFA ATHLIT
CAESAREA
ARSOUF

SAFAD

Fall of Safad
1266

Fall of Jaffa
12th March 1268

JAFFA

• JERUSALEM

Baybars takes
Kerak 1263

• DAMIETTA

GAZA

HEBRON
• KERAK

EGYPT

• SHOBEK

CAIRO

Crusader States in 1260

• SUEZ

Cilician Kingdom in 1260

R. NILE

SINAI

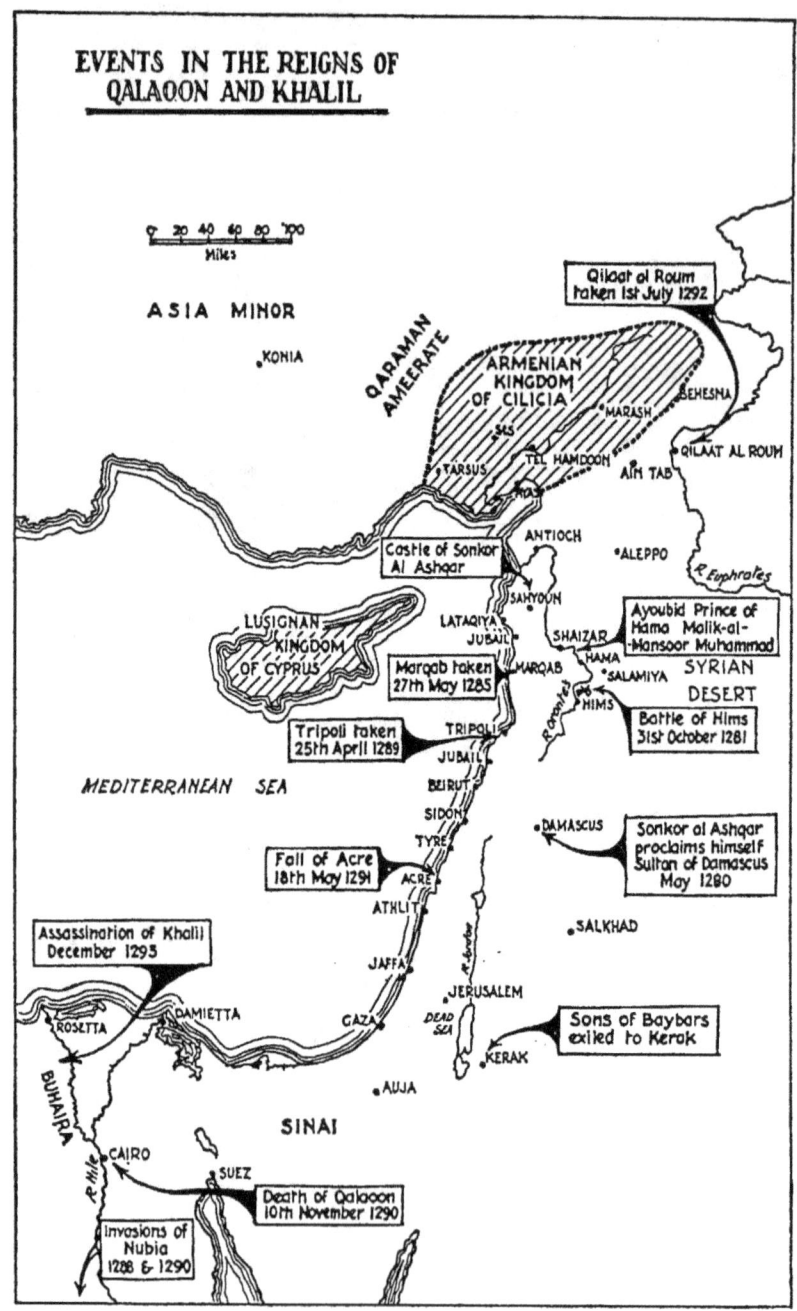

EVENTS IN THE REIGNS OF
QALAOON AND KHALIL

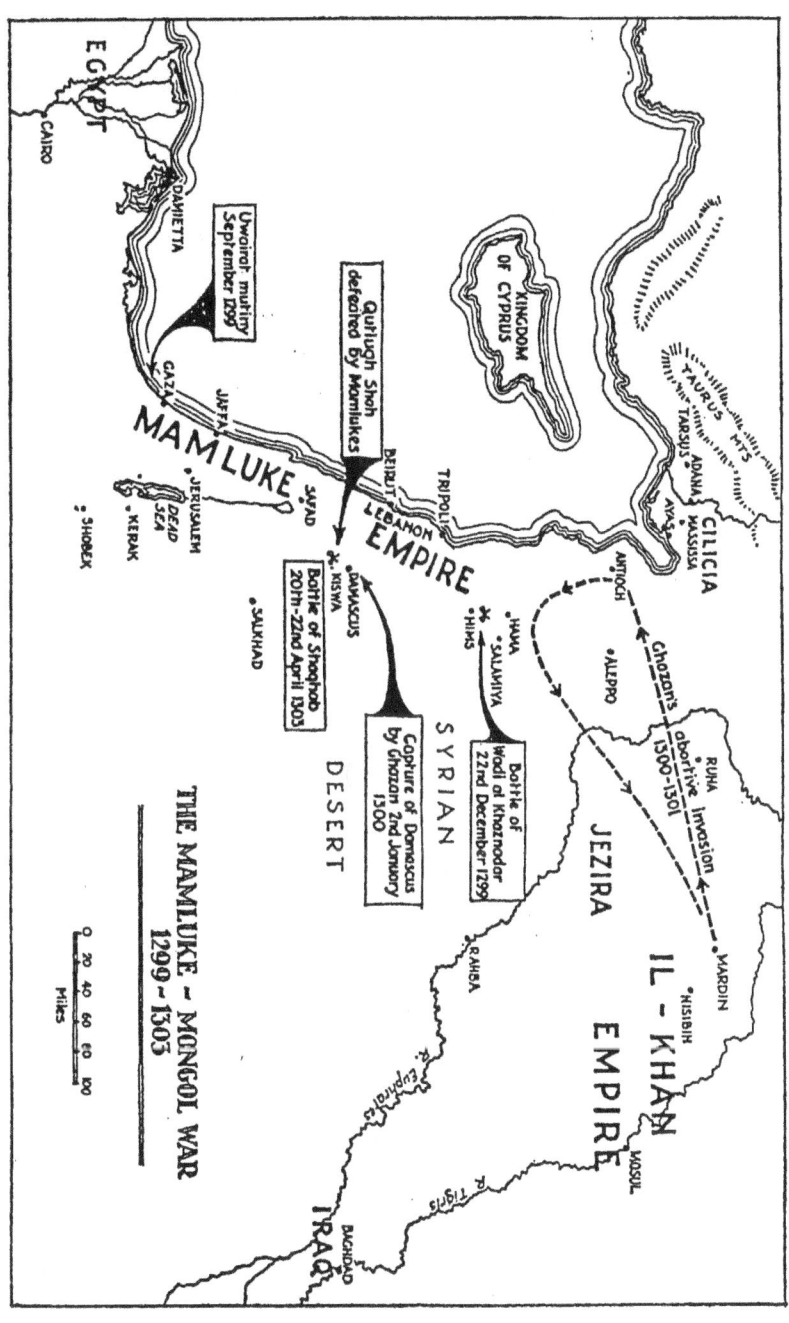

THE MAMLUKE ~ MONGOL WAR
1299 ~ 1303

MAMLUK

Preface:

The primary coin used in the book is the dinar of Baybars I, who, as the story opens, reigns as sultan. It contained approximately 4.27 grams of gold. The Baybars I dirhem, a lesser coin, contained approximately 2.97 grams of silver

The Crusaders paid their troops and workers with bezants, a coin made in imitation of the dinar. But with 3.3 to 3.7 grams of gold, it had less value. A gram is about a third, (0.035) of an ounce. At the writing of this book, gold was trading at approximately $1,250.00 an ounce, silver at approximately $16.00 an ounce. The vast expense of defense can be seen when one reads it took 1,100,000 bezants to construct just one of their many castles, the castle at Safad, plus 40,000 bezants a year to stock it and pay its seventeen hundred men.

When an Arabic word is introduced in the book for the first time, a brief phrase of definition is usually included. This definition is not intruded again, so a brief glossary has been provided:

MAMLUK

Glossary:

Al-Qalah: The Fortress (Cairo's Citadel).

Qalat al-Jabal: The Fortress on a Mountain, i.e., the Citadel of Cairo.

Jabal Esh Sharki: Mountains of Syria.

Amir Ashara: An amir in charge of 10 to 20 mamluk cavalrymen.

Amir Muqaddam: An amir in charge of 100 mamluk cavalrymen.

Amir Tablkhana: "Amir of Drums." An amir in charge of 40 to 80 mamluk cavalrymen.

Aulad al-nas: "Sons of the people." Sons of mamluks.

Bowwab: A gate keeper.

Dhalul: A racing camel.

Fellah, fellahin (pl.): A farmer.

Ghawazy: A dancing girl.

Gubba: An Arab robe.

Halaqa: Cavalry of non-mamluks, mostly aulad al-nas.

Iwan: A pavillon.

Jamaqiya: Combat pay.

Jird: An Arabian cape.

Jundiya: Common foot soldiers.

Kaba: Coat

Khafakiya: An Arab head scarf.

Khasakiya: "Specials" of the sultan, members of his bodyguard, cupbearers, armor bearers, masters of the robe, etc.

Khushdashiya: Comrades, barrack-mates.

Kindjal: A Georgian knife.

Malana: Lord, master, patron.

Malik: King.

Mantelet: A portable barricade to shield besiegers.

Meshrebiyeh: Carved, wooden windows.
Nafaqa: Pre-battle pay.
Odalisque: A slave girl.
Qa'at: An audience chamber.
Qadi. An Islamic holy man.
Qalautah. The small cap inside the turban.
Sarrajun: A mounted battle-servant.
Saulaq: A money bag.
Tawashiya: Eunuch servants.

A chronology of sultans who ruled during the life of Diyar al-Mijiri al-Baybariyya

1260-1277	Baybars Bunduqdari
1277-1279	Al-Said Baraka
1279	Al-Aadil Salamish
1279-1290	Al-Mansoor Qalaoon
1290-1293	Al-Ashraf Khalil
1293-1294	Al-Nasir Muhammad (First Reign)
1294-1296	Al-Aadil Kitbugha
1296-1298	Al-Mansoor Lajeen
1298-1308	Al-Nasir Muhammad (Second Reign)
1308-1309	Baybars al-Jashnekeer
1309-1341	Al-Nasir Muhammad (Third Reign)

MAMLUK

CHAPTER 1

Diyar crouched in a cluster of bushes as the Mongol scout rode slowly through the trees. The scout's keen eyes darted from side to side, searching for the slightest movement. His stench alone induced terror, and Diyar, age ten, struggled to keep his small bow and nocked arrow from shaking.

At the edge of the wood rose a knoll where, moments before, his slave party had fled. Now he watched with pounding heart as the scout found Diyar's lame mare nosing the ground for grass. The Mongol observed her lathered neck, and turned back to the woods, his thin, black eyes penetrating each shrub, his wide nose, thick with hair, sniffing the air for prey.

The Mongol's horse moved closer, and Diyar knew he had to act or die. He gulped a shaky breath, leaped to his feet, and let fly an arrow.

The scout grabbed for his sword but Diyar's arrow bit deep into his arm. With a scream that rattled the trees, the Mongol whipped out the sword, and his horse sprang forward.

Fighting panic, Diyar nocked another arrow, drew and shot. The arrow dug into the warrior's mail chest but merely made him grunt, and his down-swooping sword grazed Diyar's skull, knocking him into the bush. Dazed, his arms clutched by branches, he fought to tug free.

The Mongol wheeled around, then paused to tear the arrow from his chest. This gave Diyar a moment to gain his feet and place his last arrow.

The Mongol saw the boy standing once again, and cried out in rage. His horse charged, but Diyar stood steady. As the warrior bore down on him, he shot, and the arrow split the man's neck.

The man's sword dropped, and he rolled off the bounding horse. Without weight in the saddle, the horse slowed, then walked back to its fallen master. It whickered and nuzzled the corpse.

Diyar stepped over and grabbed its reins and tied them to a sapling. He held his bleeding head and, fighting to overcome his terror, knelt to examine the body.

The man's helmet had rolled off revealing a shaved skull but for two long, greasy plaits behind his ears and a thick forelock where lice burrowed. He wore a rusty chain-mail hauberk that reached to his thighs over a greasy, knee-length robe and trousers. A few strands of horse's hair fluttered from the tip of his pointed helmet.

Several times in Diyar's lifetime, Mongol raiders had plundered his yurt village, carrying off his older brothers for herdsmen, and his sister and other girls for maidservants. And though he had seen great mounds of their victims' skulls bleached white from the sun and snow, this was the closest he had ever come to one of the hated conquerors who ruled his land.

Grease and soot stained the man's leathery face, and a wispy mustache hung from the corners of his small, pursed mouth.

The Mongol's eyes blinked open, staring blindly. He gurgled and blood spat from his lips. He groped for the arrow protruding from his throat.

Terror seized Diyar. He whipped out his *kindjal*, fourteen inches of deadly steel, grabbed the arrow in one hand and slashed the man's throat. Then he fell back, watching the man's face sag into death.

Warily he approached again. He jabbed the man's arm. No reaction.

Then, like a sudden summer storm, rage erupted in the lad, a rage blinding all thought. His face twisted and he kicked the corps's skull, once, then again and again.

Finally gaining some control of his anger, he paused. He lifted the warrior's bow from its holster and tested its pull. Diyar was tall for his age, and found he could, with difficulty, draw it to his chin, so he loosed and tugged off the man's weapon belt. On the right side hung the bow's holster. On the left, the quiver and sword scabbard.

A anxious thought struck him.

Are there more Mongols?

He glanced around.

Must catch up with Yanaul before I am discovered.

He drew the horse up and leaped into the saddle. He urged it up the knoll, tightening the weapon belt to his narrow waist.

Yanaul, the Bolgarian slave trader, reined up at the top of a grassy hill. Soon, Diyar and the other youths pulled up next to him. Though the summer day was warm, Diyar wore a short-sleeved, sheep-skin vest over his kaftan. A pointed, black sheep-skin hat topped his golden hair, and a grimy scarf kept sweat out of his head wound.

The plain below ran to the edge of a river. Yanaul pointed to a wide expanse of rubble near the river. "It was once a great city." Sadness tainted his voice. "My home. Thousands lived there. Then came the Mongols. Now there is nothing but rocks and weeds." He turned to the boys. "You will spend all your lives living in fear of the godless ones."

Something moved on the far side of the valley. A lone rider moved onto the plain, then paused looking around. Horse-hair streamers wafted from the peak of his helmet, and braids trailed behind his ears.

With urgent dread, Yanaul forced his horse off the skyline, and though the rider was far distant, whispered fearfully, "There is one of them. Quick. We must go."

Diyar, reckless after his first kill, snorted. "But he is only one and we are many."

"Fool," hissed the Bolgarian, "that second bow on his saddle would cut you down before you got within hailing distance." He glanced back. "Quick, he has seen us. They have eyes like hawks. Now we must stretch the horses. Perhaps he will not give chase," and he urged his mount down the backside of the hill, the dozen youths galloping after. But after cresting several knolls, they found the Mongol warrior apparently had not followed.

These rolling grasslands that spread across the Rivers Don, Volga and Ural, were once the pasture lands of the Kipchaks, tall and proud Turks. Now, from the Baltic to the Pacific, from north of Moscow to the Arabian Sea, all suffered under the yoke of Mongol tyranny.

Had Diyar remained with his people, his fate would be the same as most young men of the steppes: absorption into the armies of the great Baraka Khan, Mongol Prince of the Golden Horde. It would have been a life of sporadic pay and early death.

Wherever the slaver, Yanaul, encountered a cluster of Kipchak yurts, he would pause and speak to the clan's chief. He painted pictures of golden streets and warming sun, of battles of glory and plunder, of fame and fortunes that could be made in the army of Baybars, the Grand Sultan of Egypt and Syria.

The lads, facing a bleak life on the snow-streaked steppes, went gladly. The amazing thing was, the tales the trader wove were true. Baybars himself had been a mamluk, a former slave from the steppes, a Kipchak, member of the Barali tribe.

The fame of this great ruler had spread far beyond the shores of the eastern Mediterranean. His dash, his powers of military organization, his daring and strength and ruthlessness, were the stones with which legend is built.

Baybars knew life on the steppes made a youth hard and resilient, eager for war and adventure as long as it could be found from the back of a racing horse. So the sultan sent his traders to scour the steppes for youths to buy, to train, and finally to free, for with discipline, Kipchaks were the best mounted warriors in the world.

Why not me? Diyar had dreamed, listening to his father and Yanaul as they sat cross-legged on the carpets in his parents' yurt. And the next morning, Diyar rode away with the Bolgarian.

But at the crest of a low hill at the edge of the village he turned to look back at his parents, his father, a tall, hard figure in a black, sheep-skin coat and cap, and his mother, fair of hair and skin. For the first time he was struck by uncertainty.

How familiar it all looked, the group of yurts, the cluster of the friends and kin he had known all his life who had gathered to see him off.

If I leave, will I ever see them again?

Tears smarted his eyes.

Yanaul, watchful for such indecision, cantered back to him. "Come, lad." He clapped him a sharp slap to the shoulder. "The world awaits," and he rode on.

Shaken from his sadness, Diyar followed.

Days later, the party approached a bustling trading settlement, and Yanaul announced, "Korsun." They passed through the remains of charred, wooden walls.

"The traders here did not know how to deal with the Mongols, to offer them the most fabulous gifts that could be found and thereby buy their lives. They boarded up the town and prayed. The Mongols swept the walls aside like parchment, and the traders had to run to their boats and sail home, back to Genoa or Venice or Constantinople. Later the Mongols allowed them to come back. They like the trinkets the merchants bring, but the Venetians and Genoese are so jealous of each other the Mongols wisely keep them in separate parts of town."

To Diyar, familiar only with brief visits to tiny fishing villages, the muddy frontier town was a great city. But once inside, he found its glowering, log houses hulking over the stinking streets unsettling.

And so many people! So many different *kinds* of people. There were Kipchaks like himself, tall, slim, light-skinned with weathered eyes from the steppe's winds, rarely off their horses; there were European traders, pasty-faced and soft, wearing shapeless clothes and fur collars, picking their way through the debris, followed by thugs for bodyguards; there were Mongols, lean and swarthy with little bearding, drunk and arrogant.

There were Greeks from Trapezunt, Seljuks from Rum. There were Armenians, Circassians, Bolgarians. He even saw a tiny, yellow-faced man in an embroidered-silk robe perched in a litter carried by four bearers of the same skin. Unlike the Mongols who were quite tall and hard as wolf sinew, this haughty, little man sat stiffly upright, immobile as an altar statue. Diyar glanced questioningly at Yanaul.

"Catayans," the trader noted, "from far to the east past the great mountains."

Diyar knew of no such place, nor of any great mountains, but he was a Kipchak Turk and too proud to admit ignorance.

The train of boy-slaves followed Yanaul through the town to a large, walled estate at the edge of the sea. The estate's plastered walls gleamed white in the sun. Red tiles topped the roofs. Heavy wooden doors opened at Yanaul's call, and the troop rode into a flag-stone courtyard.

Turcomen warriors paced the narrow battlement atop the wall, and lancers stood guard at the gate.

A thought came to Diyar. "As a slave, I must be valuable property," and he filed the thought away for possible use.

Several older women appeared and directed the boys to a long room that opened onto the court and served as the boys' dormitory. Each boy's space was indicated by several pegs in the wall, and a rolled up quilt on the floor. The women ordered the boys to undress and don the robes hanging from one of the pegs.

After pulling on his robe, Diyar tried to carry his kindjal with him. But a woman, taller than he and weighing twice as much, grabbed it and hung it on a peg.

At the doorway to a large, tiled bathing room, the boys hesitated superstitiously. Inside women waited with buckets of hot water. What strange rite was this?

Ordered to doff their robes, they did so reluctantly, and stood shivering, cupping their genitals. But the women shoved the boys into the room and attacked them with rags dipped into pots of brown, oily cream—soap from Marseilles, another new feature for Diyar—and hot water, all the while checking with keen eyes for parasites.

When the boys returned to their bedrolls, they found their weapons gone and their clothes replaced by cotton trousers and blouses, wool coats and caps.

Without his kindjal, Diyar felt naked and vulnerable. But he would not show it. He set his jaw, put his back to the wall, crossed his arms, and waited. Yanaul had disappeared, but when Diyar saw him next, he would demand his blade back.

Evening, and women crossed the court carrying jugs of soup, hot and thick with lamb and barley, and ladled them into bowls. Hungrily, the boys dug in with wooden spoons. Again, Diyar missed his blade to cut the lamb chunks, but Yanaul had yet to appear. Then Diyar saw the slaver framed at an upper-story window of the building at the end of the court.

He set his bowl aside and trotted down the courtyard to a flight of stairs. But before he could start up, a big Turcoman guard stepped in front of him. In Frankish breast plate and conical helmet, the lancer looked as wide as a Yurt's entrance.

"Where do you think you are going, whelp?" he growled in a dialect barely understandable.

Automatically Diyar's hand dropped to where his kindjal should have been. "I must speak to the Bolgarian."

"Oh, you must, hey?" the warrior said with a dirty laugh. "I think not. I think you will speak to him when he wants to speak to you. Now get back over there with the rest of the little girls." His hand flicked, and the butt of the lance cut Diyar's legs out from under him, sending him sprawling to the ground.

Diyar picked himself up, jeering laughter from the boys in dormitory burning his ears. He ignored the widening red stain on the knee of his new trousers and, struggling not to limp, stalked stone-faced back to his bedroll.

Now more than ever he was determined to retrieve his knife. It had been a gift. His father had traded a healthy, young mare, heavy with foal, to a Georgian merchant for it, and nothing was going to keep Diyar from getting it back. He had to talk to Yanaul.

He sat on his bedroll, and as night darkened the court, his

anger and self-pity subsided and a plan formed in his mind. The boys' slop buckets sat in a small chamber at the far end of the dormitory. After a woman came out and lit a few candles on holders along the wall, Diyar waited until all the boys were asleep, then tiptoed to the chamber. He squatted over one of the pots, while observing the court from the chamber's doorway.

The guard at the base of the steps had disappeared inside the doorway, and seeing no other movement, Diyar stole out to the corner of the court. There stood a great, wooden, rain barrel. Climbing onto it, and using the sill of a small window, he pulled up onto the roof. Praying the tiles would hold, he crept to the ridge and peeped over.

A guard, not twenty feet away, stood on the wall's walkway, peering out into the black space that was the sea.

Diyar ducked down and, holding onto the ridge line, made his way along the roof until it ended below the window where he had seen Yanaul. He glanced back, but the guard was lost in the darkness. Above him protruded the ledge of the window. Light from the room fell onto a narrow balcony.

Should he leap for it? If he missed he could easily slip down the roof and fall to the stone court yard below. But he had to try. He had to get his knife back.

He squatted, then leaped and grasped the edge of the balcony. Pulling himself up, he stepped over the balustrade and peered inside.

Yanaul and another man lay in the middle of the room propped up on great pillows. The other man, his back to the window, faced Yanaul over a low table where little statues waited on a board of black and white squares. Yanaul had changed to light, cream-colored trousers and blouse in the summer style of the Bolgary.

The other man wore a robe in shimmering blue of such beauty Diyar had never seen. Near the man's side, like a pet, lay a sword whose scabbard gleamed with incised lines of silver and gold. Two great red stones, one in the center of the scabbard, the other in the sword's pommel, glowed deep and dark.

Suddenly struck by doubt, Diyar hesitated. Perhaps he should have listened to the guard at the stairs and waited.

The guard at the stairs! Remembering the blow and the humiliating laughter, rage blazed in the boy's young heart once again, and he stepped boldly into the light of the room.

Yanaul's eyes flicked up and saw him, and something in them made the youth freeze. Yanaul said nothing, but, as Diyar paused, the other man's hand slid to his sword.

CHAPTER 2

Yanaul also saw the man's hand move, and he quickly stood. "Diyar, what are you doing creeping around this time of night? You are fortunate the guards of Rukn al-din Mijir did not see you or your head would be squinting from a pike-pole." Now the seated man turned slowly and with dark, hard eyes appraised the lad. "Come here, boy," he said. His voice was soft, almost a whisper, but it commanded obedience.

Diyar frowned. Who was this man to order him? He glanced at Yanaul, his owner.

A look of urgency sprang into the Bolgarian's eyes, and he gave a swift jerk of his head telling the boy to move and move fast.

His was an elegant face. Diyar, used to men with thick beards, and skin chapped from the icy, steppe winds, had never seen such a face, smooth, handsome, a finely-trimmed mustache and beard gracing his lip and chin.

Mijir continued. "God has been good to instruct the great Baybars al-Bunduqdari, Malik-al-Dhahir, the Sultan of Egypt and Syria, to appoint me as his sole eyes to find young men like you to become *mawali* in his service, and the only reason I do not kill you now for violating the sanctity of my harem, is because Yanaul has mentioned you might be of some value if, and only if, you learn to rein in your insolence." He nodded at the statuettes on the bi-colored board. "Now, do you know this game?"

Though curious, Diyar shrugged indifferently. "We had little time for games in my clan."

The slave-master suppressed a smile. "I know. I was born in a yurt too. So, attend. You must learn this game. Besides personal beauty, which you just might have—if you live—the mastery of this game is prized among the sultan's warriors. Now sit down and be quiet."

Diyar dropped onto a cushion nearby and, with growing fascination, watched the two men play. At first Mijir described with a word or two the way the pieces moved, but soon the two men sank into silence. Diyar found such deliberation tedious. Why did they not just charge each other? A good scrap would soon reveal who was the better man.

Finally, when Mijiri's horse pounced on Yanaul's woman, the Bolgarian smiled ruefully and toppled his tall man.

"You are still too good for me, master, but someday..." He glanced at Diyar. "Well," he said testily, "did you learn anything?"

He frowned, trying to assimilate. "Yes. I learned this is a very slow game."

Mijir smiled. "Your first lesson is patience." He clapped his hands softly and immediately a boy appeared at the doorway. "And now, it is time for you to find your bedroll." He raised his hand, "But before you go, know this. You have entered uninvited into my harem. If you ever do so again, you will die instantly by my hand. You live now only because these rules have yet to be explained to you."

He turned to the servant boy who, though smaller and darker than Diyar, was about the same age. "Show this slave to his bedroll, then fetch me the captain-of-the-guard."

The boy bowed and waited next to the doorway.

Diyar stood, and started around the table, but Yanaul halted him. "Have you forgotten yourself?" he said sharply.

Diyar turned. "What?"

"Thank your good master for sparing your life, for never has a lad sought to lose it more diligently."

Diyar's face went blank. "Thank you, master," he intoned.

"And now, thank him for generously taking his time to instruct you in the game of chess."

"Thank you, master," he repeated.

"And bow when you speak, you ungrateful whelp," the Bolgarian shouted. It was the first time Diyar had ever heard the man use an angry word.

Shaken, he bowed. "Sorry, master."

Mijir nodded benignly. "Goodnight, boy, and may God give you peace."

"Repeat it," ordered Yanaul.

"Goodnight, master, and may God give you peace." Then he turned and followed the servant out the door.

The servant wore a long, striped cotton shirt to his ankles, and a simple red, felt cap. They entered another room lit only by several candles on a tall stand in the corner. As they approached the far doorway, a girl carrying a water jug on her shoulder slipped in. A thin, gown hung over her slim body.

Diyar halted as if turned to stone.

The girl stood slightly taller than he, and her golden hair was held back from her soft, white face by conch combs. The candles, as she crossed in front of them, silhouetted her seductive, lithe body.

The boy had never seen anything so beautiful.

Her eyes dropped but as she passed they flicked up at him and…. Did speculation hover there? Diyar could only be certain they were blue, blue and deep as wells. He stared as she padded into the darkness.

The servant boy's nudge brought him back to reality. "Come, we must hurry. You should not be here."

"But who is she?"

"Just one of the master's slaves."

"Her name?" They trotted down the stairs.

"Uh, I do not remember. Thalia, I think. She is to be sold."

They entered the darkened court and the guard dozing at the doorway awakened with a snort and straightened up.

Diyar glanced at him with contempt. *Lazy ass,* he thought. *If he served me, I would have him whipped.*

Diyar dropped onto his bedroll and, as he wrapped the rough, wool blanket around him, the shimmering face of the girl—Thalia—drifted into his thoughts.

He became sleepy and automatically reached for his belt and the security of his kindjal. He sat up annoyed. He had forgotten to ask about getting it back.

With a yawn, he dropped back to the mat. *Maybe it was just as well,* he thought sleepily. *Tomorrow.*

The next morning, after the boys ate a meal of barley mush and mare's milk, with a generous dollop of honey, Mijir and Yanaul appeared in the court before them.

Yanaul gestured to the boys to come out. The boys scuffed forward, and Yanaul pushed them into a semblance of a line, then said, "Now, bow to your enlightened and generous master, Rukn al-Din Mijir al-Din."

The boys looked at each other, than stiffly bobbed, and he continued, "Now listen, for he has important words for you, words that could save your life."

Now Mijir had their complete attention. In the morning sun, he stood resplendent in a green silk, Tatar-styled waist-jacket heavily embroidered in gold. His crimson pantaloons were tucked into soft yellow boots. His sword hung from a belt with a silver-and-gold buckle. A bow in a tooled, leather case, and a matching leather quiver, hung on his hip.

Diyar stretched out his chest. Mijir was a master of whom to be proud, and he, Diyar, could serve him with honor.

The slave-master's eyes ran along the line of youths, then moved away languidly. He spoke in their dialect. "There are rules—many rules—you must learn and follow, or come to a painful end. And the first rule is, never enter your master's harem without invitation. The word 'harem' itself means 'forbidden', and to break the law of the harem is to die."

His arm swept over the buildings along the end of the court. "Those are my quarters. There are the steps to them. You climb those steps without being bidden, you die."

He turned and nodded to a guard standing in the doorway of the gate house. The guard entered the house, returning at the head of a guard detail of four. They led out a man, manacled and shackled, who squinted in the sunlight.

Diyar recognized the bound man as the guard who had knocked him to the ground the day before.

The guards led the shuffling man to the far end of the court, and a sense of dread grew in Diyar's stomach. The other boys, feeling the same, shuffled nervously.

Mijir continued. "There may come a time when it will be your tasks to guard your master and his family. You must learn to do so with your life."

The guards tied the man to a pillar at the end of the court. A cord encircling the pillar, bound his head fast.

"And," Mijir said, "you will learn to keep your eyes open so nothing or no one will be able to attack or harm your master or his family. If you do not keep your eyes open..." The bow leapt to his hand and, faster than they could see, an arrow, and then another, whirred down the court, and embedded in the man's eyes.

The boys' gasps mingled with the dying man's last breath. Pinned by the arrows to the column, the corpse remained upright.

Mijir al-Din's bow slipped back into its holster.

Diyar's admiration for his master soared. It had been a gory lesson, but, he was sure, a needed one. And what shooting! All Kipchaks knew how to use the horn-and-wood bow, but he had never seen such accuracy. Two arrows in flight almost as one? Wonderful! And the dog of a guard had gotten what he deserved.

Mijir was talking. "The law of the harem is inviolable. But one of you here thought he could break that law."

Diyar froze.

"Even though he had not been warned, still, he must be punished." Mijir looked away from the boys, and said quietly, "Will he come forward?"

Diyar hesitated for but a moment. Then, with his face a mask to hide his terror, he took one step.

Mijir nodded to the guards, and they grasped him by the shirtsleeves and hurried him down the court. They approached the body hanging from the column, and the horror of the visage grew. Blood drained from the shredded eyeballs and stained the man's coarse, woolen jacket. Diyar looked away and steeled himself for his own death.

But instead of turning him around to be shot, the guards shoved him into the corpse—the stench of death already permeating the body—and tied his hands around the pillar.

Then, to his soaring shame, his pants were yanked down around his ankles.

Mijir walked by heading for the harem. "Ten should be enough"

A great whack across Diyar's bottom stung him to the bone. It was followed by another and then another. The pain seem to double at each blow. Tears coursed down his face, blood down his legs.

Finally they cut his bindings and left him tottering. He stepped back. Blood from the body of the guard stained his cotton blouse. He fought the pain, bent and pulled up his pants. The soft cotton fabric chafing his buttocks felt like molten iron. He turned struggling not to fall and, avoiding all eyes, walked stiff-legged back to the line of boys. Some watched with fear, others with a look of hidden glee at another's pain.

He fought to keep his head up, his lips from quivering. But inside his chest roiled with shame. He was the son of a chief. No one had ever struck him before.

Only one thought dimly glowed in his mind.

I must...

He glanced at the main gate.

If I could steal a horse... He had to escape, to get back to the comfort of his yurt, his gentle, loving mother, his father who taught by example, never raising his voice.

Yanaul confronted the boys. "Learn from what you have seen today. Now collect your belongings. We leave for the ship."

The boys turned away, But Diyar forced out his voice. "Yanaul."

The Bolgarian turned with irritation. "What now?"

Through gritted teeth Diyar spat out, "My kindjal...I want my knife back. Did you steal it?"

Yanaul frowned in disbelief. "Steal?" he growled. "Watch your tongue, boy, or I will use your precious blade to cut it out. The master has it." His eyes softened. "Now think, do you truly believe we could allow one of our boys to carry such a killer? But do well, and you may get it back one day."

CHAPTER 3

The boys folded their bedrolls and boarded two heavy, wooden wagons. They rumbled out the compound's gate and onto a rutted road and Diyar cast about seeking escape. But a squad of horsemen trotted close behind, and he saw he would not reach the edge of the road before they swooped down on him, and wanted no more of the whip.

The procession soon reached Korsun's quay-side where an open, double-ended freighter of about twenty paces, one of many loading in the busy port, wallowed in the briny water. Its portly captain, an Armenian from Trapezunt, directed his crew in the boat's loading. They were Greek, and like the captain, Nestorian Christians. One, staggering under a great, wrapped parcel, shoved past.

Yanaul wrinkled his nose. "Ignorant infidels. See how they wear their crosses around their necks. They think if they are captured by Frankish pirates, the crosses might save them. But they are wrong. If we are captured, nothing will save any of us."

Diyar had seen people in the villages wearing crosses, though they were like the ones atop their tiny churches, with two horizontal arms, the shorter, upper one at a slant. But his father had no such belief, knowing each place, each rock, tree or hill, had its own god, its own power.

Already aboard the ship were boxes and bundles wrapped in thick, black hides; Naphtha from Tiflis; copper from Bardaa; and carpets, leather goods and boots from Ersinjam. Amidships, a half-dozen tawny-yellow mules from Derbend were tethered. Their dung added to the odorous mix of cargo.

Suddenly Diyar's interest perked up. Two girls led by a stout matron and followed by two eunuch guards, made their way up the gangplank, and Diyar recognized the honey-haired Thalia.

The Armenian captain sent the women forward to a tiny tent erected for their privacy. Throwing up the flap of the tent, the girls pulled in some of the mules' hay and spread out their bedrolls.

Diyar nodded towards the girl and tried to sound indifferent. "Who is she?"

The Bolgarian viewed the girl with the sharp eye of a slaver. "She is a Greek from Circassia. The amirs prefer to marry only women of their own tribes," his grin held lechery, "but, praise to God, they *do* love Greek girls." He frowned. "She is a little tall to gain the most gold, but she is now twelve years, the best age to get the best price."

Greek, the boy thought in wonderment. *My mother is Greek.*

A poke in the ribs brought him back to reality. "Put all ideas of her out of your head. She is slated for the sultan's harem. You try to enter *there,* boy, and you will not get off as lightly as you did today."

Last aboard stepped Mijir and several of his men, resplendent in silk and steel. Soon the ship pushed away from the quay, its lateen sail bellied out, and the captain took up his position in the stern near the helmsman.

Diyar looked past the receding port and village to the forest and fields rising above it, and was struck by a pain of hopelessness. He might sneak away from the compound, but there would be no escape from the boat. With every gust of air, he was being blown further away from all he loved. The humiliation of the beating, the searing pain burning his flayed backside, only increased his sense of loss. He swiped a tear from his cheek, and glanced along the boat's rail. Several other boys stared with bleak eyes at the diminishing strip of land. Knowing he was not alone in his anguish, gave him little comfort.

The ship ran before a south-east wind and soon picked up a current that grew stronger the closer they approached the Bosporus.

"It is good," grunted the captain to Mijir al-Din. "This wind and current happens only a few times a year, but it means all sailing will be down through the passage, with nothing sailing up." His grin revealed more gaps than teeth.

"Less chance of pirates."

Mijir al-Din and the boys lay wrapped in their bedrolls as the broad-beamed freighter bounced through the choppy sea. Diyar, after his first attack, fought off sickness by keeping his head up in the cold, clear breeze. And, from his vantage point near the ship's rail, he watched as the beautiful Greek girl, her head and face hooded by a white, wool scarf, bent retching over the ship's rail.

A strange feeling rose in his chest. *Perhaps, perhaps if I could talk to her I could help her, maybe make her feel better.*

He shook himself savagely. *Put it out of your mind. You have more important things to worry about: this new life, becoming a great warrior, winning battles, fame, fortune. This is your destiny.*

Still, something whispered in his mind: *What would her hair feel like? Her skin?*

At the docks of Constantinople the mules were off-loaded, and the boys stared in awe at the city-state's mountainous walls. Then the ship headed south through the Dardanelles, the Ionean archipelago, the Dodecanese, and into the deep blue of the Mediterranean. Now they were in Frankish waters.

The Christians—Frankish Crusaders, Pisans, Genoese, Venetians—controlled the sea from their home ports in the West to their captured lands in the Outrémere, "The Land Beyond the Sea." These territories the Crusaders had wrenched from the Moslems and defended with such savagery—Edessa, Antioch, Tripoli, Jerusalem—had never been able to sustain themselves. They depended on their home ports for supplies. Any ship falling into their clutches became trade goods. Mijir did not tell the boys, but if a sail appeared on the horizon, they might well end up in the brothels of Marseille or Rome, Venice or Pisa.

Now, though the year was still young, the air turned hot. The sun glinted across the skinned sea, scorching the ship. Diyar had never felt such heat, and along with the rest of the boys, sought refuge under the tarp shading Mijir.

From one of his trunks, Mijir broke out a small chess set, and he and Yanaul played silently, the sweat dripping off their down-turned heads onto the worn boards of the ship.

When the boys pressed their master about their new life, Mijir replied, "Your life will be what you make it," then he continued.

"The sultan becomes not only your master, but your father. If you live through your training and the sultan is good enough to free you, you will no longer be a mamluk, a slave. You will become a mawla, a warrior-servant. If you have proven yourself worthy, you will carry the sultan's name. Often the foremost mawla in an amir's house will succeed his master as head of the family. After all, he is often more worthy than a son, because of his training and loyalty."

He raised a finger in warning. "But in return, the mawla will fight to the death in loyalty to his master. I will tell you a story," and the lads settled back.

"Once a member of the Abbasid family, one of the oldest ruling families of the land, said to the Caliph al-Madhi: 'O Commander of the Faithful! We are a family whose hearts are imbued with the love of our mawali and with the desire to prefer them over all others.'

"The al-Madhi answered: 'The mawali deserve such treatment. When I sit in public audience, I may call a mawla and raise him and seat him by my side. As soon, however, as the audience is over, I may order him to groom my riding animal and he will be content with this and not take offense. But if I demand the same thing from a son, he will say: "I am your son and above such things," and I shall not be able to move him from his obstinate stand.'

"So you see," Mijir concluded, "what high esteem is placed on mawali."

One of the boys spoke up. "But what are the people like in this new land?"

"There are men like us, men from the steppes. We rule. There are Egyptians, many work for us. Christians and Jews, they make good clerks. Some Mongols, good warriors." A hint of disdain touched his handsome features. "Then there are the fellahin, Egyptian farmers. They live only to serve us." He saw their incomprehension. "It is like this, our beloved sultan owns all the land. This he divides up into fiefs. The yield of these fiefs is paid to the amirs, and they pay their mawali. Fellahin tend the fiefs. You as warriors will have little to do with them."

The days rolled on, then Diyar's keen eyes picked up something new on the horizon. Off the bow's point there appeared a thin spire peeping above the water. Curious, he crept back to Mijir. "Forgive me, master, is that a ship coming our way?"

It took the amir a time, but then he smiled. "Ah, at last, al-Manarah."

The Arabic word sounded strange to the boy. "Al-what, sire?"

Mijir's smile had a touch of relief in it as he looked down at him. "You will soon see. It is God's welcome," and he pointed out the spire to the captain who ordered the steersman to head for it.

The torpid day crept on, but the point seemed hardly to near. Then, like the tip of a gigantic candle, an immense tower rose out of the sea. But still no land could be seen. Finally the sun, hanging low in the sky behind them, illuminated a thin band along the horizon on both sides of the spire: Land!

They approached the scepter-like curve of Alexandria's harbor, and the full magnificence of the tower rose above them.

"Al-Manarah shows the ships the way to the harbor," Mijir explained. "It has been standing here since the days of the Greeks. It is said that in olden times a fire was kept burning in its peak night and day, providing a beacon of light by night, a plume of smoke by day. Hence the name, al-Manarah, the place of fire."

The huge tower stood on an island at the mouth of the harbor. Its base was a great marble building containing many offices. The tower rose over four hundred feet above the building in three tiers, first a square tier, then an octagonal, and finally a cylinder. The top two tiers narrowed slightly as they rose, their grace capped by a precious domed mosque peaked by a golden crescent of Islam. The huge monolith was covered by gleaming white marble, beautifully carved, now burned rose by the dying sun.

What a miracle! thought Diyar. *What wonder of the world could surpass this?*

Into the night, freight was exchanged at quay-side, and the next morning, the ship, along with many others, departed harbor and nosed into the broad, reed-lined waters of the Mahmudiyeh Canal which would take them to Cairo.

Diyar never imagined so many boats existed. Like a flock of butterflies, the white, cotton sails covered the canal.

Now, as they neared the end of their voyage, Mijir called the boys around him for the last time.

"You should all consider how you want to be called. You are starting a new life—you can take any name you like. But it must be in the tongue of our homeland. Only a mawla can have a Turkish name. It is one more way of staying separate from the people we rule. They speak Arabic, have Arabic names. We speak Turkic. Any mawla who takes an Arab name divorces himself from his brother warriors.

"Not even the son of a mawla can have a name from our homeland. The sons of mawali, or the Aulad al nas, must take Arabic names. Nor is anyone but we allowed to speak our language, or dress the way we do, or even ride a horse. Only we are allowed these things.

"Many mawali take Bugha, or Bull, as a name. You can add to it; Taybugha, Colt-Bull; or Altunbugha, Gold-Bull; or Kimishbugha, Silver-Bull; Timurbugha, Iron-Bull. After this name comes your father's name. It does not need to be his actual name. Pick one that describes him. Next will come the name of your jallaban, your slave-master. I will allow you to use my name if you do so honorably. Then your name could be, for example, 'Timurbugha Arslan Mijiri'. And if and when you become the sultan's mawla, he may allow you to use his name too. Then you would be known as 'Timurbugha Arslan Mijiri Baybariya'. Once you have proved yourself, you may take a title. Each one of you will be a Royal Mamluk, al-mamalik as-sultaniya. Most of the sultan's mawali take the title of 'Rukn al-Din'. Therefore, my full name is, al-Amir Rukn al-Din Mijiri Altunbugha al-Yargushi. Choose your name well. If you do not live up to it, your fellow warriors will know of it."

Thoughtfully, the boys crept away to consider.

Diyar's name had been given to him by his father, and he decided to keep it. And it seemed disrespectful to change his father's name. Still Taydumur, Colt-iron, sounded good. "Rukn al-Din Diyar Taydumur al-Mijiri al-Baybariya": a heavy weight to carry for a boy who, only a few weeks past, had little more concern than keeping his father's herd from straying.

And then one morning: wonder of wonders, the most wonderful of wonders.

One of the boys turned, and peering up the river, spied a sight that made his jaw drop. He pulled the sleeve of his fellow, and soon all the boys stared transfixed.

One of them asked Mijir, "But, master, how could they carve mountains so fine?"

Glancing at the great triangles rising above the palms, he smiled. "They were built of great blocks of stones, more stones than grains of sand in a wagon load. An ancient people even older than the Greeks built them as tombs for their kings. Someday, if you work hard, maybe you will be allowed to ride over and see them. They are farther away than you think."

Diyar, who loved to climb, whose greatest joy, next to racing a spirited horse, had been to inch his way up the sheer palisades near his settlement, now itched to explore the monuments' strange, wonderful symmetry. How long, he wondered, before the cadets would be permitted to venture out and see this golden land?

Then the city: Cairo

"Um iddunya," murmured Mijir fervently.

"What, master?"

"The 'Mother of the World,' my home."

It never occurred to Diyar his master had more than one home. How wealthy could he be?

And soon, topping a mountain beyond the city, a great fortress.

"Qal'at al-Jabal," Mijir said. "'The Fortress on the Mountain', or just 'al-Qal'ah,' 'the Fortress'. The great Salah al-Din had it built to protect the city from the Franks. He used 50,000 of the infidel Christian prisoners to construct the walls and towers, and to dig the moat. The Franks called him 'Saladin,' and it the 'Citadel'."

Diyar stared at the massive walls and towers rising above the mountain's sheer cliffs and, for the first time, felt the impact, the wonderment, his decision to leave his windy steppes and seek his fortune in this hot, dry land might mean.

CHAPTER 4

The freighter sailed past the city and tied up at a long quay full of boats and freighters. Small, brown men, their tattered clothes barely covering them, bent under heavy loads as they padded up and down narrow gangplanks. Along the quay clustered old warehouses of mud and plaster, with tall, narrow houses crowding in behind.

Flies blackened the air, crawling on every surface. Futilely Diyar slapped them away from his face. Soon two amirs and ten warriors, all on sleek Arabian mares, clattered down the quay, scattering the stevedores and caddies. Like Mijir, the horsemen wore red satin Kaba al-Tartariyyah, coats of Mongol origin with the flap cross the chest from left to right. Red kalautah caps wound with immaculately white, silk scarves topped their heads, and their bloused trousers were tucked into knee-length, yellow khuff boots. The red silk sashes around their waists were covered by decorated belts of gold and silver. Straight swords and holstered bows hung from their belts. Heavy, padded embroidery on the warriors' left trouser legs protected their thighs from the rubbing of their swords. Their polished silver scabbards, inlaid with gold, sparkled in the sun.

Bursting into the drab surroundings, the men's brilliant plumage and glistening horses created a dazzling spectacle.

Yanaul herded his slaves onto the quay—the girls to one side—and the amir in charge of the escort inspected them all carefully.

The other amir remained in the saddle. His dark-eyes sparkled as he flirted with the girls. They, in turn, drew their shawls about them and turned away, but with smiles.

The mounted amir had a thin mustache that curled at the end and, like the other amir, instead of a turban, wore a sharbush, a stiff cap trimmed with fur, rising to a slightly triangular front with a metal plaque above the forehead.

The inspection completed, the boys once more climbed into wagons, the girls crept up into a camel litter, and the procession moved off. Horses had been brought for Mijir, Yanaul and their guards, and the procession led through a narrow lane surrounded by the rundown houses of Fustat, then out onto a dusty road. Ahead of them, rising hundreds of feet above the surrounding land and nearby city, reared Qal'at al-Jabal, the sultan's fortress on a mountain. The formidable outer wall encircled it and rolled north across the hills to merge with city's wall. Behind the outer wall the Citadel rose in a succession of massive inner walls.

Mijir stayed on the main road and headed up to the Fortress's front gate, the Chain Gate, leaving Yanaul and the boys to follow a secondary road running to the base of the Fortress' cliff. When the walls of the Fortress were being erected, the mountain's side was chipped away, and now, at the base of the enormous cliff, steep steps climbed the rock.

With growing awe and not just a little fear, the lads stared up at the cliff and walls. The message in their eyes mirrored Diyar's thoughts. *Are these walls a home or a prison—or a tomb?*

A glowering gate house crowned the steps up the wall. Looking up as he climbed, Diyar saw narrow openings in the wall and towers.

Are soldiers peering through the slits at that very moment training their arrows on us?

He glanced down the face of the cliff and over the valley to the river. But who could be so foolish—or powerful—to attempt an assault on such a fortress.

Then he remembered the long, pile of rubble that had been Yanaul's home, and heard again his ominous warning: "All your life the Mongols will be your enemy."

After sweating up the zigzagging flight of steps, they arrived at Bab al-Mudarraj, the Gate of Steps. Here they paused, and while the amir ashara—amir of ten—in charge of the gate examined their papers, Yanaul read to the lads the inscription over the massive entrance: "Our master, al-Malik al-Nasir Salah al-Dunya wa al-Dan Abu al-Muzaffar Yusuf ibn Ayyub, restorer of the empire of the caliph, has ordered the construction of this magnificent citadel close to the God-protected city of Cairo on the strong hill of al-Armah, which combines utility and beauty and gives sanctuary to whoever seeks shelter in the shadow of his kingdom."

Yanaul turned to the boys with pride. "Salah al-Din was a great sultan. Throughout history, only our Sultan Baybars today can match him."

Once inside, the group passed through a succession of iron-studded gates, and Diyar learned the Fortress was really a city. The boys trooped by palaces, mosques, pavilions and courtyards. Yanaul pointed out the hall of justice, a prison, dormitories for the khasikiya, the sultan's private guard, dormitories for the palaces' eunuchs, a mint and treasury, and several baths. They even spied a bustling marketplace used exclusively for the inhabitants of the Fortress.

Coming to an opening between buildings, he pointed north, and said, "And in that direction are your barracks, baths and dining room, and below, the stables, more horses here than you have ever seen or can imagine."

In front of the largest palace, they found Mijir and the older amir waiting. Two tabardariya, guardsmen with tabars, half-moon axes on tall shafts, guarded the palace's wide entrance. Over their tunics, they wore beautifully patterned, knee-length robes.

For Diyar, stepping into the great entryway was like entering a enchanted cave: cool, dark and mysterious. The floors and walls gleamed with marble tiles woven into intricate Arabesque designs. Dignitaries in long, colorful robes and pristine white turbans glided by, accompanied by small, brown men in simple clothes carrying pen boxes, ledgers or account books.

A pair of eunuchs in cotton robes appeared and led the girls away.

Seeing the slim figure of Thalia glide away Diyar felt a pang of loss. *Will I see her again? When?*

Yanaul and the boys followed Mijir across the entryway to the wide entrance of a vast qa'at, or audience hall. On the far side, tall, arched openings in the wall welcomed in a cooling breeze, and framed the wondrous triangular mountains across the wide river.

Mijir spoke to the Hajib al-Hujjab, or Grand Chamberlain, who wore a large turban and a gorgeous blue robe over a white robe. After murmuring a few instructions, the Grand Chamberlain preceded them into the Hall of Audience.

The hall was full of men dressed in beautiful tunics and robes. At the far end rose a platform where, on a special throne of gold and gold satin, sat a tall, fair-haired, fair-skinned man: the sultan. In contrast to the row of amirs seated on his right who wore beautiful robes embroidered in gold and trimmed in fur, the sultan was dressed in a simple tunic, trousers, and boots. On his left sat a line of Judges and Ecclesiastes—the Qadi. They all wore white silk gowns with even larger turbans than the amirs.

Mijir led the way to the front of the gathering. He paused and threw the boys a look that clearly ordered, "Stand still and be quiet."

They did.

The men in the hall were listening raptly to an old storyteller. With the story completed and its teller paid, the Grand Chamberlain approached an old amir who stood near the throne and whispered to him, then nodded to Mijir and the boys. This last dignitary was the Lord of Audience, the Amir Majlic, and he, in turn, moved to the throne and spoke to the man seated in the middle of the raised platform: Al-Malik al-Dhahir Rukn al-Din Baybars al-Bunduqdari al-Salihi—Sultan Baybars.

Baybars stood, a powerfully built man in his early forties, and his booming voice carried the hall. "Good. Bring them to me."

Mijir motioned for the boys to line up at the base of the steps to the throne.

The sultan strode down the steps, greeted Mijir warmly, then turned to the boys. Passing down the line, he peered into the eyes of each. Like most of the men present, he wore a beard, full but trimmed. One of his eyes was cloudy, milky white, which gave his other eye a greater intensity with which he examined closely his latest purchases. Then he nodded to the Khazindar Kabir—the Grand Treasurer, who stood near the throne, who motioned for servants to bring a large, brass box. He presented the cache of money to Mijir, who indicated for one of his guards to take it.

Then the sultan turned to the boys and, as both an amir and a qadi noted on separate sheets of parchment, walked down the line, designating the tibaq, or warrior regiment, each cadet would be assigned. Some were assigned to the Tabaqt al-Taziya, same to Tabaqt az-Ziman, and some to Tabaqt al-Ashrafiya. When he came to Diyar, he paused. "This lad will be a member of the Tabaqt ar-Rafraf. Work hard, boy, and someday you might be a member of the khasikiya, my personal bodyguard."

A murmur of assent rumbled through the crowd of amirs, and Diyar knew something important had just taken place.

Finishing with the assignments, Baybars ascended to his throne and turned. "Young mamluks," he said in a voice that rolled over the audience, "you come to me with nothing but your courage and determination. Who you were before means nothing, only how brave and hardworking you are now. Be faithful to the Prophet, loyal to your sultan, and in return, your sultan will love and reward you. An obedient mawla is worth three hundred sons. Sons will plot to overthrow their father for the inheritance, but a mawla will give his life for a master who cares for him. When the time comes for your graduation, I as your ustadh, your liberator and master, will free you. Then you will be able to add to your names 'al-Baybariya', the sons of Baybars, and you can proudly take your place in the victorious armies of the Faithful."

The forest of tall, white turbans nodded in approval and the boys were led out.

As they moved through the entryway, they passed a group of lounging pages watching the proceedings. The teenagers wore yellow silk tunics and red conical caps. One of them, thin and taller than the rest, to his mates' delight, made a kissing noise at the boys.

Diyar could not help but stare. The young man's face was as clear and white as a girl who had never been out of the yurt.

The youth leered and Diyar looked away. Angrily he rebuked himself for giving the young man any attention.

Outside of the palace, Mijir and Yanaul mounted their horses. But before leaving, Mijir paused and looked over the boys one last time. Observing their fresh, eager faces, he shook his head. "You all have a long way to go before you are fit to be the sultan's warriors. The way will be hard. Be alert. The line between being in or out of prison is thin, the time between living or losing a hand or head, but the blink of an eye. Work, make me proud. And, if it be God's will, we may meet again."

With a touch of its reins, his horse turned and cantered down the great courtyard descending from the palace.

The amir who had inspected them at the quay, now took charge. Mounting, he led them along a wide walkway between the palace and the great square building which was the Fortress's mosque. They crossed the court, and passed through the high wall and gate separating the palaces from the administration area. Soon they entered a smaller palace and the office of Amir Sanjar al-Shujai, the Commandant of the Citadel.

Several other amirs and clerks clustered about the commandant's desk, but seeing the cadets enter, he motioned for four men wearing white cotton robes to come forward. They were smooth skinned, and dumpy shaped: eunuchs. But what Diyar noticed first about them was each carried a stout staff.

"These are your handlers," the commandant said. "Obey

them, and you will not have to come before me again." He paused. "Believe me when I tell you, you do not want to come before me again."

Even the dullest of the boys felt the weight of the warning.

The four eunuchs called for the recruits in each of their particular tibaq. Diyar's eunuch was a smallish, young man with fair skin and vibrant, red hair.

"My name is Firuz Zayn al-Din," he said. The eunuch's voice was high, and soft like a girl's, and had a strange accent. "That is not my original name." He raised his chin proudly. "Actually, I am Greek. My name was Petros. But, when I became the sultan's servant, I was renamed Firuz which means ruby." Pointing at his hair, his eyes twinkled. "I can not imagine why, can you?"

Diyar and the three other recruits who had been assigned to the Tabaqt ar-Rafraf, followed Firuz to a warehouse where they received light-blue, cotton jackets and trousers; stockings; soft, tan boots, with heavier, red-moroccan shoes which were worn over the boots; and black, goat-hair belts with a saulaq, a black leather pouch for holding their few personal possessions. A red kalautah cap, topped off the simple uniform. For cold or rainy weather, they received heavy, wool capes.

They carried their clothes to a large, single-storied dormitory made of stone. Several more eunuchs squatted in the shade of the doorway. Inside the low, dark building, Firuz assigned the boys their bedrolls.

Outside, at a chair in the barrack's shadow, a eunuch with a razor that felt as though it had been sharpened in gravel, scraped the hair from their heads. After a bath in cadets' bath house—a rambling building of many rooms, tiled and steamy—Farus walked them to a long dining room, and ordered them to sit down and be quiet.

Soon other cadets poured in, the younger ones, like Diyar and his group, under the direction of eunuchs. Older cadets, dressed in red muslin jackets and trousers, and smelling of horses and leather, swaggered in, brushing the younger boys aside. They sat down at their own tables and pounded the tables for food.

How Diyar envied them. They had been through much of their training already and gleamed with strength and confidence. He vowed to be just like them someday, but with a feeling of dread, sensed how long, how so very long, it would be.

Soon eunuchs passed between the tables laying before each boy bowls of beans, chunks of bread, and milk—and a small, orange-colored ball. Watching the older boys, he saw them bite greedily into the balls. Then some peeled them, others sucked the moisture out of them.

Tentatively Diyar bit into the ball. Bitterness sprayed his lips, but then, imitating the more experienced boys, he squeezed, and a sweet juice spurted into his mouth, and Diyar drank from his first orange.

After lunch, the boys returned to their barracks. Diyar no sooner entered the long room, when one of the eunuchs handed him a stick with long, stocks of straw tied to it. Seeing Diyar's questioning look, the little man peevishly tore it from his hands and demonstrated how to sweep. No seamless marble here, but hard stone floored the tibaq's barracks.

Dust boiled up as he began sweeping, and Diyar saw the winds blowing across the surrounding desert had deposited much of its sand in his barracks. Cleaning would be an endless task.

He looked up and saw his handler, Firuz, standing in the tibaq's doorway nodding in proprietary approval. A thought came to him, and he approached the eunuch. "I must rid myself of water," he said.

Firuz had heard the excuse before, but nodded, "Behind the barracks."

Diyar left the broom at the door and hurried around the corner. Near the wall he spied a narrow shed, open toward the barracks. Several cadets squatted on the long, holed bench. Behind it ran a stone ditch where a boy stood urinating. Diyar headed over.

He finished and decided to take a look around. He cut across the courtyard, walking with purpose as if on some important errand. Suddenly a blow struck him across the back, knocking him sprawling across the hard flagstones. Fighting for breath, he struggled to his knees. But another blow flattened him again.

Something huge and white towered over him. In its hands, it held a thick, gleaming staff—and the staff was again swinging at him.

Diyar ducked his head in his arms and jerked sideways, and the staff banged off his elbow, smashing him over onto his back.

From the barracks, eunuchs and cadets ran to see the cause of the commotion.

Now Diyar experienced real fear. If the blows kept coming, if he could not get to his feet to flee...

The monster stepped forward, his legs spread wide to swing the heavy staff. But Diyar spied a path of escape. He rolled to the right, dived between the monster's legs, jumped to his feet and shot to the crowd to try to disappear. He nearly made it when another staff tripped him and sent tumbling.

Before he could right himself, Firuz grabbed the back of his neck and dragged him to his feet.

Still in a panic, Diyar fought for escape, but the muqaddam al-tibaq had wrestled young Kipchaks before. His grip tightened like a steel trap nearly paralyzing the boy. The pain took the run out him, and the grip forced him into a bow.

From his ignominious, head-down position, pain reverberating through his brain, he glanced over and saw Firuz was also bent in a deep bow, as were all the eunuchs and cadets alike. Who was this huge, white-clad monster with his lethal, golden staff?

In a high, dry voice that scratched like fingernails on slate, the man berated Firuz in a strange language. Then he turned and, ponderous with dignity, stalked away.

As soon as it seemed safe to stand, Firuz, his grip not relaxing one notch, dragged Diyar around the corner of the barracks. Hidden from view, he took the boy by the shirt and pulled him into his face. The eunuch's placidity had disappeared, replaced by fear and rage.

"Now see what you have done. Do you know who that was? That was the Mamalik al-Sultaniya, the sultan's Chief Eunuch. He is the Master of us all. Everyone fears him, even the amirs. You he could have skinned, and me, my head torn from my body. Now, I do not intend such should happen to me. So, when you see him coming, bow low and back away. Never, do you understand me, never cross in front of him. Better, when you see him, just go the other way."

Stiff with pain, Diyar spoke through clenched teeth. "But I did not see him coming. I did not see him at all."

The hand shook his neck. "Silence. It seems you need a lesson in respect, and I know just where it can be found."

CHAPTER 5

The familiar smell of horse dung met Diyar as one of Firuz's eunuchs led him down to the stables. Inside the wide stable door, the eunuch left him and stepped into a tack room where long lines of saddles sat on frames. There, an old warrior squatted before one of them sewing on a stirrup strap. He did not look up as the eunuch spoke to him.

His report given, the eunuch, with a sniff of distaste, swept passed Diyar and hurried back to the barracks. After a time, the old-timer rose from his low stool and came out. Short and bow-legged, he moved with a limp, and his face, leathery as the saddles he tended, proudly carried a thick, grey mustache, split by a deep scar.

He observed the tow-head with a slight smile. "So, you did not show proper respect to the Muqaddam al-Mamalik al-Sultaniya. Well, he can be a great bull." He winked, "but the old bull lost his horn long ago, no?"

The meaning of the words escaped the boy, but he recognized the man's friendly manner, and his accent sounded of home.

"So, what is your name, boy?"

"Diyar."

"And your father?"

"Tani Bak."

"Tani Bak..." the old warrior said thoughtfully. "Was he not the chief of the Tetyushi clan?"

Diyar nodded proudly.

"I thought so. Our clan once wintered near yours on the river. I knew him and his father. I am Sudun Taz, the Saddle-Master of Tabaqt ar-Rafraf. The eunuchs might want you to muck out the stalls, but the sultan's mamluks do not do such work. We leave that for the fellahin."

Seeing the look of fellowship appearing on the boy's face, he added, "But do not think you are going to get out of work. There is plenty to do down here."

He led him to the first stall where several beautiful mares stood tethered. "Every warrior has his own squire, older cadets who take care of their horses and tack. These are my horses." He scooped up a handful of straw, pulled a dirk from his belt and squared off the straw ends. "Here, you know how to brush a horse. Make them shine." He tossed the knife, and it sprang quivering into the stall's wooden post. "Cut fresh straw when you need it," and he turned back to his tack room.

This was punishment? He gazed at the beauties, so clean and bright. Happily, he stepped into the stall. The intelligent animals eyed him with curiosity.

He had been working for a time, when an older cadet rode up to the stable door. He carried his lance, shield and reins in one hand, while the other arm hung limp, blood dripping from his finger tips.

Sudun Taz hurried from his tack room and took the lance and shield from the wounded boy. Striding into the stall, he grabbed a bridle from a hook, eased it onto the head of one of his mares, and leaped up on its back. Siding the youth, the two rode up the hill together.

Diyar returned to his chores. The cadet must have been at the practice field. To charge wildly into battle—what fun! What adventure!

He reached down to grab another handful of hay, and a sharp pang of pain shot up his side where the Chief Eunuch's staff had barked his ribs.

But, he thought ruefully, *I must keep my wits about me.*

A whipping in front of the other lads at Mijir's compound, and now this beating before all the cadets in his tibaq.

Not a very good start. I must become smarter. I must learn the rules—he smiled to himself—*in order to get around them.*

The act of brushing the horses brought memories of home, and he clenched his jaw against the pangs of homesickness. Still, upon seeing the splendor of the sultan's palace—he had never imagined such beautiful robes as the amirs wore, shimmering silks in gold, yellow, green, blue, scarlet—he knew this was where he wanted to be.

The sound of laughter and approaching horses broke into his thoughts. A group of pages cantered up to the stable. With a practiced eye, Diyar observed, though they rode fine horses, they sat them like sacks of grain. Then he recognized the taller youth leading them.

The young man waved airily at him. "Here boy, take our horses and give them a good rubdown."

Diyar turned back to the Saddle-Master's mares. If these fops wanted anything of him they would have to go through Sudun Taz.

The youth frowned. "Hear me, boy? Take our horses and be quick."

The group grew silent as Diyar studiously ignored them.

"It seems," hissed the youth ominously, "this little girl needs a lesson in manners." Without grace he slid off the horse. "And I would be remiss in my duties if I did not teach it to him."

He approached the stall, the rest following.

Diyar moved to the other side of the mare, putting her between him and the youth. And when the skinny page stepped into the stall, Diyar stabbed the mare in the underbelly with the sharp stalk ends. She shied away, knocking the teenager to the floor.

He struggled up, manure dripping from his fine, yellow coat. He raised his hand, saw the muck on his fingers, and rage twisted his narrow features.

"Look," he gasped, "look what you have done." He grabbed the nearest boys and shoved them into the stall. "Get him. Get the little snake."

Arms grabbed at him, but Diyar ducked under the horse's belly. He kicked a knee cap, and a scream of pain rang out. More pages crowded in the other side of the stall and soon they cornered him and dragged him out.

"Bring him here," said the thin one. He stuck his filthy hand in the boy's face. "I ought to make you clean this off with your tongue, but you would probably like it." The other boys giggled. "Instead, I will give a lesson in respect. It is time you barrack rats learn who really runs the realm. Pull off his shirt."

Eager hands tore the coat from the boy's back. But as his smooth, white skin was exposed, a hush fell over the young men.

The thin one stared, and in the stable's gloom, Diyar saw something evil enter his eyes. "Hm. I think I have a better idea. Pull down his trousers," he said breathlessly.

Diyar immediately kicked out at the nearest boy, but two more pinned his legs to the floor. And, as he bucked and writhed, hands jerked his trousers down to his knees.

The young man was breathing heavily. "Bend him over."

Wildly, Diyar tried to wrench free, but hands held him fast. He felt the boy gripping his hips, and he cringed, sick with shame.

Hoof beats pounded, and Sudun charged into their midst, knocking the boys, including Diyar, rolling. Before they could gain their feet, the saddle-master bounced to the ground, and grabbed the skinny youth by the throat of his coat. "Get out of my stable, you jackal's spawn, and take your bitches with you," and he threw him towards the stable's entrance.

Righting himself, the youth groped for the dagger at his waist, but the old warrior shook his head. "Pull a blade on me, boy, and I will cram it so far up your chute, you will have to drop your turds standing up."

The boys slunk away, and Diyar quickly pulled up his pants. At a safe distance, the tall one called back, "I will see you again, pretty boy, when you do not have that old bag of gas to protect you." Then he added with forced nonchalance, "And old man, take care of my horse. That is what a stable boy is supposed to do, is it not?"

Sudun ignored him and, avoiding Diyar's eyes, so full of shame, walked his mare into her stall. When he came out he nodded. "Yes, he is a bad one. Can not lift a sword to save his life but, with enough of his scum around him, he can cause trouble. You best keep out of their way."

As soon as he could trust his voice, Diyar said, "But Who are they? What do they do here?"

"Them? They are 'favorites', palace pages, part of the khasikiya, and they do as little as possible. And he is the worst. Abu al-Mulq. He is the son of one of Sonkor al-Ashqar's slave girls."

"Sonkor al-who?"

"Al-Ashqar, the Nayib al-Saltana, the Viceroy of Damascus."

"Damascus?"

"Yes, Damascus. More beautiful than Cairo, second only to it in importance. And its ruler, second only to the sultan. Sonkor al-Ashqar is as hungry for power as a mule for water. He has many followers, but I would not follow him anywhere, and it appears his son has inherited all his father's bad lines."

The old warrior turned and examined the handsome lad with a critical eye. "You want to be careful. There are thousands of men here in the Citadel, but few women. A true son of the steppes would never marry one of these little brown creatures who live in this country, only a woman from his own land, and there are far too few of them around."

"So who do the men marry?"

"Oh, often Mongol women."

"Mongols?" Diyar said with distaste. "Are there Mongols here too?"

"Some. They lose favor with their Khan and have to flee, so they come here. The sultan welcomes them, and gets what information he can out of them. From them he has learned the

Mongols' methods of warfare and has improved on them. But they are a dirty lot. They drink too much, and refuse to follow the words of the Prophet. Still the sultan has taken their women for wives."

"The sultan?" Diyar said aghast.

The old man smiled. "Yes, and beautiful women they are." He became serious. "But there are not even enough Mongol women around, so guard yourself."

Soon the new cadets' training began in earnest. After a light breakfast of milk and barley gruel, the boys were led to the mosque where, in a corridor along the edge of the great hall, they sat under a row of windows, and listened to an old qadi, Ibn bint al-Aaz, explain that all learning, all education, all the law they will ever need, came from the Prophet and was contained in the holy book, the Koran. Ibn spoke in the language of the steppes, and he promised, if diligent, they too would be able to read and write their own language.

Diyar could see that most of the score of boys squatting on the beautifully woven carpets were hardly interested. As warriors, what need had they for reading and writing? Besides, one could always find a qadi to write for them. Still, the old qadi seemed a wise man, and Diyar listened with half an ear as the man counted out the duties of a true Muslim.

1. The acceptance of the Creed: There is no God but Allah, and Muhammad is his prophet.

2. Prayer, preferably five times a day, but at least three.

3. Almsgiving.

4. Observance of the fast of the month or Ramadan.

5. The pilgrimage to Mecca, at least once in a lifetime.

But when the qadi began speaking about the sultan, all the boys gave him their whole attention.

"When Malik-al-Dhahir—the sultan—mounted the throne, the world of Islam was in retreat on all sides. The Frankish knights had come from over the seas and stolen our lands, making great kingdoms for themselves over the graves of the Faithful. And from the East came even a greater threat, the godless

Mongols. They murdered the Caliph in his palace in Baghdad, burned the thousands of books that were the repository of all learning, and destroyed the most beautiful city on earth. Then they marched on Cairo. If it were not for the valiant troops of the Faith, under the guidance of our beloved sultan, Islam could have been lost forever, and darkness would have descended over the whole earth. But God was merciful, and His servants won the day, and now the defenders of Islam are fighting back, stronger each year. The sultan rescued the next in line to be the Caliph, and in turn, the new Caliph has anointed the sultan as defender of the Faith against the encroaching infidels.

"The sultan is very keen on his men learning the teachings of the Prophet. Islam means submission, obedience, and you will learn to submit to the articles of faith, and to be polite and respectful of others. Now repeat after me the Kelimeh or credo, 'There is no God but Allah. Muhammad is the apostle of God.' To which is the reply, 'Wherefore exalted be God, the King, the Truth! There is no God but He, the Lord of the Glorious Throne.'"

He repeated the Kelimeh, and the lads began a mumbling reply. One of the eunuchs swatted a couple of heads, and the boys spoke up.

After lessons, the boys had an early lunch in the cadet dining room, then tromped down to the vast dining room in their tibaq's warriors' barracks. Cooks, bakers and servants prepared the food, but the warriors preferred to be served by the boys.

Now Diyar saw what Sudun Taz had meant by his warning to be watchful around the warriors. As Diyar hurried down the rows of men bent over their meals, many leered openly at him. Several suggested he return to their barracks with them after the meal. Occasionally a solid pat on the bottom helped him along. Ashamed, he knew he had to get off the floor.

An older boy was sawing bread into thin circles, and when he laid the knife down, Diyar scooped it up and continued slicing.

He observed that some of the cadets enjoyed the attention of the warriors, but he found the intimacy disturbing.

How could anyone become a great warrior if he allowed himself to be another man's pet? Diyar shook his head. Not good enough. He stretched taller, a look of defiance in his young eyes. *I will become the best warrior in the sultan's army by skill alone.* A swarthy Turk caught his eye sending him a knowing grin. *But first I must get out of this mess duty.*

His opportunity came after lunch.

From the tibaq's dining hall, the boys marched down to the stables. It would be some time before they received horses and began the training that made the mamluks the finest light cavalry in the world. For now they had to ride less exalted beasts.

Next to the stables stood a rank of frames the height of horses. Each held an ancient, sun-cracked saddle. Against the side of the stable leaned discarded swords, lances and shields, rusted and dented.

From the shade of the stables emerged an old warrior, his tunic and trousers worn from constant riding. Three or four younger horsemen followed him.

The older man stood in front of the boys. "I am Baqtimur al-Hasami. I and these men will be your Riding Masters. Pay attention. What I tell you may save your life." This last phrase would preface much of the instruction the boys would hear in the next few years.

"How fast you are able to mount your horse could determine if you live or die. You will now learn to mount a horse properly. You will learn to mount from both sides, and from the back. You will learn to mount without using your hands, and in time, in full armor with a shield in one hand and a sword or lance in the other. Then you will learn to loose an arrow from the back of a horse at a full gallop, from under the belly of a horse, even riding backward. Then you will be a member of the world's finest horsemen, the Sultan's cavalry. But first you must learn to mount."

The Riding Master nodded to one of the younger men who picked up an old shield and sword and, with a blood-curdling shout that startled the boys to their toes, dashed for the nearest frame. Leaping, the warrior descended solidly into the saddle, the sword and shield raised high in the air. He then spun around, and sat backwards in the saddle grinning at the boys.

Wearily, Baqtimur al-Hasami gestured to the young warrior to dismount, then turned to the boys. "We do not expect you to do the same right away. For now, just run up—you will notice there are cords where the horse's mane would be—grab the mane, not the saddle—and jump into the saddle. Practice from both sides."

As the boys lined up behind the frames and began practicing, Sudun Taz stepped out to watch. Seeing Diyar he nodded.

A thought came to Diyar, and after taking his turn, he trotted over to Sudun Taz.

"You remember what you said the other day about those palace pages?"

"About you being careful? I remember."

"I know what you mean now."

Sudun smiled. "Yes, I did not think it would take long."

"But could you help me? I dislike having to serve in the dining room."

He nodded. "Ah, yes, the dining room. But you are in no danger there. The eunuchs are always watching. Even I eat in the dining room."

"I know, but maybe I could work for you down here in the stables."

He looked doubtful but shrugged. "If it be God's will."

A shout from the riding-master forced Diyar to break off the conversation, but the next week Firuz stopped at his table in the dining room.

"The Muqaddam al-Mamalik al-Sultaniya mentioned you again. He wants you to report to the stables after lunch instead of having the easier duty in the warrior's dining hall."

The looks of superiority on the other boys' faces did not faze Diyar.

This was exactly what he wanted.

CHAPTER 6

After the evening meal, handlers marched the boys to the baths. The building was a labyrinth of rooms, large and small. In the main room, the boys doused themselves with buckets of water from large basins along the walls, while the handlers stood watching from the dressing room.

Diyar enjoyed the evening baths for, once clean and in his bedroll, he fell instantly to sleep. But one evening, as he finished washing, a hand from behind grabbed his mouth to stifle any cry, and other hands dragged him to the back of the washroom.

Frantically, he looked to the other boys for help, but they were too startled to speak.

Several young men, as naked as he, shoved him into a narrow passageway and stretched a rolled scarf across his mouth. They dragged him through a maze of passageways to a small, tiled room. Light from a single candle in a wall-holder reflected off the shiny walls and the pool in the floor.

Under the candle, his captors spun him around, and he faced the gaunt, leering face of Abu al-Mulq.

Al-Mulq wet his lips. "Now no bandy-legged barbarian is going to interrupt us. I intend to have your pretty, little hole, and what I want, I get."

Dipping his hand into a pot of soap, he nodded to his companions. They spun Diyar around and, twisting his arms up his back, bent him over.

Eagerly Al-Mulq lathered the boy's rectum, then inserted.

Diyar tried to fight but the pain in his arms paralyzed him.

When Al-Mulq had grunted to a climax, another pushed in to take his place. The lad was grinding away, when a whispered warning stopped him.

The candle was snuffed, Diyar shoved to the floor, and the pages scuttled off into the darkness.

He rose stiffly and staggered down the hall, his bottom feeling slimy. Wrenching the gag from his mouth he wiped his rectum. The scarf came away smeared with blood and feces, and he tossed it away with disgust.

Somewhere in the passageways he heard a voice call out for him. He answered, and in a moment, Firuz hurried up, his staff striking the floor irritably at each step. "I should have known it would be you." He grasped the boy's arm and jerked him along.

Entering the main washroom, he dragged him through the bathers, boys jumping out of his way. He spied his assistant handlers near the entrance, stalked over and slapped them both soundly, then spoke to them in the strange tongue. The men hesitated. Firuz raised his hand again, and the two handed over a few coins.

That the eunuchs had been bribed gave Diyar no solace. Stone-faced, he struggled not to let the boys see a tear. But the shame! Would he ever again gain their respect?

Nor did the shame end in the baths. He staggered back to the barracks, but word of the rape flew ahead of him. The younger cadets stared with curiosity, the older cadets leered and laughed. In the mess hall the shame was worse.

When finally the sun set and the few candles in his barrack were snuffed, he lay head covered on his mat. But when he felt sure all were asleep, he crept to the door, slid past the dozing troop handler and stole outside.

Keeping to the shadows, avoiding the mounted guard patrolling the barracks, he sought a place, anyplace, of refuge. Behind his tibaq's stable, next to the wall above the practice field, he knew he would be hidden. Across the distant desert, the fading light outlined the rolling orange dunes in purple shadows. A memory pierced his wretched heart: the steppes.

The vision of his mother swam into his moist eyes, so beautiful, so comforting.

His face felt strange, and as hard as he fought against it, it crumpled into tears. Head down, he sobbed with misery and longing.

Why did I ever leave home? Why? Why? Why?

In his anguish, his father's tall, commanding frame appeared. *If he were here, he would tear the eyes from that evil snake*, he thought savagely.

Then the misery overcame him again. *But he is not here. There is no one here who will help me, no one who cares*, and the well of anguish opened up for him once again.

Suddenly an arm across his shaking shoulders startled him, and he twisted to see the grainy face of Sudun Taz staring out over the desert.

Quickly Diyar tried to swipe the tears from his cheeks, but Sudun Taz stared only at the deep red horizon. "Looks almost like home, does it not?"

After a moment he glanced at the boy, nearly as tall as he. "But it is not. This is our home now. And with the great Rukn al-Din Baybars, Malik-al-Dhahir, we will make it great."

He gave the boy's shoulders a gentle shake. "And you will be a part of it. You will see." He almost smiled. "Why, I make a wager right now, you will become a great amir, even an Amir Muqaddam, leading your thousand into battle." He gave him a nudge. "Will not that be a great day, lad?"

Head down, Diyar managed a nod.

Sudun reflected the nod with emphasis. "Yes, a great day. And I will live to see it."

Then he stepped back with a frown. "But, what are you doing out here when the night bell has already rung? Have you not had enough beatings, you are searching for more? Why, if I did not have to see about the mending of an amir's saddle, I would turn you over to the Duty Officer myself." He jerked him toward the barracks. "Now, back to your mat before I change my mind."

But as Diyar moved away, he heard the words behind him in the dark tinged with concern, "And make sure the Night Patrol does not catch you."

Now, dodging through the night, he somehow felt better. He would have to live with the shame, but perhaps he was not totally alone in this strange land. And when he finally slipped into the barrack and stretched out on the floor, one thing burned into his mind: revenge.

One day I will be full grown. I will have my kindjal. I will catch Abu al-Mulq, and turn the royal bastard into a eunuch—for the few seconds I allow him to live.

The thought lent him some relief from the humiliation. Still he ground his teeth in rage.

But I must be patient, and careful. Be on my guard. Can not make so many mistakes.

He sighed as sleep drifted over him. *To be sure, life as a mamluk is far harder than I could have ever imagined.*

Morning brought no relief from the humiliation. The whole barracks knew, their side looks cutting his heart. And when the cadets met in the brief period the eunuchs allowed them for play in the evening, he was ignored. In the ball game, a battered semi-round ball of sewn horse hide stuffed with goose feathers was chased and kicked from one end of the court in front of the barracks to the other. In previous games, Diyar had created his own crew, directing them with a shout or a shove. Now his place was taken by an older boy.

Diyar trotted up. "I want to play. These are my men."

"You're too late."

Aware others were watching, Diyar tried to grab the ball. "I said, I want to play."

The boy flicked it out of his reach. "And I said you're too late." He dropped the ball, kicked it, and the boys charged after it, screaming their delight. The lad trotted after them.

Desperation gripped Diyar. Everything was slipping away. He had to play. He had to save face.

He chased after the pack swirling around the ball, and tried to push in front of the taller youth. "I said," he panted through gritted teeth, "I want to play."

The boy gave him a sharp shove. It caught him off balance, and he tumbled across the rough stones. Brays of laughter erupted among the cadets at the edge of the court, and the lad threw him a backward glance of superiority, and ran off.

The rage of self-pity and injustice exploded in Diyar. He recognized that look and he wanted to smash it, grind it into the dust.

He bounced to his feet and, blind to all but revenge, dashed after the boy. He struck him full force in the back and sent him sprawling.

Angrily the boy rolled over. He started to rise, but Diyar dived on him, his fists flailing.

One blow struck on the boy's ear, another smashed his temple. Stunned, the boy's arms drooped.

Diyar, in a frenzy of white-hot hate, grabbed the boy's head and smashed it against the flagstone. The head lolled, and he grabbed it again. He had to crush the smirk and arrogance out of him, out of all of them, all his attackers.

He slammed the head down again. But before he could a third time, a staff knocked him sprawling. He tried to get up to strike back, but the butt of the staff struck him full force in the chest, blasting the fight from his lungs.

Firuz stood over him, his face as livid as his hair, forcing the boy down. "Stay! Do not move or I break your skull." He then turned to examine the semiconscious boy whose mates where helping him to sit up.

He examined the boy's eyes and, seeing light return to them, turned back to Diyar. He grabbed him by the shirt and wrenched him to his feet. He stared into the boy's face, still twisted with hate and anger. After a moment his eyes narrowed and he shook his head and released him. "You have been cursed. Your temper will kill before any enemy's sword." Then he shoved him away, giving him a sharp poke in the back. "Now get to your mat. You are through for the day."

Diyar stepped from the barracks into the Spring morning

sunlight. Clouds of water birds winged high above. The air hung still and heavy.

Soon other cadets tumbled out, rubbing the sleep from their eyes, and formed up to march to the dining hall. As they ate, a wisp of north wind swirled around the courtyard. Soon it grew stronger, driving with purpose. In moments, a great, brown wall of dust rolled across the desert and broke like a tidal wave over the Citadel.

The eunuchs hurried the boys back to the barracks, then scurried to wedge shutters over the narrow windows and stuff rags under the doors. Still, the dust penetrated every crack, covered every surface. The sky darkened to a burnt umber, and a slashing rain assaulted the rock-sided fortress. Tumultuous whirlwinds turned everything to chaos. The torrential downpour cascaded off the walls, forming wind-strewn pools in the corners of the courts. Water streaked the inner walls.

The handlers, frightened and superstitious, huddled near the door, whispering in fear. But the boys relaxed on their pallets. While the hurricane raged there could be no classes. Grateful to catch any moment of much-needed sleep, Diyar rolled over on his bedroll and nodded off.

With Spring, al-qhamaseen appeared, the hot wind from the south, blowing steadily, oppressively, for days. Its weight, so prolonged, exhausted the people, and the plague, always lingering at the edge of the city, began creeping over victims.

But finally al-qhamaseen waned, and the trees, including date trees, burst into blossom, their gentle scents drifting out from the palaces' gardens.

Now struck the fire of summer. The land dried and cracked, and flies, hanging, circling, crouching on every surface, drove the boys to near madness. A stench, the miasmata, stinking and putrid and so strong it could be tasted, rose from the drying swamps, covering all with lethargy.

At night, clouds of mosquitoes drifted on the odorous wind, and in the day, fleas, tiny, yellow parasites hardly bigger than a speck of dust, appeared in the crevices of the skin. Soon, throughout the city, pustulated corpses were found rotting in the morning streets.

The valley grew hotter by the day, by the hour. The heat hung on the body like a great, heavy robe, weighing down the spirit. Only the baths gave relief. There the boys lingered, pouring the tepid water over themselves in an attempt to escape the heat. The eunuchs, even more spiteful than usual, were too lethargic to carry out their threats, and the boys languished in peace.

And all waited for the Mother of Rivers to rise.

Once, when Diyar had asked Sudun Taz about the farmers, he snorted. "The fellahin, the 'cutters of the soil?' They do not have to be 'cutters' to farm here. Just stick a seed in the ground and it grows, so rich is the soil. They are really just 'waterers.' They spend more time watering than anything else. But they and the great river keep us alive. Without what we get from our fiefs, we would all starve."

The Nile fell—"The Night of the Drop"—auguring the river's forthcoming rise, and so total was the heat, the night brought no change in temperature.

Throughout the Fortress nothing moved. No breeze stirred. All waited.

But the river did not rise.

Within days, fresh vegetables disappeared from the market places. A few days more, and famine crept into the hovels of the poor. Soon each morning's sun fell on flies gorging themselves on corpses rotting in the streets. Disease slunk around the city on the stench from the cracked bodies.

Sultan Baybars ordered the government's granaries be opened, but restricted the sales to only the poor, at a fixed price and in small quantities. Thus the speculators were unable to buy up large amounts of grain to profit from the city's tragedy.

Now in the depth of summer struck the samoon, a hot, south wind that roared in off the desert. Unlike al-qhamaseen which could drag on for days, this blast from the desert's furnace roared through the valley quickly, forcing sand and dust into everything, permeating clothes and skin with abrasive grime, then left just as quickly. During such an attack, the boys could only dive into a corner and wait for the monster to pass.

As the summer wore on, the temperature abated somewhat and the city's climate became more livable. Daily, the sultan himself, after morning prayers, took charge of the drills on the practice field, galloping everywhere, barking out instructions in a voice that could tear the hide off a dreaming warrior. He was determined to have the finest cavalry in the world. His reign depended upon it. The Mongols had never been stopped before. They would be back.

Finally the heat of summer broke, and the sultan decreed his eldest son, Baraka, would be his heir-apparent. Baybars had become sultan by simply murdering everyone who could claim the crown. Now he hoped that by crowning Baraka, while he, Baybars, still reigned, his son's succession would be assured.

Celebrating the coronation, Baybars ordered a review of the Fortress's troops in full armor and regalia. With other cadets of his tabaq, Diyar cheered at the sight of the dazzling warriors, and clapped to the beat of the many drum bands. How they wished to be a part of the spectacle.

With the festivities over and the passing of summer, the boys woke to cool mornings. And occasionally rain fell, washing the stolid walls, and bringing a sense of relief and purity.

Winter. Hot food every meal. The snakes, insects and vermin disappeared. Frost, then severe cold. The water of the Nile flowed clear and sweet.

Word came that Mongols, sent by Hulugu, the Il-Khan of Persia, were once again on the march and had attacked Bira, one of the cities on the Sultanate's northern border.

Quickly the sultan sent a division of 4,000 light horsemen racing north, and amassed the rest of the troops on the parade ground, this time not for games, but for war.

Diyar ran to the wall behind the stables to watch. Leading off the procession came the sultan's great band, nearly two hundred drums, rows of soaring trumpets, singing flutes and shimmering cymbals. The power of the beat shook the ground.

The sultan followed his band on his prancing warhorse accompanied by a high ranking qadi, a representative of the Caliph, to show the holy relationship between the sultan and the Faith.

Ranks of the sultan's elite bodyguard, the khasikiya, followed. Next trotted the band and the warriors of the most senior amir-of-a-hundred, an amir muqaddam, whose regular regiment had been swollen to a thousand horsemen by halaqa, sons of mamluks. Behind them rode the regiment's servants with strings of camels laden with supplies. Altogether the army was made up of twenty-four such reinforced regiments.

After passing through Cairo's cheering throng, the sultan cased the pennants, covered the drums, and spurred his men into a forced march through Syria to Bira on the Euphrates. Arriving at the city, he found the Mongols gone, and his 4,000 cavalry in control. He ordered the city be repaired and equipped with war-machines, arms, and provisions sufficient to sustain a siege of ten years.

Soon word arrived that Il-Khan Hulagu had died and was succeeded by his son, Abagha.

Now the sultan turned his attention to his other enemy, the Franks. Leading his army down to the Mediterranean, he besieged and conquered the fortified cities of Caesarea, Haifa, Athlit, and the Hospitallers fortress at Arsouf.

Throughout the sultanate important messages were sent by carrier pigeon. Before a pigeon carrying a message of victory was sent, his feathers were perfumed. Many were the sweet smelling birds that flew into the Fortress's roost that spring.

CHAPTER 7

In late spring, the sultan, at the head of his army, made a triumphant entry back into Cairo through the famous Bab al-Nasir, or Gate of Victory. In celebration, his amirs covered the sultan's entire route through the city with pure silk, hence arose the saying when Cairenes invite close friends to visit, "Afresh al-ard harir," I will spread the ground with silk". After the procession passed, the silk was left for the people to divide among themselves.

With the army garrisoned, every evening the amirs, most of whom lived in the city, ordered their bands to play outside their houses. The cacophony across the city pleased all but the most sensitive ears. It proclaimed that a mighty army sat in residence protecting the townspeople, and they were grateful.

By the time Diyar turned thirteen, he had grown to near his full height, over six feet, the tallest youth in his tibaq.

Horses were provided for the squires' training, older mares, patient and forgiving, and the cadets began the practicing of the furusiya exercises. These exercises embraced all aspects of working with a horse: its maneuvering, training, and care. Furusiya also included mastery in all weapons of war, plus wrestling and hunting, even chess, everything that made up a well-rounded warrior.

Diyar's duties included standing watches on the towers and battlements of the Fortress. After forming up at the base of a tower, the squad of cadets followed an amir ashara through tunnel-like passageways. Every dozen paces or so, a candle in a simple brass lamp burned a dim hole in the dark, and the amir would clap his hands to frighten away the poisonous snakes slithering along the cracks in the stone floor. Over the months, Diyar struggled to learn the maze of stairways, the labyrinth of narrow galleries and endless passageways within the walls.

Now it was Diyar and his cohorts' turn to swagger into the barrack's dining hall and receive the envious glances of the younger cadets.

When he rode out for practice, he carried himself proud and erect. And always he kept his eyes open for Abu al-Mulq. He had "acquired" a knife from the dining hall which he hid in the stables and carried in his boot.

If I can just corner him on the field, I will make sure he never leave alive, he thought with a tight smile.

The lads' training was hard and exhausting, the discipline quick and merciless, but most strove to improve. They knew their survival depended on how well they learned on the practice field.

* * *

The boys stood around a blanket spread out in the corner of the training field. A Mongol warrior squatted at its edge and struggled to explain in broken Turkish, the items in row across the blanket.

Diyar, like most of the young mamluks, could not totally keep from being disdainful of the Mongol, but since displayed on the blanket were the weapons that could kill them, he, with the other cadets, listened closely.

The Mongol pointed out his two bows, the heavier one for longer shoots, and his three quivers, each containing various kinds and lengths of arrows: armor-piercing, whistling, message-bearing, even arrows carrying explosives. He allowed the boys to finger the arrows, their eagle-feather flights, and their iron, bone or horn heads, three-fingers broad. From demonstrations, the cadets knew the heavier bow could hurl an arrow as far as three hundred and sixty paces. But they also knew the mamluk bows were more accurate in close combat.

The Mongol archer showed them his thumb ring, a piece of metal that fit over the thumb and allowed a more efficient release of the bow string and arrow.

Next, he emptied his saddle bags displaying needles and thread, a file for sharpening arrow heads, extra bow strings, and a shirt of strong, raw silk to wear in battle as an under-garment.

Each of the cadets fingered this last item. They knew most deaths from arrows occurred when the barbed head was torn from the flesh and the battlefield surgeons were unable to mend the wound properly. But an arrow was unable to sever the heavy silk, and the Mongol doctors could extract the arrow without tearing the wound.

As the great, brown eyes of the horses watched, Diyar walked through the dusty, still air of the stables. Ahead, a tall figure stood combing the forelock of a beautiful, mahogany mare. Hearing Diyar's tread, Amir Ashara Kizil al-Suduni turned and squinted. "Who is it?"

"It is I, sire, Diyar, your new squire."

The warrior paused, remembering. "I have seen you before, have I not?

"Yes, sire. You and your men met us at the ship when we first arrived."

"You have come a ways since then, but now the hard work begins." He untied the line across the stall. "Walk," he murmured to the mare, and the intelligent animal stepped out of the stall. "Stop" She stopped. Effortlessly, the warrior leaped onto the horse's bare back. The mare stood as if rooted to the floor.

Diyar's heart swelled with admiration at the well-trained animal. After Mijir, his slave-master, Kizil was the first amir Diyar had ever seen, tall, handsome, with dark, flashing eyes, and the boy never forgot him. He felt the man possessed all the qualities a Royal Mamluk should have. He was a fine horseman, respected both in battle and in camp, and Diyar was proud to serve him.

When Kizil would take a break supervising his troops on the practice field, he would often spar with his apprentice. Diyar liked competing against Kizil, although, in hand-to-hand combat, he scored few hits.

He fared better in chess. He found it fascinating how quickly he could determine the expertise of an opponent. Like swordplay, it took no more than a few moves, several blade crossings, before he had analyzed his opponents prowess.

He liked playing fast, and found he could beat a seemingly superior player often by simply getting on the attack and staying there. And by playing the older men, Kizil, Sudun Taz, Riding-Master Baktimur, and Stable-Master Taghri Birmish, he learned the importance of patience.

One afternoon, the Royal Equerry, an amir muqaddam and close advisor of the sultan, rode up to the stable door. Observing the tall, tow-headed youth defeat old Sudun Taz in chess, he challenged a game. Soon a group of warriors gathered to see if the lad would lose to the influential amir. And when Diyar won by getting the old warrior to fall into an elegant trap, the queen as bait, they held their breath.

The Equerry scratched his graying beard, then stood. "Your name?" he asked in a quiet voice.

"Diyar Taydumur al-Mijiri, my lord."

The man nodded and turned to Amir Taghri, the Stable Master. "When the shipment of horses for the sultan's khasikiya arrive, pick four of the finest mares. They should be beautiful yet of a quiet spirit. They are for the sultan's daughters to ride when accompanying their mothers to Mecca."

Several days later, the horses arrived, beautiful animals lovingly trained by clansmen of Isa Ibn Mahanna, King of the Syrian Bedouins. Their pedigrees were filed in the Royal Equerry's office and copied. Usually, the amir would simply send the pedigree papers over to the sultan's palace by one of his servants, but remembering the tall squire....

The amir smiled ruefully. How he had jumped at the chance to capture the boy's queen. But the capture had opened up a long diagonal run right into his own king's castle. Clever. And fearless. The boy needed watching.

Diyar received word Stable-Master Taghri wanted to see him.

What have I done now, was always his first thought, and he quickly reviewed his past actions. Could it have been that chess game with the Royal Equerry? He cursed himself for being so rash as to defeat an amir muqaddam.

He found the Stable Master conferring with Sudan Taz, and it was as Diyar feared. .

Tagri turned to him, his face stern. "The Royal Equerry wants you in his office immediately. Be quick, keep your mouth shut, and watch yourself."

Needless advice, Diyar thought, as he mounted and rode for the gate to the upper Citadel.

It would be the first time since arriving five years before, that he had been in the upper level of the Citadel's complex. The offices of the Equerry lay between the upper wall and the main cluster of buildings around the sultan's palace. Diyar reined up and walked inside. An Egyptian clerk led him to the amir's secretary, a Christian, as seen by the small, ornate cross he wore around his neck, and, in a minute, Diyar stood in front of the amir.

The Royal Equerry perched on a high divan along the side wall. A round, inlaid table sat before him, scrolls pyramided on one side. From his vantage point by the window, the amir could look out and observe his responsibility, the vast rows of stables.

The amir picked up several scrolls, but before handing them to Diyar, he paused. "Tell me, did you plan that trap in our chess game, or did it open up as you moved?"

Diyar's expression went dead. "Just luck, sire."

The amir nodded. The boy was diplomatic, but it was as he suspected. The lad had played him just right. Nothing showy, but still, always one move ahead until, in frustration, the amir had tried to even the sides with one decisive move. It had been his undoing.

He examined the youth, so tall and full of promise, and something stirred in the old warrior. He moved closer and said quietly, "You were good there on the board. And you may find glory on the battlefield. But hear this, and never forget it, it is the palace you must fear. There is treachery there enough to snuff out any warrior, and has. And the higher one rises in the service of our beloved sultan, the more danger there exists." A hint of a smile crept into his eyes. "I should know. It was not so long ago since I, like you, rode free across the steppes. We have both have traveled a long journey to get where we are, yes?"

Then his brusque demeanor returned. "In any event, put these into the hands of Sultana Ola, and no one else's."

He called in a young clerk, and handed him a pass containing his seal. "Take this man to the sultan's harem."

The sultan's harem! Diyar kept his face blank but his mind roiled. *Thalia. Perhaps I will see Thalia again.*

More and more in recent months, he had awakened, his body throbbing, his groin wet, and the beautiful blond girl haunting his dreams.

Trotting on foot ahead of Diyar's horse, the clerk led the way through a succession of gates and courtyards, until they reached a guarded side entrance to the sultan's palace. But as Diyar and the clerk ascended the steps, warriors with lances stopped them. An amir ashara appeared from the shadow of the entrance. Hearing the cadet's errand, he sent for a eunuch.

"Give me the papers," the eunuch lisped when he arrived. "I will see the sultana gets them."

Diyar did not move. "I am to give them to the sultana personally."

The sun glinted off the sheen of the little Abyssinian's black features. "Now see here..." he sputtered.

Diyar's gaze moved lazily away.

"Do not look away from me," the little man screamed, and a tiny blade flashed in his hand. But before it could reach its mark, Diyar's eyes, the heavy shaft of one of the guard's lance smashed the eunuch's forearm. The stiletto skidded away on the tiled entryway.

The eunuch screeched and clutched his broken wrist. "What have you done?" he cried, but the guards ignored him and gathered around Diyar.

The young amir spoke for them. "You should know better than to take your eyes off an opponent," he said sharply. The other men nodded.

Diyar turned his hand over. In it he clasped a blade no longer or wider than a finger. "I was not completely fooled, sire."

A bellow of laughter erupted from the men. Rough and ready, they all appreciated a good jest, especially if bloodshed was involved. They shoved the eunuch cradling his arm into the palace and, slapping Diyar on the back, ordered him to follow.

Diyar left the men chuckling and retelling the incident, men happy to have the tedium of guard duty broken.

Sniffling, the eunuch scuffed through the wide entryway, up massive steps and down a hallway. At high, arched, finely-carved doors he stopped and nodded to the guards standing in front. They opened one of the doors, and Diyar stepped into a large, empty room with white, marble floors. Two more guards stood at the doors opposite, but unlike the first two guards who were mamluks, these were smaller, darker men, smooth-faced and dumpy-shaped: eunuchs.

"Wait," the eunuch ordered, and hurried through the doors and down a long corridor of successive arches, the doors shutting behind him.

And Diyar waited for what seemed a very long time. Meanwhile the two guards watched him impassively. Growing uneasy,—it would be just like the little man not to mention to anyone he was there,—he thought about speaking to the guards but doubted if they understood Turkish, and he knew no Arabic.

Then the door opened and a woman in a richly embroidered, blue-silk robe and carrying a golden goblet, entered somewhat unsteadily. Neither short nor tall, the skin of her square face possessed a softly yellow-white luster, her eyelids an Asian fold.

Next to her moved a eunuch official wearing a white, silk robe. Behind the two, several more women followed. They too were Mongols. And to her right, within easy reach, walked a beautiful girl, blond, carrying a golden pitcher.

As Diyar bowed to the sultana, his heart leaped. The cup

bearer was Thalia.

The sultana spoke in uneven Turkish. "You hurt my tawashiya?" she said, trying to frown.

But Diyar was staring at Thalia. She had changed. She always drifted into his dreams thin and lithe, as he had first seen her. Now the silk brocade vest she wore accented her full breasts, and her near-transparent pantaloons outlined her long legs.

The sultana saw where the cadet's attention lay, and she reached back to the girl to have her goblet filled.

The girl's attention seemed also arrested by the handsome youth, and it took a sharp stamp of her mistress' foot to make her start to her task.

Huffily the Chief Eunuch spoke up. "Her Supreme Highness wants to know why you broke her servant's arm."

Diyar's face became a mask, and he did not look at the eunuch. "I did not break the servant's arm."

The eunuch pursed his lips in annoyance. "Can you prove it was not you?" he hissed.

Finally Diyar looked at him. "Yes. If it were me, I would have killed him."

The eunuch sucked in his breath with shock, then turned to the sultana for support.

The woman squinted hazily at the boy, then started wheezing. The wheezing turned into a deep, guttural laughter, the ornate combs bobbing in her hair. Behind her the ladies-in-waiting covered their mouths to hide their mirth.

"Such impudence," exploded the Chief Eunuch. He turned to the sultana. "Give him to me, Your Highness, and I will make him more respectful."

Coughing, the Tatar queen struggled to catch her breath. With a silken sleeve, she waved him back into the harem. "Go. We will talk of this later."

After he had stomped off, she turned to Diyar. "You know this girl?" she said, nodding to Thalia.

"Yes, Majesty. We had the same yasarjiya, Amir Mijir al-Din."

She nodded. "Amir Mijir al-Din was your slave master, hey?

He always brings the sultan good boys and girls." She paused, then said, "Give me the horses' pedigrees. Did Isa Ibn Mahanna send good mounts?"

"Yes, Majesty. Gentle and well-trained."

She stiffened. "What difference does that make. No horse has been foaled I can not ride. Is that not correct, ladies?" she said, turning to the women behind her.

"Yes, Majesty," they chorused.

"Yes, Majesty," the sultana mimicked grumpily. Her eyes went from the young cadet to the pretty handmaiden. She took a draught from the goblet, then held it out to the girl for more. But when Thalia reached to pour, the sultana dropped the goblet, and wine spattered across the floor.

The ladies gasped.

"Now look what you have made me do, you clumsy girl," the sultana said without anger. "Get down there and clean it up." She turned to the door. "Come ladies. Let the goose tend to her chores. Go, go," she said, shooing the women before her.

At the door she turned, shook a finger, and said softly, "Only a moment now, or I will send the Chief Eunuch for you both." She slapped the lance of one of the guards. "Come, you two, on the inside of the door."

With the door closed, Thalia set down the pitcher and, using the cloth she used to rest the pitcher on, began wiping up the spilt wine.

Diyar stood awkwardly for a moment, then to help her, began to undo the rolled scarf binding his waist. But before he could get it off, she finished and stood.

To pry his eyes away from her, he glanced down to tie his sash. When he looked up she was standing close to him, watching him with quiet eyes. He tried to speak, but could not.

Her head canted to one side. "I remember you on the ship. Have you been well?"

"Yes, thank you. Uh, I remember you too. You were sick. I wish I could have helped you somehow."

"You are very considerate," she said with a smile, and he felt the warmth of saying the right thing.

She glanced at the door. "I must be going, or they will be coming for me."

He lurched forward. "I would like to see you again."

Fear sprang into her eyes. "Shh," she whispered. "Do not speak so. I am not allowed out of the harem."

"Please."

She quickly shook her head and backed toward the doors.

He grabbed her arm, panicked he would lose her again. "There must be a way." Desperation nearly made his voice crack.

She looked down at his hand in wonder, but still shook her head. "Not unless you can climb the wall."

His heart filled with hope. "There is no wall I cannot climb."

As the doors swung open he released her arm. The two guards stepped in and took up their post next to the entrance. Thalia picked up the pitcher and smiled weakly. "Goodbye."

He grabbed her arm again, her body shielding his hand from the guards. "I will not let you go until you tell me when," he whispered.

Fright tensed her soft features, and she tried to twist her arm from his grip. "Please," she hissed. "You do not know what they will do to me."

One of the guards stepped forward, the butt of his pike striking the stone floor sharply. "Are you all right, girl?" he said, suspicion in his high, thin voice.

"Yes." She tried to keep her voice natural, but her eyes on Diyar brimmed with fear. Her voice dropped and the words came out a groan. "Oh please, let me go."

"Not until you..." he started to say between clenched teeth.

Quickly she leaned close and whispered. "Watch for a red rug on a balcony. Come after the mid-watch change."

She wrenched her hand away and hurried through the door.

It was not until he was in the hallway outside the harem did he allowed himself to think about what she said.

"...red rug...balcony...mid-watch."

And, one evening a few days later, he looked up from the

practice field, and spied a red rug hanging from a small balcony high up in the sultan's palace.

MAMLUK

CHAPTER 8

That night, with snores resounding through the barracks, he stole to the door and slipped past the dozing eunuch into the night.

Even after sundown, the heat continued heavy and oppressive. Sweat trickled down inside his cotton shirt. Creeping from barrack to barrack, he worked his way to the curtain wall separating the lower area of al-Qal'ah from the palace complex. Showing the sleepy guard the pass he had bought with a bribe to the servant of the Royal Equerry, he hurried through the gate and, once out of sight of the wall, ducked behind the palace bathhouse, the Hall of the Pool. There he paused.

Fear and excitement made his pulse race, and he struggled to breathe in the liquid, hot air. The stench of the miasmata tainted the air, its vapor carrying clouds of mosquitoes.

He glanced up at the moon, its waxing crescent descending. It was well into the mid-watch. He would have to hurry.

In the shadow of the palace eunuch's bath house, he glanced up at the great wall that loomed to his left. It disappeared into the night. He knew guards, invisible in the dark, prowled its balustrades, and the amir in charge of the night watch could come riding past at any moment.

And, creeping around the corner of the bathhouse, he almost ran into a horse's rump. The night-watch amir was sitting looking up at the wall.

Diyar ducked back and held his breath. Had he been discovered? He heard the horse whicker softly, but after a moment, its hoof beats clicked across the stones toward the palace entrance.

Diyar sucked in a deep breath and tried to calm his vaulting heart. Still, such was the fire burning in him, he did not ask himself if the escapade was worth imprisonment, torture, castration, and death. His desire drove him on.

Again he slipped around the corner and found the well-trimmed shrub tree the Egyptian lad had described. He extracted the small grappling hook.

Taking a deep breath, he bolted to the shadows at the base of the great wall. Every score of paces along the wall, torches burned throwing pools of flickering light that spelled discovery and doom. Trotting toward the palace, he circled the deadly light. After a time, the wall angled, moving to within twenty paces of the rear of the palace—and the window with the rug.

He ducked around the corner of the palace and into the shadows, then paused to listen. No sound.

He pulled up his undershirt and unwound a cord wrapped around his chest and waist.

High above him perched the narrow balcony. A curtain, lit dimly from within, hung over the balcony door's opening. He tied the cord to the hook, its tongs wrapped with cotton batting to deaden the sound of impact.

He twirled the hook and let fly at the rug over the balustrade, only a dim square in the dark. It struck the wall above the balcony and fell onto the balcony with a thump.

He froze, waiting for someone to break through the door's curtains and cry out an alarm. But no cry came.

He pulled the rope, and the hook traveled up the balustrade and caught on its railing.

With a deep breath, he began the hand-over-hand ascent, walking up the wall. He had done this exercise enough times on the tall, wooden partitions on the practice field to know how exhausting it was, and this balcony was far higher than the partitions.

Finally, gaining the balcony, he pulled over the balustrade and edged to the curtain. He opened it a crack, peeped in—and saw the most breathtaking sight of his young life.

Bodies. Feminine bodies. Young, white, brown, black, in sheer bodices and pants, lit softly by a few candles in tall stands; sprawled in sleep, some enwrapped around each other. Some slept on the low, wide bench that followed the walls around the room. Some slept on the floor; girls and sleeping pads strewn everywhere.

In one corner, partially hidden by a screen, a girl squatted over a pot. She finish and after a couple of swipes with a cloth, crawled back to her pad, rolled over and with a sigh, fell asleep.

Entranced, the wondrous sights swept everything from his mind, why he had come, the peril of his position, everything but he had to get a closer look. He opened the curtain and began to creep into the dim room.

A sharp "shh" stopped him. He looked down. Thalia lay across the entrance to the balcony. Blinded by the vision of entrancing girls, he had not seen her right beneath his feet.

She wore nothing but gauzy pantaloons, and the sight of her full, round breasts froze his mind.

She stood quickly and pushed the gaping youth back onto the balcony. They stood, he straining to see her figure in the dim light, she peeking down at his protruding trousers.

She moved closer. "What was that sound I heard?" she whispered.

Even her breath smelled sweet. "Uh." He could not think clearly. "Must have been the hook."

She glanced at the grapnel hanging from the rug, then back to him. "Oh."

He held his breath, and softly ran his fingers over her nipple. She pulled a knot at her waist, stepped out of her pantaloons, then slid into his arms. Quickly, he untied his waistband, dropping his trousers.

She leaned back against the wall, pulling him closer. But when she reached down to take hold of him, he climaxed in her hand.

Curious, she raised her hand to examine the semen. Then, raising one leg and resting it on the low balustrade, she guided him in. As soon as he felt the warmth of her womb envelop him, he erupted again, and lay shuddering on her shoulder.

She held him close by his hard, round buttocks, and waited. After his gasps had softened, she started to gently pump against him, their breaths commingling.

He pulled back and stared at her in the dim light. She did it so well, she must have done it before. The thought of her not being a virgin had not occurred to him. But then, his full erection returned, and all thought ceased once more.

This time it was longer, sweeter, and he discovered a greater joy than he had ever known. Her womb felt like—like home.

This time she worked with him, moving with him, pulling him into her. And when his ejaculation came, such was the exaltation, he groaned despite the jeopardy.

Fearfully she clapped her hand over his mouth, but all he wanted was to do it again...and again.

Finally she pulled back. "My leg is getting tired," she whispered.

Still panting, he tried to speak normally. The words came out harsh, strained. "Can we not lie down?"

"The balcony is too small."

"We can go inside. No one will see."

Fear made her breath catch. "Oh no. Someone would see and tell the eunuchs. They are vicious."

That he knew.

Even as she talked, he caressed her warm body, her breasts, the curve of her bottom. Her vagina was wet. His fingers came away with the soft, salty scent of the sea.

"Do not even think about coming in," she insisted, and turned and peeped through the curtains. With her back to him, he cupped her breasts.

She turned back, his mouth capturing hers. She pulled away and whispered, "You must go. Now, before it is too late."

But desire still drove him. "Can we not do it again?" The words came out a whine. He hated the sound, but he wanted her so.

He could see she wanted to, but she said, "I am getting awfully sore."

He did not understand. "Why? Did I hurt you?"

"It was my first time."

Doubt assailed him. How could that be? She knew exactly what to do.

She saw his doubt and reached down, then held her fingers to the light. A faint color of blood stained them.

Something altered in his mind. What was it? He more than wanted her. He...

"I love you."

She stared at him, trying to understand. Then fear rose in her eyes and she shook her head. "No, you must not. To do so could only mean death for us both. You were wonderful, but we can never meet again. It could only mean..." She tensed, listening.

He heard it too, footsteps—soft, padded footsteps.

She split the curtain, then jerked back, horror twisting her face. "A eunuch! Go," she whispered in terror, and almost shoved him off the low railing.

He jerked up his trousers, grabbed the line and dived over the edge just as the curtain burst open and light from the doorway shone out into the night.

"What are you doing out here?" The voice was thin and spiteful.

As Diyar twirled in space, Thalia kept herself between the eunuch and the hook.

"It is so hot," she whimpered. "I wanted more air."

Her pleading tone speaking to the eunuch angered Diyar. Who was this house dog that he should have such power over his woman? He itched to climb back up onto the balcony and throw the worthless-one off, but he knew that would mean disaster for both her and himself. He could only grit his teeth and swing helplessly.

"More likely you were out here dropping your water. We have pots for that, and for the next month you can clean them." A sharp slap echoed in the night, and Diyar heard the girl gasp.

"Now get back in here," hissed the eunuch, "before you wake everyone, and I must tell the mistress." And then it was dark and quiet.

Fuming with anger and frustration, Diyar slid to the ground. He flipped the cord to dislodge the hook and jerked it over the railing, then flatten against the wall when he could not see its falling in the dark. It struck the flagstones with a muffled clang.

From high up the great wall, a voice shouted, "Who is down there?"

A torch was waved from the darkness of the wall-top, and Diyar jumped back against the palace wall.

"Speak up whoever is down there," another gruff voice repeated.

A third voice approached asking, "What is it?"

"I thought I heard something."

A second torch made rippling shadows on the palace wall.

Suddenly the curtain on the harem balcony opened, and the eunuch's voice piped out. "Quiet. People are trying to sleep here. Just because the master is away, does not mean you can keep us awake all night," and the curtain swung closed again.

The gruff voice snorted. "It sounds like the little tawashiya is bitchy tonight."

When the light from the torches faded, Diyar quickly gathered up the hook and cord, and dashed for the base of the main wall.

Twenty minutes later, he lay panting on his bedroll. The hook was hidden in the shrub, and the question burning in his mind as sweat ran off his body was, when could he use it again? His body still tingled from the touch of her soft skin.

He groaned. Praise be to God, I want her again already, and as he slipped into fitful sleep, one thing burned in his mind, When can I have the beautiful Thalia again?

He strutted into the stables. Seeing Sudun Taz, he slapped him on the back. "And how are you this fine morning, my friend?"

The old warrior frowned at the impertinence of the adolescent. "I am fine, far better than you will be if you do not mount up and get down to the practice field."

He ignored him. "Sudun, I must ask you, how old were you when you took a wife?"

His frown deepened. "A wife? Why are you talking of such things? You have a long road to ride before you come to that place."

"My question is an honest one. How old?"

The man could see the lad was serious, and he scratched his scarred lip as he remembered. "It was after the battle at Ayn Jalut the first time we turned back the godless Mongols." He looked at the lad proudly. "Nobody had ever done it before, but we did it. My master, Rukn al-Din Baybars, the sultan's most powerful amir, was the leader of the army. Afterwards I used my battle pay and petitioned the amir to bring a woman from my village." He shrugged. "She was my first."

"You have more than one wife?"

"Of course. I have three." He gave him a wink. "And I might just get a fourth."

He shook his head with certainty. "I shall never have four wives. One is all I want."

Sudun examined him with suspicion. "What is all this talk about wives? What have you been doing?"

Now it was Diyar's turn to give a knowing wink. "There are some things a man does not tell."

"A man," Sudun said with a snort. "You have a long..."

"I know, I know, a long road to ride, but it just might be..."

A bellow exploding from path to the practice field startled the lad to action, and an older warrior, a lance instructor, galloped up. "Grab a lance and get on a horse before I take my lance to your backside."

And Diyar, spurred by many memories of what punishment

an angry instructor can deliver, dashed down the stable to fetch a practice horse. But as he galloped by Sudun Taz, he gave him a jaunty wave. "Ah, love, it is something to fight for."

Clearly concerned by his young friend, Sudun called after him. "Staying alive is a far better one."

MAMLUK

CHAPTER 9

The sultan and the army returned from their victorious Spring campaign, and made a triumphal march down the wide Main Street of the capital. Exultant, the people showered their heroes with welcome.

Besides being a great tactical general, Baybars was also a politician and knew the importance of these parades. War was expensive, and the people paid for the victories with their hard-earned dinars and dirhams. The triumphal parades, the gallant warriors, the waving pennants, the booming bands, the crestfallen captives, showed the people what their high taxes and austere life paid for. They were also devout Muslims. The victories displayed the supremacy of their faith over that of the intruding infidels.

But in the barracks, Diyar observed how weary the warriors, including Kizil, appeared. Sleeping on the ground, suffering from poor and often infrequent food, took its toll on the men. But the greatest toll was having constantly to live with death.

In the next few years, the sultan attacked and conquered the walled cities of Shaqif, Jaffa, and Antioch. With the fall of Antioch, the rest of the Frankish Northern Syria tumbled after. The fortresses on the Orontes River, Darkush, Kafardobin, Belmis, all surrendered. Then Harim gave way, and the Templars abandoned Baghras, Hajar, Shoghlan and Port-Bonnel.

With each year the reputation of the great mamluk sultan grew until it reached near superhuman levels. All mamluks could live in the saddle, but the riding feats of Baybars became legendary.

Treasuring secrecy, he allowed few to know his plans. While his army besieged Jaffa, he remained in his tent, claiming to be ill. But when night fell, he and four of his most trusted men stole out and rode for Cairo. Riding one horse while leading a second, they covered three hundred and sixty miles in three days.

For three more days, Baybars walked the city in disguise, analyzing the status of his rule. Then the cadets were startled to find him riding unescorted onto the Citadel's practice field, checking to see if his military training instructions were being carried out. After eight days of being absent from the battle, he struck out at a gallop for Jaffa again, and on the thirteenth day of his absence, entered his tent dressed as a courier with a dispatch bag.

While he was gone, an amir described his symptoms to the doctors who prescribed medicine for him. On the next day after returning, he appeared before his staff. He apologized for his illness, and examined their work, finding the bureaucracy had continued smoothly during his absence and all correspondence had been kept up to date.

Next, in the garb of an Arab, he rode to the fortress of Karak, inspected its fortifications, spent one night there, and headed for Damascus. The Viceroy of Damascus, hearing rumors that he might be coming, called in his officers and warned them to be on the lookout for their illusive leader. But by that time, he was already walking in the city square, alone and on foot.

He took a bite of food at the Viceroy's palace, and before the local amirs could assemble to reaffirm their allegiance, he had vanished once again.

He headed for Aleppo far to the north, and the garrison there was alerted to his arrival. A ceremonial parade was drawn up, but when he arrived, alone and in casual togs, he passed through the gate without being recognized. He then inspected the city's defenses and left as quietly as he had arrived.

Back in the Citadel Diyar chafed against his restrictions. The thought of the beautiful Thalia was seldom far from his mind.

Nearly every night he relived the tender moments with her. The remembrance of the feel of her slim body fevered his dreams. He knew he could not marry, could not take an apartment in the city or even to ride down to the city alone, and he fought against impatience. And the fact he had the world of al-Qal'ah figured out, knew how to move about without being seen, or get out of duty he did not want to do, was little consolation. He had developed into something fairly unique in a military society: a loner.

After the rapturous night on the balcony, the red rug had not appeared again on the balustrade, and once, while on an errand to the palace complex, he had checked the bush where he had hidden the hook and found it gone.

Even had the rug appeared, he was not sure he would hazard another such escapade. He was nearing the end of his training, and had worked too long and hard to jeopardize graduating now. He knew if he wanted Thalia, indeed, as Sudun Taz once said, if he just wanted to survive, he had to live only to hone his fighting skills.

Constant practice with sword and lance had made his shoulders thick and broad. He looked, it was said, much like the sultan himself. His height was certainly as tall as the sultan, but he was, due to the mixture of Rus and Greek blood in him, fair and blond. And in the mamluk hierarchy, to be fair and handsome was a great advantage.

One day as he rode out to form up with Kizil's cadets, a young warrior cut across his old mare's path, forcing her to stumble and fight for her balance. Diyar grabbed the mare's mane, but the battered helmet he wore went flying, and revealing his plaited blond hair.

The warrior laughed. "What have we here? With such hair, you should stay out of the baths," and he loped off.

Anger exploded in Diyar, blinding him to all reason and caution. He kicked the mare forward and dashed up to the warrior.

The warrior saw the youth's face contracted with rage, his

raised lance, and automatically brought up his shield. But Diyar drove his lance into it with such force it knocked the older man from the saddle, sending him sprawling in the dust.

Diyar sprang on him, striking him again and again with his stout hardwood sword.

The young warrior, kicking away under his shield, desperation growing in his eyes, tried to block the blows. But with madness in his eyes, Diyar struck again and again, only one thing in his mind, to bring death to the smirking face, the leering lips he hated so deeply.

Beaten to unconsciousness, the warrior could no longer defend himself, and Diyar raised the sword one last time to crush his skull, when a hand grabbed it and shoved him away.

With a growl of rage, Diyar spun to continue his attack on anyone who would try to stop him, and found himself confronted by Kizil, hard-faced with anger.

Kizil shifted the sword to his other hand, and slapped his protégé sharply. He saw the blind anger remained, and he slapped him again with such force it spun Diyar's head around.

He staggered back. Kizil grabbed the neck of his padded jacket and, as others rode up to examine the crumpled warrior, dragged him away from the crowd.

When they were far enough not to be heard, Kizil spun him around. "Do you want to die, you fool? Do you know what would happen to you, you still a slave, if you killed one of the sultan's warriors? I have seen this in you. You have an anger, an anger that wants to kill. Something must have happened to you, I know not what, but anger of such heat will get you killed. It is a wolf. Allow it to run free and it will turn on you. Master it or it will kill you." He grabbed the front of his jacket and jerked him close. "Do you understand me?"

Diyar fought to get his breathing under control. "Yes, master."

Kizil continued to glare into the youth's eyes, then he nodded. "It had better be so. I have no time for such madness. It is a madness that can not learn." He gave him a push. "Now, get your horse and join the others. You have wasted enough of my time."

At the age of seventeen, 1270 of the later Gregorian calendar, it was time for Diyar's graduation. On the practice field there was no cadet he could not best with sword or lance, and few veterans who dared compete with him. Only Kizil could hold his own against him. With the bow, however, no one was the equal of Diyar Taydumur al-Mijiri.

The lavish ceremony took place in the winter when the sultan and troops were in garrison at the Fortress. In the Audience Hall, with the sultan flanked by his advisors and judges, the cadets were awarded their papers of manumission. And then came the honor Diyar had been hoping for since the beginning of his training. When the names were read off of those cadets being accepted into the sultan's elite bodyguard, the khasikiya, Diyar's was the first on the list. There were only two others.

Now each cadet was presented with a suit of armor—chain mail, light and supple—a new sword, lance, bow and quiver, a mace, and a robe of silk with a silk band for his turban. With the armor came a pointed helmet with a silk ribbon—the khasikiya's color was yellow—streaming from its tip, and a small, round shield with sayings of the Prophet embossed in its surface. And each warrior wore tiraz bands, the silk band woven in gold and silk attached to the upper arm of their tunic containing an honorific formula with the name of the sultan and the warrior's amir, and a pious phrase from the Koran. This writing helped to distinguish one regiment from another.

Following the manumission ceremony, the cadets assembled on the parade ground and each received several Arabian mares. Diyar's best, a fine-bone, dune-colored mare named Saba, possessed a blood-line far more royal than any of the men on the field.

Unlike the Franks who rode stallions, and used high, sharp bits to make them enraged in battle, no bit had ever touched the mouth of these Bedowy-bred beauties. A light touch of the bridle was all it took for an instantaneous response.

After the ceremony, it was time for the games. As his great

drum band kept up a constant din, the sultan led off. Small balls were suspended on poles around the parade ground. The sultan, galloping at full gait, dashed by each pole loosing arrows at the balls and hitting each one. Next came the cadets. Each had at least one miss, each save Diyar. Only he had the skill, or audacity, to challenge the sultan.

And the sultan did not like being equaled. No warrior did. He approached Diyar at a gallop and reined up, his one sharp eye blazing. The crowd held its breath. He examined the lad closely, taking in his newly wound turban with the yellow tip. Then he laughed grandly and slapped him on the shoulder. "It is good you are on my side. Come, to the stand. You deserve a reward for such shooting."

Dignitaries and notables in gleaming robes graced the stand. The sultan's great band crashed into a fanfare. Coming from demure yurts, growing up wearing unpretentious clothes, how the Kipchaks had grown to love ritualistic display!

The sultan raised his hand for silence, received a bundle tied in a beautiful gold cord, and handed it to the newly-manumitted Royal Mamluk. The robe of honor was of a deep blue silk with simple embroidery along the seams and was cut so it could be worn over armor.

The drums thundered again, and Diyar made his way off the platform.

At the edge of the dignitaries, his old teacher, Ibn bint al-Aaz stopped him. "I must speak to you," he shouted over the blast of the drums. "Come with me," and strolled away from the noise.

Curious, Diyar followed.

At the edge of the hippodrome, the qadi turned. "Amir Mijir gave this to me to give to you. He said your love for it almost got you killed," and he drew from his sleeve Diyar's kindjal.

With delight, Diyar reached for it, but the qadi held it back. "The amir said to give it to you only when you were mature enough to receive it. Therefore, I have two things I need to say. First, your father is dead, killed fighting a Mongol raiding party. That makes this blade the last thing you have of him. Second, I know what Ibn al-Mulq did to you. But if you go for him while his father is Viceroy of Damascus, the sultan will be forced to execute you, and the life of a fine warrior for the Faith will be lost. Now, I ask you, are you mature enough to receive this weapon?"

Diyar paused, and the swirling scene of the festival field disappeared. He saw the face of his father—he had always hoped to return to his clan dressed in warrior finery to display his success—and then the evil face of al-Mulq. Again he felt the welling up of bitter rage that always accompanied the thought of the pederast, and fought to suppress it. Mamluks by nature were vain and proud, quick to take an offense at any slight, especially at such an outrage as al-Mulq had perpetrated. There were few things more he wanted in life than a chance to revenge himself against the vain bully. But Diyar knew the qadi, Amir Kizil al-Suduni, was right. If he wanted to succeed, if he wanted to rise in the ranks, he would have to wait.

"Yes," he growled, "I am mature enough to receive the weapon."

Ibn bint al-Aaz examined the young man's eyes, then said, "Yes, I believe you are," and handed it to him.

He pulled the knife from its leather sheath. The blade gleamed from sharpening and a light coat of oil. Ibn bant al-Aaz had kept it in fine shape.

He made a swipe with it. After the years of training, it felt light but lethal in his hand.

The qadi saw the glow in the young man's eyes and smiled. "In truth, lad, this is the first time I have seen you smile since you came to Qal'at al-Jabal."

Diyar thanked the holy man warmly, and tucked the long knife into his belt.

* * *

The newly manumitted cadets also received a purse of gold coins. And after the games, and a quick bath, they all, including Diyar, donned their graduation robes with one thought in mind: a visit to the flesh pots of the capital. The sultan had banned most of the sinful pursuits, but an enterprising young warrior could always find something tempting.

The memory of the rapturous night with Thalia had never left him. He would have her for his own someday, but if not now, he would find a girl he could have.

CHAPTER 10

"So where did you hear about this place?"

Diyar might be a loner, but for his first taste of nightlife, he wanted the company of friends. The three new warriors rode through the Chain Gate of al-Qal'ah into the village of Roumaila which had sprung up to cater to the Fortress.

Tanin al-Ajani, shorter, fair-haired, spoke up. "I asked a couple of pages from the palace. They said this one quarter has wine and ghawazy, Greek girls, plump as pigeons. He said they were the most beautiful dancing girls in the world."

Greek. Diyar exhaled. That was all the encouragement he needed. "I doubt that," he said gruffly, "but," and his eyes twinkled, "I am willing to find out," and Sungar as-Sadi, the third member of the triad, nodded with enthusiasm.

The three cantered onto Main Road. The sun had set, and across the river, only a dull glow lit the edge of the desert. Soon, after passing the huts and shops surrounding the slaughterers' corrals, the walls of the city loomed ahead. They entered the city's main southern gate, Bab Zuwaylah, guarded by troops of the Viceroy of Cairo, and continued to the vast market place, now rimmed with shuttered stalls.

A boy of the streets ran up, bowing as he approached. His face was as grimy as the rags that barely covered him. Examining them with shrewd eyes, he bleated in terrible Turkish, "Oh, noble warriors, you want beautiful girls? Ghawazy? I take you. Wine, too. Hashish? Pretty boys? Anything you want."

The men were young, but they knew a sale's pitch when they heard it. Tanin al-Ajani spoke up, striving to sound in command. "We are interested in only one place, the Mansouri Quarters."

Something changed in the boy's eyes. "No good," he said quickly. "I take you better place."

Tanin dug his heel into his mare, shouldering the boy to the ground. "If you can not do as you are told, be gone."

The boy rolled quickly away, coming up into a wary crouch. His eyes narrowed. "I do. I take. One silver dirhem each."

Now all three laughed, and Tanin spoke for them. "One coin for the three of us, and a copper one at that."

The boy smiled thinly. "I take you Mansouri Quarter, and gladly, sires," and he started off at a trot.

Soon they were winding through streets so narrow two horses could barely pass, and they had to keep alert so as not to ride someone down. Once, in rounding a corner, they almost collided with a turbaned gentleman on a burro. No mamluk warrior would be seen on such a mount, but for gentlemen of the city, these little animals were ideal for the narrow streets.

Against the approaching night, the city's quarters, each no more than two or three streets closed by a wall, were locking up, their gates guarded by a bowwab, gatekeeper.

Following the urchin, the young men found the lanes growing darker. The Egyptians kept lamps lit by their gates, but few broke the night here. And by now, though they would not admit it, they were hopelessly lost.

Diyar glanced back and saw the look of uneasiness in his companions' eyes. He called to the boy. "How much farther?"

"Soon, sire. Soon."

Just as Diyar had decided to turn back, the lad stopped and pointed. By city law, a wane torch burned next to an old gate. The plaster on the gate's wall was cracked, revealing its mud brick skeleton.

Diyar nodded. "Knock."

"Me, sire?"

"You. Tell them we want to enter. We have money."

The boy walked to the gate and rapped. Inside, dogs erupted into raucous howls. After a moment, a voice called out over the din.

The boys could not understand the Arabic, but the lad, eyeing the Kipchak youths, muttered an answer, then turned.

"To enter, a silver dirhem for each," he said, a look of triumph in his eyes.

Diyar glanced at his friends, and they nodded. "Tell him one dirhem, and you come in too."

The boy stepped back. "Me, lord?"

"You. I want you to watch our horses. For that we will each give you another copper."

The money was too good to turn down, and the boy reluctantly followed them through the gate as it squeaked open.

They rode in and the gate slammed shut. The dogs, locked behind the walls of the surrounding houses, became hysterical.

The bowwab was a gaunt little man with eyes rheumy from disease. Except for a rolled, silk scarf around his neck, his clothes were filthy. Eyeing the richly turned-out lads, he smiled a gap-toothed grin. He motioned for them to dismount.

A shack of a gatehouse stood next to the gate. Diyar pointed to it, held up a coin, and said to the boy over the noise of the braying dogs, "Stay here with the horses, understand?"

Tight-lipped, the boy nodded.

Again the gatekeeper grinned evilly and motioned for them to follow. They headed down the dark street and more dogs along the way took up the unholy howl, then drums within the houses began to boom, and tambourines rattled, adding to the raucous charivari.

Uncertain, the boys sought each others eyes in the gloom, but before they could hesitate, a door opened ahead of them, and light fanned out over the dirty street. A great sack of a man stepped out.

Instinctively, Diyar's hand dropped to the pommel of his

sword. The man was just too big not to take seriously.

The gatekeeper grinned again and gestured them in. The big man also smiled reassuringly and beckoned. As Diyar stepped through the narrow gate, he noticed, though the man wore a filthy housecoat, his silk scarf was immaculate.

The boys entered a small court where a single torch burned. Two skinny dogs, tethered to the wall, tore at their leashes, barking insanely.

The big man bowed to the boys, and raised his hands in question. Speaking in fair Turkish, he said with a thick smile, "What may I get for you?"

Tanin al-Ajani stepped forward. "We want wine and to see the girls," he said loudly to cover his nervousness, and to be heard over the shrieking dogs.

The big man's eyebrows arched and he leered. "Ah, wine, girls." He nodded. "Good. Come. Come."

He led the way to a doorway off the court. "Girls," he said with assurance. "Here are girls."

The boys stepped into the room but saw nothing in the gloom. Suddenly, a hiss of silk dropped over Diyar's head, and jerked tight with deadly assurance around his neck.

Instantly he dropped to his knees and whipped out his sword. The big man struggled to pull him up again, but Diyar twisted around and hacked at the man's legs. The blade chopped flesh, and a roar of pain cried out in the dark.

The hold on his neck relaxed, but the big man fell on him, and they both crashed to the floor. He kicked the man away and leaped to his feet. He plunged his blade deep into his body and spun around to the doorway. More assassins with scarves were choking his friends.

He lunged, stabbed one of the assassins and slashed the other. For a moment the three men were free. But now a mob of men, each carrying silk scarves gripped for death, streamed screaming into the court.

The boys cast about for an escape. The stairs.

They bounded up to the next floor, but slammed into a gaggle of women clustered around the top, all carrying drums and tambourines. Seeing the charging boys with their swords waving, they scattered screaming.

A large, inlaid, copper cabinet stood near the top of the stairs. When his companions were clear, Diyar lifted it, staggered to the head of the stairs, and pushed it down. It crashed into the leading assassin, crumbling him and bowling through the men following, wedging in the narrow stairwell.

Diyar turned, searching for an escape but saw only a locked meshrebiyeh, the latticed window that projected out over the street.

"This way", he cried. He sprang to the window and kicked out its finely carved doors. He boosted up Tanin, who clambered up the meshrebiyeh to the roof. Sungar as-Sadi was right behind him.

Diyar prepared to follow, but several men clawed over the cabinet and charged the window. Diyar's sword lashed out at the nearest man. A scream rang out, and a twitching hand bounced across the floor leaving a bloody trail. By then Diyar had gained the roof.

A thin moon gave little light as the boys leaped over the roof's rotting timbers and debris. When they reached the gate house, they were stunned to see men strangling the boy who had been holding their horses. He fell quivering to the ground, and the assassins grabbed the horses to lead them away.

Now real panic gripped the youths. To lose their graduation prizes would be the ultimate shame.

Without hesitation, Diyar leaped down to the gate house roof, hit, rolled, and jumped to the ground. The boys followed, urgency destroying their fear. They charged after their horses, the crowd of men falling away to a sword's length.

Diyar reached the ruffian dragging Saba, and his sword sank deep into the man's arm. The man rolled away with a scream, clutching his wound.

The men leading the other mares saw the grisly sight, dropped the reins and bolted.

Instantly the boys leaped into the saddles and wheeled the

horses around. But now the assassins in the house poured out.

Swords flailing, the boys fought to get back to the gate.

Rocks and bricks began to rain down on them. The women had taken to the roofs, and were hurling debris to kill them from above. A brick struck Sungar on the brow. He slumped forward in the saddle, and the assassins surged forward.

Diyar grabbed Sungar's tunic lest he be pulled from the saddle, but a stone crashed down on his shoulder, and his grip went limp.

A brick glanced off of the head of Tanin's horse, causing her to scream and veer to the side. Tanin grabbed the mare's mane to keep from falling, and men lunged forward to grab him.

Amid the noise and confusion, more men boiled out into the street, and Diyar felt the panic of inevitable doom.

Then a cry rang out in the street. "Open this gate," and pounding reverberated above the tumult of barking dogs and drums.

"Open this gate," the voice cried again, and Diyar knew he had to get to the gate and unlock it. He slapped Saba on the flank with the flat of his sword, and forced her to charge into the seething mass before her. Hands grab for her reins, and more than one was lost to Diyar's blade.

He reach the gate, leaped to the ground, sword flashing, and grabbed the crossbar. A mighty heave, and he pushed open the gate.

In charged Sudun Taz, Kizil, and Stable-Master Taghri, their lances down to skewer anyone who got in their path. Instantly the street cleared, and in the confusion, the pelting from above abated somewhat.

The warriors grabbed the bridles of the boy's horses, turned and surged out of the quarters. Diyar leaped onto Saba's back and followed.

Outside the gate, waited a servant with a torch.

"Go," shouted Taghri Birmish, and the Egyptian took off running at full speed, the men galloping behind.

CHAPTER 11

When the din of the evil quarter had faded behind them, the men slowed their horses to a trot. They entered a small, deserted marketplace, and paused under a wall torch. Sungar as-Sadi slumped in the saddle, blood dripping from his forehead.

Sudun Taz reached to wipe his head, but Sungar pushed his hand away.

"I am not hurt," he said brusquely. Still the older warrior closely examined the lad's eyes before turning away.

Then he hopped down to appraise the gash in Tanin's horse. He nodded. "Yes, this will need tending. We will have it washed as soon as we get to the cabaret."

"Cabaret?" Diyar said, still panting from the throes of the riot. He pulled a cotton handkerchief from inside his tunic and wiped the blood from his new sword. He was proud of it. It had served him well.

Sudun Taz grinned as he mounted. "Of course. Unless it was a fight you wanted, I am sure you did not find what you were seeking there at the Mansouri Quarter. Now we will take you where you should have gone in the first place."

They started out again, and Diyar said, "How did you know to come looking for us?"

Sudun Taz grimaced. "Abu al-Mulq and his friends were

watering their horses at the stable, and I heard them saying how they told one of the newly freed cadets to take his friends to the Mansouri Quarters if he wanted to find dancing girls. So we thought we had better go down there and make sure that nothing happened. Besides," he said with a grin, "we were looking for a little excitement. I should have known you would be in the center of it."

Diyar's face tightened with anger. "Abu al-Mulq. If there is evil afoot, he is leading it. But why did the Mansouri want to kill us?"

The old warrior's face pulled a look of distaste. "They too are an evil bunch. The last remaining followers of an evil holy man, Abu Mansours, a fanatic who lived some four hundred years ago. It seems the old man thought anything new was an affront to God. His followers think they can attain everlasting life if they kill all users of new weapons. That is why they use the silk scarf as garrotes. They especially hate us foreigners. We are new to the Faith, and not to be trusted."

"But surely this is not a worthy reason to kill."

"To the Mansuriya it is. To them the act of murder is legal and worthy. They use dogs and drums to cover the screams of their victims." He grinned in triumph. "But that is what led us to you, the noise of the dogs and drums."

"So where are we going now?" They had entered a narrow lane which confined them to two abreast.

His eyes twinkled. "You will see."

Soon they reined up at a double wooden gate. Light and the whining sounds of a band filtered out from the meshrebiyeh in the adjacent building, occasionally interrupted by gales of laughter.

"It sounds," said Sudun Taz, "as if some of your khushdashiya have already arrived," and he pounded on the gate with the butt of his lance.

Bowwabs immediately threw the bolt of the gate, and the men rode into a well-lit courtyard lined with horses. They dismounted and tied their animals to rings embedded in the wall. Sudun called a bowwab over and instructed him on how to cleanse the wound on Tanin's mare.

Inside the cabaret, several shallow landings ascended from the carpet-covered floor. Warriors of the Tabaqt ar-Rafraf, lounging around low tables on the landings, sent up a cry of greeting upon seeing the men. Brass goblets and pitchers sat on the tables, and several of the men gestured for the new arrivals to join them.

But at that moment, a naked, black dancing girl entered from a beaded doorway to the carpeted area below, and the room erupted with a roar of pleasure. The five-piece band sitting on the floor whined into a deeply erotic rhythm.

Sudun Taz grabbed Diyar's arm. "Tonight will be your night, lad. You are going to get some of your reward for all the hard work you have done for the last few years," and he pulled him, the other boys following, to the front row.

As they stared transfixed by the writhing creature, goblets of wine appeared at their elbows, and after their brush with death, they drank greedily.

Diyar had never seen such a girl. She was sooty black, so black she seemed but a weaving shadow in the dim light. And how she moved! Every beat of the drums vibrated off her perfectly curved buttocks, jiggled the small, round globes of her breasts. In the sultry night, sweat glistened her skin and coursed down her chest and back.

In trance-like intensity, she twirled near the low divan where the boys had sprawled, and Diyar made another discovery, a strange scent, unlike anything he had ever sensed, surrounded her. It was heavy, musky, not altogether pleasant, but uniquely hers. He shifted to relieve the pressure in his groin.

Sudun chortled and gave him a shove. "She is something, no? A Sud, new and young." He motioned over Mustafa, the cabaret's owner, and whispered in his ear. The fat Egyptian hesitated as if unsure. Sudun raised the price, and now the saloon keeper smiled obligingly, allowing the silver to be slipped into his hand.

Finally the girl spun and dropped to her knees. The dance was over.

Cheers broke out, and silver rained down on her. The girl ran off through the doorway and a boy scurried about retrieving the coins.

Sudun pushed the goblet closer to Diyar. "Drink up. The girl's name is Ittifaq, and she wants to meet you."

Diyar gazed at him with stupefaction. "Me? What for?"

Sudun finished off his wine with a gulp, slamming the goblet down. "What do you mean, 'what for'? You're a man, yes? A member of the sultan's elite guard, yes? Why would she not want to meet you?"

He stood, pulling Diyar up. To Tanin and Sungar, he said, "Wait here. You will have your turn soon enough."

Diyar disliked being controlled, but he allowed himself to be shoved through the doorway.

"What better for your first time," Sudun Taz said happily, "than a Sud dancing girl, right?"

He began to protest. "This is not my first...," then he saw the Sudanese girl. She stood at the bottom of a narrow stairway listening to instructions from the manager. She saw the young warrior and she started up the stairs, glancing back at him with black, unreadable eyes.

Sudun gave him a shove. "The prey's afield," he said with a chortle. "After her, lad, before she is away."

Diyar started up the stairs behind her, and with her bottom inches from his face, he smelled again her pungent aroma, so seductive he had difficulty climbing.

The next floor seemed to be a storeroom, with a row of cracked wooden doors running along one wall. And from behind one door, a woman's laugh was followed by a man's satisfied chuckle. The girl continued up a second flight to the roof. Here, in the darkness, she took his hand and led him across to a shack in one corner. She pushed open the door to a low-ceilinged room with a single candle burning on a dish on the floor.

She drew him in, then walked over to her sleeping pad on the floor, sat down and stared at him with dark, unfathomable eyes.

After a moment, he stooped and pulled off his boots, and carefully placed them side-by-side at the foot of her bedroll. He then undid his waistband, and took off his sword, placing it next to the bed. Next, off came his tunic and trousers, their removal made awkward by his throbbing erection. Seeing no pegs on the walls, he folded the garments neatly and placed them on the toes of his boots, topped off by his turban.

The girl followed each movement with great interest. When he came to stand over her, she rose and went to the corner. She returned with a small earthenware basin which she gave to him to hold beneath his genitals. Her gentle washing was just about the sweetest thing he had ever felt, and he climaxed in her hand. Now she smiled for the first time.

She rinsed and wiped him off, and indicated he lay down on the bedroll. She stood above him and wiped herself off, her face, breasts and loins, her toweling almost as sensual as her dance. Then she slid down beside him.

They were grinding together, she too becoming aroused, when the door burst open and several gaping faces led by Sudun's, grinning widely, jutted into the room.

Diyar grabbed for his boot, and his knife hissed through the air, sticking with a quiver in the door jamb but a hand span from Sudun's nose.

Sudun jerked back, and the door slammed shut.

Howls of laughter outside taunted Diyar.

"We just wanted to see if you knew what to do," Sudun called.

"I know what to do, and the next blade will find an eye," Diyar answered.

He turned back to the black girl, just a shadow in the darkness, and found her waiting for him.

CHAPTER 12

"NO!" Sudun Taz spun and stalked back into the tack room.

Diyar followed. "Please, Sudun. Just until Pay Parade. Then I will return all I owe you."

Sudun raised a hand of dismissal. "I said no and meant it. I know what you will do with the money, and she is not worth a copper. She is but a whore."

Diyar winced. "I know, but she has never had anything. Besides, you owe me."

Taz skidded to a stop. "I owe you. What strange logic tells you that?"

Diyar put an arm on the shoulder of the smaller man. "It is like this: You saved my life, therefore I belong to you, forever, or until I can save your life in return. See?"

"And where did you hear such philosophy?"

"Uh, I think it was from a Mongol."

Taz snorted. "That I can believe." Grumpily he pulled out his leather pouch and wedged it open. "Only a couple of dinars, and I will be first in line when you get paid. You owe every man in the tibaq."

Diyar plucked a third out of the old man's hand. "And one more for a bit of food and wine," then danced away as a bow-leg swung at his bottom.

Minutes later, as Diyar threw a saddle onto Saba, Taz sidled over. "You are not in love with this black whore, are you?"

He forced a grin. "Of course not. I just like being with her." But as he rode out of the stable, he mulled over the question. *Why do I like her?*

He loved seeing her excitement when he brought her things, pretty things, a silk scarf, gold earrings. And he loved her lack of inhibitions. Compared to the Egyptians who were so conservative, so restricted by their religion, and the mamluks who revered pomp and ceremony, she seemed not to have one self-conscious thought. In her room, she never wore clothes. She happily threw herself onto her back at his slightest suggestion, and fornicated with total abandon—provided, of course, he first paid.

They could not even converse. She knew no Turkish, he certainly knew no Sudanese, and neither of them spoke much Arabic. And yet, when she wrapped her strong legs around him and writhed under him, making strange, whining noises, he knew exactly what she meant. He felt the same way.

Though afternoon, the cabaret's gates were open and horses lined the wall including a beautiful bay mare. A little, grey burro stood stolidly next to it.

Diyar dropped Saba's reins to a bowwab, jumped down and strode inside. Not wanting to see any of his friends, he did not look around, but walked through the beaded doorway and doubled up the stairs to the roof. He knocked and pushed open the door, then halted in astonishment.

Ittifaq stood before him completely covered in a pink tob, a shapeless, floor-length gown with sleeves as wide as the garment was long. A white muslin burko, face-veil, fell from her eyes nearly to the floor. A habarah, a voluminous, white-silk outer-garment, covered her head and flowed over her arms and shoulders to the floor. Yellow, pointy-toed, moroccan slippers peeped out from under the habarah. Only her black eyes were recognizable. A black slave girl in a sleeveless tob stood nearby.

He had never seen Ittifaq in anything but sheer pantaloons, and occasionally an antaree, an embroidered vest.

He frowned. The traveling garments did not bode well. "Where are you going?" he asked. He suddenly remembered the grey donkey and his apprehension grew. "What is happening here?"

"Old nimrod buy Ittifaq," she mumbled behind the veil.

Diyar knew the Egyptians called mamluks "nimrods" or hunters. "Who bought you? What is his name?"

The girl shrugged, whether from not knowing or not understanding his question, he could not tell. "Stay here," he commanded. He pointed at the floor. "Here," spun and strode out.

He entered the cabaret and spied Mustafa on an upper landing. The Egyptian hovered over the table where an amir reclined.

With purpose, Diyar mounted the steps and grabbed the saloon keeper's arm. "Come, Mustafa, we must talk."

With an oily grin, the Egyptian drew his arm away. "Perhaps later. Now I speak with an important client."

"Now, Mustafa. It is about Ittifaq."

"Ah, but sir, the slave is no longer mine to talk about." He nodded unctuously to the amir. "If you have any questions concerning the girl, you must ask the honorable amir here, Amir Rukn al-din Kazan al-Baybari. He now is her patron, and a fortunate one she is," he said, smiling at the amir.

Diyar glanced at the amir. A grey-white beard, sharply trimmed, pointed the man's gaunt face. A dark scar drew the corner of his eye. His small mouth pursed with petulance as he raised a silver goblet, and a servant quickly stepped to fill it.

Years of respect had been drummed into Diyar, yet he could not let the girl go without protest. He had pictured himself returning from a campaign laden with victory loot, purchasing the girl, taking her to their own house.

He pushed Mustafa aside and spoke to the amir. "You see, sire, I intended to buy the ghawazy myself, and..." His voice trailed off. The man seemed not to hear him.

Mustafa tried to draw Diyar away. "Please, sire, it is too late."

Angrily Diyar turned on him. "How much was paid?"

Mustafa smiled and shrugged. "An honorable merchant does not discuss such things."

Diyar gripped the man's vest and growled, "How much, fellahin. Speak or you will feel a blade between your ribs."

A heavy hand dropped on Diyar's shoulder. A man every bit as tall as he, and much heavier, gave him a bemused smile. "My amir now owns the slave. Mustafa will be happy to you find another."

Anger flashed in Diyar's eyes, and he jerked out of the man's grip. Instantly a half-dozen warriors encircled them, all wearing matching turbans.

The big man continued to smirk. "Now, I am sure you do not want to trouble the amir any longer." He jabbed Diyar in the stomach with his sword's pommel, pushing him down a step, then another. And the warriors moving with him, the big man forced Diyar out to his horse.

Diyar mounted and the big man slapped her on the rump, causing her to leap for the gate. Jeering laughter chased Diyar from the courtyard.

He reined up in the narrow lane, revenge seething in his mind. *Who is this arrogant amir who would not even look at me?*

He had to know more.

He backed Saba into a tiny cul-de-sac, and soon, Kazan, sitting stiffly against the wine he had drunk, trotted out of the cabaret's gate, followed by the big man. Behind him clipped Ittifaq atop the donkey, then the amir's bodyguards.

Diyar trailed them as they transversed the city and rode to the canal. There, behind a high, white wall, soared a palace. The gates in the wall swung open, the party entered, and the gates slammed with a clang of finality.

For a long time, Diyar sat observing the palace. Up until that moment, he had always seen the difference between himself and amirs as one of military rank. Now he saw there was something more than rank. There was wealth. And there was power.

He etched a vow in his mind, then turned back to the cabaret.

He arrived, sought a dark corner, and called for wine. After a time, a movement of white caught his eye.

A woman reclined behind a tiny table in the corner. She was tall with fair skin, her pantaloons and vest, dark maroon. A wide, bronze bowl containing a white gardenia sat on the table. Languidly she stirred the flower, the movement of which had caught his attention.

She smiled at him, and pushed forward her goblet. "Can the mawla spare a drop?" she said in Turkish.

He shrugged, and carried over his cup and pitcher.

After she had taken a drink, she said, "You looked like you were thinking about someone, a pretty girl, perhaps?" She moved the flower in a slow circle.

Unaccountably, the visage of Thalia appeared before him.

The woman seemed to read his thoughts. "I am sure you would like to see her again. Am I right?"

The wine had made him lustful. He would like to see her, and right now.

She caressed his inner thigh. "For but a few dirhems, I can make it so you will believe she is right here with you." The gardenia moved hypnotically, capturing his eyes, dulling his mind.

In a trance, he dug into his saulaq.

Then, on a cot in one of the tiny rooms at the top of the stairs, Thalia seemed to be laying under him, soft and indistinct in the light of the single candle. And then he was loving her, too dazed to wonder how she came to be there. How delicious it was, just like on the balcony, only better here, safer, the wine making everything warm and hazy.

He was soaring to a rapturous eruption, when someone slammed a door nearby, and he awoke to find himself panting atop the prostitute. She stank of garlic and stale sweat.

He jerked back, but she held him in a grip of steel.

"Finish it, my warrior. Close your eyes and just dream."

The fight drained out of him. As bidden, he shut his eyes and relaxed, and in a moment, he collapsed into a shuddering climax.

Ashamed, as if he had sullied the precious bond he had with

his beloved Thalia, he slunk away, vowing never to be lured into such degradation again. But, following the next pay parade, after much wine, he found himself sitting down at her table again.

CHAPTER 13

In the cool of winter, Baybars once again prepared a strike against the Crusaders, and Qal'at al-Jabal stirred into action. This being Diyar's first campaign, he took special care in readying his gear.

The vast army, bands blaring, marched through the city and out the Gate of Conquests. It took hours for the full army to pass through the capital, cheering throngs lining the boulevard.

The sultan was clad in a resplendent gold robe that radiated in the brightness of the sun. How the people shouted and waved when they caught sight of him. And Diyar, riding behind him as a member of his bodyguard, watched his master and swelled with pride. He stretched tall in the saddle, his face a mask of warrior's determination. And even the intelligent Saba pranced higher, her tail a raised pennant of pride.

The sultan's adversary was once again the Frankish King Bohemond VI. Having dislodged Bohemond from Antioch, Baybars now determined to complete the king's downfall by wrenching Tripoli, that great port on the Mediterranean, from his grasp. But before he could lay siege to the walled city, he had to take the two huge fortresses that guarded its eastern flanks, Safita, and the mighty Husn al-Akrad or, as the Crusaders called it, Crac des Chevaliers.

The long column stretched northeast to Salihiya, swung under the Nile's great draining pool, Lake Manzala, and entered the Sinai

Desert.

Diyar had never seen such barrenness. White dunes rolled and broke across a sea of wasteland. By day, the army baked, at night, it froze. The winter wind blew the stinging, white sand into the men's eyes and clothes, and Diyar's excitement at being on campaign quickly faded.

From the Sinai, the army moved into the Negev Desert which was little better. The great army camped below the cliffs of Jerusalem, continued north to Damascus, then along the base of the rugged Syrian mountains, the Jabal Esh Sharki.

Diyar had become one of Amir Kizil's ten, and shared with another warrior a sarrajun, a mounted servant. Often fine fighters, sarrajun were dubbed "Killers of their Patron's Enemies." Diyar's sarrajun, Kareem, was a quick, young Syrian. Reaching Hims, he went shopping in the walled town and rode back carrying a plump chicken, fresh bread, and oranges for his patrons.

From Hims the army began the climb into the mountains. The castle of Safita, an important strategic stronghold from which Tripoli could be harassed, was the sultan's first target. This castle was one of the eighteen that, at one time or another, were manned by the mighty Templar knights.

These warrior-monks' reputation for aggressiveness had grown until one Frankish chronicler stated, "When the Templars were called to arms they did not ask how many the enemy were, only where they were," and indeed, Templar law stated if the odds were less than three to one against them, they could not retreat.

The expense of maintaining their fortresses in the Outrémere was enormous. By the time of Baybars, the Templars had as many as 9,000 estates throughout Europe where their holy brethren labored to provide the funds to continue the struggle against the hated Muslims in the Holy Land. Over time the order grew richer than any king. Indeed, it answered to no king, only the Pope, and not always then.

The ground beneath Safita's walls was rocky and steep, and the sultan's men pitched tents anywhere they could find a purchase. That night their countless campfires dotted the darkness like stars in the sky.

After dinner it was time for stories around the fire. Kizil called out to Kareem, "It is said you are a wise and brave sarrajun. Prove yourself with a story."

Happy with the attention, the handsome, young Syrian moved into the circle of men. "There was once, in the palace of the world, a king," he began, and the men sat back, their eyes drifting in the fire's flames, and allowed the age-old words to capture their minds.

"The king had two wazeers, one of whom was wise and learned, and one of whom was foolish and ignorant. When the king requested counsel concerning the management of the state, the ignorant wazeer said, 'O king, give not money to the soldiers and warriors, for when thou hast money on the battle day, many will be soldiers to thee: where the honey is, there surely come the flies.' His words seemed good to the king, who one day said to the learned wazeer, 'Get me a few men who will be content with little pay.' On the learned wazeer's replying, 'Men without pay are not to be had,' the king said, 'I shall have money when anything befalls, and shall find many men.' Quoth the wazeer, 'So be it, I shall find men who will take no pay and stir not day or night from your gate.' The king was glad and said, 'Get them. Let us see.'

"The learned wazeer went and found a painter and brought him, and he painted a large room in the palace so the four walls of the room were covered with pictured figures of men, and he decked all the figures with the implements of war. When it was completed, the wazeer called the king, and the king arose and went with him to the wall of pictures, and he showed the king the whole of them. The king looked and said, 'What are these pictures? Why hast thou ranged these here rank on rank?' The wazeer replied, 'O king, thou desiredest of me men without pay. Lo, these youths want no pay. So they will serve the king.' The king said, 'There is no life in these. How can they serve?' The wazeer answered, 'O king, if lifeless pictures will not serve, no more will payless soldiers serve. Fief and pay are as the life of the soldier. When thou givest not a man his fief or pay, it is as though thou takest away his life. Judge if a lifeless man could serve.'

"Then the learned wazeer laid a dish of honey before the king. As it was night, no flies came to it. And the wazeer said, 'They say where there is honey, thither will the flies surely flock. Lo, here is honey. Where are the flies?' Quoth the king, 'It is night, therefore they come not.' The wazeer said, 'My king, it is necessary to pay soldiers money, for bringing out money only on the battle day is like bringing out honey at night.' When the king heard these words from the wise wazeer, he was ashamed. He greatly applauded the wazeer, and thenceforth did whatsoever he advised."

A murmur of assent rose from the reclining warriors. And from the edge of the firelight, a man on horse chuckled deeply.

"So make sure each one of you earn your dinars tomorrow," Baybars said, and moved off into the night.

When the siege began the next day, Diyar stood with the rest of the khasakiya around the sultan on a low knoll just out of arrow range from the fortress's walls. At all times on the field, the sultan wore a bright-yellow silk robe over his armor so all could recognize him.

The garrison of Templar Knights with their Syrian mercenaries put up a stubborn resistance but, following the recommendation of their Grand Master of Knights, finally capitulated.

When the surrendered Grand Master and his knights rode out from the walls, his banner, black and white with a red cross emblazoned on it, was carried by his servant on foot. The Templars wore chain mail to their knees covered by white silk surcoats with a cross in red, defiant on the chest. They carried their barrel-shaped helmets under one arm.

Diyar observed his enemy closely. In their heavy armor they were like individual fortresses, unwieldy and slow. They fought bravely enough, but treated their great, wide-backed chargers cruelly. Their heavy, sharp bits tore their horses' mouths, and their pointed spurs shredded their flanks.

"It is to drive their horses mad so they too will attack the enemy," Sudun Taz had once said, shaking his head, not understanding such cruelty. "And they only ride stallions, thinking it unmanly to ride a mare."

Still, the Franks had fought well, and the beneficent sultan, after relieving them of weapons, had them escorted to the sea where they could find ships back to France.

Now the great army turned east to Husn al-Akrad, the most formidable fortress in Syria.

Husn al-Akrad was manned by Hospitaller Knights, or the Order of the Hospital of St John. The garrison also included many knights who joined them temporarily or with allied contingents. Even some Muslim mercenaries fought with them, though if captured, these latter suffered terrible retribution.

After several days of climbing through the mountains, the army entered a narrow valley where, at the upper end, protected by a walled town, the huge fortress waited. As soon as the first of the army spied the castle, a roar of defiance erupted, to be repeated again and again as each regiment entered the valley. It was the 21st of February.

The sultan ordered raiding parties destroy all habitation outside the city's walls, then directed his engineers to roll forward the war machines. Trebuchets were especially effective.

A trebuchet consisted of a long timber balanced on a fulcrum between two tall triangular supports. A great box filled with nearly two tons of rocks and debris was affixed to one end of the timber. A wide sling was tied to the other end. Horses strained at large wheels to pull down the sling end raising the box of rocks. The sling was loaded, usually with sculpted round boulders but occasionally large pots of Greek fire, the lines holding up the weights were loosed, and the boulders screamed through the air to crash on, or over, the walls.

The Hospitallers and their mercenaries made a good account of themselves on the town's walls, but by the 22nd of March, a breach was made, the Muslims poured through, and the town was taken, the Franks and their allies retreating to the castle.

Gazing up at the castle, Diyar shook his head. How could

such a fortress be conquered? It sat high on a mountain surrounded by a double set of walls reinforced by high towers every thirty or forty paces. A deep, wide moat lay between the enceinte and the great wall of the fortress itself. The great wall sloped upward and inward for more than 80 feet, and its base was nearly 80 feet thick. The walls and castle squatted on the mountain's solid rock, making it impossible to use sappers to tunnel under and undermine them. At the base of the walls, the mountain continued to slope steeply down to the valley below.

The sultan commanded, the trumpets cried and drums thundered, and the war machines let fly salvo after mighty salvo. Such was the mamluks' distaste for their heavy armor, only then did they don their chain mail.

Though the sultan used trumpets to direct general troop movement, he sent riders of his khasakiya to carry individual messages. Most of the khasakiya watched the battle, but Diyar watched the sultan. And seeing the ruler squint with thought, he moved into his line of sight. After a moment, Baybars beckoned to him.

"The sultan has called for me," he shouted to Kizil, and steered his horse out of ranks. He rode through the last circle of dignitaries surrounding the sultan, leapt from his horse and knelt in the dust in front of the ruler's horse.

"Yes, O Malik al-Dhahir?"

The sultan continued to study the assault. "Ride to Amir Sayf al-Din. Tell him to throw now the largest boulders. Concentrate on the corner tower. And when it falls, he should have his archers keep the enemy away from the breach."

Shield in hand, Diyar leaped into the saddle and raced to where the amir stood next to the largest trebuchet. He reined up and shouted the message.

"It will be done," the amir replied, and turned to his men.

Now Diyar had to pass on the message to the amir's archers nearer the wall. Galloping into arrow-range, he serpentined through the open ground as arrows from the wall above stabbed the dust around him. A courier was always a prime target.

A row of mantelets shielding the amir's archers spread the length of the wall. Diyar rode up to the nearest and pointed at the great tower. "When it falls, keep the enemy away from the breach. Pass the word down."

His duty completed, Diyar allowed himself a moment to observe the great wall looming over him. Though he knew it perilous to stand exposed so close to the wall, he could not help his fascination.

High above him, something moved in the narrow open space of a crenel: a knight in a black cape. Then an arrow sped down. Diyar had only time to get his small, circular shield up when the arrow struck, piercing the steel.

Instantly, Diyar's bow leaped from its holster, and an arrow arched up in return. A scream rang out, quickly followed by more arrows streaming down.

Amir Sayf gestured angrily. "Back to the khasakiya with you so we can get to work," but as Diyar dashed away, he heard the veteran shout, "and nice shooting."

As he took his place among Kizil's ten, he glanced at the sultan. The man's good eye flicked over and Diyar thought he saw a faint smile play across his lips.

On March 31 a breach was made in one of the towers of the fortress. Finally overwhelmed, the Franks and their mercenaries grounded their weapons and gave up. But many of the Hospitallers took up a defense in the castle's great, round tower, the keep, and continued the fight. Now the catapults were dragged inside the citadel to be directed towards the keep.

But here Baybars used cunning instead of might. He ordered his scribes to forge letters from the fortress's commander in Tripoli ordering the men in the keep to lay down their arms. When the most senior knight of the keep received the letters he appeared on the parapet and called down, requesting leniency. The sultan agreed to spare their lives providing they promise to return to their homelands.

The knights abandoned the keep, were given horses and escorted to friendly lines, and the sultan took possession of the greatest castle in the Outrémere. The Syrian mercenaries who fought alongside of the Hospitallers were slaughtered to the last man.

Baybars then wrote a letter to the Grand Master of the Hospitallers: "This letter is addressed to Frere Hugues, Hugh of Revel, to inform him of the conquest, by God's grace, of Husn al-Akrad, which you fortified and built out and furbished, you would have done better to destroy it, and whose defense you entrusted to your Brethren. They have failed you. By making them live there you destroyed them, for they have lost both the fort and you. These troops of mine are incapable of besieging any fort and leaving it able to resist them."

The sultan then ordered the collapsed corner tower be rebuilt, and a great, square, gate tower constructed, making the fortress even more formidable. Meanwhile he had the fortress restocked. Over a thousand mules burdened with wheat and barley plodded up the road to the castle. Another thousand bore fodder for the garrison's horses and camels, and nearly as many wagons carried all forms of meat, fish, vegetables and fruit.

With the capture of Husn al-Akrad, the sultan's prestige soared, for the castle had resisted all other monarchs, including the legendary Saladin.

Now the sultan sent troops into the territories around Tripoli, their orders: kill and destroy. Amir Kizil and his men were allowed to join the plundering. But Diyar soon found raiding held no glory.

Warriors, swords and maces held high, swooped down on the poor Christian peasants scraping at the rocky dirt. In shock, the farmers fell to the dust and awaited death. In a trice, they were crumpled heaps of bloody rags.

After the charge, Diyar paused at a peasants' shabby hovel. Inside, he found the room devoid of furniture except a tiny hearth, stones embedded in the dirt, and straw along one wall for a bed. A rude wooden cross hung above the bedding.

Something moved in the corner. A girl, shapeless in a coarse shift, shook with terror.

Diyar stared at the quivering creature for a second, then walked out.

"Anything?" asked one of his squad members.

"Nothing but straw."

It was not the first order he ignored. It would not be the last. And as they rode away, he thought, *Do not even Christians have a right to live?*

Even to ask such questions, he knew to be treason. But killing an enemy soldier was one thing; killing a defenseless child another.

He was glad when Kizil signaled a return to camp. So completely had the land been ravaged, it looked as if locusts had descended on it.

CHAPTER 14

Baybars was now ready to mount a major attack on Tripoli. But his plans were thwarted by the arrival of Prince Edward of Cornwall—later to become King Edward I, or Edward Longshanks—with his troops at the great seaport of Acre. Always scheming, the sultan immediately sent an embassy to Tripoli and secured a ten-year truce.

With the treaty, Baybars was left free to attack Al-Qurain, Montfort to the Franks, the only castle in the coastal territory belonging to the knights of the Teutonic Order. The Teutonic Knights were the third great Military Order in the Outrémere. Exclusively German, their full title was The Teutonic Knights of the Hospital of St Mary of Jerusalem.

Al-Qurain was one of the most heavily fortified castles in the region and was a menace to the Muslim city of Safad. But by June, the town and citadel had fallen to the mamluks, and the Teutonic Knights who survived sent back to Germany.

Back at the Citadel in Cairo, it was time for the army's happiest event, Pay Parade. Each warrior dressed in his best robe and rode proudly behind his amir's banner to the pay platform. To guarantee the loyalty of his private bodyguard, the khasakiya were paid first.

After collecting his jamaqiya, his additional combat pay for the expedition, Diyar found his sarrajun, Kareem. Receiving his coins, the Syrian dropped them into his saulaq without glancing at them.

"Are you not going to count your money?"

The man looked at him with level eyes. "I trust you, sire."

Diyar paused. "It comes to me I will need a sarrajun on all my campaigns. Perhaps you would care to serve me."

Kareem's bright smile flashed. "I will live to serve you, and die defending you."

"Hmm, not too soon, let us hope." He dropped more coins into the servant's quick hand. "We will need a house, a place that is quiet. Take care of it without costing me too much, and I will consider keeping you."

The sarrajun leaped into his saddle and bounded off with a laugh, his departing words, "I live to serve."

The small house overlooked the canal in Fustat. It was old but cheap and clean. Though many of the houses in Cairo contained as many as six stories, it had but three, built around a tiny court, and stood shoulder to shoulder with homes of equal modest size.

Diyar found the luxury of keeping a servant and a house took most of his small wages. With the little money left, instead of buying clothes, the showy silks and satins the mamluks so loved, he decided to learn Arabic, the language of the people they ruled, and sent Kareem to the Medina Mosque to hire a teacher.

Throughout the Islamic world, from the Atlantic Ocean, to the Philippine Sea, from the Pyrenees to the Himalayans, the mosques were the centers of all learning. In the larger mosques, often hundreds of scholars lived, studied and taught. As a gift of patronage from the sultan or governors, anyone wanting to learn the Koran, Koranic recitation, intonation, Islamic law or jurisprudence, could come to a mosque, be given a room, and be paid to study or even just to read. Even the gentle old men who walked the children to and from the mosque for school were provided a room, bed and board. It was a national educational system while the rest of the world slumbered in ignorance.

Ali Darwish, who came to Diyar's house in the evenings, was a quiet man, loving his Koran. But he was wise enough not to try to force on the young warrior only spiritual works.

***

They sat on a corner divan, a table between them, candle holders at their elbows.

"Try this one," Ali Darwish murmured, and placed a book of rough-cut parchment, its covers slices of wood, on the table.

Diyar opened the volume and began slowly, following the graceful script with his finger. "'Wake! For the sun, who scattered into flight the stars before him from the field of night, drives night along with them from heaven, and strikes the sultan's turret with a...'"

"'A shaft...'"

"'...a shaft of light.'"

He looked up with a smile. "Such beautiful words."

"Yes. This was written by an astronomer from Persia, Omar Khayyam, very wise."

Diyar turned the pages, all written laboriously in beautiful calligraphy. "I like this book. I would like to buy it."

Ali coughed discretely. "I am sorry, sire, but it would be quite expensive. Few people buy books. They rent them, usually in pages of ten, then copy them. This book I copied myself. However, I will loan it to you, and you can copy it for yourself. It will be good practice."

"Thank you," Diyar said sincerely, and read on.

The next year, the sultan once again sallied forth at the head of his army, arriving in Damascus in September. The next month, the Mongol Il-Khan of Persia sent a raiding party of 10,000 striking into the sultanate as far as Harim. Baybars immediately dispatched a strong counter-force, and the Mongols were obliged to withdraw.

Since the sultan himself did not depart from Damascus to take part in the fighting, his bodyguard also remained bivouacked there. Diyar did not mind at all. He had been paid his nafaqa, pre-battle pay, at the beginning of the campaign. While other members of the bodyguard sought out the cabarets, Diyar could be found seated in the back of some book-merchant's stall, examining manuscripts, while Kareem undertook the haggling.

Prince Edward took advantage of the Mongol incursion into the sultan's territory and attacked the Muslim fortress of Qaqum. But the sultan ordered a regiment of his fleetest horsemen to speed to the fortress where they caught the Franks by surprise and drove them away.

Now the sultan decided to eliminate Prince Edward in the cheapest way, by assassination. So, on the 16th of June, as the prince rode through the streets of Acre, a man dashed from the crowd and stabbed him.

Instantly the assassin was chopped down by the prince's knights, and the prince was dragged away. He survived, but upon recovering well enough to travel, left the East, never to return.

When the army returned to Cairo, Baybars sent troops to open a campaign against the Ismailis—the Assassins—the very people he had negotiated with to kill the prince. No ruler had been able to extract these Arab clans from their pinnacle fortresses in the Jabal Esh Sharki, the mountains of Syria. From these aeries, the Ismailis would swoop down to harass passing caravans, or steal down to commit what they were most feared for, assassination.

Now, through threats, promises, and siege, armies under Baybars' command began taking over their dozen or so fortresses.

Diyar's squad had remained in Cairo. The operations against the Ismailis dragged on for a year, and through boredom and need of cash, he requested permission to join one of the armies.

His comrades thought him crazy. Cairo was the most sought-after billeting in the empire. For a warrior to be sent to serve in some other area was tantamount to banishment, and to actually volunteer for such duty seemed ludicrous.

The task of attacking the Ismaili fortresses was relegated to the Viceroy of Hims, Amir Badr al-Din. As Diyar tied on his saddlebags, Kizil strolled over. "Be aware, the mawali of the viceroy have no love for the sultan's khasakiya. It might be wise to leave in the trunk your robe and khasakiya turban."

Before leaving, Diyar was summoned to the office of the Deputy Chief of Corps. As he entered the office, the amir was examining a bundle of arrows.

He turned to the amir in charge of the Fortress's armory and shook his head. "Not bad, but not good. There was a time when we had so many arrows our bowmen could eclipse the sun. Now to get good shafts, the sultan must pay dear."

The Chief Armorer shrugged. "We have used up all the good trees. The fletchers must go farther and farther to find good wood."

Seeing Diyar, the amir said, "Ah, yes, Diyar al-Mijiri, the sultan wants you to carry a message to Amir Badr al-Din." He handed him a baton wrapped in yellow silk. "It is sealed. It will arrive that way," he said, ominously, "or you will find no place to hide. Do you understand?"

Diyar stiffened to attention. "I understand and will obey," he said, reciting the first speech he had learned upon entering al-Qal'ah.

Being a courier allowed him to exchange his weary horses at the sultan's post houses. Here fresh horses awaited to carry him on. In this way, dispatch riders could race to the ends of the sultanate, traveling farther faster than anywhere else on earth. Now Diyar utilized the network to speed for Hims.

At the last post house before Hims, Diyar learned Amir Badr al-Din and his army had left for the mountains, so Diyar headed northwest. He knew he neared the army, when he came across poor farmers scraping the precious horse and camel dung off the road. When he encountered the army's rear-guard, he was escorted up the line of troops from one amir to another.

The road was narrow, choked with cavalry, foot-soldiers and camels. The camels moved out of the way with haughty reluctance, the foot troops moved to keep from being run down, but the proud mamluks begrudged the right-of-way to no man. Finally, an amir ashara ushered him to the side of Viceroy Badr al-Din who, as he broke the seal of the dispatch baton, eyed the young man suspiciously. He read on the move, then glanced up.

"These papers say, among other things, you are good with the bow. But you will find there are many here who can fly an arrow just as true as the sultan's pets—including many among those who fight against us. You can practice your skill with Amir Jantimur and his men who are leading the column," and he waved Diyar forward.

Again he was passed from unit to unit until he reached Amir Ashara Jantimur who headed the avant-guard. The amir, short, stocky, was skeptical. "You are from the sultan's khasakiya? So, why are you here?"

"The viceroy assigned me here, sire."

"That is obvious. My question is why."

"He must think I can be of service to you."

"More likely he wanted to get rid of you quickly." Not seeing a lance, he demanded, "Where is your gear?"

Diyar patted a sheepskin duffle tied behind his saddle. "I rode without a servant. All I need is here."

The tough little amir gentled somewhat. "A member of the khasakiya without a servant? Hm..." He glanced up at the road curving up into the barren mountains. "I hope you have armor in that bag. You will need it."

"Only a short dir, mail shirt, and my khaudha, helmet."

Jantimur nodded approvingly. "All right, but stay alert. Ambush is the Ismailis' meat and bread."

As the road wound higher into the mountains, it narrowed, often hacked out of the mountainside. No tree broke the mountains' sky-lines, but many boulders and ridges offered fine cover for Assassin archers. Diyar looked back and saw the army, now single file, curving around the edge of a mountainside—and far distant, curving around the edge of another.

The troops had just rounded a bend when arrows buzzed down on them. One dug deep into the ear of a horse. It squealed in pain and lunged blindly over the cliff's edge. Its rider leaped to the rocky slope, and the horse rolled disjointedly down the mountainside. The rider slid several yards down the mountain then, arrows ricocheting all around him, began crawling back up to the road.

Meanwhile, the rest of the squad had wheeled their mounts and started back down the trail. But more arrows met the men from behind.

Jantimur waved to the men and shouted, "Take shelter against the hillside." The men immediately leaped from their horses and, in the low cover offered by the inside of the trail, forced their well-trained mounts to lie down, and began pulling on their armor.

Donning his helmet, Diyar scanned the rocks above. Behind one boulder, sunlight glinted dully off conical steel. He scuttled over to where Jantimur knelt, bow in hand, peering above for a target.

"There are two groups of them, one on the far edge of the ridge, the other just above us."

"I know that," the amir growled with impatience.

"With your permission, I will climb to their level."

The warrior next to them spoke up. "I will go with him."

Jantimur nodded. "Go then, but hurry. The viceroy will be wanting to know what is holding up his army." To the man whose mount had fallen off the trail, he called, "Stay there and wait for our arrows."

He turned to his men. "Ready....Now," and they all stood as one and fired a volley. As quick as his arrow flew, Jantimur leaped to his feet, ran to the edge of the trail and jerked the fallen warrior up, and they scampered back to the shelter of the trail's inner edge.

Instantly as the arrows were loosed, Diyar ran to his mount. He urged it to its feet, leaping on its back as it stood. Jantimur's man was mounted right behind him, and they raced down the trail, arrows whining after them.

Out of range, they came upon an amir tablkhana, an amir of forty, and his men.

"Why the delay?" the amir asked.

"Double ambush. If we climb from here, we may be able to target them," and he and his riding companion leaped to the ground and started scratching up the hill.

The amir grabbed the reins of Diyar's horse, then turned to a man nearby. "Don armor, take your men, and follow them."

"Thank you, sire," Diyar called back, "We will meet above."

MAMLUK

As the two struggled up the rocky slope, slippery with loose gravel and dust, a merciless sun beat down on them. Soon sweat coursed down Diyar's cheeks from under his helmet, and he wished he had left it in his pack.

When the two reached the top of the ridge, they found the hilltop surprisingly flat. They hunkered down behind a boulder, and Diyar's companion whispered, "They must be down that way. You stay here. Count three score, then move toward them. I will move to the right and hit them from that side."

He nodded. It was as good a plan as any.

After the man disappeared over the edge of the ridge, the ridge fell silent. He pulled his helmet off, and wiped his face with a cotton kerchief.

Time paused.

After a while, a tiny mouse peeped out from a hole in the rocks. As Diyar watched, it froze, only its minuscule nose quivering. Then it leaped from its hiding place, scampered across several rocks and disappeared into a crevice.

Diyar had not thought to count. Now he drew on his helmet, rose to a crouch, and trotted toward the brow of the ridge. He had nearly reached the edge, when the sound of rolling rock came from his right. Had his companion fallen?

Ahead of him, two battered helmets popped up, peering in the direction of the sound. Diyar let fly with an arrow, then another. The first arrow embedded in one man's neck, the other, the forehead of the second man when he turned to Diyar's direction. The men fell without a sound.

In their place, two more popped up, bows pulled, and Diyar dived for the shelter of a boulder as the arrows zipped past where he had just been.

Pulling off his helmet, he propped it up at the edge of the boulder. As soon as an arrow knocked it over, he leaped up and fired. But one of the Ismailis was also standing, and he and Diyar fired at the same time. Diyar's arrow was true. The Ismaili's glanced off his temple.

Dazed, Diyar remained standing. As in a dream, his hand went to his quiver, pulled and nocked an arrow, pulled and, as the last man stood, let fly. The arrow went in the surprised assassin's mouth and out the back of his neck.

Diyar staggered to the men's hiding place. Had not the sound of falling rock attracted their attention, he would have walked right into them. These men had been lookouts protecting the ambushers. The latter, about a dozen of them, were hiding about a hundred paces below him. Farther down, around the curve of the ridge, perhaps twice as many were scattered among the rocks. They were the ones who had fired the first volley to hold up the column.

Even as he watched, several of Jantimur's men tried crawling up the slope from the trail. The Ismailis let loose a volley down on them. One fell with a yelp, another without a sound.

From their vantage point the ambushers could hold the army for hours, or until the mamluks massed enough men for a charge.

Diyar heard more tumbling of rocks from his right, and stood to investigate. His companion approached and Diyar hissed, caught the man's attention. In a moment, the soldier dropped into the lookout post.

He saw the dead men, arrows protruding from their skulls, and nodded approval. "Good eyes."

"Thanks, but if you had not made so much noise, I would not have seem them." He pointed. "There are the ambushers." He gathered up the Ismaili's quivers. "I am going down,." and, bent in a crouch, started down the slope.

"Wait," called his companion.

Diyar twisted around. "In the name of God," he whispered, "be quiet."

"But..." The man hesitated, not knowing how to ask whether the man really wanted to do such a foolhardy thing. Finally he reached for his quiver. "Here, you may need more."

Diyar grinned. "Me? You jest, of course," and continued on.

Now surprise was impossible. He slipped down the slope as

far as he could before the rolling rocks caught the ears of the ambushers. Instantly they turned and began shooting up at him.

Dropping behind a boulder, he peeked out. The Ismailis had moved to rocks that hid them both from him and Jantimur's men. They were at least seventy-five paces away, perhaps too far for accuracy for them, but not for him. And the sun sat on his shoulder, grinning into their eyes.

He stepped out and stood next to the boulder, a tantalizing target. One poked his head out to shoot up at him, and Diyar let fly. And the man died. He then moved a few paces so they could not get a fix on him, and repeated the process.

After his arrows had split several heads, the men kept down.

He picked up a heavy rock and rolled it down the hill. Another Ismaili heard the noise, stood, and died for such foolhardiness.

Soon the Ismailis in the other ambush position spotted Diyar, but he was beyond accurate range, and they could only curse and shake their fists at him. Several tried to work their way to the beleaguered men, but Jantimur's men, firing from below, forced them to duck to safety.

The last two assassins below Diyar made a dash to join the their comrades below, only to be caught by Diyar's arrows. They did not stop rolling until they dropped onto the road.

Cautiously, his bow drawn, Diyar crept down to the Ismailis' protected ledge. Among the corpses he found a leather bottle. Suddenly struck with thirst, he snatched it up. Whether it contained water, wine, or camel piss, he cared not, and jerked the stopper and greedily upended it.

Diyar's companion and a squad of mamluks came skidding down the slope. They glanced at Diyar surrounded by corpses, shook their heads, then fanned out, and advanced on the main party of ambushers.

The Ismailis saw the impossibility of their position, mamluks above them, mamluks below them, and a marksman of near demonic accuracy to the left of them. That left them only one escape and they took it. With backward looks, they abandoned the rocks and skittered away down the ridge.

Below, Jantimur ordered his men into the saddle, and chased after the fleeing ambushers. Carefully, Diyar began the descent to the trail. Soon the amir tablkhana rode up, and his servant returned Diyar's horse.

Over the next few days, as the army snaked deeper into the bald mountains, it was struck frequently by ambushes. Though he had earned the right to leave the avant-guard, he remained with Jantimur, repeating the process of weeding out the ambushers.

Finally the mamluks came around a bend and saw, wedged in between two pinnacles of rock, the Ismaili fortress, as if part of the mountain itself.

A chasm, once spanned by a bridge now drawn into the fortress, separated the fortress from the road. The Assassins had chosen a perfect spot for a stronghold.

Who were these Ismailis, these Assassins who even the great Salah al-Din could not pry loose from their rocky nests?

That night, an old warrior told their story.

CHAPTER 15

Campfires in the night snaked down through the mountains. The army had set up camp on the road and the warriors clustered around early-evening campfires.

Diyar's near inhuman accuracy with the bow, and his willingness to clamber up the crumbly slopes after ambushers, had made him a welcome comrade-in-arms with Amir Jantimur's squad. On the battlements of the Ismaili fortress, torches flickered as its lookouts watched against a mamluk night attack. Eyeing the rocky fortress, Diyar now wondered aloud about their enemy, and an old warrior gave the reply:

"Who are they, you ask?" The wan flames lit his craggy features. "They are the devil's spawn. As long as these fanatics live, no one is safe. They seek heaven through the slaughter of the unsuspecting. Their leader, though long dead, still leads them like camels around a threshing wheel."

He leaned back, and the men settled for the tale. Behind them, sarrajun leaned forward to hear.

"Two hundred years ago, an old man, Hassan ben Sabbah, a holy man, wandered out of the mountains of Persia preaching the word of the Prophet. He chose the kingdom of Alamut in mountains on the southern shore of the Caspian Sea as his residence, and created a secret sect. His following grew, and erelong, his word became all, and the word of the Prince of Alamut became nothing, and the holy man sent the prince away.

"Being now Lord of Alamut, Hassan built a paradise in the mountains. It contained embedded fortresses, gilded palaces, tropical flowers, precious fruit-trees, and shady palms.

"He chose young men and, being wise in the way of drugs, captured their minds with hashish. While they were drugged, he had them carried to a lovely garden. Beautiful maidens entered and catered to the lads' fantasies. Later, when the boys awoke again in their bedrolls, they were told, because they were the followers of the Lord of Alamut, they had experienced paradise. And if they died in his service, in the service of the Sheik-al-Jabal, or 'King of the Mountain,' they would live forever in such a paradise.

"From that moment, a young man in the lord's service became a Fedai, one of the Devoted. In disguise, he would go and slay any victim ordered by his master. He carried only a dagger, and was to kill openly so all would see the power of Sheik-al-Jabal and be afraid. The Assassin was so intent on making his kill, he etched the name of his victim on his blade.

"The Mongols were determined to put the sect to the sword, 'down to the children in the cradle.' But even they were not strong enough. For three years they were held at bay by the Assassins in their impregnable fortresses, until, after the death of the reigning Sheik-al-Jabal, his weak successor surrendered. Even then, a hundred of the fortresses in the Elburz Mountains still held out.

"Then Il-Khan Hulagu forced the imprisoned sheik to send the order to the commandants of the fortresses to open their doors and destroy their fortifications. But when the demolishers got to work upon Alamut itself, the walls proved so strong they resisted pickaxe and sledge. Hulagu sent the dethroned ruler of the Assassins to Khakan Mangu at Karakorum, but the ex-Sheik was murdered before he reached his destination—certainly not by Mongols, who would never dare to touch the person of a prisoner on the way to the Khakan. Who killed the Sheik, no one knows.

"Some of the Assassins escaped to these very mountains and built new fortresses. They continued their devilish rites, bought young boys, and once again grew strong. Other monarchs tried to drive them from these peaks. All have failed. Only our great leader, Malik al-Dhahir Baybars, may his reign be glorious, has been powerful enough to accomplish the destruction of the Ismailis. But will the vermin ever be completely killed?" His eyes traversed the circle of rapt listeners. "It is doubtful." He leaned back on his blanket and closed his eyes. "It is doubtful."

Uneasily the men glanced out into the inky darkness. Were the Assassins creeping up on them at that very moment?

Jantimur snorted. He was one amir who was not to be frightened by fireside tales. Even so, he stood and went to recheck his guards on watch, and presently the men around the dying fire heard a sharp reprimand coming from up the road.

The next morning, behind the protection of mantelets, engineers began chopping away the mountain opposite the fortress. Camels, some carrying in tandem, bore timbers up to the construction site, and engineers constructed a bridge and a siege tower. Archers, including Diyar, shielded by mantelets, tried to give them protection. Still, arrows rained down, and any part of the body exposed risked a wounding.

The completed bridge, built with a stout roof, was rolled on massive wheels out over the chasm to the fortress's entrance, and a battering ram, a timber headed by an iron ball, was hung from the rafters inside the bridge.

The fortress's entrance was closed by a great door, sheathed with an iron face. For the rest of the afternoon men sweated in the close confines of the bridge, slamming the ram against the iron door. However from the first blow it was evident to everyone the door would never yield.

The viceroy knew why.

Spies had informed him the Ismailis secured the iron door with a huge boulder that no battering ram could budge. He ordered the tower be brought up.

The ram was pulled out, the roof of the bridge dismantled, and the great tower pushed across the bridge. Thick hides protected the tower's wooden timbers from fire arrows. Mamluk warriors waited in its lower levels. When finally in place, the siege tower stood higher than the fortress's wall. Then all fell silent.

Behind the curve in the road, hidden from the fortress, the viceroy rode down two long ranks of warriors on foot, quietly encouraging them to victory. He nodded to his flag bearer, who dipped his flag. Drums thundered and trumpets blared. The engineers on the highest level of the tower dropped a catwalk onto the fortress parapet, and with a roar, the soldiers in the tower leaped onto the Ismaili wall and began hacking away at the waiting Assassins. From along the road more mamluk warriors dashed for the bridge, scrambled up the tower, following the ones on the wall, brandishing sword and mace.

The timbers of the bridge groaned under the combined weight of the huge tower and the crush of men trying to get up the tower and into the fray.

Bored with the weeks of inactivity, the men lusted for action. Was there gold in the fortress? Beautiful women? They would brush the fanatics aside and plunder their treasures.

It was not that easy. The Ishmailis fought with the ferocity of fanatics who did not fear death. But slowly they were hacked back by the superior numbers.

Diyar stood on the side of the hill and watched as the fortress's parapets filled with the viceroy's men, clashing against the defenders. Then he pushed through the stream of troops until he found Jantimur's servant who safeguarded his horse. He left a message for the amir, "If there is any loot coming to me, please send it on to the Citadel. I have enjoyed sharing a fire with you."

CHAPTER 16

In the capital once again, Diyar's life returned to normal: a day on the practice field, then home to his little house and a meal picked up from street vendors by Kareem. Many of the Cairenes procured their meals in this way. The food was cooked expertly, was hot, spicy and multi-varied.

The arrival of a modest cache of dinars and several jewels, booty from the Ismaili campaign sent by the Viceroy of Hims, was a welcome surprise.

Diyar considered how best to invest it, and approached his teacher, Ali Darwish, with a proposition. The sage, though not interested himself, recommended a nephew, Abd ar-Rahman. The young man had recently graduated from a zawiya, a monastery, where he studied theological law, and eagerly desired to enter business.

Abd ar-Rahman was slim, of medium height, and he kept his short beard well trimmed. He wore clothes clean and modest. Though too diplomatic to correct the mamluk's rudimentary Arabic, he would occasionally repeat the Kipchak's statement with improved syntax. Diyar sensed he could learn much from the young scholar.

And when Abd heard Diyar's proposition, he smiled, bowed, and quickly agreed. So Diyar turned over the spoils of his latest campaign to the Egyptian, and became the partner of Cairo's newest book stall. But it had to be a silent partnership. No mamluk would give up the status of warrior and ruler to become something so common as a merchant.

When Taninl-Izz, the ruler of Nubia, became blind, he was dethroned by his nephew, Dawud. Dawud refused to pay the baqt, the annual payment of slaves, Nubia's greatest export, to Sultan Baybars, and foolishly began raiding towns along the sultan's southern frontier.

The Baybars immediately sent a force of 3,000 horsemen south up the Nile to capture Dongola, the Nubian capital and depose Dawud. A contingent of the sultan's khasikiya rode with the generals' entourage as couriers to carry messages back to Qal'at al-Jabal. Diyar was one of the contingent.

To transport the army up the Nile, hundreds of boats were hired. With Amir Kizil and the rest of the ten, Diyar lazed on board and let the days slip by.

The days grew hot, stretched on, and grew hotter. When the boats approached Dongola, the generals ordered all men to the shore and into the saddle. Soon the high, sloping walls of the city by the river appeared. Made of mud bricks, in the hot, equatorial sun, they glowed dull-gold like the desert.

Eyeing the height and solidity of the walls, the generals were about to issue orders for the assembly of the siege machines, when the great gates opened, and the Nubians, brandishing spears and sitting atop tall camels, loped out with a shout of attack.

As the camel cavalry rolled closer, the veteran army of the sultan waited quietly. Upon orders, they nocked arrows, drew their bows, and let fly. The cloud of arrows darkened the sky, struck, and the Nubian army fell thrashing to the ground. The battle was over.

Diyar observed the hundreds of men and animals whose blood stained the sand and shook his head. This was no victory, this was slaughter.

A detail of mamluks rode into the city to capture Dawud, only to return with the news he had escaped. A company of riders was dispatched to bring him back, Diyar included as courier.

Into the desert the men raced following the telltale tracks.

Soon they came across Dawud's family and servants abandoned by the pretender's headlong flight. The amir in charge quickly issued orders for them to be escorted back to Dongola, and he and the rest of his men pressed on.

Diyar loved the chase. Under him, Saba, her blue blood coursing, stretched her legs. This was the desert, her home, and the home of unnumbered generations of her ancestors. She cared not where she was going, as long as she could fly. Diyar gave her her head, and she arched her neck and stretched her nostrils to the sky, an "Eater of the Wind."

In a few bounds Diyar and Saba pulled ahead of the regiment. As a member of the khasikiya, Diyar had no authority. But being a favorite of the sultan, Diyar knew he was hard to rebuke, and took advantage.

Soon he approached thick walls squatting on the crest of a low, rounded hill, the fortress of the Lord of al-Abwab. The rest of the mamluks reined to a stop, but Diyar, reveling in his invincibility, dashed up to the gate and demanded, in his best Arabic, for an entrance. To the men's amazement, the gate creaked open, and the impetuous young warrior galloped in.

He drove to the center of the courtyard and reined in Saba. Filled with the exhilaration of the chase, she reared up, her hooves clawing the air, sending the brown-robed people scurrying.

Diyar peered around, shield up, sword in hand. In one corner, a handful of camels drank at a trough, their masters backing into the shadows.

"I demand to see the lord of the castle," Diyar bellowed in Arabic. They pointed to an open entrance in the tall building at the end of the court, and Diyar rode for its darkness. Two spearmen guarded it.

"Stand back or die," he cried, and they leaped back as Saba raced past, found wide steps, and bounded up. The top of the stairs opened into a dim hall where tall, black courtiers tumbled out of the horse's way.

Instantly Diyar's eyes took in the scene. At one end of the hall was a low throne. On it sat a heavy-set man of about forty, wearing a dark blue robe. A golden dagger jutted from his belt. In front of him, accompanied by several attendants, cowered a tall, thin man covered with dust.

Diyar pointed his sword at the cringing man, and roared, "In the name of al-Malik al-Dhahir Rukn al-Din Abul Fath Baybars, I demand the surrender of that man."

The Lord of al-Abwab appraised the young man quietly for a moment, then said, "Take him, and may God's blessing be on you and your sultan."

In June 1276, the Nubia contingent returned to Qal'at al-Jabal with Dawud in chains. Baybars and the army were bivouacked in Damascus. He had been informed of Dawud's capture but wanted to hear the tale firsthand from the arresting warrior, and Diyar was ordered to ride north to Damascus.

In the Hall of Audience in the splendid Piebald Palace, Diyar told of Dawud's capture to an enrapt court. When he finished, the sultan stood and stepped down to him. "Rukn al-Din Diyar al-Mijiri al-Baybariya," he said, "you have done well. For this, and in the name of God and his most learned Prophet, I now make you amir ashara." At the young age of twenty-three, Diyar had become an Amir of Ten.

When he returned to al-Qahirah he resisted the temptation to move to a larger house and instead bought a larger book stall nearer the city square. His partner, Abd ar-Rahman, delighted with his burgeoning fortunes, went out and found a bride.

In February, 1277, the sultan headed up another campaign into the rugged mountains of Asia Minor. Soon the sultan's armies met a combined force of Seljuk Turks and Mongols at Albistan. Because of the steep, rocky terrain, the mamluks grudgingly dismounted and attacked on foot. No mamluk liked to be afoot. If only crossing a courtyard, he would mount and ride.

The mamluks won the battle, but soon reports arrived Il-Khan Abagha was advancing with his whole army. The sultan dared not risk being cut off in the tangled mountains, and led his army back to Albistan.

By June, he and the troops were back in Damascus where a

huge reception was mounted. Many games were contested and, though Baybars forbade the consumption of alcohol in public, kumiss, the fermented mares' milk of the steppes, was served.

Diyar and his ten were in charge of guarding the sultan's pavilion. In the shade of the awning, he watched as the sultan, with every quaff of the foamy drink, became more agitated. Then, Diyar saw why.

During the campaign in the Taurus Mountains, an Ayoubid prince, Malik-al-Qahir (Conquering King) Abdul Malik, and his men had joined the sultan's army. In several hand-to-hand grappling with Mongol warriors, he had distinguished himself by outstanding bravery. Now, as he entered into a game of polo, the crowd screamed their adulation. The sultan, accustomed to monopolizing the public's applause, seethed with jealousy.

Embarrassed for his leader, Diyar stepped inside the pavilion. There awaited the sultan's portable throne, gold covered and encrusted with jewels. To one side lay his bedroll, on the other, stood a table, usually used for eating, or for plotting military plans, now laden with jugs of kumiss. Well disciplined, Diyar ignored the drink. But, seeing several books piled on a low stand, his resistance wavered.

What did the sultan read? He glanced out the entrance, then sidled over to the stand. But before he could pick up a book, hooves pounded up outside.

Diyar quickly stepped to the entrance, then fell back as the sultan, followed by an older amir, lurched into the tent.

The amir was speaking. "But, Malana, this is wrong, and will appear so before the people."

"No man can make a fool of me," the big man said, his words slurred.

He strode to a stack of beautifully carved, mahogany boxes. One opened to become a cabinet. From it he snatched a small blue bottle and hurried to the table. Filling two golden goblets with kumiss, he poured the contents of the vial into one of them.

The amir spoke up. "Malana, if you do this, all will know."

A crafty look twisted the man's drunken features. "Do you not remember what the old astrologer said when we started this campaign? This year, he said, a king would die of poison in Damascus. And the whole court heard him say it. Now his prophesy will come true."

He turned back to the goblets. "Now, which one was it? Ah, yes, this one," and he grabbed them both and strode out of the tent.

Springing into his saddle without spilling a drop, the sultan rode off, guiding his mare with his knees.

Diyar stared after the two men. They had been so intent, they had not seen him. He glanced back at the table, crossed quickly and pocketed the blue vial.

Soon Sultan Baybars left the playing field complaining of stomach pains. Later that day he died, and was carried back to Qal'at al-Jabal on a litter. The astrologer's prophesy had come true—a king had indeed died that day.

Baybars was fifty years old, and from then on the poets would forever sing his praises.

He had been brave in battle, full of initiative, quick to make decisions, revered by his men, feared by his enemies. His leadership had thwarted the double-threat of the Franks on one front, and the Mongols on the other. During the seventeen years of his reign, he undertook thirty-eight campaigns, rode the equivalent length of a circling of the globe, and had personally fought nine battles against the Mongols, five against the Armenians, and three times against the Assassins of Syria. Most of all, he defeated the Franks twenty-one times. They lost all the strongholds they held in the interior of the country. The only land still possessed by the Franks was the coastline from Lattakieh in the north to the Castle of the Pilgrims in Athlit in the south.

Now the Atabeq al-Asaqir, the Army's Commander in Chief, mustered all amirs and officials in the Hall of Audience. There they passed in front of the throne and pledged their loyalty to Baraka, Baybars' son. First came the nobles of the court, all amirs of a hundred; followed by the remaining Amirs of a Hundred, all totaled, twenty-four; then the amirs tablkhana (nearly a hundred), the amirs of twenty (several dozen), the amirs ashara (nearly fifty counting Diyar), and finally, a few amirs of five.

Baraka, nineteen, sat haughtily on his throne flanked by his father's advisors. Diyar, always near Sultan Baybars in campaigns, had observed Baraka and knew him to be foolish and vain. In battle, like his father, he was cruel and treacherous. However, unlike his father, he had little ability to command.

Diyar remembered the counsel of the old Royal Equerry, "Never forget, it is the palace you must fear."

Other amirs were also aware of the youth's failings, and plotting to gain the throne began immediately throughout the city.

CHAPTER 17

Steam swirled throughout the bathhouse. Diyar and Kareem, after a morning working out with their squad on the practice field, were scrubbing off when Diyar became aware of someone near the door watching him. A small, fair-faced youth dressed in palace yellow stood staring. He held a roll of parchment.

Diyar nodded to Kareem who stepped over to the page.

"Yes? What do you require?" said the sarrajun.

"The amir is required in the palace," lisped the youth. "He is to follow me. He should hurry."

Diyar snorted with distain, but as he returned to his bucket, he suspected the worst. In the few short weeks since Baraka had donned the sultan's robes, many of the older amirs had been banished or imprisoned, replaced by young courtiers. Now beautiful young men learned the road to power ran not through the battlefield but through the sultan's bed chambers.

Diyar dressed and followed the page. They entered the palace from the side entrance and mounted the stairs to the harem. The last time Diyar had come this way, he had found Thalia. He wondered where she was now.

The sound of a drum, soft and sensuous, interrupted his thoughts. The bowed whining of a kemengeh joined in.

Padding down a carpeted hall, Diyar moved into a haze of hemp, dusty and demonic. Ahead, a couple of khasikiya lounged sleepily at a room's entrance. They saw Amir Diyar and straightened up. The boy turned in and Diyar paused at the threshold.

The room's only light came from a small window high on the wall. It tunneled through the smoke, and glanced off the multi-colored rug, highlighting bare legs.

A naked black boy twirled into the beam, undulating to the pulsing rhythm. His penis, long as his forearm, whipped and snapped as he danced.

As Diyar's eyes grew accustomed to the dark, he could see young men lying along the walls watching the dancer, or sprawled entwined in the murky corners.

The page moved to one wall where most of the men congregated, and bent to whisper to the young sultan. Lazily, Baraka gestured for Diyar to enter.

The sultan was of medium height, and sported a wispy mustache. The room, heavy with the dry stink of hashish, was stifling, and he wore only a loin cloth, his swarthy skin shiny with oil and sweat.

Setting his jaw, Diyar walked over and bowed.

The sultan held up a lethargic hand. The music trailed off, and the dancing boy drifted off to waiting arms.

Baraka tried to frown. "Why have you kept me waiting?"

Diyar did not look at the page. "I came as soon as I received your summons, sire."

In one corner an orgiastic groan erupted, and some of the naked courtiers giggled. Diyar's face did not move.

The sultan tried not to smile, and seeing Diyar's hard eyes, his face slid into a petulant frown again. "Word has reached us you have been less than loyal to your sultan. Is that true?"

Diyar bowed again. "As a loyal member of our most exalted Sultan's khasikiya," he recited, "my only purpose in life is to serve."

Blearily, the young monarch tried to read his expression. "Hm, yes. But we have decided you are far too young to be an amir ashara."

He waited to see how the warrior would react, but Diyar said nothing.

Peevishly he continued, "In reality, you do not look trustworthy at all to me. I do not even want you in my khasikiya."

Still the young warrior remained silent.

In exasperation the sultan waved him away. "So? You have your orders. Get out."

Stepping back with a bow, Diyar looked up and saw, for the first time, the tall, thin man smirking at the sultan's elbow: Abu al-Mulq.

Now Diyar knew why he had been demoted. He kept his jaw set, but his hand itched to grasp his kindjal. It would take but two quick steps, and the man's skinny throat would be opened.

He turned and strode out, feeling fortunate to have escaped with only a demotion.

Soon he received orders from the Nawbat an-Nuwal, the Chief of the Corps of Mamluks, to report to Amir Ashara Mukbil as-Sirghitmishi. Mukbil was just smart enough to realize he had been deeply fortunate to have gained his promotion, and was determined never to do anything that would jeopardize it. He was hidebound and duty-driven, often angry, always worried. Diyar took one look at him and determined to stay as far out of the man's reach as possible.

But Mukbil had heard about Diyar's numerous exploits, knew he had been an amir ashara, and immediately felt threatened. "You might have been well-thought of as one of the old sultan's pets, but now you are just another mawla to me. You do what I tell you, or I will have stripes laid on your back, stripes that will stay with you."

"I understand and will obey," he murmured, and meant it.

Amir Mukbil drilled his men unmercifully. To keep free of the amir's ire, Diyar did nothing to call attention to himself. Only when it came to the bow drill, firing at a suspended target at full gallop, did he refuse to diminish himself. This rankled the insecure amir who hated to be seen as inferior.

Diyar's only consolation in being in Mukbil's ten, was he was reunited with his old friend from his training days, Tanin al-Ajani.

"You must not make Mukbil look bad," Tanin said as they rode to the stables after a morning's lance drill. "You know the old saying: 'In combat with your amir, the last thrust is his.' No matter how good you are, you cannot win. Especially with someone like Mukbil as-Sirghitmishi."

Then orders came down for Mukbil's squad, orders direct from the sultan's office: Amir Mukbil and his men were to relieve a squad on duty at a frontier fortress deep in Nubia.

Diyar knew such orders, the equivalent of banishment, had to be the work of Abu al-Mulq.

But Mukbil was elated. Always nervous about making a mistake in garrison, he was relieved to take to the field.

Again, Diyar carefully led Saba onto an dhow and they set sail south on the lazy waters of the Nile.

The Aswan fortress, a characterless blockhouse of mud bricks, overlooked the village and river. Passing through the gates of the fortress, blown sand heaped against its walls, the squad was met by the commanding amir.

Mukbil leaped off his horse and bowed low. "We are proud and happy to be here, sire. Just command me, and I and my men will obey."

That was all it took for the fortress commander, Amir Nadjm al-Ahdab, a quiet veteran of many campaigns, to ascertain Mukbil's character. "I am sure of it," he murmured.

Shouts from the village made them turn, and they watched as a large contingent of mounted Beja tribesman raced through the village street, forcing the villagers to dive for safety. At the gate, the Arabs skidded to a stop, their horses rearing.

They wore blue vertical striped gubbas, long sleeved robes of camel-hair wool, soft boots, and turbans wrapped so one strip allowed only their eyes to be seen. They carried lances and swords but, Diyar noticed immediately, no bows, and they wore no armor.

Laughing derisively, they taunted the guards manning the

walls. The mamluks, though knowing not the words, knew well their intent.

A shrill call from the nomad's leader, and they spun and charged back down the hill. As they galloped past the merchants' meager stands, their lances jabbed out, spiking fruits and vegetables and knocking over the rickety structures. Outside the village, the riders curved away and disappeared into the desert.

Mukbil spun around to the amir. "Send me after them, sire. Let them feel your servants' steel."

Diyar winced. *Dear God*, he thought, *spare us from ambitious amirs. Ten men with a dullard for a leader against a whole tribe of nomads out in the desert?* He did not like the odds.

Fortunately, Amir Nadjm was more realistic. "I appreciate your zeal, Amir Mukbil, but first, I am sure you want to see your quarters and get your men settled in."

"But, sire..." Mukbil sputtered.

"And please turn over any messages from the Commander-in-Chief." Relieving Mukbil of the rolled dispatches, he turned and headed for his offices.

The warriors' billets were a pair of tiny rooms of crumbling brick against the fortress's wall. Here, amid the fleas and scorpions, they slept face to each other's feet.

But the men were not to be in the cramped quarters long. The papers from the sultan ordered more raids against the Beja, and Nadjm al-Ahdab was forced to send the squad on constant forays into the desert. They were often in the saddle for days, scouting and investigating allegations against the tribesmen.

One evening, when the mamluks had pitched their camp for another night under the stars, a clutch of naked Ababdeh children approached the campfire, standing silently at a respectful distance. The Ababdeh was a poor tribe, performing menial tasks the haughty Beja refused to touch.

Though in pathetic condition, the children did not beg, and after a time, Diyar sent Kareem to invite them in.

Immediately Mukbil was on his feet. "Why are you bothering with the little beggars? As soon as you sleep, they will slit your throat for a crust of bread."

Diyar shrugged. "Perhaps the best thing to do is give them the crust of bread first and get a good night's rest," and he poured a little honey on a fatireh, folded it, and held it out to the shy group. The children bounded over with such happy eagerness, the hearts of the warriors went out to them, and many shared their left-overs.

Soon, however, one boy, older than the rest, spotted a cloud on the horizon, and murmured something to his mates. The children quickly finished the remainder of the men's food, and silently disappeared over a dune.

Another lump of camel dung was dropped on the fire, and the men prepared for sleep. Mukbil ordered Tanin al-Ajani to take up a post as sentry, and soon everything fell quiet in the tiny bivouac.

In the black of night, Diyar was awakened by the sound and fury of a dust storm. Wind shrieked over the dunes and blasted his face with sand. In the dark, the horses nearby cried out in fear.

Diyar stood and wrapped his blanket over his head for protection. He kicked the nearest man and cried over the wind, "Up. We must get the horses behind the shelter of the dune."

He staggered to the smoldering fire and dropped on another camel's turd for light. Then, bending into the biting sand, he fought his way to the horses. He did not see Tanin al-Ajani in the darkness, and called out, but his words were blown away in the storm.

He found Saba and began untying her, when a terrible pain cut down through his side, a pain far greater than he had ever felt or could imagine, and he knew he had been stabbed from behind.

He dove forward, rolled, and came up sword in hand. But a blow exploded on the side of his head, horrendous. The pain dimmed as he fell insensate.

Several times, in his nightmare of fever, he nearly clawed to consciousness, but finally soft, urgent voices seeped into his mind. A tug on his loin cloth roused him more, and the stabbing pain that shot through his side made him retch.

He opened his eyes. It was day, but his vision was blurred red.

He tried to blink, but the effort exhausted him. His head drummed with a dirty-grey pain, and he wanted only to escape the torment by sinking into unconsciousness again.

"This one still lives," came a voice speaking Arabic, "Give me the knife."

Diyar fought to sit up, but a spasm shot through his head with such excruciating intensity, his hand jerked involuntarily to his skull. The movement caused the wound in his side to rip open.

He struggled to see, but his eyes were glued shut by sand and dried blood. He dug at them, and saw a slim, dark figure in white approaching. The Arab carried a curved dagger.

Feebly, Diyar put out his hand. "Wait. Please wait."

Still the man came on.

Why does he not stop? Diyar thought desperately. Then he heard his words. He had spoken in Turkish. As the man raised the blade, Diyar racked his scrambled brains.

The dagger arched down, aiming at his neck.

Instinctively, he crossed his hands over his face and croaked in Arabic, "Stop. Gold."

The knife paused. No other words would have stayed his execution.

The young man peered into Diyar's eyes. "You have gold, sire?" he said politely. "Where?"

The man's coloring was deep bronze, almost black, and his long, black hair fell in curls over his shoulders and gleamed with grease. A tuft curled atop his forehead. His nose was long and narrow, and thin, gold rings hung from his earlobes.

Diyar struggled to think in Arabic. "You spare my life, I give you much gold."

The man tipped his head to one side and regarded him pleasantly. He smiled without guile. "How much gold?"

Several other of the men in white smocks wandered over.

Diyar forced himself to one elbow and held up both hands, fingers spread. "That many."

The man held up his hands. "That many, and again that many," he said.

But Diyar was too weak to bargain, even for his life, and collapsed.

He awoke slowly, his head pulsing with fever. He lay on crude mats. At arm's length above him, another mat covered the crossing of a few poles. Involuntarily, he hacked a dry cough, and his head felt as if it had been struck again.

At the sound, a slim woman seated nearby slid closer. She was as black as the man, and wore only a skirt of the same white wool. Necklaces of glass, brass and shells, rustled as she bent over him. A gold ring pierced her nose.

"Are you alive?" she asked.

He gazed at her fine features for a long moment. "Am I in Paradise?"

The woman looked startled, then quickly glanced around fearfully. "No, sire," she whispered. "You are still on earth. Do not speak so rudely, and you may stay here a while longer." Then she smiled shyly. "Are you thirsty?"

"Oh, yes. Please, for just a taste of water..."

She nodded, slid away, and presently returned with a calabash of water. Several naked children entered to peek at him. She motioned them away, but he recognized a couple of them as ones he had fed.

The woman held his head, and he drank ravenously, the throbbing pain in his head never ceasing. Then he sank back.

A thought came to him. "The men...my friends?"

She shook her head. "All gone but you, and another. But he is hurt bad too."

He clutched at her arm. "Who? Which one?"

She shrugged, then touched his hair. "Like you, same color—yellow."

Blond hair, he thought. Could it be Tanin al-Ajani?

"Who did this? Who attacked? You?"

Shock struck her eyes. "No, sire. The Beja."

"The Beja..." he gasped, but she ran her hand slowly over his eyes. His exhausted mind gave up, and he collapsed into sleep once more.

When he awoke again he seemed alone. He glanced around. The flimsy shelter was no more than two or three paces wide. At one side, a baby lay sleeping, partially covered with a wool cloth. He tried to twist around to see out the opening, but his wound tore, and he eased back down.

He slept.

The woman woke him. "I must clean your wound again. Can you move?"

Aided by her gentle hands, he rolled over on his good side. She dabbed at the slash with water, then brought out several little earthen pots. Using a mixture of strange-smelling herbs: senna leaves, colocynth, wormwood, and a gum arabic from acacia bushes, she ground a poultice, and rubbed it softly over his wound. It felt cool and soothing.

She gave him a drink, and he said, "Where is my friend?"

"In another tent."

"I must see him."

She shrugged. "He cannot move. You cannot move. Are you hungry?"

Weakly, he shook his head.

"Then sleep."

The woman watched as his eyes fluttered closed, the look of anguish etched in his face, and she shook her head. He had lost so much blood. Would he live through the night? Would the men kill him?.

She glanced over at a low shelter nearby. And the nimrod's wound there was even worse.

CHAPTER 18

He lost time. Sleeping most of the day, he woke at night to find himself wedged in among the woman's sleeping family: Iwah, the young man who had spared his life—at least for the moment—and the woman had several children, all sheltered under the few sandy mats.

One afternoon he awakened to see Tanin peering into his face with intense, feverish eyes. Madness hovered at their edges.

Diyar coughed to clear his parched throat, and said, "My friend, how are you?"

He held up a hand swathed in bloody bandages. "It is my hand. The marauders hacked off my fingers and it will not stop bleeding."

Two women hurried in and led the delirious man away. In a moment the woman appeared over him. Seeing his anxiety, she spoke soothingly. "Try not to worry. The nimrod will recover."

But later that day, a scream in the next hut wrested Diyar out of a delirious dream.

In his fever-racked nightmares, the sneer of Abu al-Mulq pressed down on him. Diyar's throat and nostrils seemed coated with the stench of hashish and oily bodies. Al-Mulq was the cause of his suffering. He was a rotting cancer that had to be hacked out of the body of humanity. But every time Diyar raised his kindjal against the mocking grin, he was stabbed in the side, and his head crushed from an ambusher's blow. He awakened to find several women holding him so his thrashing would not tear open his wound again.

Then one night he awoke to feel a cool breeze wafting across his brow. He had a terrible thirst, but the fever was broken.

Daily, the woman meticulously bathed, doctored and bound his slashed side. And daily, he slowly improved.

Tanin came again to his hut. He was calmer, but his arm was short a hand.

Diyar, driven by the need to urinate, finally crawled out into the daylight. The woman spoke to one of her daughters, a girl perhaps ten, to lend him support. She led him to behind the hut and idly watched as he, stooped and shuffling like an old man, relieved himself. These outings became regular. Still it was weeks before he could stand upright.

When he finally asked for food, the woman offered him milk and durah, unleavened cakes baked over a camel-dung fire. He rarely saw meat. The Ababdeh owned cattle, bony creatures that barely survived on the desert scrub. But these they raised only for trade. For the first time in his life, Diyar learned what it was to go to sleep hungry.

Though the men toted javelins and knives, Diyar soon saw they possessed little skill with them. But any animal they did kill, they considered eatable, including gazelles, foxes, hares, jerboas, or hyenas. They owned little, their sleeping mats, a clay pot or two for cooking, skins for water and milk, wooden bowls, grinding stones, perhaps a leathern bucket. Often the women walked all day to fetch water.

The cauterization of his arm a success, Tanin's health also improved, but neither he nor Diyar mentioned the obvious: few mamluks remained in the sultan's service without a sword-hand. Tanin might find an administrative position, but that took a friend in court, something neither of the men had.

Iwah, seeing Diyar staggering about in only his loin cloth, brought him one of the coarse, white gowns to wear. Diyar found it quite comfortable. The white color repelled the sun's heat, and the deep arm wells caught whatever breeze stirred through the dunes.

And then came the day he was able to climb onto a camel. At a trip to the river to bathe, he had found a dried branch thick enough for a bow. He borrowed Iwah's knife and began to whittle. The bow completed, the making of arrows was more difficult. Still with time, shafts straight enough were found. Obsidian for the heads, feathers from an egret, then he rode out into the desert for a hunt with Iwah.

Seeing a small herd of gazelles, he wanted to give chase.

"What is the use," Iwah said. "Before we can get close, they will have run away."

Diyar eyed the little animals for a moment, then nocked an arrow. "We will try anyway."

Slowly they allowed the camels to drift towards the half-dozen grazing antelope. Several of the gazelle raised their heads and observed the larger beasts with uneasiness. And as the animals shifted in preparation for flight, Diyar let fly an arrow.

The distance was impossible, yet when the arrow completed its arc, it fell into the flank of one of the little beasts, knocking it to the ground, where it lay kicking in silent agony.

Before their loping camels could come to a stop at the downed gazelle, Iwah leaped to the ground, ran over and slit its throat. Diyar, conscious of his wound, forced his mount to drop to his knees before sliding out of the saddle.

Looking down at the gazelle whose color was so like the dune, the Ababdeh shook his head. "Are your arrows magic? What spell do you call upon them to make it fly so far?"

Diyar smiled. He knew the hit was more luck than skill, but he would not tell that to the Ababdeh. "Keep the skin, and do with the meat as you will."

Iwah stared at him in amazement. "You give me the skin too."

"It is the least I could do for saving my life."

With the gift, Diyar had bought a friend, but he had another motive in mind. He had plans, and he would need the man's help.

The small Ababdeh clan, no more than four or five families,

was constantly on the move following its herds. Besides camels, it kept small flocks of goats and sheep, a few cattle, but no horses. One or two of the families had an ass, each had a dog.

As soon as the two mamluks were able to travel, the Ababdeh packed up to search for new grazing land. The two men of the steppes, wearing the long, white smocks and being burned to bronze by the desert sun, grew to look more and more like Ababdeh—but for their long, golden tresses. And therein lay their danger. If any Beja or Nubian warriors spied such hair, the man would be dead in a heart beat. Iwah attempted to mask the danger.

The Ababdeh men were proud of their hanging curls which, woven into long plaits, fell over their shoulders. These they stroked liberally with grease which shone in the sun. Curling pins and pomade bowls were essential articles of the Ababdeh's meager toilet materials. Now Iwah ground a mixture of dyes in a bowl and soaked the two warriors' hair. A thick coat of grease, and the typical braiding completed the disguise.

Still, Diyar's height and broad shoulders stood out among the thinner Ababdeh, and whenever they encountered passing Arabs, he kept to the far side of his camel.

After several months of slow migration, one of the Ababdeh shepherd girls came weeping into the camp reporting two tribesmen from a nearby Beja clan had raped her. As Iwah questioned her, they learned it was the same clan that had ambushed Diyar's squad. It was time to act. But first he needed the help of the weather.

Diyar knew the Beja could track a shadow across a rock. So, before attempting to go near their camp, he would have to await a night with winds strong enough to cover his tracks. He dared not leave a trail which could be followed back to Iwah and his people. He only hoped such a wind would arrive before the Beja broke camp.

Then one afternoon, a dust devil danced across the desert, and Iwah nodded. "Winds are coming."

Soon a breeze sprang up and by evening winds blew streams of sand across the desert.

Time for revenge.

The girl said the Beja camp was located near the river. Though approaching during the day would be dangerous, Diyar had to examine the camp in the light. The Ababdeh girl bravely consented to show him the way.

She clung to his waist as the camel swayed through the dusk. He carried his bow, a quiver of arrows that had taken months to fill, and an ancient short sword provided by Iwah. A small, goat-skin bag hung over his shoulder.

Nearing the Beja camp, he skirted their herds to avoid being seen by their herdsmen. But he knew the camp itself would be guarded by dogs, half-starved mongrels which would cry out at the first scent of a stranger.

At a safe distance from the camp he jumped down, leaving the girl the camel and instructions to go at dawn if he had not returned.

Evening's last light outlined the camp as he crawled to the top of a tall dune and peeped over. The tents curved around in the shelter of the dune. To one side of each tent, one or more horses were tethered. It took him a moment, but then he saw, at the far side of one of the tents, a golden mare standing patiently, picketed with two others. Saba. And, staked out behind the tent, a scrawny dog stood guard.

He searched along the dune. Somewhere there had to be lookouts. And sure enough, not a hundred yards down, he spotted two dark-cloaked figures squatting in the sand hunched against the wind.

Diyar slipped back to the girl and sent her home, then returned to the dune to watch the lookouts. When the black of night eliminated the men's dark silhouettes, he crept along the camp side of the dune until he was below them, then moved up behind them. The wind, coursing over the dune, carried away the sound of his approach.

With a short, powerful shove of the sword, he stabbed one in the back, just to the left of the backbone, deep in the heart. The other Beja twisted around, his hand darting to his sword. But as he drew it, Diyar jerked out the sword and slashed his throat.

Diyar stripped the dark blue cloak off the taller of the two, and threw it over his shoulders. It stank, but not enough to suit him.

He worked his way down the dune, and approached the tent where he had seen Saba. The pup who stood guard at the rear of the tent picked up the scent of the cloak, but growled with suspicion. Diyar pulled a goat joint from his bag and tossed it to the him. The hungry animal snatched it greedily, forgetting all else. Did they have another dog?

Diyar avoided the tent's support ropes, and sneaked around to the horses. He had just reached Saba, when a man stepped out of the tent heading for the dune, and he had to duck between her and the next mare.

When the Beja passed, Diyar stepped out and grabbed his mouth. The man clutched at the hand, but Diyar shoved the sword into his back, giving the pommel a kick with his knee, severing the man's spinal cord. He died without a sound.

Diyar cut the horses' picket line, leaped on Saba's back, and with the other horses in tow, rode for the dune.

When he galloped into the Ababdeh camp, Iwah jumped from his shelter, javelin in hand.

He reined up. The smoldering fire reflected off his grin. "Be not afraid. It is only I, and I have brought you gifts."

Iwah's wife added fuel to the fire for light, and when the people could make out the horses, Iwah's eyes widened with fear. "What have you done?"

Diyar slid to the ground. "I have retrieved my horse."

"But you have stolen from the Beja."

Others, including Tanin, crawled from their lean-tos.

Diyar felt no compulsion to justify his action, but he said, "True, as they have stolen from you."

"But horses?" Iwah gasped. "Now they will come and destroy us," and he lifted the spear.

"My friend," Diyar said quietly, "you know it would be foolish to raise a weapon against me."

Sullenly the Ababdeh nodded and dropped his hand.

"Now," Diyar continued, "we have horses, and my friend and I will leave you. I promised to pay you for my life. Come with me to the river, and I will give you your money."

Minutes later, he, Iwah, and Tanin rode with a camel in tow east to the Nile.

CHAPTER 19

The small dhow floated down the river, Diyar laying in its bow. The headaches that had plagued him since the ambush had abated somewhat. But the ringing in his ears continued, diminishing to a hiss, often unnoticed, never disappearing.

He kept Saba and sold the other three horses, giving Iwah the most gold the poor man had ever seen. With the remaining money, he bought clothes and passage for Tanin and himself to Cairo.

Once on board, he borrowed a boatman's old rusty spear and, with a fury barely controlled, practiced his lance drills, shredding the imagined figure of Abu al-Mulq. But when he flopped down to rest, it was the vision of Thalia that slipped into his dreams.

Will I ever see her again?

He had hoped to win such favor with Baybars as to be able to request her hand. But now Baraka ruled, and there seemed little chance of receiving favors from that pederast.

The dhow tied up at the docks of Fustat and the merchants and porters took little notice of the two Arabs who disembarked, the bands of their turbans masking their faces. When they neared Diyar's little house he wondered what they would find. He had departed in the summer of 1277. It was now the spring of 1279. He had left Kareem in charge. Would the sarrajun still be there?

At his gate, he banged the heavy, brass clapper.

"Who is there?" came an aged voice.

A bowwab? This is new, thought Diyar. "It is I, Rukn al-Din Diyar al-Mijiri al-Baybariya," he said sternly. "This is my house. Open this door or I will have my horse kick it in."

A passing merchant perched on the rump of a burrow paused at the sight of a shabbily clad Arab with a mamluk's name demanding entrance to a house. Diyar turned and glared at him, and the little man urged his beast on.

The wooden lock clapped, the door swung open, and an old bowwab peeked around. "Are you really the master?"

"I am, and who are you?"

The man bowed humbly. "I am Abd Alla, your servant, sire."

"My servant, huh. And where is Kareem?"

And hurrying out of the house came his answer. Kareem beamed widely. "Master, glory to God, is it really you? Word came back months ago your squad was killed and you had disappeared. I feared you had been killed too."

"Your fears were close to the mark. But how have you been?"

The man nodded enthusiastically. "Good, good, as good as can be expected in these times. Mornings I go to the practice field hoping to hear some word about you. I often practice with the other sarrajun. Several of the warriors have asked me to become their servant, but I waited to hear of your fate."

Diyar and Tanin strolled with him into the dim interior of the narrow house. He saw several improvements: a rug on the floor, used but well cared for, and a small bronze cabinet in the corner.

He nodded at the old gate keeper who followed the two with curiosity. "I see we can not be faring so badly if you have taken on a bowwab."

Kareem nodded eagerly. "It is the book shop, sire. Abd ar-Rahman is a magician. Everyone is talking about him. They come from all over to ask him for books, and if he does not have them, he makes them. He seems to have relatives in every town in the realm, and they all search for books for him. He has even rented a room above the shop where he has four clerks copying books to sell. I go down every afternoon to help out as much as I can, and when he has a moment, Abd ar-Rahman is even teaching me to read...."

His chattering trailed off, seeing the speculation in his master's eyes.

"He has hired clerks?" Diyar said. "I see I must look into this. And what news from court?"

Now Kareem frowned. "About that, the news is not as good. The young sultan has surrounded himself with companions who flatter him, but only cause mischief. You remember Amir Ak Sonkor al-Farekani, a man of wisdom and experience who was regent? Not long after you left, the sultan's evil companions convinced him the regent was out to steal power, and the sultan had him arrested and executed."

Diyar was shocked. He had seen Amir Ak Sonkor often on the parade ground and exercise field. He was a good man, prudent and wise.

Kareem was talking. "Then the Council of Amirs appointed Amir Sonkor al-Mudhaffari as regent, but now the sultan has imprisoned him too. So finally all the amirs and their men marched up to the palace. In the Hall of Audience, they said to the sultan, 'You have alienated the loyalty of all hearts. You have treated the most prominent amirs as enemies. You must either abandon this attitude, or there will be a clash between us.'

"He imprisoned no more amirs, but he and his favorites have squandered the treasury on huge banquets. Now he puts great pressure on the merchants for more taxes. He even sent one of his young friends demanding the Viceroy of Damascus, Sonkor al-Ashqar, to pay him thousands of dinars, but the Viceroy put him off. As a result, the young sultan threatened to dismiss the viceroy."

"Has he yet?" Diyar remembered his promise not to kill al-Mulq until his father, Sonkor al-Ashqar was off the viceroy throne

"Not yet, sire. And I do not think the viceroy would go if ordered. It will probably mean war between the sultan and viceroy."

Civil war! That is all I need now, thought Diyar sardonically. He turned to Tanin al-Ajani. "With all that has been happening it may be unwise to go near the palace. Still, if we want to be paid, we must report to the Commander-in-Chief."

Diyar donned his best robe, loaned one to Tanin, and the two cantered up to the offices of the Commander-in-Chief. They were about to enter when a page intercepted them.

"You are ordered to present yourselves immediately to the Major Domo of the Great Audience Hall," he said haughtily.

The two warriors looked at each other. Things had come to a pretty pass when a page could be arrogant to warriors. But there was no avoiding the order, and they fell in behind him.

They were being passed from lower to higher officials in the ante rooms preceding the huge qa'at, audience hall, but the two men recognized few of the old amirs. Most were like Baraka, young aulad al-nas, sons of mamluks, men who had never seen battle. The Major Domo himself was little older than Diyar, and had none of the carriage expected of the amir in charge of the Audience. But he was green-eyed and fair-faced.

At the entrance of the Great Hall, the Major Domo raised a hand. "You must wait. The sultan is listening to a recitation," and they were forced to listen to a young sycophant lisp about the bravery and virtue of his beloved sultan.

The recital over, the two men were led into the Audience Hall and announced. The first thing Diyar observed was the row of chairs for ecclesiastical advisors at the sultan's right was empty. And those chairs at his left were no longer filled with white-bearded advisors, but young men, gaudily dressed, goblets in hand. And, leaning against the side of the young sultan's throne, grinned Abu al-Mulq.

The young sultan squinted down at them, trying to focus. "What do you want?" he said testily. Al-Mulq leaned over and whispered in his ear. Baraka's jerked up. "Oh, yes." He tried to frown. "Are you not the men I assigned to Amir Nadjm al-Ahdab at Aswan? So, why are you here?"

Diyar sensed impending criticism and steeled himself. But Tanin al-Ajani spoke up.

"O Great Sultan, may your reign be glorious. As fortune would have it, we return because we had no choice. Over a year ago, we were attacked at night by a large number of Beja tribesmen. Our amir, Amir Mukbil as-Sirghitmishi, and all the rest of the men and servants were killed, and all our horses and weapons stolen. We lived only because Diyar al-Mijiri al-Baybariya here bargained for our lives, a bargain, I hasten to add, he paid off at considerable risk to himself."

The young sultan tried to look imperious. "You bargained with the enemy?"

"Oh, no, Your Majesty, not the Beja, but a small tribe of Ababdeh. They found us and nursed us back to health."

Baraka starred at the two for a long moment, his head swaying, then al-Mulq whispered again. Again the man's head jerked. "Correct. You still have not told us what you are doing here. Why did you not go back to the fortress at Aswan?" Al-Mulq's head bent nearer the ear of the sultan, and Baraka pointed at Diyar. "Yes, let us hear from you."

Diyar nodded and bowed. "O Great Majesty, may your reign be glorious," he recited. "As Tanin al-Ajani has said, the reason we returned was because we had no choice. The Beja were in pursuit of us, and we had to board the first boat that happened along. Its master was sailing down river, not up, but since the Beja were in sight, and we had no choice but to pay his price and get aboard as quickly as possible."

Now Abu al-Mulq, spoke up. "You could have transferred to another boat going upstream. Was not your proper place to be at your fortress?"

Diyar bit his lip. He hated having to defend his actions to this sycophant. But the sultan nodded. "Yes, what about that?"

Diyar forced himself to be patient. "Sire, we only had enough money to buy passage on the one boat."

The room grew ominously silent. Any hope the two warriors had their escape would be applauded or even accepted, Diyar sensed, was lost.

Finally Abu al-Mulq stepped in front of the sultan and bowed low to him. "Beloved Malana, Most Wise of Rulers," he said in a heavy tone, "I feel it is my duty to speak out against what I sense may be a foul crime."

The sultan frowned hazily. "Uh, speak on, Amir Abu al-Mulq."

"Sire, these men say they stole horses from the Beja tribe. Now, we know the Bejas number in the thousands. They are fierce warriors, and their horses are among the fastest. If a man steals from them, the desert is eating his bones before the sun sets. No, I say these two led their fellow warriors into an ambush. They were probably aided by these Ababdeh, weak men who live off the leavings of stronger tribes."

"Your Majesty," Tanin protested, "that is not true."

But al-Mulq hurried on. "And Malana, if not leading their own comrades into an ambush, the least they are guilty of is being absent from their post, and refusing to return when they had the opportunity. And, of course," he said with a thin smile, "we all know what the punishment for that is."

The young sultan tried to think. "Death?"

Al-Mulq's voice rose over the crowd. "As always, sire, your grasp of the law is impeccable." He raised a hand dramatically. "But wait. Lest any man feel our glorious leader lacks compassion, it is only fair we investigate their stories, no matter how implausible they sound, in order justice can be done. Until we get to the truth, I am sure you know what should be done."

The Assembly Hall waited.

Finally Baraka said weakly "I do?"

Al-Mulq smiled. "Imprisonment, sire, imprisonment."

Baraka ibn Baybars nodded slowly. "Of course. Imprisonment."

Tanin al-Ajani gasped. "But, sire..."

Baraka lurched to his feet. "Silence," he cried. He gestured to guards. "Take away these traitors."

"What?" Tanin screamed. "Traitors?" He raised his arm. "You think I got this by being a traitor to my sultan?" and he jerked back his sleeve revealing the scarred stub.

The great room fell silent.

Abu al-Mulq spoke up quickly. "Sire, you have ordered these men to prison, and rightfully so. Are they not being disloyal in not carrying out your orders as quickly as they can?"

Disloyalty! The greatest threat to an insecure sultan. He nodded slowly. "It is true." He slumped back onto the throne, exhausted by his outburst. "They are disloyal," he mumbled. To the amir and five that surrounded Diyar and Tanin, he waved a limp hand. "Take them to prison."

A scribe with pen and scroll stepped forward. "Which prison, sire?"

"Um, Al-Zardkhana until we decide what to do with them."

The feisty Tanin spoke up again. "What? Al-Zardkhana!" But immediately one of the sultan's guardsmen shoved him with his pike handle.

Tanin spun on him, but Diyar spoke quietly.

"Do not give them the pleasure of seeing your anger, my brother."

Tanin relaxed and allowed himself to be marched out.

Al-Zardkhana, "The Arsenal", stone built, spread thick and ugly among the royal stables at the lower end of the vast al-Qal'ah complex. Stable dung was heaped up against its back wall, and the stench hung over the prison.

The prison's heavy, iron door stood open. Just inside was the tiny office of the amir in charge. Under a small window, the aging amir sat behind a cluttered desk and read, then signed the men's orders and nodded to the guardsmen. "You can go. They are my responsibility now."

He glanced at the orders. "Imprisoned because of disloyalty to the sultan. How unusual," he said dryly. "Do you carry any money?"

At the men's hesitation, he gestured. "Come, give it to me. I will keep it for you, and it will keep the guards from stealing it from you. You will be fed the same as the troops in the dining rooms, but you will need money for other amenities."

He turned to a young Jewish clerk sitting on a stool in the

corner, "Fetch Bugha, tell him to bring four men."

The men who appeared belonged to one of the lower tibaqs. Big men, powerfully built, chosen to be guards because of their size, rather than battle prowess. Unlike most mamluks, proud of dress, their tunics were stained and slovenly worn.

The amir hooked a thumb. "To the blacksmith."

The men fell in around the prisoners, and they marched off, led by Bugha, Amir of Five.

The blacksmith, a giant Turcoman with a great, black mustache, bent heavy iron collars on the two, then ankle braces. But attempting to attach manacles, he found Tanin al-Ajani had no wrist.

"Now," he asked with a heavy accent, "how is a man to do his job when the prisoner has no wrist?"

"Today," Tanin muttered, "everyone is having problems."

The Turcoman stared at him for a moment, then laughed roundly. He slapped him on the shoulder. "Good man. You lose your freedom but not your humor." He chuckled. "You will need it."

He fashioned a thick arm band and hammered it on above the elbow, and the two shuffled back to the prison. The guards led them past the office to a door of woven steel slats, and shoved them through into darkness. Heat and stench fell on them like a sodden blanket.

Diyar, blind from the bright sunlight, stumbled over someone's leg. The man kicked out. "Careful, fool, or this day will be your last."

While the two men waited for their eyes to adjust to the dark, a voice at Diyar's elbow whispered, "Give me your boots."

Diyar jerked back and pushed the figure away. "Come," he said to Tanin, "let us find a place to sit." But someone poked Tanin and took up the cry, "Give me your boots."

"What are they talking about?" Tanin whispered.

"I know not," Diyar said stoutly, "but no man is getting my boots." He stepped on another leg, and received a curse in return.

The old Arsenal was one great room with heavy, circular

pillars curving up to the low ceiling. A steel-latticed wall divided the front third where the guards slept, from the back where the prisoners lay on the stone floor. Slivers of sunlight cutting through a few loopholes in the thick walls were the chamber's only light.

As their eyes sharpened to the gloom, the men saw bodies lying against the walls and pillars. Most lay near the front. And, picking their way towards the back, they learned why. The closer they neared the back wall where the dung was heaped, the hotter grew the room and worse the stench.

At Diyar's feet, something skittered through a strip of light on the floor—a cream-colored scorpion, its lethal, black tail hooked over its back.

He paused, eyeing the patch of light. It took a moment to discern, but the filth on the floor appeared to move. The stones were alive with fleas and vermin.

He jerked back. "Let us find a place nearer the front."

This proved difficult, but men, also bound in chains, grudgingly moved, and the two sat down against the latticed wall. One nudged Tanin. "Give me your boots. Soon you will have no need of them."

The man, as did all around him, wore only trousers, no robe or boots. "Nor do you, it seems."

In the enervating heat, the semi-naked men moved only to dig at vermin that covered their bodies. Observing their agony, the fastidious Diyar felt his skin crawl.

The man at Diyar's side spoke low. "If not your boots, give me your robe. Surely it is too hot in this sump pit to wear such a fine robe."

Diyar fought to control his temper. "Now why should I give you my boots or my robe?"

The steel door clanged open and guards kicked their way in. "Those last two prisoners...get up here," one shouted.

"Too late," the man whispered, and slid away.

Tanin started to get up, but Diyar held him back. "Wait," he whispered. "They can not see us here."

But soon the two guards spotted them and started over.

These lizards must never see the light of day, Diyar thought, and stood to meet them.

"Did you not hear my call," yelled one, and swung a heavy truncheon.

Diyar easily side-stepped the blow. Surprised by the Diyar's quickness, the big man twisted and tripped over an inmate's leg.

Laughter erupted, laughter which, Diyar knew, could only bode ill.

The guard found his footing and turned with enraged fury. "Trip me, will you. Now you will pay."

Diyar set himself to meet the maddened man's charge, but before he could, a blow came out of the dark, smashing against his fractured skull. He fell like a stone.

Steady pushing awakened him. He first became aware of sound, a guttural grunting. Then pain, the terrible, familiar pain in his skull. And there was something else. His sphincter felt like it was being torn apart.

He opened his eyes. His face ground into the rough stone floor. Hands held down his arms, and near his face he could make out grimy knees, then a semi-erect penis. Then he knew. He was naked and being raped.

He tried to rear up, but the strong arms held him helpless.

"Ho," called a panting voice, "He bucks like a wild mare."

"How fair she is, like a Greek. Come, Arslan," a stinging blow from a riding crop tore open the back of Diyar's neck, "ride her until she becomes a good little mare."

Effeminate giggles.

Diyar reared up. He knew that voice—Abu al-Mulq. The man was here, a spectator to his degradation.

More blows from the whip shredded Diyar's back. "Stand still and take your punishment," al-Mulq growled. "Be grateful I am using only guards on you, not a fiery lance."

Diyar gritted his teeth and waited for them to finish. *Abu al-Mulq,* he vowed silently to his soul, *when I kill you, it will be slow, very, very slow.*

When one guard groaned to a climax, another mounted him, until it felt like he was being split open.

Finally Al-Mulq's voice came from above. "Enough. Stand him up."

The guards jerked him to his feet. In the dingy gloom, Al-Mulq's face shone yellow and waxen. He shook his head. "Watching you has become boring." He turned to his gaudily clad companions. "Come, we will go observe the castration of some bulls."

He swung and viciously slashed Diyar's cheek with the crop. His eyes brimming with evil, he said, "Be thankful it is not you we castrate." Then he smiled lazily. "Maybe next time."

Rough hands threw him, stripped, back with the prisoners. Out of the shadows came a voice. "Perhaps next time you will part with your clothes."

He dragged himself to the back vowing there would be no next time. But he knew better. With power-mad amirs wrestling for domination, no one was safe from prison, rape, torture or death.

The next day, guards dragged in Tanin unconscious, and dropped him like a sack of meal. Raped continuously, the mind of the handsome young man had ceased to function.

Diyar, still sore and with pain in his skull that blinded one eye, crawled over to his friend. Tanin reeked of sweat and excretion. Someone had vomited onto his back, and he stank of stale wine. No matter. Diyar dragged him to a pillar, and cradled him in his arms.

When the meal arrived, Diyar poured a little water down his friend's throat, and he responded somewhat. Diyar tore the fatireh into small pieces and soaked it in water, but the semi-conscious young man could not swallow.

For several days, while other men were dragged out and beaten or ravaged, the two friends were left alone. Then the clerk appeared at the steel door, two guards at his side, and read out their names.

In the dark, Tanin trembled and clutched at Diyar's arm.

"Courage, my brother," Diyar counseled. "The worst it can be is death, and that would be a relief," but they both knew there were far worse things than death. They had seen evidence of it in the bloody and broken bodies that had been thrown back into the prison.

The clerk led them to the amir in charge. "You are being taken to Alexandria," was all he said, and the guards pushed them out, blinking and blinded by the sun. A young amir, and two members of the khasikiya awaited them on horse.

To display their fallen status, the two were forced to ride burros, sitting sideways because of their shackles. A page with a drawn knife, symbol of the men's demotion and imprisonment, followed along behind.

They descended to the Fustat docks, and the whole party boarded a dhow. On the slow cruise down the canal, Tanin, lying in the warmth of the sun, began to mend somewhat. Still he remained listless.

Nearing the sea, the dhow put in at a quay. Above it, a low stockade of stone glowered over the river. The page acted as messenger from the arrogant, young amir.

"You will be kept here for the night, and tomorrow morning you will be driven through the streets to the main prison." He did not need to add, this last was to magnify their shame.

Inside the walls, the men were led down to cells deep in the bowels of the prison. An occasional candle provided the dank passageway's only light. The cell they were thrown into was one of many along one side of a narrow hallway. Enclosed by three stone walls, a steel-latticed wall with a gate sealed the fourth. The cell held nothing. Muddy slime covered the floor.

After the guards had gone, a voice whispered from the next cell. "What news from the Qal'at al-Jabal?"

Before Tanin could speak, Diyar shook his head, then said guardedly "About the same."

"Is that jackal, Baraka, still on the throne?"

"Sultan Baraka still reigns, yes."

"No need to be cagey with me. I have long ago given up caring whether I live or die."

"But we still care," Diyar replied harshly, "so leave us in peace," and the hallway fell silent.

The men slumped down on the fetid stones and, after a time, dozed.

Diyar was awakened by something scuttling across his ankles. Instinctively, he jerked back, and several crabs fell to the stone floor.

Coughing with shock, he grabbed the steel lattice and pulled himself to his feet. The nearby candle showed the sleeping Tanin was also covered with the little, black-shelled creatures. Diyar quickly shook his friend.

"What?" Tanin mumbled sleepily, then screamed as he saw what crawled on him.

A chuckle came from the next cell. "It gets worse," said the voice.

Soon several rats skittered by the cells, heading up the passageway. They were followed by more, and even more, until an army of the vermin streamed by.

Peering down the hallway, the two saw why. Water, greasy and black with filth, slowly crept up the hall.

"What is happening?" cried Tanin.

Mad laughter erupted from the adjoining cell. "This? This happens at every changing of the tide. Sometimes it fills the cells." The laughter trailed off hollowly. "Be glad your cell is not at the low end."

For the rest of the night the two clung to the lattice work, while the water lapped at their legs. Then, as slowly as it came, the water retreated down the hall, leaving a thick coating of fresh, rotting mud on the floor. Exhausted, the men slumped to the slimy floor. And one by one the rats sneaked back down the passage way, creeping into the cells, sniffing for the carrion of those who did not survive the tide.

Mid-morning, the two men were dragged out, stinking and filthy. Entering through Alexandria's great walled gate, they rode atop burros through the streets. Most Alexandrians, catching sight of the degraded mamluks, shrank away. Only children and the demented stared in flat-faced wonder.

Tanin, suffering from the degradation of the guards, found it hard to keep his head up. But Diyar closed his mind and stared straight ahead.

The street turned and followed a high, stone wall The procession entered a wide, open gate guarded by lancers. Inside, a stone barracks for the guards and officers extended along the wall.

The amir in charge was a lean and handsome grey-beard with a look of shrewdness. *A survivor*, Diyar thought. *A man who, perhaps, could be trusted but only so far.*

The amir took the two men's orders from one of their escorts, broke the seal and read.

He looked up. "My name is Amir Tablkhana Yunus al-Asiridi. I am in charge of the day watch of the outer walls. My orders from the sultan say that I am to keep you here until further word."

Diyar knew the answer to his question but asked it anyway. "With respect, sire, do the orders say how long that will be?"

"Until you are released, die or…"

"Or?"

He shrugged at the obvious. "Or I receive orders for your execution." He wrinkled his nose. "In the mean time, you men look terrible. No mawla should look like this. Do you have money?"

Diyar hoped to hear that. "Yes, sire, but not with us. We can get it as soon as I can send word to my servant in the capital."

"I will trust you." He turned to a servant. "Get them decent robes," and to a couple of guards, "And get those chains off them. To the forge and then the baths."

They were led to the gate in the main, and even higher, wall. This great gate remained closed, but a door in the gate opened and they passed through.

Inside, on a wide flagstone yard, men walked casually in

groups, chatting. They wore various garb. Most, since summer approached, wore long Islamic coats, qaba al-Islamiyya, white cotton or satin, and white turbans. But a few wore the Tatar coats, qaba al-Tatariyya of colored silk, and the kalautah cap.

Diyar felt a surge of hope. Perhaps this prison would not be as bad as the hell-holes they had just survived. He was right—and he was wrong.

The huge prison was a self-contained city. Diyar soon learned it housed not only mamluks, mostly amirs and Royal Mamluks, but government officials and notables who had fallen out of favor, or been caught in corruption. Important prisoners of war, such as Frankish knights awaiting ransom also moved among the prison's inhabitants.

With Baraka's ascendancy to the throne, the prison's population had increased. Still, for internment, it was not a bad life. The amirs were allowed apartments where their families and servants lived with them.

The quality of food a prisoner enjoyed depended upon the money he had to spend. A bustling market place had grown up outside the walls.

Kareem soon arrived bringing much-needed money, and Diyar procured a small corner room. Tanin found lodging in a cubicle nearby.

Diyar immediately set out to explore the prison. He soon observed wealthier amirs had created small domains of their own. Although they were not allowed to carry a sword, every bodyguard sported a wicked-looking dagger. One entered into the quarters of these amirs by invitation only.

He also saw that, although mamluk guards prowled the battlements of the prison's double walls, escape from the great complex would not be difficult. Still, no one tried. Walls did not confine the mamluks as much as their class and training. They were foreigners in their own land. Their lives, the only lives they were trained for, depended on the sultan. If they escaped, where could they go? By the way they looked and dressed, by their inability to speak Arabic, they would soon be discovered. At least in prison they retained some status. And if, as many did, they had business partnerships with the merchant class, they could continue to live moderately well. Live, wait, and hope for a change of rulers. But for many, the prison was their last home.

When Diyar learned the prison contained some Frankish warriors, he said to Kareem, "I would like to meet one of the Infidels. Find out where they are living."

Kareem was cautious. "Master, you must be careful who you are seen with. There are spies everywhere. The sultan is sure to get word."

"A plague on that pederast," he said stoutly. "I will meet whomever I choose. Do as you are told."

Later in the day the sarrajun entered the room. "They are located in the far north-eastern corner." He wrinkled his nose. "They are a filthy people, never bathe, fleas play on their bodies."

Diyar, the nightmare of al-Zardkhana prison still haunting him, felt his skin twitch. "Surely they all cannot be so bad. I would like to speak with one."

Diyar remembered how he had balked at taking his first bath at Amir Mijiri's villa. But such fear was well founded. Living on the steppes, one looked upon water with fear and superstition. When the freezing wind blew across the grasslands, water on the skin caused chapping. The skin cracked open, and the wounds wept blood, ripe for infection. Mongols in the Gobi often lived their lives without washing.

Still, since accepting God as his Father, and the teachings of Muhammad as his Most Holy Prophet, he, Diyar, was grateful for the availability of the baths, and felt repulsed meeting someone who did not exercise daily ablutions.

A few days later, Kareem entered. "I think I have found an Infidel for you to talk with. It seems he was a knight who fought with the armies of their King Louis when he attacked Damietta."

"Damietta," Diyar exclaimed. He calculated for a moment. "That was twenty-eight years ago. Has no one ransomed the poor man yet?"

"I would think, it is because he is a poor man that no one has ransomed him."

Diyar tried not to smile. "Thank you for such insight. Now, where can I find this knight?"

"He usually comes to the bath just before the morning prayer."

"His name?"

"Juff."

"Juff? What means such a name?"

The Egyptian shrugged. "Who can understand the Franks?" he said in dismissal.

The next morning Diyar stood in the main room of the bath, bucketing the oily soap off his back, when a fair-skinned man entered who stood taller than average, wore an Egyptian qaba of blue over a long, white muslin shirt, and a white turban. His garb was threadbare but clean. A gray-white beard surrounded his face, and when he unwound the turban, a full mane of white hair sprang forth. An Egyptian servant boy of ten followed.

Later, as the man was departing the bath, Diyar moved in next to him. He bowed slightly. "I am Rukn al-Din Diyar al-Mijiri al-Baybariya," he said in Arabic. "May I ask your name, sire?"

A slight smile played over the big man's full lips. "I am Gouffre, Count of Perros-Guirec. How can I be of service to you, sire?" he said, his Egyptian Arabic, Diyar noted, superior to his own.

"Of what service, I know not," Diyar said, "it is only..."

"It is only," Gouffre interrupted, "that you are a young mawla who is curious about what an enemy knight might be like. Is that not correct?"

Diyar did not like the man's manner. He was too cocksure by half. Worse, he was right. "True. I saw Frankish knights in defeat when we conquered Marqab and Husn al-Akrad..."

"You mean Crac des Chevaliers, do you not?"

"I mean what I say," Diyar said, steel in his voice. "The victor can call a place what name he pleases."

Gouffre nodded in concession. "True. Only history will have the last word. But you still have not told me how I can be of

service to you."

He shook his head. "In no way I can think of."

"Oh. I thought you might have some translating for me to do."

The role of a "Man of the Pen" did not sit convincingly on the big man's shoulders. "You do translations? What do you translate?"

"Anything in Arabic or French."

"You read Arabic?" he said incredulously.

"I read Arabic before I read French. When I arrived in this land, I could not read at all, but living nearly thirty years behind these walls, I had to do something to keep alive."

"Could you teach me the language of the Franks?"

"I could, but why would you want to learn it?" He snorted. "It is a tongue that seems to be dying here in the Outrémere."

"'Outrémere,' what is that?"

"Hm. Perhaps you are interested in the language. 'Outrémere' means 'beyond the sea'. To us, the Kingdoms of Jerusalem, Tripoli, Antioch and Edessa were kingdoms beyond the sea, and we had to cross the sea to come here."

From then on Diyar began taking lessons from the count. The walls of the man's tiny room were stacked with books. "Copies," he said. "Each by my own hand. All money I have been able to earn has gone for parchment and vellum."

Diyar hated prison, hated any form of confinement. He wanted to be free once more to ride Saba across the sands. Still, if he had to be caged, he decided he might as well learn something. He had Abd ar-Rahman send what few books in French he could find, for which the count was truly grateful.

The Frenchman had a great and easy laugh and liked nothing better than telling what Diyar sensed were rude stories. But often, when explained, he had to laugh too.

When Diyar expressed an interest in the Count's home, Gouffre replied, "My friend, why do you care? Let me tell you, it is nothing like this."

"You mean prison?"

He waved his arm in a wide sweep. "No, no. This city, this country. A few years back, a merchant received permission for me to come to his home to teach his sons and clerks the tongue of the Franks. The man wanted to open trade at Marseille, Bordeaux and perhaps, Le Havre. I relished going to his house. To me it was a palace."

"You are a man of the nobility. Was not your home a palace?"

"A palace?" Gouffre laughed contemptuously. "It was a great pile of stone. This merchant had beautiful carpets on his floors, not one but many laying one on another. His walls were of white marble with beautiful blue mosaics. The house had beautifully carved windows which let in the breezes. I mentioned how pleasant his house was, and he threw open the meshrebiyeh and pointed out a score of houses he knew to be far better. At his meal he served delicate wines, as light as a flower's nectar. His meats were spiced with innumerable tastes of the Orient, served by servants in silk. And the meals consisted of many dishes, and were always served hot. And the vegetables, so many different vegetables. And fruits: melons, pomegranates, peaches, oranges. He even served a frozen sherbet, a lemon ice, cold and sweet." Gouffre's mouth wetted at the thought.

Diyar shrugged. "But, surely, you had the same in your home."

The Count smiled wearily. "The Omnipotent God has blessed your land with a benign and plenteous climate. Whereas the walls of my father's castle rarely saw the sun. Rain and snow beat on them constantly. The castles in my country are cold and damp, and the wind whistles through them. Glass for windows is rare. Some noblemen, when they travel, carry their own windows with them, or at the very least, tapestries to cover the open windows. The floor of the main hall was covered with rushes filled with bones and droppings from the table. Dogs left their waste, rats scratched for food, and fleas set up housekeeping. Our food was cooked in hearths in the courtyard outside. It always arrived at the table cold. And the wine, so sour it was barely drinkable. And the ale was worse. Even the Duke's ale had to be forced down. And the whole place stank. The garderobes were built into the walls and dropped to cess pits which were seldom emptied. Here, even in the prison, the 'night soil' is removed every morning."

He looked around. "My room here is small, but far more comfortable than my room in the castle." He smiled with a touch of sadness. "Still, I would like to see my home again, at least once."

Diyar remembered the steppes. "We all would. Why have your people not sent money for you?"

He shook his head. "I no longer have any people. The Duke, the Duke of Roscanvel, coveted our land and lay siege to our castle. The Duke's son was killed when his soldiers stormed the walls, so he killed all of my family. I survived only because I had come to the Holy Land with My Lord, King Louis. I was barely sixteen, but was knighted on the field of battle." He shook his head sadly. "But I was a knight without land or home to go to. So, when I was captured...." His voice trailed off, and Diyar saw the sadness in his eyes.

Twenty-eight years, Diyar thought. Could I stand that?

One day, as he sat in Gouffre's cozy alcove struggling with French verbs, a guard fill the doorway. A chill of apprehension ran through Diyar.

"I am here to take you to the Watch Commander," the man said quietly.

Amir Yunus al-Asiridi awaited him in front of the Watch Commander's office. Four guards formed a square around Diyar, as Yunus unrolled a scroll.

"Attend my words," and Diyar snapped to attention. "Diyar al-Mijiri al-Baybariya, you have been accused of being disloyal to the sultan. How do you plead to this accusation?"

Shocked, Diyar tried to think. Disloyalty to the sultan—the most damning accusation that could be made against a mawla, and one that carried only one sentence—death.

If he pleaded guilty, he would be executed, and all his possessions would be forfeited to the sultan. But if he did not plead, there was no telling what means of torture would be used to make him condemn himself.

He took a deep breath. "I have always been loyal to my sultan."

Yunus turned to a scribe. "Record the prisoner refuses to admit to the guilt of being disloyal." He faced Diyar. "Then I have no choice but to carry out the sultan's order." He read from the scroll, "The prisoner will be bound and a large stone will be placed on his chest. Each day another stone will be placed upon his chest until he either admits his guilt or dies. He shall have no sustenance but the worst bread and water. He shall not eat on the day in which he drinks, nor drink on day in which he eats."

MAMLUK

CHAPTER 20

"Peine forte et dure."

Gouffre held the candle close and gazed down on the Diyar's insensible face.

The dark cell was little wider than a man's reach. Chords from Diyar's wrists and ankles stretched to iron rings imbedded in the corners. Chains securing the corners of a thick, iron plate on Diyar's chest which also ran to the rings. A great mound of rocks was heaped high on the plate.

A grubby little man pushed past Gouffre. "It is time for his drink," he said.

"Let me," said the count.

The guard shrugged and handed over a small, earthen cup.

Careful not to spill, Gouffre splashed a few drops on Diyar's cracked lips. Dried blood coagulated in the fissures.

With a moan, Diyar's swollen tongue pushed out, seeking the saving liquid. His hollowed eyes flickered open. "More," he whispered, his voice as dry as sand.

Gouffre dribbled more drops into his open mouth, and the prisoner's eyes cleared somewhat.

He recognized his friend and a tear ran down Diyar's cheek. He turned away. "Ashamed..."

"Mon ami," he whispered beneath the guard's hearing, "it is your ruler who is covered in shame."

Diyar turned back. "Please," he pleaded, "water. So hot..."

Gouffre gazed at the pale countenance, touched the man's filthy brow. A thin sheen of sweat lay across it, but it held the clamminess of death. "But you are cool, my friend."

Diyar's face quivered with pain. His eyes closed and his breath caught, then stopped. For a long, suspended minute he ceased to breathe, and Gouffre thought his friend had finally died. But then, in short, panting gasps, his breath came again, his face contorted in anguish.

His voice came in gasps. "My face...covered with rock."

"No, no," the Frenchman spoke quickly. "There is no rock on your face," but Diyar had fallen into unconsciousness again.

Gouffre was about to attempt to wake him, but thought the better of it. The little guard at his elbow, shook his head. "He is a strong one. It is days and he still lives. We have piled more stone on him than any prisoner and yet he lives."

"What about the bread?"

"You mean, will he starve? No, the bread is just to keep him alive so he will suffer longer. It is the weight that kills. Tomorrow, if he still is alive, he gets bread." His chuckle held a tone of sadism. "They would all trade it for water." He winked. "It must be hard to eat with so much on one's stomach."

The count turned away.

Every morning after prayers, Amir Yunus toured the cells with two of his guards. At Diyar's cell, he chose a rock, perhaps the size of a horse's skull, from the bank of boulders in the passageway, ordered it be placed on the pile rising above the prisoner, had his clerk note its placing, then went on to the next cell. To one side of the pile squatted one of much greater size, the "Rock of Death". When Yunus judged a prisoner would never plead, would die before he pleaded, he ordered that stone be placed, and death ended the ordeal.

The amir had already made up his mind. If the young warrior still clung to life after the next day of water, the "Death Rock" would be used to crush the last vestige of it out of him.

The following day when Amir Yunus appeared he examined the prisoner's face. It was twisted into a frozen mask of pain as gaunt as an old man.

"How did he do yesterday?" he said.

"He refused the bread, sire."

"Refused?"

The little guard hedged. "Uh, he would not speak, and when I tried to push it into his mouth, I could not force open his teeth."

"I see. Bring me water."

A cup of fetid liquid was handed him and he poured it on the man's face. After a moment, the pallid eyelids twitched but did not open.

Slowly the amir stood up. He motioned to his bodyguards. "Come," he pointed to the "Rock of Death," "let us have an end to it."

The two guards squatted over the boulder. With a grunt, they lifted and shuffled sideways into the cell. At the prisoner's side, they were about to heft it onto the pile, when the amir spoke up. "Wait."

He turned to the little guard. "Make a space on top of the rocks so the big one will not roll off."

The cell guard did as bidden then stepped out of the cell. The amir nodded to the men. "Put it on and get out."

As the great boulder settled, the sound of cracking bones issued from the body. Amir Yunus knelt down to watch the man's face. He was about to stand, when the sound of running steps echoed hollowly down the narrow corridor.

The guards immediately grabbed their swords. Yunus stepped out into the passageway.

A guard ran up. "Sire," he shouted breathlessly, "the amirs have forced the young sultan to abdicate. He and his mother have been exiled to the fortress at Karak."

The amir stood for a moment, assimilating the news, then started. He spun around and shouted, "Quick. Get those stones off him."

The little guard shrugged. "But, sire, surely it is too late..."

Yunus grabbed the man's neck and threw him into the cell. "Do it now," he said, his voice shaking the stone walls, "or you will take his place."

The amir worked with the guards To remove the great boulder, and to throw the remaining stones into the passageway. Then he whipped out his knife and cut the cords binding the plate and Diyar's limbs, and they propped the plate against the wall.

He held the candle over the naked man and bent down. No signs of life stirred Diyar's waxen face. He turned to the cell guard. "Do you have any liquor?"

The man raised his head with staunch piety. "Of course not, sire. We abide strictly by the sacred laws..."

"Get it, and get it now," roared the amir, and the man scuttled away. He returned in a moment carrying an opaque bottle. Yunus sniffed the distillate and winced with a look of distaste

He forced open Diyar's mouth, poured in a dollop, then waited. No reaction. He leaned over and was examining the man's face once more, when a weak cough from Diyar's throat sprayed the cheap cognac into the amir's face.

Diyar's eyes fluttered open and he whispered without focusing. "Water..," and his eyes closed again

It was quickly fetched, and the amir held up Diyar's head as he drank. Then Diyar slumped back, a twinge of pain contorting his face. "...chest...something, uh..."

Yunus nodded. "Broken? I am sure of it. But yet, with the will of God, you may live."

He turned to one of his guards. "Get a stretcher and take this man to infirmary." Then he confronted the little cell guard. "And you," he said sternly, "you, I do not know whether to lock up for having liquor while on duty, or thank you for helping save a good man's life. If nothing else," his features softened, "you should be punished for possessing such poison. Surely you can afford better than such swill," and he slipped him several coins.

In May of 1279, Baraka ordered Qalaoon and Baisari, the realms two most respected generals, on a campaign north to Cilicia. Then awaited their return in Damascus. When the armies neared the city, the sultan once again listened to his degenerate sycophants, and ordered the two generals arrested. But the generals ignored the arrest orders and declared themselves in revolt.

Baraka panicked, and sent his mother to the generals' camp to plead that they obey her son's orders. The generals refused, detoured Damascus, and marched for Cairo.

Baraka gathered an army and pursued. But soon his men began sneaking back to Damascus. He saw the hopelessness of his cause, slipped by the generals' armies during the night, and sought sanctuary in Qal'at al-Jabal. But even there, his own mamluks deserted him.

When the generals arrived at the base of al-Qal'ah's walls, the sultan stood on one of its towers and asked for terms. Their answer: Abdication and exile to Karak.

He could but comply. On the 18th of August, 1279, Malik-al-Said Baraka left Cairo under escort for Karak. He had reigned for two years and nineteen days which he had spent in frivolity. The revolt had been bloodless. No warrior was willing to fight for such a monarch.

To survive the harsh life of the steppes, the brutal military training, the countless battles, mamluks had to be tough. And the sultan who ruled them had to be tougher. He had to be feared by both his enemies and his own amirs. The mamluks would pledge their loyalty only to someone more ruthless, more cunning, more daring than themselves. In a kingdom where succession was not assured, only the strongest survived. Baraka, having been raised in the plush confines of the palace harem, was not that man.

With Baraka banished, the amirs immediately offered the sultanate to General Qalaoon. Qalaoon, though Baraka's father-in-law, did not hesitate to lead the revolt against him, nor dispatch him to Karak. But he was too shrewd to allow himself to be named sultan. The presence of the great Baybars still loomed over the sultanate. Many of Baybars' appointees, senior amirs and governors of provinces, still held office.

In stead, Qalaoon suggested Baybars' second son, a child of seven years, be proclaimed sultan, while he, Qalaoon, be appointed Atabeq, or Commander-in-Chief, with extended power over the whole civil government. This was done—the boy's name and title became Malik-al-Aadil Salamish—and Qalaoon immediately set about quietly to remove all amirs who might oppose him, including even Baybars' appointees. He also released from prison all those whom he felt could be trusted to support him.

It was in this atmosphere of transition Diyar, his broken ribs bound tightly, and accompanied by Tanin and Kareem, returned to Cairo. Upon landing, the three went first to the office of the Ustadat to see about back pay. Then Diyar and Kareem returned to Fustat and the little house by the canal.

With a great sigh of relief, Diyar stretched out on his couch which also served as a bed, a couch he had seen very little of in the last few years. He began to reflect. He was twenty-six. He should be at the height of his powers. Yet he felt exhausted, looked ten years older. The harsh life with the Ababdeh, followed by the deathly ordeal in prison, had aged him.

Deep in his heart there still burned a flame of hate and revenge against Abu al-Mulq. But with Baraka exiled, al-Mulq had fled to the safety of his father's palace in Damascus.

Perhaps it was just as well, he mused. *In my condition, I could not seek revenge on a flea.*

The cool breezes wafted in off the canal bringing with it thoughts of retirement. *No more wars. No more killing. Just surround myself with books, perhaps open another shop, a number of shops.*

While in prison, he had received word from Abd ar-Rahman saying he would like to start up a book stall in Alexandria. The Egyptian had saved enough money, and only needed his patron's permission. He even had a relative who would run the stall.

Now Diyar considered the idea. Then a thought came to him, and he called for Kareem to bring him a table, parchment and pen. He had just completed a letter to the wazeer in charge of prisons, when a bang on the gate door echoed throughout the household. In a moment, Kareem, a worried look in his eyes, appeared. "Two men of the khasikiya await you."

Diyar went down.

He recognized the older of the two. They had served together at the siege of Husn al-Akrad. The man held a scroll. "You are hereby ordered to appear immediately before the sultan at the Audience Hall. We have been assigned to accompany you."

Upon entering the great audience hall, he saw no pretty young faces among the dignitaries, but mostly grey-beards. As in Baybars' day, the line of seats on both sides of the throne were filled with mature men. But the throne itself was empty. No matter. All the room knew where the power lay.

In the heavy chair to the left of the throne sat a handsome, broad-shouldered man who looked to be in his fifties, Qalaoon al-Elfi. Like Baybars and Diyar, Qalaoon was a Kipchak. When he was brought to Egypt as a boy to be a mamluk, the Amir Ala-al-Din ak Sonkor saw great potential in the lad, and purchased him for the high price of a thousand gold dinars, hence his nickname "Al-Elfi", "The Thousander".

At Sonkor's death, he was bought by Al-Salih Ayoub who was then forming the River Mamluks, or Bahris, whose most famous member was Baybars himself. Now Qalaoon, like Baybars, had clawed his way to the throne, by ability, not ties of birth.

With cool eyes he looked down on Diyar and Tanin al-Ajani. "Many rumors have passed about you in the desert and in prison. Before we decide what to do with you, we will allow you to tell your own story."

Diyar knew his future, indeed his life, balanced on his words. The robed amirs drew closer.

"Oh, great Amir," Diyar began, "thank you for letting us speak. Know first, wherever we were, whatever we did, please believe we were never disloyal to our sultan or our fellow warriors. It happened this way..." and, knowing the Kipchaks love of a good tale, he began to tell Tanin's and his story.

Qalaoon paid especially close heed to the story. He had an advantage the rest of the amirs did not have. He knew the truth.

When Diyar came to the part of the story where he and Tanin where condemned to prison in Alexandria, he realized the impropriety of speaking against Baraka, his sultan. Instead he lay the blame for the prosecution on those who advised him.

All present assented to that.

And when he spoke of his days of torture, he modestly understated the ordeal. He concluded with praise for Amir Yunus who saved his life. Only on this final point did he sense a misstep.

The general's eyes regarded him thoughtfully. He looked to Tanin whose robe covered the stump of an arm. "Do you have anything to add?"

"No, sire. All he says is true. I owe my life to Rukn al-Din Diyar."

To Diyar, he said, "And you say you are grateful to Amir Tablkhana Yunus al-Asiridi?"

"Yes, sire. I owe my life to him."

"You feel he would be loyal to his new sultan?"

Everyone present knew what he really meant was to himself. Now Diyar began to get a feeling of what might be happening. He knew, all of Baybars' former mamluks knew, Qalaoon, though a Bahri Mamluk like Baybars, still did not trust Baybars' warriors. As the sultanate's new leader, he wanted his own army, an army loyal only to him. Consequently, as a counterweight to the Kipchaks, he had been raising another mamluk force, Circassians. The Circassians, unlike the steppe-dwelling Kipchaks, were from the Caucasus Mountains, fierce fighters, but not the great riders like the nomads.

"I do, sire."

Qalaoon turned to his scribe. "Find Yunus al-Asiridi's name and read what resolution we made concerning him."

The clerk ran down a list on a scroll, then read: "It is resolved Yunus al-Asiridi be exiled to Jerusalem at one-hundredth pay."

Qalaoon's attention returned to Diyar. "And you say this is a good man?"

Diyar knew he was on trial. To speak for Amir Yunus was to speak against the most powerful man in the sultanate. But he sensed something else. "I must remain loyal to my opinion of him, just as I know he would remain loyal to the sultan."

The well-turned phrase elicited a murmur of approval from

the congregation of amirs. The general too, seemed to accept it. He nodded to the clerk. "Remove Amir Yunus's name from the list. He may keep his position at the prison." A faint smile played over his lips. "And let us hope he remembers what has happened here if the prison doors ever open to you again," the smile grew wider, "or to me."

A roar of laughter erupted from the host, all who knew the threshold between being in or out of prison was a narrow one.

Now Qalaoon raised his voice so all assembled could hear. "Diyar al-Mijiri, Tanin al-Ajani, you both have suffered grievous wrong. We feel, after what you have experienced, if you still want to be members of the Royal Mamluks, you will be so reinstated. How say you?"

All thoughts of retirement flew from Diyar's mind. "I will serve my new sultan and his amirs willingly and loyally," he said.

Abu raised his stump proudly. "As will I."

A few weeks later, Diyar was on the practice field when word spread throughout the men that Qalaoon had dropped the pretense of having a child-sultan. He deposed Salamish and assumed power himself. On the 4th of December 1279, a great parade of all the Royal Mamluks passed in revue to their new sultan whose full title became al-Malik-al-Mansoor Qalaoon al-Elfi al-Alai, "al-Malik-al-Mansoor" meaning "The Victorious King."

On the proclamation of his Kingship, he ordered the words "Al Salihi" be written under his name whenever he signed a document, indicating his devotion to Al-Salih Ayoub, showing once more the mamluks' oath of loyalty to the master who trained and freed them.

MAMLUK

CHAPTER 21

Spring, and the skies over the Nile were darkened by flights of migrating birds. News rocked the city that the ex-sultan, Baraka, had been killed at Karak. At first it was reported he had fallen while playing polo, but soon rumors spread that poison was the real cause of his fall during the heat of the match.

Sonkor al-Ashqar, the Viceroy of Damascus, Abu al-Mulq's father, and second only to the sultan in power, saw the rumor of Baraka's assassination as the opportunity to vie for the sultan's throne. He summoned all his amirs and demanded their allegiance and, after a glance at the lancers lining the hall, the amirs gave it.

Sonkor then assumed the name of Malik-al-Kamil, "The Perfect King," and rode in state to the Damascus hippodrome surrounded by the symbols of royalty, including the Royal Parasol borne by his most trusted amir. Preceding him were those amirs loyal to him, garbed in their best and brightest robes of honor.

Such an indignity could not be tolerated by Qalaoon, and the Citadel once again prepared for war, this time not against other countries and people, but against its own.

Diyar, riding with the army through the capital, felt his blood course at being in action again, and in Qalaoon he found a sultan worth following. But time had matured his zeal. The life of a sultan was perilous. How long this one would last no one could say. And then what, another Baraka?

Still, Diyar felt encouraged. He was gaunt but his ribs had healed. And only occasionally did he suffer from the debilitating headaches. But the hissing in his ears never ceased.

Early in the Summer of 1280, the two armies squared off at Ashqar, a few miles south of Damascus. The Tibaq ar-Rafraf with Diyar among its files lined up along the front lines. The sultan kept his new regiments, the Circassians, well back in reserve.

After the first flights of arrows thinned the ranks of the charging lines, the warriors fell on each other with flailing swords and maces, mamluks fighting mamluks. Having died twice, Diyar no longer felt the nervousness that preceded a battle but fought with a calm, clear eye. He conserved his energy, striking only when he could do the most damage, slaughtering without emotion. And always in the corner of his eye he searched for Abu al-Mulq.

Where is he? Where is the bastard.

He parried a lancer's thrust, and rammed his sword through the man's mouth.

Surely he will be here willing to vie for a crown, even if it first is his father's.

But in the broiling confusion, al-Mulq was nowhere to be seen.

Viceroy Sonkor al-Ashqar, to his credit, rode into the heart of the battle, fighting with the desperation of a man contesting for a kingdom. But it was hopeless. Even as Diyar arched to hack at the neck of a rider, the man raised his hand in submission.

"Hold," the warrior pleaded. "I care not so much for the usurper to die for him," and he sheathed his sword. Diyar glanced around. Others of Sonkor's army were also dropping their weapons.

Diyar nodded toward the rear of the battle line. "I am Diyar al-Mijiri al-Baybariya. Give up your horse and armor, and I will let you live."

The man nodded. "They are yours for my life."

"Go. Give them to Kareem, my sarrajun," and he urged Saba on to the next rider, always working his way toward the battling viceroy. Perhaps there he would find Abu al-Mulq. But before he could reach Sonkor, the viceroy stand in his stirrups and look around, gauging his chances. Then he whirled his horse and galloped off the field. Just that fast, the battle was over.

As the scribes and qadi picked their way through the battlefield to identify the dead, Qalaoon reassembled his army and led a march of triumph into Damascus. On Sonkor's throne, he appointed a new viceroy, then returned with his army to Cairo.

Meanwhile, his riders tracked Sonkor and the remnants of his army. The rebels sped north, finally taking up residence in the castle of Sahyoun in Lebanon. The fortress was surrounded by the fortified town of Shaizar on the Al Aasi River, known in the west as the Orontes. Soon spies sent back the word: Sonkor had contacted the Mongol Il-Khan, Abagha, in Persia, urging him to invade Syria and to war against the mamluks. Such treachery!

Three months after Sonkor's defeat at Asqar, the pigeons brought the word to al-Qal'ah: Mongols had crossed the Euphrates. They were commanded by Mangu Timur, a younger son of Hulagu and brother of Abagha.

In October, 1280, they stormed Aleppo, taking the city without a struggle, the populace and the garrison having fled. Still the Mongols massacred all the country folk they could find, then looted and burned the city to the ground. Satiated with loot, they returned back across the Euphrates.

But the question that continued to haunt Syria, indeed, the whole sultanate: When would they return?

CHAPTER 22

Diyar lay gazing out his meshrebiyeh. Usually, at that time of day, mid-morning, he would have been at the practice field. It was important, indeed a matter of life and death, that he keep in shape. But the exercises, unlike when he was younger, now took on the ritual of duty.

The newly recruited Circassians, shorter, swarthier men, strutted about the field, secure in their station, lording it over the older warriors.

He sighed. *Was I so arrogant as a youth? Probably.*

The reason there was no practice that day was because the sultan was meeting Isa ibn Mahanna, the Grand Sheik of the Al-Fadhl, the Arabs of the Syrian desert. The sheik had been one of the Arab leaders who had joined Sonkor al-Ashqar in his revolt. Now, with Sonkor hiding in exile, he was coming to seek the sultan's pardon, and Qalaoon, with his whole retinue, had ridden out to meet him with full royal honors and gifts.

A look of disgust played across Diyar's face. Why honors for a traitor? Since his encounter with the Beja, he had little respect for Arabs. They raised beautiful horses, the "Drinkers of the Wind," but they were dirty and devious, not to be trusted.

"To turn your back on an Arab is to invite the tickle of his blade," he muttered.

But he knew enough about politics to understand the reason

behind the courtesies to the Grand Sheik. The Eastern Bedouins were a source of insecurity to the sultan. They wandered the deserts, the no-man's land between the Mamluk and Mongol Empires, living free and calling neither factions master. They had roamed the desert since time immemorial, long before either of the steppe-dwellers came, and they looked on both as foreigners. So if one side treated them harshly, they simply offered allegiance to the other.

The earth-shaking rumble of the sultan's band marked his return with his guest. The strident boom was magnetic to the city's populace, and from all corners of the city they ran to Main Road to see the show.

"Not me," Diyar said. "I will not ride out just to observe some fawning, little Arab.

Soon the blare of trumpets could be heard.

Diyar folded his arms stubbornly.

Ranks of hautboy cried out.

He leaped up. "Kareem," he called, "have Saba saddled," and hurried to don a clean tunic.

By the time he arrived at the Main Road, the avant-garde had passed, and the band was riding by. Behind it came the sultan and the Grand Sheik, the Arab on a dazzling, white mare.

Isa ibn Mahanna sat tall on the beautiful horse. He was garbed in a loosely wrapped turban of white silk embroidered with gold and, unlike the men of his bodyguard who wore red-and-white striped gubbas, he was garbed in a silk, light-green-and-white gubba that shimmered in the sunlight.

Something about the way the Arab king rode, his stately bearing, drew a memory from Diyar's past, and his eyes misted. Isa ibn Muhanna reminded him of his father, tall, straight of back, eyes weathered from scanning a distant horizon.

Diyar, on horseback, sat above the surrounding crowd, and as the procession passed, the Grand Sheik's eyes fell on him, and an almost imperceptible smile played across his lips. He nodded slightly, acknowledging a fellow warrior. Diyar steeled himself not to respond, and the sheik's gaze passed on to others. Still, Diyar had to acknowledge as he reined Saba away, the Bedowy had a presence, almost worthy of meeting again. His back shivered with a twinge of pain where the Beja blade had torn it.

Perhaps not.

He had no sooner returned home, when pounding on the outside door echoed in the courtyard. Instinctively he tensed. One never knew if the knock was not the first step to exile, prison, torture, or even death.

The bowwab ushered in a stocky warrior with a black curly beard and eyebrows to match: Amir Kounduk al-Dhahiri.

Diyar became wary. Kounduk had been one of Sultan Baybars most loyal followers, one of the Dhahiris. If he had arrived unannounced, it meant he did not want Diyar to be forewarned of his visit. Such bode ill.

Diyar bowed slightly. "My house is honored by the visit of such a distinguished guest, Amir Kounduk al-Dhahiri. How may I serve you?"

The amir's face glowered with barely repressed rage. "I must speak to you privately."

Diyar ushered him inside to a seat on the first floor's divan which extended along two sides of the room, and he sat diagonally across from him. Kareem slipped in and received an order for juice-flavored water.

When they were alone, Kounduk leaned forward. "Did you see the sultan with the Arab, that camel herder? It must have rankled you to see him fawn over the cursed Arab."

"Perhaps," he said mildly, "But it is better to have the desert tribes with us than against us."

"Yes, but you cannot approve of the way the sultan has been treating us, we who have served the sultanate so faithfully."

Diyar remained silent. Being reinstated to service, he would not be drawn into a tirade against the new sultan. Most warriors, when exiled or imprisoned, guilty or not, were rarely seen again.

The amir forged on, his anger growing. "Surely, you have noticed the way these new recruits," his lips curved into a sneer, "these 'Men-of-the-Mountains,' have treated the old warriors. We men of Malik-al-Dhahir Baybars have been demoted, our fiefs taken away. We are daily subjected to humiliations at the hands of these goat herders."

His voice dropped. "There is only one answer. We must rid ourselves of this upstart, and elect a new sultan."

There it was, what he feared, revolt. He had to tread carefully. Just knowing about a plot to kill the sultan could mean death— from both sides.

He stood and bowed formally. "I must ask the amir's pardon. I cannot involve myself in any conspiracy against the sultan."

Kounduk stood, his hand resting on his sword. His eyes narrowed, his tone ominous. "But it is too late. You already know our plan."

He shrugged. "What plan, amir. Nowadays there are more plots than flies in summer. I do not know what you intend to do, and I prefer it that way. If asked, I could only say you came to share a cool drink with me which, by the way, you have yet to do. Please be seated and I will go see where my lazy servant can be."

The man moved to block his way and started to draw his sword. "You are not going anywhere."

Immediately Kareem stepped through the door, a lance in hand. "I have your repast right here, sire." He moved closer to the amir, the lance pointing at his heart. "Did you want anything more?"

Diyar smiled at the amir. "You must forgive me for having such an indolent servant. It is so hard to find a reliable sarrajun these days."

Kounduk slammed his sword back into its scabbard, and aimed a finger at him. "Be warned: Speak about our discussion, and you die," and he spun and headed for his horse.

Diyar called after him. "I thank the amir for the advice."

Later, as he sipped the cool orange drink in his room, he pondered. What will the outcome of such plotting be? These are desperate men struggling for power. Only two possible outcomes exist for them, success or death. With such stakes, it is unlikely the amir will trust me to remain silent. He sighed.

We will have to guard our back even more closely in the future.

One thing he had learned with the changing of the sultanate's leadership was the precariousness of being a warrior in a sultan's army. So far in his career, he had fallen from the exalted height of the sultan's bodyguard, to the dust of the sultan's prison, only to be raised to the position of a journeyman knight, grateful for the position. Faced with such vagaries of fortune, he knew he had to have extra income to fall back on in case fate made him a civilian again. It was time to open a book stall in Alexandria.

Abd ar-Rahman politely suggested a nephew for the position of its manager, but Diyar had someone else in mind. He did not realize how much paper-work it would take, but after riding to-and-fro between a half-dozen different bureaus throughout the Citadel, he set sail for Alexandria.

When he and Kareem rode into the great prison again, Amir Yunus strode from his office, a smile of welcome on his face. Diyar jumped to the ground, and Yunus clutched his hand in friendship.

"I will always be grateful for what you did for me," Yunus said. "Had you not spoken up to the sultan, I would be one of the prison's guests, rather than its guard. Is it true the sultan had the orders already inked?"

Diyar smiled. "I believe so. But I could not have done otherwise than speak up. Were it not for you, I would be unable to speak at all. To do less would be unthinkable. Now, where is my prisoner?"

"Ah, yes, your prisoner. You know, I will miss him sorely. He is one of the few who could beat me in chess. Do you have his papers?"

Diyar handed them over. "You will never know how much trouble these took. I had to ask favors of several old amirs to have these expedited. And, as you know, there are not many left who still have influence."

"I do know first hand," he said ruefully. He motioned to a couple of his men to follow. "Come, let us go see if he is ready?"

Gouffre, Counte de Perros-Guirec was ready, and eager to

leave. His books and scrolls were bundled into wicker baskets which several porters hefted and carried down the corridor. But as he was about to step out of his cubicle, he paused at the threshold and looked back.

"I have spent more time in this cell than any other place in my life. Thirty years." He turned to Diyar with a smile. "Who would have thought it would be one of the hated Saracens who ransomed me?" His eyes clouded over. "My friend, how can I ever thank you?"

Diyar put a arm on the knight's shoulder and gave it a shake. "Friendship had nothing to do with it. This was business. You want to thank me? Sell many books," and he gave the thick shoulder a squeeze.

And the count did. With the book stall located near the docks, Gouffre was in a good location to contact ships' officers and travelers. He could offer to buy their books, copy them for a fee, and/or sell them more books to take on their voyages. His knowledge of a half-dozen languages proved invaluable.

He, too, hired a staff of copyists, and transcribed all new works he acquired.

In the spring, the army was once again marched into Syria. The Mongol sweep through the north and destruction of Aleppo meant Qalaoon had to shore up the sultanate's defenses.

In Palestine, he had a formal meeting with the leaders of the Knights of Saint John, the Hospitallers, under a pavilion in the middle of a flower-carpeted field, the opposing knights eyeing each other warily at the field's edges. Qalaoon offered a truce which the under-manned Franks accepted gratefully.

The sultan and his army then rode north to Tripoli where King Bohemond VIII who, since his loss of Antioch, was Count of Tripoli only, signed a similar treaty. These truces benefited both sides. They offered some assurance the Muslims would not attack the Crusaders, and the Muslims would, in turn, be free to face their greater foe, the Mongols, without fearing an alliance between the Mongols and the Crusaders.

The sultan's great army turned east, then, inexplicably, halted as it neared the River Jordan. Rumors rippled down the ranks and files. A detachment of riders from the khasikiya pounded past Diyar and Kareem.

"Why do we stop?" a warrior shouted at them as they rode by.

"The sultan has uncovered a plot. We go to capture the traitors now."

Kareem turned to Diyar whose face went blank. They could only wait and see who would be accused.

In time, a contingent of the sultan's bodyguards returned with a group of Baybars' old amirs at their lance tips. Kounduk was among them. The rest of the conspirators had made a dash for freedom.

With the amirs assembled, Qalaoon accused Kounduk of fermenting a plot to overthrow him. The sultan's guards tore the amir from the saddle. A sword arced, and the black, curly head rolled across the ground.

Twenty-three other amirs were stripped of weapons and armor, and clapped in chains. On the back of asses they were led back to Qal'at al-Jabal. The troops looked away in shame. All knew too well the depths of pain that would be inflicted upon them. Death would be their only mercy.

But the sultan could feel little assured. Two amirs and over three hundred warriors had escaped. Qalaoon had them tracked, but knew where they headed—north to Sonkor al-Ashqar.

Kounduk's body was left at the side of the road, its severed head on its chest. Diyar rode by and viewed the grisly remains with apprehension. It was said the sultan knew everything that occurred in the sultanate. Did he know about Kounduk's visit to Diyar's house?

As always I can only wait and see.

In May, 1281, the sultan entered Damascus at the head of an army of nearly sixty thousand men. A public holiday was proclaimed, and the people, wild at seeing their protector, draped the army's parade route with multi-colored bunting that billowed in the breeze.

Upon reaching the Piebald Palace, Qalaoon mounted its

throne. Amazingly, his first decree was to award the former Viceroy of Damascus, Sonkor al-Ashqar, a large principality extending from Lattakieh to Antioch. The unspoken reason he made such a seemingly strange decree was he hoped it would keep Sonkor from joining the Mongols. Such were politics.

Diyar loved exploring Damascus. The beauty of the city had won it many titles: "Bride of the Earth", " Queen of Cities", and in Arabic "Al-Fayha", "The Fragrant" because of her many flower-filled gardens. But his ramblings were cut short by an order to appear before the Commander in Chief.

The Commander, an old campaigner from the days of Baybars, had taken over the office of the palace's Major Domo. He looked up from behind a beautiful ivory-inlaid desk.

"It has come to our attention you can speak Arabic."

"Perhaps a little, sire."

The amir's words sharpened. "Can you or can you not speak Arabic?"

"Enough to get by in the street."

"We all can do that. But can you carry an important message if called upon?"

A tickle of excitement awakened in his chest. "Yes, sire."

The amir examined him for a moment, then nodded. "Good. We have just learned Mangu Timur is preparing to invade Syria with an army of over eighty thousand. Consequently the sultan is sending messages to all contingents in the realm and ordering them to report to him here in Damascus." His eyes glinted. "War is afoot." He motioned to him. "Come around here."

A vellum map covered the desk. "This is the Eastern Desert." His finger circled an area. "The Al-Fadhl tribe is usually here this time of year. I want you to find them and give Sheik Isa ibn Mahanna the sultan's command to muster here to join in the war against the godless ones'."

Diyar squinted at the map. It contained mostly featureless expanse.

The amir read his thoughts. "Do not worry. We are not sending you out into the desert alone. You are to go to the home of Mustafa ibn Hasan. He is a sheik of the Al-Fadhl and, in his old age, is now living in the city. He will give you a guide to lead you through the desert."

Arabs? The desert? Diyar's back twitched.

"Sire, I must speak honestly. I do not hold Arabs in very high regard."

"What you think of them is of no importance. What is important is we get as many warriors here to defend the realm as possible, and as soon as possible. You are going whether you like them or not."

CHAPTER 23

At his knock, two Arabs, lances in hand, pushed open a double-door gate, and Diyar rode into a large courtyard. In front of him an Arab major-domo stood waiting, sword on hip. A dozen or more desert warriors nearby watched him narrowly, their blue-black jirds—capes—thrown over their right shoulder.

Diyar set his jaw and dismounted, his hand never leaving the pommel of his sword.

The major-domo led the way up several steps into a large garden with flowering shrubs. In the center, water mushroomed up from a fountain in an octagonal pool.

The two men crossed the garden and passed through a portal, also guarded by lancers, and ascended wide stairs to an expansive room. At the far end, a man reclined on the floor near open meshrebiyehs. He was propped up by rugs heaped against a saddle. Several more layers of rugs thickened the floor and hung on the walls. Other than a small, low table at his elbow, and chest along the wall, the room was devoid of furniture.

Sheik Mustafa ibn Hasan rose slowly and nodded his greeting. "Welcome to my humble home." He gestured and a black slave hastened over with cool drinks. The sheik motioned to the floor. Diyar sat and the sheik dropped back into place against his saddle.

The old man sighed. "So, the godless ones come again." He

glanced around the room, and shook his head. "No, I will not be put out of my home. If they come, they will meet me at the gate."

"Yes, sire, but I hope you will allow us to bring your clan to help you."

"My clan," he said resolutely, "indeed, the whole Al-Fadhl tribe will come." He nodded to the servant. "Call Fuaz."

In a moment, a lean young man entered and bowed in front of the sheik. "O Protector!" he said, head down. "God grant thee long life, most magnanimous of all Arabs."

Sheik Mustafa smiled and replied, "And peace be with thee, my son."

The sheik took a small, sealed scroll from the table and handed it to Diyar. "Give this unopened to Sheik Isa ibn Mahanna." Another roll of parchment he opened. "And this will pass you through Al-Fadhl lands. As you can see, it has my seal on it. With this letter you will be safe."

Diyar took the two documents, but remained silent. The perceptive sheik noted his hesitancy. "If something troubles you, speak it now."

Diyar's eyes quickly ran through the flowery language of the passport. Then he said, "Sire, this document, for which I thank you deeply, will allow us to pass through Al-Fadhl lands, but I was told we must also pass through the lands of the Murra. Is it not true the Al-Fadhl and Murra are enemies?"

Sheik Mustafa nodded. "Since the ascension of the Prophet, or so it seems."

"Then how am I to pass through Murra lands?"

He raised his hand proudly to the young man. "That is why I have commanded Fuaz here to guide you. He is the son a sheik of the Murra. With him you will be safe."

Momentarily confused, Diyar said, "But the Murra are Al-Fadhl enemies."

"They are," agreed the sheik, "and to the death." An expression of pride fell on the old man's face as he looked on the handsome young man. "But who could be an enemy of Fuaz Shalan?"

Diyar let it pass. Perhaps the riddle would be answered in time.

Since he was aware it was customary among the Arabs to exchange trifling gifts before departing, he now drew forth from his waistband a pretty blue bottle from Acre full of rose water. In exchange, the sheik nodded to his servant who produced what appeared to be a dark-blue bolt of cloth.

Diyar was about to thank the sheik, when Fuaz spoke up. "You are honored. Sheik Mustafa, in his great generosity, has bestowed upon you the jird of his house. Here I will show you how it is worn."

He grasped the corner of the cloth and made a loop. "Put your right arm and your head through here. In town the long end goes under your left elbow, and is then thrown across the right arm and shoulder. But", and he drew the mantle over Diyar's head and shoulder, "in the desert, this will give you cover and warmth."

Diyar observed how the fringed end of Fuaz's jird fell down his back to just above his boots, and he gave his wrap a casual, albeit somewhat awkward, toss to clear his shoulder so that it would hang like his companion's.

The sheik nodded his approval, and the two men, with a bow, departed.

Back in the entry-court, the sheik's warriors were readying supply camels and mounting their horses to accompany the two. As they all rode up the hill-road east of Damascus, Diyar turned to the young man. "Now, let me understand. You will get me through the Murra, and the passport will get us through the Al-Fadhl."

A dazzling smile split he young man's face. "True."

"But are you not afraid, as a Murra, the Al-Fadhl will do you harm?"

"Not with the old sheik as my patron. Besides, no man would dare kill me, I am a sharif. That is a..."

"I know, a descendent of the Prophet. So?"

"So, if any member of a clan kills a sharif, they must forfeit five of their own men. It is the law."

Diyar felt little comforted.

The well-worn road passed through walnut, olive, and apricot orchards and entered grasslands. After a couple of days, the steppes dried up and became desert: Murra country.

The party paused next to the road, now barely a track, and dismounted. Riding camels were led forward, and Saba and Fuaz's horses taken away. A throat of a young camel was slashed three times. Herbs were dipped into the dead beast's blood and tribal emblems painted on the riding camels' necks to say to all whom the riders met they came in peace.

The sheik's guard turned back to their first responsibility, protecting the old man, and the two men continued alone on the riding camels and leading two supply camels. The Hamad, the North-Arabian uplands lay before them, flat, hard soil for hundreds of miles southward and eastward.

Birds whirred out of the camel-grass, flew several hundred paces, then disappeared once again in the grass. Clumsy, desert bustards and coveys of pintail grouse, startled while feeding on flaming red caterpillars, rose in clouds, only to settle as the riders passed by. A small wolf crossed their path, paused to examine them without fear, then trotted on. Foxes could be seen darting among the rocks. Delicate stems of wild lavender and chamomile broke under the camel's padded feet.

Diyar learned how to wrap his jird against his body for warmth, or to pile it on one shoulder as a barrier against the remorseless sun.

After several days of seeing no one from dawn to dusk, three men on camels appeared.

Fuaz nodded. "No need to worry. Not my clan, but still Murra tribe."

Even so, Diyar shifted his jird to uncover his bow holster and quiver on his waist. When the men neared, Fuaz called out a greeting. The men, eyeing Diyar, mumbled a reply.

Fuaz shouted angrily, "Do you not recognize me? I am Fuaz,

son of Sheik Jirad ibn Jeneyb, leader of all the Murra's."

The tribesmen made no reply until they were nearly on them, then the lead rider pulled his sword and whipped his camel forward, the other two men right behind him. Diyar's bow sprang to hand and an arrow flew, piercing the first man's neck. Dead instantly, he plummeted to the ground. The second man fell too, the arrow in his chest breaking as he bounced on the rocky dirt.

The camel of the third man crashed sideways into Fuaz's camel, its rider attempting to dislodge him. But Fuaz's sword was too fast, and the camel ran on, his rider's severed head bouncing along behind. The body toppled from its perch.

The two men chased down the dead men's camels then returned to examined the bodies.

Fuaz shook his head. "These men are thieves, and died the death of thieves. We will leave them for the vultures. Even their camels smell bad."

"True," mused Diyar. "I only hope all your kinsmen will not greet us in such a manner."

The next afternoon, a slim figure was silhouetted on a mound ahead. When they neared, the girl called out her soft demand, "Who is with you?" to which Fuaz replied correctly to etiquette, "Only God."

"His countenance be upon you, and peace," she said, thus allowing them to enter into her little camp. Closer, they saw the girl had been crying, the reason apparent. A hyena had attacked several of her little flock of goats and wantonly torn their guts out. Even as the girl spoke, a kid limped by, struggling to graze though its entrails hung from its belly.

"And I fear the beast will be back to kill the rest of the flock," she said, and began to sob again.

The young Arab prince's blood ran hot, and he jumped down and began circling the camp until he found the hyena's tracks. He followed them to a burrow in the side of a dried rill. He snatched a cord from his saddlebags, and to Diyar's amazement, dove into the hyena's burrow, disappearing in the dark.

Diyar dismounted and squatted by the evil-smelling den.

Hearing snarls, he stepped back, sword drawn. In a moment, Fuaz came backing out, pulling on the cord. Together, they hauled out the hyena.

Struck by the light, the beast fought wildly, until the two hacked it to death.

Diyar examined it, its jaws powerful enough to crush a man's leg. "It took great courage to go in after it."

Fuaz shook his head. "The trick is to catch him in the dark. He is a coward in the dark. I simply felt around in there until I found him, tied the cord around his neck and dragged him out. It took no special courage."

Diyar knew otherwise.

They returned with the hyena to the girl's camp and the grateful girl invited them to stay.

She was a lovely creature with thick, smooth hair and fine features. She had a small fire of twigs burning among a hearth of rocks. The men sat, and she placed before them a bowl of fresh goat's milk, and said, "Swear to thy sister, no harm will come to her at thy hands."

She took a twig from the fire. "Take this in thy hand and swear by the life of the Lord, the giver of all life."

Fuaz answered with the ancient Ismaili formula, "In the name of God: as He took the life from this piece of dead wood, thus may the Lord take life from me if I do not honor and protect thy soul and thy body, O my sister!"

Night was coming on, and the two men worked to slaughter the mortally wounded animals to let their blood run. Then they carried them closer to the fire to protect them from predators. With the remainder of her herd settling at the edge of the camp, the girl smiled shyly and went to her shelter, a small tarp of woven goat's hair slung between the rocks. She returned with all her food: bread, milk, butter, and dried dates.

The men munched the girl's humble meal, learning her name was Tuema. She was of the Al-Fadhl tribe who were camped nearby, and she was the daughter of Sheik Isa ibn Mahanna himself.

A light rain began to fall, and Tuema offered to share the slim protection of her tarp. When the men were settled, she took out her dagger.

"Let this dagger rest in my lap," she said, the symbolic gesture a request that they spare her maidenhood.

Diyar knew, among Bedouins, a girl's chastity was sacred. If it was violated, a father could kill his daughter and carve her flesh into pieces.

"You need have no fear from us, my sister," replied Fuaz with sincerity, and the three huddled together out of the rain. Within minutes, the girl's two dogs, lean as twigs, crept into the crevices between their bodies.

The next morning, the men woke to the enchanting sight of the morning rays outlining the beauty of Tuema's body through her thin black garments as she prepared their breakfast: thin leaves of flour mixed in cold water and baked in glowing coals, dates dipped in butter and rolled in the warm bread, and goat's milk.

As she moved about the fire, Fuaz's eyes never left her. When it was time to leave, Diyar gave her parting gift of a leather bookmark with a saying of the Prophet tooled into it. But Fuaz took her aside and, from his arm, pulled a fine silver bracelet etched with gold.

"This has been mine for good luck. Now that I have found you, I need it no longer."

The two men mounted and headed away, but Fuaz looked back at her standing highlighted in the morning sun. "Saba," he said dreamily.

"That is the name of my favorite horse."

"Horse," he snorted disgustedly. "'Saba' means 'Morning', but it also means 'Virgin Bride'."

He glanced at the young man. "Have you forgotten? You are a prince of the Murra, and she is the daughter of the Al-Fadhl's chieftain?"

His smile flashed. "Stranger things have happened, my friend."

Soon their camels were floating through a stream of dusty sheep. The men topped a low hillock and below, as far as the eye could see, stretched a city of black tents. Ahead, a group of riders awaited them.

The two approached, and their greeting was returned by a young man, who said, "I am, Ali, the second son of Sheik Isa ibn Mahanna. Welcome to our humble home."

"Thank you," Diyar said. He held out the scroll. "I have a message from my Sultan, al-Malik-al-Mansoor Qalaoon al-Elfi al-Salihi al-Alai, and I have been charged to put it in the hand of your sheik, Isa ibn Mahanna."

The young man quickly drew back his hand.

"I am not able to touch the message and my revered father is not here. Just this morning he departed on a hunting party and might not be back this day or even the next."

"It is imperative he receive this as soon as possible."

The man nodded. "I understand. Come. We will go find them."

The men were given horses and lances. The sheik's son followed the tracks of the party with no difficulty, and by mid-morning they came across a small tent and several of the sheik's slaves. Hoof prints led off in several directions and, following the pointed finger of one of the slaves, the group continued east.

Soon they saw two men squatting eating fatirehs as their horses wandered nearby. Two sleek greyhounds impatiently paced nearby.

The taller of the two men stood, and Diyar recognized him as the dignified old sheik he had seen in the parade to Qal'at al-Jabal.

The men dismounted and Ali made the introductions.

"Yes, I remember seeing you when I visited Malik-al-Mansoor," said the sheik. He took the paper, read it, then looked up. "Yes, I understand your sultan's need but unfortunately I can not come now."

Stunned, Diyar saw prison gates opening for him once again

when he failed to return with the sheik and his men.

"But, sire, the battle could be lost without your fine warriors. And the godless-ones are far more ruthless allies than the sultan."

"Perhaps, but it can not be helped. I am the sworn protector of my tribe, and I will not leave until I have rid the land of these damnable wolves."

Diyar could scarcely believe his ears. The man would let a nation fall rather than miss a hunting party. There was only one thing to do. "Perhaps, sire, you would allow my friend and me to join in the hunt in order that we may quickly dispatch the wolves and move on to the battle."

The old man brightened. "Fine idea. We were just finishing our meal. Take food, then we will continue the tracking."

Diyar glanced at Fuaz who spoke up. "Many thanks, sire, but we ate before we arrived at your camp. If you wish to resume the hunt, we are ready to ride with you."

The men mounted and, following tracks, spotted several wolves on a rise ahead. The animals bounded away and the men gave chase.

One of the wolves, an old male, large and rangy, veered off, and Diyar dashed after him, a greyhound leading the way. The wolf could have crippled the delicate hound with but a bite, but he dared not turn with the lancer right behind.

The lance Diyar had received from the sheik's son was a primitive weapon of bamboo. Tufts of black-and-grey ostrich down decorated its shaft back of its triangular steel head, and its red ribbons fluttered in the wind.

Though Diyar closed on the wolf, every time he was about to run it through, it dodged away. Then the animal stumbled and, exultantly, Diyar lowered his lance to make the fatal stab.

Black. Darkness engulfed him. Slowly light drifted in, and he opened his eyes. He lay on the hard, sandy ground. The dog stood guard over him, his muzzle but inches from his face. Diyar heard an ominous growl. He raised up to see the wolf creeping toward him.

He pushed the dog aside and awkwardly hurled his kindjal at

the wolf. It missed, and the wolf turned and loped away.

Diyar creaked to his feet shaking his head to clear it. Sheepishly he looked around. There was no greater humiliation to a Kipchak than to be unhorsed.

Stiffly he walked to his browsing horse. And as he did, he asked himself, How had it happened? His lance work was too practiced to miss such a target. Yet all had gone black.

He probed his head wound. Pain still throbbed, deep and festering.

Atop a distant knoll, the old wolf paused, raised his muzzle, and a soulful cry sang across the desert, ending in a series of barks.

"Your laughter makes it worse, old-timer," Diyar groused. He climbed into the saddle, and scanned the horizon. Fortunately, no one had seen his debacle. It was getting late. He turned his mare back toward camp. Doubt and fear gnawed at him. He had lost consciousness in a hunt. What if it happened in the heat of battle?

When he returned to the sheik's tent, several of the hunters had already arrived and their kills lay in a line, the wolves throats carefully cut.

Fuaz sat on a rock munching a date, and he tossed one to Diyar as he dismounted. Soon Isa ibn Mahanna rode up, the body of a wolf draped over his pommel. He stepped down and inspected the row of dead beasts. Then he turned to Diyar.

"And how was your hunt?"

"I had bad luck, sire, but then, if I did not have bad luck, I would not have any luck at all."

The old-timer looked at him for a moment, then tipped his head back and laughed loud and long.

Diyar spoke softly to Fuaz. "This is the second time today an old wolf has had a laugh on me."

By dark, the hunting party returned to the tribe's encampment. After they ate, the tribal leaders assembled in the sheik's tent. It soon became obvious the sheik would honor the sultan's request for assistance. Nevertheless the men began discussing the campaign. It was then Diyar learned Arabs rarely did anything without every man expressing his views, often many times over.

Sometime during the night, Tuema arrived in camp, peeking into the male side of the sheik's great tent to see if Fuaz was there—and to be seen by him.

But there was now no time for love to blossom. In a few hours the morning sun emblazoned the horizon and the whole Al-Fadhl tribe erupted into action as it broke camp and the migration began.

The commander in charge of the move was a big man garbed all in black, shirt, trousers, jird. His saddle and bridle too were black with some inlaid bits of silver. And even though the Arabs preferred not riding a black horse, his mare was as raven as his saddle and clothes.

Despite the heat and dust, he was constantly on the move, sending riders galloping the width of the tribe—it extended to both horizons—directing herders, answering questions, giving orders. So great was the camel herd, startled gazelles ran ahead of it as before a desert fire. The air resounded with the roaring and squealing of camels, the neighing of horses, the curses of the herders, scolding women, laughing children.

As Sheik Isa ibn Mahanna rode along, tribesmen trotted over to hail him good fortune. Slaves dismounted to kiss his feet and murmur a blessing. Women and girls cried shrilly, "God strengthen thee!" "Go thee before the countenance of the Lord!" "Long life to thee, our Prince!" "God grant thy wishes!"

And when the great Arab nation of Al-Fadhl neared Damascus, the sheik led an army of hundreds of well-mounted horsemen, all wearing helmets and breastplates, and carrying swords and lances. Behind them came their slaves on camels, leading spare horses. The rest of the tribe, women, children, flocks, baggage camels, followed. And all were led, even the sheik, by the most extraordinary structure in the nomadic Arab world, the Marqab, or the "Ark of Ishmail."

The Marqab was a large framework of acacia wood balanced atop a tall camel. It was adorned with hundreds of small tufts of black ostrich feathers. Barbaric decorations, votives and thank-offerings, festooned its sides. And inside, Tuema, the chosen virgin, sat on a special seat. In the left fore-corner stood the sacred standard. Women lodged in "riding tents" made of tall, curved horns rode along side in escort camels.

Sultan Qalaoon had ordered all troops converge outside of Hims, north of Damascus, and as the great Al-Fadhl nation approached the battlefield, Tuema untied her head cloth and her glorious tresses fell over her shoulders. Then she stood in her lofty frame, her face transfigured in an ecstasy of joy, and as the escorting women took up the high trill of the desert, she, to the dazzlement of the troops, tore open her dress. With bared breast, her supple body straining forward, she held aloft a bouquet of snow-white ostrich plumes. Looking like a goddess—the bravest and most beautiful maiden of her tribe—she burst into jubilant song, crying to the warriors words of passionate eloquence, singing psalms of heroism and strength, inflaming them to warlike ardor.

Diyar, riding at the sheik's left, glanced at Fuaz. The youth stared at the princess, transfixed with adoration.

A princess of the Al Fadhl, Diyar thought, *and a prince of the Al-Fadhl blood enemies? This is how tribal wars began.*

CHAPTER 24

The Murra Arabs had already arrived at the battle site; also the Governor of Karak, Malik-al-Mansoor Khidhr—a younger son of Baybars—and his warriors; the Ayoubid Prince, Malik-al-Mansoor Muhammad from Hama; and the Turcoman tribes of Aleppo. By late October, 1281, the whole army was encamped. At the last minute, even Sonkor al-Ashqar from Sahyoun and his troops appeared at the edge of the encampment. These included the band of warriors who had deserted after the assassination attempt on the sultan. And there, among the ex-viceroy's bodyguard, Diyar spotted Abu al-Mulq.

He ground his teeth in frustration. Nothing would give him greater pleasure than to challenge the arrogant bastard then and there. But the night before a battle was not the time to settle old grudges. If he tried he knew the sultan would make sure he never saw the morning.

The progress of the great Mongol army of Mangu Timur as it traveled south from Hama had been monitored. It consisted of fifty thousand Mongols, and thirty thousand Cilicians from Georgia and Armenia, Mongolian tributaries. When the Mongols left the captured city of Hama, they ordered its Mamluk governor to release a pigeon for Damascus. Its message read: "The enemy numbers eighty thousand. Tell the sultan to strengthen the left wing of the mamluk army."

In Damascus, the people collected in the mosques to implore

God's protection. A copy of the Koran alleged to have belonged to the third calif, Othman, was carried in procession through the city, many people weeping and praying to God for help as it passed.

On the morning of the 31st of October, Qalaoon rose early, walked to the opening of his pavilion and looked over the battlefield. These plains had seen a thousand battles over the millennia, and was about to see another. After a moment, he called to couriers to marshal his troops.

On his right, he placed the Ayoubid Prince of Hama, Malik-al-Mansoor Muhammad, and his men. In front of the right wing, he positioned the Arabs, both the Al-Fadhl of Isa ibn Mahanna, and the Murra. He had Sonkor al-Ashqar take the left flank with the Turcomans in front of him.

In the center stood the sultan, with four thousand Royal Mamluks plus various other units. Qalaoon himself, with his khasikiya of two hundred, took a post on a small hill from which he could overlook the battle.

Diyar, having received orders to act as a courier to the Arabs, remained near the command post.

Soon the Mongol units appeared and, screaming their fury, fell upon the mamluk right wing. The message the governor of Hama had been forced to send, stating the Mongol's target would be the left wing, had been a ruse. To their credit, the Arabs and mamluks on the right repulsed the charge, driving the Mongols back into their center.

At the same time, the Mongol right were attacking Sonkor al-Ashqar's troops. But they immediately dropped their weapons and fled. From his vantage point near the top of the knoll, Diyar watched as Abu al-Mulq led the wild retreat from the battlefield.

Exactly what one would have expected, he thought, a sneer twisting his lips. He itched to ride in pursuit, but had to stand fast.

The fleeing troops scrambled into the town of Hims, the enemy hot on their heels. The gates of the town were slammed shut, but the Mongols wreaked havoc among the dwellings outside of the walls, massacring men, women and children.

Many of the panicked mamluks fled to Damascus, some continuing on as far as Gaza. Wherever they rode they proclaimed the battle lost, spreading terror throughout the countryside.

Back at the battlefield, the mamluk right flank was pushing the Mongols back, penetrating almost to their center, which had begun to advance against Qalaoon's position. In the midst of the cries of fury and screams of death, the sultan ordered his great war drums to begin beating to rally back the stragglers from Sonkor al-Ashqar's retreat.

A khasikiya galloped up to Diyar. "The sultan orders that you ride to Sheik Isa ibn Mahanna, get as many men as he can spare and you ride back and gather up the broken units and bring them back to the center." But as Diyar rode down the mound, a group of mamluks galloped past him toward the oncoming Mongols. But instead of attacking, they cried out to the Mongols that they were deserters and they wanted to be taken to their leader, Mangu Timur.

Stunned, Diyar sped after them and nearing the amir who seemed to be leading them, Amir Azdemir al-Haj, he shouted, "Sire, do not give up. The battle is far from lost. Remain loyal."

Amir Azdemir, squat, powerful, glanced at him with furious eyes. "Ride away," he shouted back. "Ride away before it is too late."

"Not without you, sire," he said, and reached for the man's reins.

Azdemir struck Diyar's arm with the flat of his sword. "You fool," he hissed, "we are riding to assassinate, not to desert. Now, ride off before it is too late."

But it was already too late. A wave of screaming Mongols fell on the handful of mamluks, engulfing them. Rough hands ripped them off their horses, jerked their swords from their scabbards, their bows from their holsters, and prodded them at lance-point to where the great Il-Khan, Mangu Timur, waited.

As the chaos of battle raged on around them, Mangu Timur eyed the men without curiosity. Like his bodyguard and officers, he wore a steel helmet with leather coifs, mail corselets and lamellar body armor. His helmet left his face uncovered, revealing a long, thin mustache and scraggly beard.

He was about to raise his sword for the deserter's execution, when Azdemir pulled free from his captors, leaped on Mangu Timur, dragging him from his mount. The amir pulled a dagger from his sleeve and fell on the fallen king, tearing at his armor.

Mangu Timur's men reacted instantly and hacked to death the struggling amir. His comrades lunged forward and were also cut down. But the damage had been done. Mangu Timur lay wounded, bleeding and senseless.

From his vantage point, Qalaoon saw the confusion around the Mongol leader and called out to his royal bodyguard to charge the enemy's center. But the slaughter of the assassination party continued. Diyar dived under the horse of the nearest Mongol, lunging up into its belly with his pointed helmet, causing the animal to rear and create a diversion. He dodged and rolled in the dust to escape the blade swipe of another mounted Mongol, when from nowhere the back of his head exploded, his helmet went flying, and he crumpled under the flailing hooves.

A Mongol warrior leaped from his horse, his sword raised to decapitate the golden-haired warrior, when his captain called. "Leave him. The Muslims charge. We must get the Leader to safety." He had one arm of Mangu Timur, another man had the other. "Grab his legs," he ordered.

Diyar never knew it, but over him the tide of the battle turned.

Behind the sultan's headquarters, old Sudun Taz labored ministering to horse and horseman alike. When a cry rang out that Azdemir had struck down the Il-Khan, he mounted and rode to the crest to see the cause of the excitement. He heard the sultan call out for the Royal Mamluks to attack, drew his sword and joined the charge.

Where Azdemir and his warriors fell, he found Diyar crushed in the dust. He fingered the pulpy wound on the back of the man's head, and saw him wince. He was alive!

He shoved him over his saddle and rode back to where the surgeons labored.

***

Diyar drifted in a sea of grey confusion, then thirst drove him awake. He tried to sit up.

Kareem bent over him. "Easy, Master, you must rest."

"Thirsty," he croaked. "Help me up."

With Kareem's help, he pulled to his feet and looked around. He stood among prostrate men, many bound in linen dressing, sprawled across the grassy ground behind the hill. His head throbbed and, reaching up, he found it also wrapped in linen.

A thought came to him. "Saba?"

"I have her here, master," Kareem answered.

The sun squatted on the horizon, burnishing red-golden the mare tethered to a line. He approached her but spotted a goat-skin water bag hanging from a tripod. A wounded man sat next to it with a earthen cup.

"Please," Diyar said, "may I have the cup?"

"Take it in God's name," came the reply.

Diyar drank and his mind cleared somewhat. He turned back to Saba.

"Do not worry," Kareem said. "Like a faithful lamb, she came back. I have given her water and fodder."

Sudun Taz rose from tending a comrade and walked over.

"So you are on your feet again. Good."

Diyar gazed around. "The battle...?" He fought to remember. "I saw Sonkor al-Ashqar in retreat."

A look of scorn bent the lips of the old Kipchak. "That hyena's spawn? He and his men ran for the sea. I pray they fall in and drown." He brightened. "But the sultan's regiments are even now chasing Timur's troops. The Mongols should be in Aleppo soon, as fast as they were running."

Diyar handed the cup to Kareem and untied Saba. "I think I

will go to the sultan's pavilion to seek news."

His head pounded as he rode, and he was grateful the sultan had silenced the drums.

At the peak of the hill stood the pavilion, a wide tent of red and cream stripes, its sides rolled up to give view of the whole plain. Men of the khasikiya stood or squatted on the ground around its edges, their horses and servants nearby. Inside, the sultan sat at his desk with several advisors while other men stood or sat on the rugs.

In front of the pavilion, men were casing the flags, tying tight the silk cords around the envelopes.

Diyar walked to the edge of the tent, scanning the men inside. One of the seated figures wearing a white jird—Prince Isa ibn Mahanna—leaned forward and called out to him, "Is that you, my friend? Are you still alive?"

All eyes turned to him, and he knew when he was being bidden. He entered, and bowed, the action making him momentarily dizzy. "It has been God's good pleasure to spare me," he mumbled.

He straightened and saw Fuaz standing behind Sheik Isa, a smile of relief on his face.

Qalaoon appraised him. "Yes, we saw how you joined in the assassination. You may have saved the battle."

He struggled to remember. "With all respect, O Victorious King, it was Amir Azdemir al-Haj, may he rest in paradise, who deserves your praise."

Qalaoon nodded. "Your modesty becomes you, still you should be rewarded...."

At that moment several khasikiya galloped up the hill and bolted into the tent.

"Sire, forgive our interruption," one said breathlessly, "but a large force of Mongols approach from the south-west."

The sultan leapt to his feet. "It is the return of the force which routed Sonkor al-Ashqar," he said angrily, "and me with but barely a thousand men for defense. How long before they are upon us?"

"Burdened by their loot, they move slow, sire."

The sultan glanced into the vanishing sun. "Let us hope it is dark before they get here." He turned to an older man who had remained seated. "Now, Caliph, would be a good time to lead us in prayer."

The man stood, an imposing figure, from turban to boot, garbed all in black. As the Caliph began to pray for deliverance from the Infidels, Diyar started to move away. But Isa ibn Mahanna caught his eye and motioned for him to come and stand behind him. So Diyar fell in among the amirs next to Fuaz who gripped his arm in a silent welcome.

The prayer completed, Qalaoon turned to the Commander in Chief. "Tell the amirs to set up along the upper sides of the hill. They know the drill, bows, then lances, then sword and mace."

The commanders strode out, the orders were executed, and soon all grew quiet.

After a time, a few Mongol warriors ahorseback approached.

In the pavilion, all waited for the blood-freezing scream that preceded their charge but no scream came.

Tension gripped the knot of men, and grew. One young palace page began shaking. "We will be overrun," he whimpered.

The sultan shot him a steely eye. "Silence, fool," he whispered. "Wait and see."

More Mongols passed only several hundred yards distant, slouching in the saddle, leather wine flasks hanging in their hands. Many rode asleep.

An advisor seated near the sultan started. "Sire," he whispered, hope in his voice, "they do not..."

"I know," he hissed, "they do not see us. Put out all light and pass the word—everyone is to remain absolutely still. And the servant who lets a horse speak, will lose a hand for it. Now go."

Soon the lethargic soldiers ghosting by in the dark grew to be an army, then after an hour, diminished to a few.

Qalaoon spoke softly to an amir, "Give the order for all men to stand by to mount."

The look of tension on the men's faces eased. With luck, they might just be able to creep away to safety. This look turned to astonishment when Qalaoon, the canny old general, continued. "May God protect us, we are going to attack."

And attack they did. A thousand men, outnumbered ten, fifteen, perhaps twenty to one, with the sultan leading, charged screaming down the hill, shocking the somnambulant riders and panicking them into flight. Burdened by their loot, wearied by battle and debauchery, the Mongols bolted and were easy prey.

At first Diyar rode with the vanguard of leaders, Sheik Isa and Fuaz at his side, but soon the men became separated in the twilight as they chased the fleeing Mongols.

Finally, when the night grew too dark to distinguish between friend or foe, the mamluks turned back to the Command Post.

Kareem, his lance held wearily upright, flanked him as they neared the hill. "I believe God, praise His holy name, has given us the victory," the sarrajun said.

Totally spent, Diyar could only nod. All he wanted to do was find a drink of water, and crawl into his bedroll. But as they skirted the sultan's mound, a call rang out for Diyar al-Mijiri al-Baybariya to report to the sultan.

"Now what?" he mumbled, and rode to the front of the pavilion and dismounted. The sultan, his armor shucked, sat at his table writing letters to provinces proclaiming the day's victory. Nearby a few amirs sat cross-legged munching on chunks of lamb.

Diyar waited as his sultan worked. Finally finishing, Qalaoon stood, stepped to a large iron chest and pushed back the lid. Gold coins mounded to the top. To a clerk nearby he said, "Call all amirs and the khasikiya. Divide the treasury into saulaqs and issue one to each, and record the man's name and amount. We may be overrun tonight and perhaps enough men will survive to save the treasury."

He turned back to his desk and noticed Diyar. "Ah, Diyar al-

Mijiri, for your exploits today, I have decided to make you an amir ashara. When we return to Qal'at al-Jabal, you will be assigned your ten men." He picked up a scroll and handed it over his desk.

Woodenly, Diyar stepped forward and took his promotion. Finally he mumbled, "Thank you, sire."

"And one thing more," he continued. "It appears you are the only one of the assassination party who lived. It would please me to grant you a gift. Any requests?"

"But, sire, it was Amir Azdemir al-Haj..."

"I know," the sultan said patiently, "it was Amir Azdemir al-Haj who led the charge, but he is gone, and you remain. Now, please, we may not have much time. Your request?"

A request of the sultan was unprecedented. Usually it pleased a sultan to award gifts, but to give the privilege of a request... He struggled to think.

The amirs sitting nearby paused in their meal to watch with interest.

Something ran through his mind. *Amir Azdemir al-Haj....* He spoke up. "If it pleases Your Majesty, I would like to beg for the wife of the fallen amir, Amir Azdemir al-Haj."

Silence fell over them all. Though it was not unusual for the sultan to give permission to a man who had gained his favor to ask for the hand of a dead warrior's wife, still Amir Azdemir had been one of the wealthiest men in the sultanate. A prize of such size could be used by the sultan in securing an amir's loyalty.

But the sultan smiled. He felt magnanimous. Good fortune, discipline, and quick response had given him a victory over a far larger foe. He could afford to be generous.

He was about to speak, when an older amir stood. "But, Malana, it was my intent to ask for the wife of the amir."

Diyar stared at the man. It took a moment to recognize him. Amir Kazan al-Baybari, the man who had bought Ittifaq, the beautiful, black dancer.

He remembered the man's palace, its white walls rising high above him. Diyar gnashed his teeth. What greed! It was obvious to all present Kazan had not thought about acquiring Amir Azdemir's property until Diyar spoke of it.

He felt the familiar taste of anger creeping into his mouth. Before, he could not kill the arrogant amir, but now...?

No! He had to keep his anger in rein. To draw a sword in the sultan's pavilion meant instant death. Again, he had to bide his time and await the sultan's decision.

Now the sultan had a dilemma. The rule was a widow could reject a suitor. But a suitor, especially if backed by the sultan, could sit in her house and refuse to leave until she assented. The young warrior deserved a try for Azdemir's widow. On the other hand, Kazan was a powerful amir and had been a friend to the sultan since they both were tibaq-mates.

An idea lit the sultan's face. He cleared his throat.

"I am sure you both are equally worthy of the amir's widow. So I will give you an equal opportunity to win her. The first one who asks and receives her permission to wed has my blessing," and he sat down and returned to his dispatches.

Silence followed the pronouncement. Then Kazan strode out of the tent, calling to his henchmen. It took Diyar, his brain weary from a day of death and dismemberment, a moment longer to grasp the sultan's words.

The sultan glanced up. He spoke quietly. "He who would acquire a fortune must move faster than greed,"

Diyar started. "Uh, yes, sire. Thank you, sire," and he turned and left.

CHAPTER 25

Kareem awaited him outside the tent. "What are you going to do, master?"

Crushed with exhaustion, Diyar pulled into Saba's saddle and they trudged down the slope. Away from the lamps in front of the sultan's tent, darkness engulfed them, and the mare picked her way carefully around the sleeping and wounded troops.

"Do? I am going to find my bedroll and sleep."

"But what about the amir's widow?"

"Even if we had a half dozen fresh horses, which we have not, she is still many days away, even if I could sit a horse that long, which I can not. No. There is but one thing to do, sleep." He snorted wearily. "I have heard men in battle say they would give a fortune for a good night's sleep. Now, it has actually happening with me. Ah, I think this is our gear," and he fell onto his bedroll, instantly unconscious.

Insistent shaking woke him. The faintest grey smeared the eastern sky. He looked up to see the fine smile of Fuaz above him. Kareem squatted at his side.

"What, ho," said Fuaz. "Do you intend to sleep all day?"

Chill hung in the desert morning. The pain in his skull beat like a drum, his joints ached. Every fiber of his being cried out for more sleep. He pulled up his sheepskin. "Yes," he said emphatically.

Fuaz laughed. "Oh no. Not today. Today you ride for a fortune."

The events of the previous night seeped into his mushy brain. He forced himself up. "The widow of Azdemir al-Haj."

"God be praised, the man lives. So, what do you intend to do about it?"

He shrugged. "Unfortunately, there is nothing I can do. I have no horses."

"Ah hah. But that is where you are wrong. Prince Isa ibn Mahanna has graciously agreed to sell you nine fine mares, the finest of his herds, or so he says. You are not in a position to be choosy."

"Nine?" he exclaimed. "What am I to do with nine?"

"What? You would not include your friends to ride in your race? We Arabs love a race even more than you Turks. Now up, Amir Diyar al-Mijiri, we ride. Amir Kazan departed several hours ago."

By rotating mounts, they rode as long as there was light. Kareem, on the weaker horses, fell farther and farther behind as they headed into the hills toward Khatmia Pass. Diyar and Fuaz continued on and spent the sixth and, with luck, final night in Salihiya, east of the tip of Lake Manzala.

Now, as they raced toward Cairo, they caught glimpses of three men and their string of horses ahead. Diyar and Fuaz reached the gates of Cairo at dusk and remounted for the last time.

Azdemir al-Haj's estate lay south of the city on the river, so, like Kazan and his men, the two young men circled the walls rather than try to gallop through the crowded Main Avenue.

Only a hint of light remained on the western horizon as the two pounded past walled palaces. But Diyar reined up when they approached a grove of trees.

Fuaz circled back. "Why do you stop?" he said panting. "We

almost have him."

Wearily he tried to catch his breath. "The woods. If you were them, ahead in a race and about to be caught, what would you do?"

Fuaz glanced over his shoulder at the grove. "I see what you mean, an ambush." He wheeled his horse around and sprinted forward. "You go around," he shouted over his shoulder. "Let me take care of whatever is there."

Diyar wanted to follow, but knew it would be a mistake. Instead he cut into the desert. As his horse waded through the sand, he heard first a whinny, then shouts from the darkness of the grove. He set his jaw. If anything happened to Fuaz, Kazan would pay, even if he were an old friend of the sultan.

Ahead in the night appeared the white walls of Amir Azdemir's estate. Reining up at the double gates, Diyar peered through the crack in the center. Servants were walking a panting horse around the front court to cool it off. Kazan had already arrived!

Riding to a side wall, Diyar stood on his saddle, then leaped up to catch the top of the wall. He pulled himself up, and peered around. Fatigue nearly overcame him, and he teetered dizzily. His vision cleared and he made his way atop the wall across the garden to the palace and an open meshrebiyeh. Here he crouched down, took in several deep breaths, and sprang, catching the sill of the meshrebiyeh. He hauled himself up onto the window seat inside.

He rose to his feet, swaying with exhaustion. Before him shimmered a vision, a beautiful, dark-eyed woman sitting on a divan staring at him. She wore a golden silk gibbeh, and a lacy, shear tarhah was draped over her head and shoulders.

He took two steps, gulped for a breath and said, "Madam, my name is Amir Rukn al-Din Diyar al-Mijiri al-Baybariya. I have the deep sorrow to inform you your husband, the estimable Amir Azdemir al-Haj, has given his life in the service of the sultan. I therefore request your hand in marriage," and he fainted dead away onto her lap.

Lady Shajar looked down at the tall man sprawled across her. She pushed away his dusty cap and observed the golden curls. A dog with soft, red hair who had been watching from a rug across the room walked over and rested his head on the unconscious man's arm.

"What do you think, Tarfa," said Lady Shajar, "should we keep the handsome amir?"

Tarfa allowed his tail a brief wag.

A maid hurried in, gasped at the sight of a man in the harem, but stuttered out her message. "Madam, Amir Kazan grows angry. He says he will not leave until you accept him. And there is some Arab at the gate wishing entry. He says he is the companion of an Amir Diyar al-Mijiri."

Lady Shajar brushed the man's locks aside and looked into the heavy-lidded blue eyes, dark-rimmed with fatigue. His breath came in short, labored pants.

"Have the Arab enter, and inform Amir Kazan I have already chosen my next husband. Tell him he graces my humble home, but it now grows late and we wish to retire."

The girl hurried out, and in a moment, a roar emitted from below, and contrary to all rules of etiquette, Kazan charged up the stairs and burst into the room. To his rage, the young man who was supposed to be found dead floating in the Nile the next day, if found at all, was floating in the arms of the beautiful widow.

He reached for his sword, but four great, black Abyssinian eunuchs pounded into the room, their swords already out. Tarfa twisted around and growled ominously.

Lady Shajar spoke calmly. "How dare you, sire, break the sanctity of the harem. Go, before harm befalls you."

The eunuchs moved closer.

"I will go, Madam," Kazan shouted, "but not until I curse that man, and all who come near him," and he spun and trounced out.

She made a brief gesture to the eunuchs. "Make sure he is out, and the gates are locked," and as they hurried out, she continued caressing the tall man's golden hair.

MAMLUK

In the Battle of Hims, the Mongols lost more men during their flight than in the assault. Even the folk of the countryside fell upon the panic-stricken warriors, striking them down with the vengeance of people too-long abused.

When the Mongols reached the Euphrates, unable to cross, they hid in the riverside reeds. The mamluks set fire to the brush, burning to death many, and lancing those who tried to escape the holocaust.

Pigeons arrived in Damascus with the news of the victory and the populace went wild with joy. The streets were bedecked with garlands and ribbons, and exuberant music could be heard throughout all neighborhoods.

During the Mongol rout, one of the captains of the Royal Mamluks, Amir Torontai, captured a warrior with a haversack containing secret papers of Mangu Timur. The were sent them back unopened to Sultan Qalaoon at the Hims' headquarters.

Among the letters in the haversack, the sultan found letters to the Mongol leader, Mangu Timur, from Sonkor al-Ashqar, encouraging him to attack Damascus, and that he, Sonkor, would aid the Mongols in any way possible if they would just reinstate him as viceroy upon their victory.

Now the sultan knew why the mamluk right flank with Sonkor in command had crumbled so readily. But, being the consummate politician, he burned the letters. And, when Sonkor was finally found, the sultan allowed him to return to his castle in Sahyoun. By doing so, the sultan avoided a rift in the sultanate, while consolidating his victory.

When the sultan returned to al-Qal'ah, his son, whom he had left in charge, and his staff were in formation in front of the palace to meet him. In attendance with the palace amirs stood Amir Ashara Diyar.

The sultan dismounted and started up the steps, but seeing Diyar he paused and motioned him over.

"So tell me, who won the race for Lady Shajar?"

Diplomatically, he replied, "Kazan won the race, sire, but I won the lady."

Qalaoon paused, thinking, then tipped his head back and laughed. "That should be good enough," and he turned and held out his hand to his chief advisor, an old, white-bearded amir. "Come, you heard the man. He won the lady. Pay the wager."

The amir scratched his beard. "Ah, but Malana, it was as I predicted, Kazan won the race."

Qalaoon returned to Diyar with a wink. "See the trouble you have caused. Now the arguments begin," and he, chuckling, continued up the stairs into the palace.

Several weeks later, as Diyar rested in his room below the harem of his newly acquired palace, Kareem entered, and said, "Several amirs have been arrested in their homes and have been imprisoned. Rumor has it they are the ones who joined with Sonkor al-Ashqar in a conspiracy with the Mongols against the sultan. One of the names the rumor carries is yours."

"My name? What does my name have to do with Sonkor al-Ashqar? I am certainly no follower of his—or his worthless family."

"But does the sultan know that? You barely survived that last arrest. Perhaps it is time we visit the desert. Perhaps Prince Isa ibn Muhanna would give us sanctuary."

He thought for a moment, then shook his head. "No. We must have faith the sultan will see any rumors about me are lies."

Kareem only answered, "Yes, master," but his doubt was obvious.

CHAPTER 26

Diyar, as an amir ashara, was issued ten warriors, half being solid veterans of the old Bahri regiments, the rest, recent tibaq graduates. These last, Circassians, were obviously the least apt of their class, but Diyar set out to improve their horsemanship, and weapon skills.

After a morning at the Citadel's practice field with his squad, he would ride into the city to confer with Abd ar-Rahman, to see how his book stalls were faring. Amir Azdemir had been the head of a far-flung trading network, and Diyar and his clerk worked hard to continue the relationship with the amir's partners in trade.

And he became acquainted with his new, dark-eyed wife. Lady Shajar was Kipchaki and about ten years older. The Lord had not blessed her with children with Amir Azdemir, so Diyar began to rectify that oversight, and soon she whispered to him the joyful news.

Diyar saw the combat skills of his eunuch guards needed honing. The squad consisted of a score of men and several officers. He found the men willing but inept. And he discerned a certain peevishness among some of them. He called for Hital Zayn al-Din, his chief eunuch.

It was difficult to assess the age of the Abyssinian. His black face was smooth and beardless. He spoke with a high, soft voice and carried himself with dignity. His manner to the odalisques could be overbearing, yet to the master and mistress of the house, he was respectful and seemed genuinely desirous to serve.

When Diyar pressed him for information about how the men had become eunuchs, he looked away. "It is not a story to pass on as gossip."

"Please know that I will keep your confidence."

The man nodded. "I believe you, master," and began. "I was but a child of ten when slave-thieves raided my village and stole me. As you know, master, the Faith forbids the cutting of a man's manhood, so the deed must be done outside of the world of Islam. They carried me and several other boys to a town named Washalaw, an evil place, one without religion or God, and cut us there. But because no treatment for our wounds was done in that filthy town, we were carried to Hadya where a second operation was done to open the channel to clear out the clogged pus. This trip was made on mules, very hard on us, and most died and were left along the way in shallow graves. Bones which wild animals had dug up littered the road.

"After the second operation, we were buried in the hot sand of the desert to get well. More died in terrible pain because their channel was plugged and they could not make water. But those who survived were sent down the river to the slave market in Cairo. I was bought by the late amir, and in time, rose to my present position by dedicating myself to serve him, my lady, and now you."

"But I notice some of the eunuchs are gentle, while others often get angry. This is not the case when a horse is gelded."

The chief eunuch raised himself up. "We are not horses, master. We are men." Then he relaxed somewhat. "But often the behavior of a man is dependent on what is done to him and when. If a youth is very young, and the operation is one where his eggs are removed or crushed, he seems to accept his lot with more grace, never knowing any other. If he is older, has enjoyed the use of his tool, and then it is cut off, you can understand why he might well be angry. Still, if his eggs remain, he can still enjoy the climax of mating without penetrating his mate."

"Then that is what has happened to..." Diyar's voice trailed off.

"To me, Master?" Hital Zayn al-Din concluded for him. "Yes. I have several wives, all of which have learned the art of satisfying me. Those boys who are just becoming men and endure the operation, and have only their eggs crushed or cut off, can still get hard. They can get hard and stay hard as long as they are aroused, which due to their inability to give seed, can be as long as their heart beats. These, of course, often become harem favorites. And," he shrugged, "there are other devices."

Diyar took a deep breath. "Continue."

"Sire, we are a society within ourselves. We meet and talk in the marketplace. Many such servants learn herbs and potions than make one more vigorous when lying with a lover. And many who have lost their manly tools purchase false ones and strap them on. And also they become good at using their mouths and tongues. Often—and this is only a rumor, and certainly does not include the wives of warriors like yourself, but..."

"Say what you have to say."

"It is rumored wives who enjoy the company of such servants who can stay hard for a long time, often become unhappy with their own husbands. I know of incidents where odalisques, when freed to marry, were unhappy with their husbands because these men could not perform as well as the servants in the harems whence they came, and their husbands divorced them."

"And do I have any such eunuchs in my harem? Tell the truth."

Fear sprang to the eunuch's eyes. "Be it my life, you have not, master."

"If you lie, it will be your life, and that is the truth."

Usually Diyar spent the heat of the afternoon in his office in the salamlik, the men's section of the harem. If a caller came to the palace gate whom he did not wish to see, the visitor was informed the Master was "in the harem", which meant nothing less than a message from the sultan or the Commander in Chief, would be sufficient to interrupt him.

His office was a small room with a wide divan along the wall, rugs on the floor, and a copper brazier in the center. In one corner stood a large carved cabinet containing books and the palace's accounts, and a small, round table holding a ledger sat near his elbow.

In this office, Diyar could eat, receive friends, even take a nap. Lady Shajar, or any woman for that matter, was not allowed in the salamlik, although it was separated from the harem by only a narrow corridor. The palace, in this regard, was like two different houses. Different servants served the two sections, and each section had its own kitchen. The harem's roof terrace was the favorite place for the women to watch the boats go by, nap, and enjoy refreshments.

Lady Shajar had frequent guests, other women of rank. They brought gossip, recipes, embroideries, and showed off their new gowns and jewelry. Often these visits were unannounced. If Diyar found slippers at the entrance to the women's harem, it was an indication Lady Shajar was entertaining guests, and he knew not to go in. Guests often stayed for several days.

The harem was made up primarily of a large room with many smaller rooms around it. Rugs covered its floors, and a wide divan surrounded its walls. Tortoise-shell tables were its only furniture. Little alcoves cut into the walls held flowers, juice glasses and cups.

The women servants slept in many smaller rooms off the large room. Odalisques slept on the floor or divan in the main room.

Lady Shajar's apartment was found nearby. Also nearby, closer to the kitchen was located the women's bath, and a room where the children of the concubines congregated.

From Diyar's divan in his office, he could look out the window into the harem's court. There a half-dozen semi-nude women servants and odalisques lay around a tiled pool. A slim girl stretched in the sun. Turning to Tarfa laying nearby, Diyar mused, "Difficult to concentrate on numbers with a view like this, is it not, Tarfa?"

The dog opened an eye, then shut it again. Then his head came up. He rose quickly to his feet and hurried to Diyar's knee. At first he peered intently into Diyar's eyes, and when he received no attention, barked sharply.

The sound pained Diyar's ears and he glanced down at him....

He floated in a grey-black fog. He vaguely recognized the nauseating sense of lightheadedness, but could not remember when....

He awoke on the floor. Tarfa stood above him in a posture of readiness. The table lay on its side with the papers strewn across the floor, and Diyar's elbow stung from knocking it over. But a far greater pain beat in his head.

It had happened again. He had become intent on something, then fell unconscious.

Somehow the dog knows when...

He pulled a pillow off the divan and remained lying on the floor.

I must do something. But what?

He knew he could not keep running away from his pain. Death festered inside his brain. He carried it with him wherever he went.

Finally he climbed back up on the divan. He picked up a little brass bell that had fallen from his desk, rang it, and sent a servant for Hital Zayn al-Din.

When the chief eunuch arrived, Diyar said, "You know everything that stirs in the city. I must speak to a doctor."

Nothing changed in the eunuch's smooth face, but Diyar added, "And I do not want anyone to know about it."

"I understand, master. What kind of doctor do you require?"

Diyar took a deep breath. "One who knows about problems of the head. But he must be the best. The amount of his fee is not important."

Hital Zayn nodded. "There is a physician, Qutb al-Din al-

Shirazi. It is said he was a student of the great Nasir al-Din al-Tusi. I believe he is visiting the city. It is said he knows everything in the world, mathematics, astronomy, philosophy. But, it is rumored he is a Sufi."

Diyar's head throbbed mercilessly. "I do not care if he makes the devil his bed partner," he said with irritation. "If he can cure my headaches, he can have half my fortune, you included. Fetch him immediately." He paused. "And send someone who will not draw attention to himself. I do not want anyone to know I am having any difficulty."

"I understand, master," and he hurried out.

Kareem knocked and entered, panting after a hard ride. "I have just come from the marketplace. I knew something was amiss when a pair of servants of amirs ignored my greeting. So to find out what was wrong, I went to the Tibaq ar-Rafraf's cabaret. Amir Kazan was already there. He saw me and called out saying traitors and the servants of traitors should not be allowed in among honorable men. Several of his men came for me, so I felt it advisable to leave quickly and return with the news."

"Kazan. I should have known it would be he who spread the lies. But he can not drive me from the city."

He went to the bronze cabinet and opened a stout bronze box. He withdrew a saulaq of gold coins and tossed it to Kareem. "Return to al-Qal'ah. Fetch the rest of the ten and bring them here with full gear. Tell them they will be staying here until I give them different orders."

He lay in a pool of hot water up to his chin, trying to relax the pain from his head when the chief eunuch entered. "I have the visitor you wished to see, sire."

Diyar rose reluctantly, toweled off, and donned a cotton robe.

The man standing in the bath's tiled anteroom was short and slight. In his late fifties, he appraised the tall warrior without fear, and Diyar sensed his examination had already begun.

"How may I serve you, O Amir?" Qutb al-Din said. Nearby his attendant stood with a large, rectangular box of finely tooled leather.

"Since being struck on the head, I have had headaches, and my ears buzz constantly." ·

"And?" the physician prompted.

Diyar bit his lip. "And I have fell into unconsciousness several times."

Qutb al-Din nodded. "I understand. Open your mouth."

He frowned. The man addressed him without the respect he was used to. Still…

Diyar opened his mouth.

The doctor peered in, then mused, "You have struggled with great anger in the past."

"Be careful what you say. I will tolerate only so much."

Qutb al-din continued unintimidated. "Yes, it is obvious. Your back teeth show distinctive wear, a sure sign of an attempt to control your anger." He gave him a hint of a smile. "Prudent, I should think, for a man of your exalted position."

The anteroom to the bath had a domed roof and ceiling with an opening to the sky. The sun shone in, highlighting one side of the blue-tiled floor. The physician pulled a dressing stool over where the sun shone. "Sit here, sire, and let me look at your wound."

Diyar sat, locking his jaw as the man's gentle fingers parted his hair and probed the back of his skull. Soon Qutb al-Din called his attendant over and opened the case. "I will need hot water," he said to Hital Zayn, and took out a curved razor, the length of a hand, from its leather case.

Diyar eyed its gleaming edge. "What are you going to do?"

"I must shave your head, amir, if I am to know what is to be done."

That he would lose some of his long, golden hair had never occurred to him. "Oh, all right," he grumbled, but the doctor had already begun lathering his skull.

So sensitive was his wound even the light touch of the razor caused him to jerk away.

Qutb al-Din reached into his case and withdrew a small vial. He turned to Hital Zayn who stood at his elbow. "Fruit juice, please. Pomegranate, if you have it."

"Immediately," murmured the eunuch, and stepped to the door. And just about as quickly, he returned with a brass pitcher and goblet.

"Drink this," he said to Diyar after carefully allowing several drops to fall into the juice."

"What will it do," Diyar asked suspiciously.

"Simply make you relax so we can proceed without injuring you."

Diyar drank, and soon a feeling of heaviness overtook his limbs, and he quietly allowed Qutb al-Din to scrape his skull clean of hair.

After a time the physician appeared before him. "The blow has crushed your skull and the broken bone is pressing on your brain. If you are to have any hope of relief I must open your skull."

Open the skull? Diyar struggled against the drug to think. "And what if you do not? What if you leave it as it is?"

"The headaches will worsen, the fainting will continue, and one day you will not wake up from one of them. Now, am I to continue or not?"

"You mean, you will do it now, here?"

He glanced around. "Yes. The light is good."

After a moment, Diyar said, "If you go into my head, what are the odds I will die?"

"The odds? I should say about the same as if you flipped a coin," he said without emotion. "But, if I do not, you will surely die, and soon."

The toss of a coin. He had better odds in battle. "Oh, be at it, then," he said with irritation, "and watch you make no slips."

Unimpressed, Qutb al-Din sent his servant to his house to

bring more attendants, then ordered a table be brought into the bath, placed in the sunlight, and covered with clean muslin. He had Diyar drink a more potent mixture of the drug, bitter even in juice, then helped him to stretch out face down on the table. Soon the patient was snoring comfortably.

When the attendants arrived, they braced Diyar's head with small bags of sand. Then, using a small blade on a thin handle, Qutb al-Din began cutting the scalp. At first touch, blood began flowing.

One of the doctor's attendants, an old, wrinkled man in a worn qaba, squatted nearby with his arms folded and stared in boredom at the floor: a "blood-stauncher." With the presence of the "blood-stauncher," the blood from the incision soon slowed, then stopped.

The doctor cut three sides of a large square in Diyar's scalp and peeled back the flap. Wiping the skull, he observed how far the cracks extended. Then, with a fan-shaped saw attached to a thin handle, he began sawing the skull. As soon as he had penetrated the bone blood spurted out splattering his face. Impassively, he wiped his eyes and continued sawing.

Nearby, another attendant lit a small lamp and began heating slivers of silver in a steel crucible where it hardened in a curve. Gauging the size of the square the doctor was removing from Diyar's skull, he formed the silver over a tiny, iron anvil with a small hammer.

With the broken shards of bone removed, the doctor picked out the clots of dried blood wedged in its folds and washed the exposed convolutions of the brain. Then he took the silver plate, shaped it with a file and, after a last examination, fitted it into the square hole in Diyar's scalp, and sewed closed the flap of skin.

When Diyar awoke, for the first time in many months, there was no pain throbbing in his head. Along with the casket of gold he sent to Qutb al-Din al-Shirazi, he included a letter expressing his most profound gratitude.

Even as he recuperated, he supervised the widening of the palace's walls. He topped them with a walkway and balustrade, then began the construction of towers in the corners. And he ordered all trees and brush cleared from the land outside the walls to rid it of cover.

Even with the completion of the reinforcement of the walls, he did not allow his men to return to the barracks or work out at the hippodrome. It was simply too easy to be forced into a fight there. Instead, as soon as he felt strong enough to ride, he led them in mounted drill on the hard ground outside wall.

One day the men were exercising, and a pair of khasakiya rode up. Two of Diyar's oldest warriors, Djanin and Karsuh, sided him, their hands on their sword handles.

"Stand easy," he said quietly. "We can not challenge khasakiya."

One of the khasakiya, a young Circassian addressed him. "Amir Diyar al-Mijiri?"

"Yes."

"We have been sent by order of Malik-al-Mansoor Qalaoon al-Elfi al-Salihi al-Ashqar, the supreme ruler of the lands of Egypt, Syria, and Nubia."

Diyar did not betray his tension. "And what does the sultan order?"

"No orders, sire. Our beloved sultan, may his reign be glorious, has ordered us to convey an invitation to you to join him at polo tomorrow after the mid-day prayer. How say you?"

He struggled to understand. "Polo?"

"Yes, Amir. Tomorrow afternoon. What answer shall we give the sultan?"

Polo with the sultan, only amirs solidly in favor were invited.

"You may tell the sultan," Diyar said, his face blank, "I would be honored to play polo with him."

He turned to his men who waited behind him, struggling to keep their exultation in check. "And you, you sluggards. One more pass at the targets, and its inside and baths for all you horse thieves."

MAMLUK

The cheer that echoed off the palace walls startled the two khasikiya. As they turned, one said to the other. "He must drive them without mercy so eager are they to stop."

CHAPTER 27

In November of 1282, the Sharif of Mecca took an oath of loyalty to Sultan Qalaoon, thus bringing Mecca into the sultan's sphere of influence and protection. Mecca contained the Ka'bah, the small stone building in the court of the Great Mosque that contained the holiest of holies, the sacred black stone that was the goal of Islamic pilgrimage and the point toward which all Muslims turn in praying. He granted the sultan the added privilege of providing the Ka'bah with its embroidered covering. This covering or kiswa had to be renewed each year, and by being chosen to provide it, a tribe or ruler derived great political prestige.

Not long after the battle of Hims, the Mongol Il-Khan, Abagha, died and was succeeded by his brother, Tekudar. In December, 1282, an embassy from him arrived to inform Qalaoon of the new Il-Khan's conversion to Islam. And he had assumed a new title: Sultan Ahmed. However, the long letter went on to state he and his council intended to continue "the conquest of the world, sending out such vast numbers of invincible troops all the peoples of the earth will freeze with terror."

Unimpressed, the sultan replied, "It is good the Il-Khan sent a letter rather than his armies, because when it comes to fighting, it is God who gives the victory," a not-too-subtle reminder of who won the Battle of Hims.

After his initial invitation to play polo with the sultan, Diyar was asked regularly. One day, as they waited for fresh horses to be saddled, the sultan moved to his side.

"I knew you were not among the traitors who conspired with Sonkor al-Ashqar against me. It was my old friend, Kazan, who spread the rumors. I suppose his holding a grudge against you is natural. To his way of thinking, you cheated him out of a fortune. Not that the Lady Sanjar would have accepted him." He leaned closer and winked. "And apparently the choice was right. I hear she is with child."

Is there nothing this man does not know? thought Diyar. "Yes, Malana, the birth could come at any moment."

"Good. I await to hear. Now, I want you to take your men and ride to Jerusalem and bring back a pair of prisoners."

"Yes, Malana."

The sultan's mount was led up, and he swung into the saddle. "I know you will perform this task well, Diyar al-Mijiri. You had better. You will be escorting a king."

Earlier in that year of 1282, the Christian King of Georgia made a pilgrimage to the holy city of Jerusalem. His country was a tributary of the Il-Khan's empire, and a large portion of Mangu Timur's army at Hims was made up of Georgians. Consequently, as an enemy of the sultan, the king traveled in disguise, taking only one companion.

Of course, the sultan not only knew of the king's plan but had a complete description of him: the king was forty years old, had a scar on his neck, a pale complexion, narrow forehead, black eyes, and wore a large gold ring on his right hand.

The two pilgrims were identified as soon as they crossed the frontier. But rather than capture them there, they were followed and observed. Only when they arrived at Jerusalem were arrested.

Diyar rode next to the king. The king and his bodyguard, a fellow knight of the Georgian court in Tiflis, had been given red silk tunics and red-and-white striped, silk qabas to replace the

Turcoman merchant's garb they were wearing.

"With respect, Your Highness," Diyar said, speaking Turkish, both their native tongue, "why did you enter the land of your enemies? Do you not know the sultan's eyes are everywhere?"

In the dark depths of the king's eyes burned the fire of an ascetic. "Truly I did not know the length of the sultan's reach. But even knowing, I would have come."

"I am sorry, sire, but that I can not understand."

"I am sure you, an infidel, can not. But had it been through hell itself, I would still have hazarded the journey to see where the Son of God was born, where he and his disciples walked, and where the evil Jews crucified him."

"Again, with respect, sire, it is you Christians who are the infidels. We follow the laws of the Prophet. We do not drink wine or eat pork, both of which I know the Christians do."

The king smiled patronizingly. "Not all Christians do, as I am sure not all Muslims do not."

"But, sire, why are the Christians so intolerant? In our Citadel, al-Qal'ah, there are Mongols, Jews, Christians, all laboring under the sultan's banner. But you Christians, in the name of your Prophet, Jesus, kill everyone who does not draw a cross on his chest. When they captured Jerusalem, they killed so many of God's children, the Frankish soldiers had to leave the city because of the stink of the dead."

The king's jaw set. "There is room in this world for only the adherents of the true Faith. All must either convert or be thrown into the pit. There is no other way."

Diyar decided silence was the best policy when dealing with royalty, silence and patience.

When he returned home, he learned he had become a father. Lady Shajar had given birth to a healthy son. Diyar named him Ismail.

In the Spring of 1283, the sultan and a large contingent of the Royal Mamluks with accompaniment of the Prince of Hama and his mamluks, rode to the province of Buhrain in the Nile delta.

Their mission? To complete the digging of a new irrigation canal. All working together, the haughty warriors completed the canal in ten days and opened up a vast new area for agriculture, increasing the prosperity of their adopted land. Egyptian city-dwellers and fellahin alike were enchanted.

The Egyptians, although subjugated by this fair-skinned people from the north, derived great entertainment in observing them. Their conquests, antics, dress and processions were the first subject of their conversation.

Diyar and his men labored with pick and shovel with the rest, and he returned to his palace to spend his thirtieth birthday on his stomach, Lady Shajar massaging perfumed ointment into his sunburned back.

From Persia, in August 1283, came reports of wrangling among the Mongols. Arghoon, the son of Abagha, proclaimed himself the true Il-Khan and captured and killed Tekudar.

There now arrived in the capital word that Prince Isa ibn Muhanna, the great leader of the Fadhl tribes, had died. During his lifetime he had kept the usually turbulent Bedouins at peace, and the sultan expressed sadness hearing of his death.

Diyar, too, felt the pangs of loss at the prince's passing. He had seen firsthand the prince's nobility, had been a recipient of his generosity and beneficence. In commiseration, Diyar sent to the sheik's son a gift of a gold-embossed shield. Sayings of the Prophet curved around the top, and the exploits of the prince around the bottom.

The next Spring, the sultan and his army marched once again into Syria where they destroyed the Hospitaller fortress at Marqab. When they returned to the al-Qalah, the sultan found many embassies from the world's capitals awaiting him. All vied to offer him the most lavish gifts.

The German Emperor's gifts included rare furs—miniver and sable—robes of scarlet, of yellow silk and Venetian cloth. The Genoese embassy conveyed silk, hunting falcons and a dog the chroniclers claimed was as big as a lion—a Saint Bernard? The Byzantine emperor from Constantinople also sent silk and many carpets. The embassy from the Yemen brought seventy camels laden with spices, thirteen eunuchs, ten horses, an elephant, a rhinoceros, eight parrots, three large pieces of amber, and many chests of textiles.

This attention from these countries showed how the Mamluk Sultanate had become one of the world's great powers.

Early the next year, the sultan took a contingent of Royal Mamluks including Diyar and his ten, and inspected the fortress at Karak. He ordered it to be provisioned sufficiently to last a long siege, and placed in it a garrison of Bahri mamluks, those warriors which once belonged to Baybars.

As the Royal Mamluks prepared to depart Karak, a messenger from the sultan appear at the doorway of the cubicle in the town's citadel which had been allotted to Diyar. With a sense of dread Diyar unrolled and read the scroll. There, in the beautiful script of a sultanic command, were his orders: He and his men were to remain as guards in the Karak citadel.

Banished!

Diyar stood atop the gate tower and watched as the sultan's troops rode through the castle gate and down the hill.

I though I had gained his favor. Why did he do this?

Banished from his family, his palace, the capital. And for how long? Some banishments lasted a lifetime, amirs being ordered to some distant post and simply forgotten.

Many amirs in exile sent for their wives and servants. But he knew Lady Shajar would hate to leave her palace. Ismail was now three, toddling around the harem, everyone's favorite.

When will I see him again?

The reason why the sultan had posted the Bahri Mamluks to Karak, was because the Bahris had been Baybars' troops, their first loyalty directed to him. They were named Bahris because they had been trained in a fortress on an island in the Nile. The Egyptians called the Nile, Bahr al Nil, the "Sea of the Nile," and the troops on the island, the Bahris.

Qalaoon, on the other hand, when he began training his new

Circassian army, housed it in the Citadel. They were dubbed the "Tower Mamluks."

Though the great Baybars was gone, many of his mamluks remained, still a cohesive force, and an influence in the capital and the sultanate. They could choose to follow whomever they wanted, whomever they thought would treat them the best.

Qalaoon could never fully trust warriors trained and owned by some other leader. They had to be banished to keep them away from influence. Though Diyar had proved himself loyal to Qalaoon, the suspicion of a sultan had to be long if he wanted his reign to be.

Diyar's eyes wandered over the countryside. Fields and citrus groves bespoke sufficient water, and a few trees still topped the surrounding hills. The town below lay at the crossroads east of the Dead Sea. The road north ran on to Amman and Damascus, south to Aqabah and Mecca, west to Cairo. When the Royal Mamluks marched north, they passed through it, as did all of Egypt and Syria in their pilgrimages to the holy city of Mecca. As such, the castle bore the responsibility for travelers' protection in its area. To feed and house the pilgrims, coin changed hands briskly in the marketplace.

Diyar and his men were assigned to guard the main gate, and had space in the circular top room of one of the gate towers. He was sitting with several amirs in the citadel's bathhouse enjoying a late-morning scrub-down, when a clerk peered through the humid air. Seeing Amir Tagri Birmish, the citadel's commander, he sent a bath attendant over to page him.

The amir draped a robe over his shoulders, and went to see what could be so important as to interrupt his ablutions. In a moment he returned. Diyar leaned forward to hear, as did the others.

"A force will be passing through here enroute to Sahyoun to arrest Sonkor al-Ashqar," Tagri said. "It seems the sultan's patience with the traitor has finally run out."

Diyar quickly spoke up. "If the sultan is requesting troops, I would like to volunteer my men."

The other men looked at him suspiciously. Karak was no Cairo, but even garrison duty here was better than being bivouacked in the field.

Amir Tagri could find no reason to deny the request, and nodded. "I suppose it could be done."

Exultantly, Diyar toweled off. *Am I finally going to corner Abu al-Mulq?*

The army heading for Lebanon paused outside Karak for food and supplies, and when it started north, Diyar and his men rode with it.

CHAPTER 28

The walls around the town of Sahyoun were manned not only by mamluks loyal to Sonkor al-Ashqar, but by the mamluks who had fled the sultan's army after the assassination attempt. Also Sonkor had also pressed into service thousands of local Syrians.

After a few of the young Tower Mamluks rode too close to the walls in order to hurl insults at the defenders, and were felled by the veterans' arrows, the rest remained at a more respectful distance.

Soon Qalaoon's great war machines were constructed around the town wall and the siege began. But it was all a sham. The Sahyoun defenders had been in enough battles to know they could not hold out against the sultan's engineers. And, before too many were killed, Sonkor ordered the gate opened and its drawbridge lowered.

Diyar and his men had been protecting a trebuchet, but when the castle's gate creaked open, he was among the first to gallop through.

Sonkor al-Ashqar waited in the audience hall.

Diyar motioned his men to one side, and allowed the Amir-in-Charge and his advisors to climb the steps to the hall. He had something else in mind. Then he motioned for Kareem, and a pair of his veterans and they ascended to the crowded hall. He paused at the entrance and searched among the castle's defenders. Sonkor sat on the castle's throne, but there was no sign of Al-Mulq.

Diyar was not to be deterred. He led the men up another flight of steps and along the landing to the entrance to the harem. Two eunuch soldiers stood at both sides lounging on their lances. Diyar nodded to his men, and in a blink, they had their swords at the guards' throats.

Diyar tore away their lances. "Sit down, be silent, or die."

They squatted immediately.

He ordered Djanin to watch them and he entered the harem.

A single eunuch with sword in scabbard stood at the first door watching the maids inside scurrying about as they bundled up robes and carpets. Diyar drew his kindjal and moved up behind the guard. He tapped the knife against the base of the man's jaw, and whispered, "Not a sound, or I will open your throat."

The guard froze, and he cut the cord holding the man's sword and scabbard.

"Now you may live until tomorrow if you show me where the apartments of Abu al-Mulq are."

The man moved only a trembling finger and pointed further down the corridor.

Diyar grabbed his arm and pulled him from the light of the room. "Show me," and he shoved him down the hall.

When they neared another door, the eunuch whispered, "Sire, Abu al-Mulq's rooms."

"Do and say exactly what I tell you." He stepped to the door and knocked. Presently a voice tinged with irritation answered. "Yes? What do you want?"

Diyar grabbed the guard and shoved him close to the door. "Tell him," he whispered, "you have a message from the Master."

The guard repeated the words, and the voice said, "Oh, all right, enter." A heavy bolt clanked back, and the door cracked open.

With a mighty kick, Diyar drove it open, knocking Abu al-Mulq back.

Abu al-Mulq rubbed his reddening cheek and squinted at his attacker. Recognition crept into his eyes, and he drew himself up. "How do you dare to break the sanctity of Lord Sonkor al-Ashqar's harem? Your death is assured."

Finally, finally Diyar stood only a sword's length away from the one man he hated more than all others. Finally he could release the rage he had penned up for so long

Diyar stepped closer, his sword pointing at the man's eyes, a maddened smile playing over his lips. "Mind your own death, jackal. You will never see mine."

The arrogance in the man's thin face wilted. Once tall, his narrow shoulders stooped. He was nearly bald, and grey streaked his stringy beard.

Fearfully he glanced around. His sword lay cradled in a lacquered stand in the corner. "But I am unarmed," he whined. "Surely you would not attack a fellow-warrior without allowing him a defense."

"You are no warrior," Diyar sneered. "And being the bastard of a traitor will never make you one. Still," he nodded towards the stand, "get your sword. It will make my pleasure in killing you all the greater."

Al Mulq unsheathed the sword but drew back in fear, the blade drooping in his hand. "But I am no match for you." He gestured to a chest on the table, dinars heaped to the top. "Surely gold can buy my life."

Diyar's jaws tensed with hate. "I have gold, but I do not have your life—yet." His sword slapped Al-Mulq's. "Fight, or die where you stand."

Tears of hopelessness welled in the coward's eyes, and he slowly raised his sword. The glint of a smile on Diyar's lips spread. He had waited so long.

The door to the adjoining room opened, and a tall, blond woman with a child on her hip started in. She Diyar, sword in hand and halted.

Diyar paused, then froze as recognition dawned.

"Thalia?"

She moved closer, her eyes on his blade. "Please, sire, do not kill my husband."

His chin dropped. "Your...your husband? You are married to this..." he flicked his sword toward al-Mulq, "this thing."

She stepped in front of al-Mulq. "Yes, sire, and he has always been good to me and the children."

A maid appeared into the doorway with a tow-headed boy in hand. She saw the sword-wielding stranger and clutched the boy to her side. But Diyar saw only Thalia.

How beautiful she is.

Motherhood had ripened her. She stood taller, her breast fuller, and she moved with quiet dignity.

How could he do her harm? But how could he let al-Mulq live? To do so would mean waiting an assassin's blade.

He hesitated too long. Al-Mulq leaped for the side door, knocked aside the boy and maid, and bolted out into the corridor. His cries for help could be heard as he pounded away.

In confused pain, the boy erupted into a wail, which was immediately taken up by the baby.

Kareem stepped into the room, urgency in his voice. "Master, we must leave."

Rage twisted Diyar's face as he heard the calls of the guards echoing up the corridor.

Kareem peered out the door. "Quickly, Master. They are upon us."

Again his quarry had escaped. Again he had found, but lost his first love.

The screams of the terrified children assaulted him. With a roar of frustration that shook the walls, he kicked the table with the chest of gold sending dinars flying throughout the room. Then he stalked out.

In the corridor, Kareem urged him along. His men fell in behind, and they all doubled down the steps and out into the bailey. They leaped on their horses and galloped for the gate.

They had no sooner reached their campsite, when two mamluks from the Commander-in-Chief rode up.

"Now what?" Diyar muttered, seething with pent-up anger.

One of the couriers handed a scroll. The orders stated that when the army began its march home, he and his men were to ride rear guard—all the way back to Cairo.

Good news, but bad news. He was finally going home, but he would have to be constantly on the alert for rear-guard ambushes.

As the miles stretched away from Sahyoun, the vision of Thalia played on his mind.

Can I finally put her away to a place in my memory?

But what a lovely memory. From the first time he saw her slim figure outlined by a candle, to the exquisite moments when he caressed the lovely figure on the harem balcony, to now, a statuesque beauty of motherhood, these memories were worth cherishing.

He thought of his own marriage. Memories are one thing, but reality lies now with Lady Shajar

But what about al-Mulq? At the very name his anger surged again. Those dirty memories might not buried by the snake's death, but it would help. And it certainly would lessen the threat of assassination.

Lady Shajar stood waiting as Diyar rode into the courtyard. With the sun shining through the filmy, white-silk tarhah that flowed over her black hair, she looked like an angel. She held the hand of little Ismail, who stared in wonder at the mighty warrior.

Diyar leaped from the saddle, raised the startled little boy in his arms, and kissed him. Then he turned him over to a maid, and drew Shajar into the shade of the palace.

After a quick bath, he donned fresh silks, and made for the harem. As he wedged Shajar down into her pillows, he found she had acquired an added softness, and he lost himself in it. He impregnated her on the spot.

Several days later, as he practiced cavalry movement in one of the Fortress's hippodromes, the Maydan al-Qabak, a pair of khasikiya trotted up with orders. Back to Karak.

One Spring day a call from one of his men drew Diyar to the gate tower parapet. The sultan and his army approached from Cairo. For several days, the regiments passed through the village, and on the 9th of March, entered Damascus, then headed north to the Christian seaport of Tripoli.

Immediately upon reaching the city, the mamluks opened a massive bombardment with nineteen trebuchets, while one thousand, five hundred sappers drove galleries beneath the walls. Other engineers sprayed the besieged troops on the walls with Greek fire. Soon two towers collapsed.

The army surged through the rubble of the fallen towers and cascaded into the town, hacking down anything that moved. Every man in the town was murdered, every woman and child carried off to slavery. And then, under a blazing, copper sky, the army methodically razed the city and its walls to the ground, stone by stone. Another Christian city exterminated, another trading rival of Cairo, Damascus and Alexandria obliterated.

Tripoli had been a successful textile manufacturing city. It was said there were four thousand looms in the city which created beautiful luxury textiles, silk, camlet and cloth of gold, that fetched high prices in the West.

When the word reached Karak the sultan's prey had been Tripoli, Diyar sent Kareem racing for Cairo with a message for Abd ar-Rahman. The clerk was to rent quarters, build looms, and hire weavers. He was to pay extra for experienced men. Where there was a vacuum, there was opportunity.

With Tripoli sacked, the rest of the County of Tripoli surrendered to the sultan, leaving the Franks, who once commanded the whole of the Mediterranean's eastern seaboard, now controlling only the cities of Acre, Beirut, Sidon, Tyre and Athlit.

In July, 1290, the sultan gave orders for the dismissal of all Jews and Christians from appointments in the civil government. These restrictions were regularly reenacted. But within a short time, the bureaucrats were back at their posts. These office-holders, Christians in administration, Jews in finance, were irreplaceable. To function, the government departments were obliged to reappoint them as soon as the sultan's decree had blown over.

Later that summer the Venetian Council sent a fleet of twenty galleys to Acre with a volunteer force of Italian men-at-arms to bolster the city's defenses. These volunteers were poor Italian peasants, without money, training, or discipline. When they arrived they had little to do but lay about, drinking and gambling—when they could find the money. When they saw Christian merchants mingling freely with Jewish and Muslim tradesmen they set to grumbling.

Then one hot day in August, a fight erupted in the market. A Christian man learned his wife had been having an affair with a Muslim. That was all the Venetian peasants needed to start a riot.

The volunteers burst out of Acre, killing and robbing the farmers and merchants who were bringing their wares to the town. Then they returned to Acre and started massacring all whom looked foreign to them, striking down both Orthodox Christians and Muslims alike.

The knightly orders garrisoned in the city, the Templars, Hospitallers, and Teutonic Knights, rushed to rescue the victims of the Italian rioters, and to save as many of the Arab merchants as possible. But the damage had been done.

The relatives of the dead ran to Cairo where, amid much wailing and rending of clothing, they spread the blood-soaked garments of the victims before Qalaoon. He had just completed a ten year truce with the rulers of Acre, and was now speechless with fury.

Instantly messages winged to all provinces of the realm ordering the preparation of siege machines. The Muslim world was about to unleash its vengeance on the treacherous Christians.

On the 5th of November, the sultan made camp outside Cairo and began to form up his great army. Suddenly, news flew through the camp and then to all corners of the sultanate: the sultan had taken to his bed with fever. The amirs stirred nervously. Nothing so endangered the sultanate as a sultan's death and the struggle for succession that followed it.

Five days later, the end came to the old warrior. He was seventy. Hardly a year had gone by since his manumission he had not ridden out in a campaign. He had fought and scratched his way to the sultanship by working harder, and being more ruthless, than his fellow amirs. He had been shrewd, patient, and careful to rid himself of possible enemies. Consequently, his reign of eleven years had been without internal rancor.

His foreign conquests climaxed in the defeat of the Mongols at the battle of Hims in 1281, and the elimination of the Frankish County of Tripoli. At home, it was said he doubled the cultivated area of Egypt.

He pushed aside the Kipchaki Bahri mamluks, of which he was one, by creating the Burji or Tower mamluks, and at his death, the Qal'at al-Jabal housed three thousand seven hundred Burji.

He left one wife, three sons, two daughters. But what he did not leave was a definitive line of succession.

CHAPTER 29

In November,1290, Khalil, the son of Qalaoon, assumed the sultanship, taking the name al-Malik-al-Ashraf Khalil, or "The Most Noble King" Khalil. But when the decree appointing him heir to the throne was brought out, it was found Qalaoon had never signed it.

On Karak's gate tower, Kareem whispered to his master, "The old sultan said, 'I will not give the Muslims a king like Khalil'. But the son tore the decree to pieces, saying, 'My father refused to bestow on me what God had ordained to give me.'"

Diyar said nothing, but his mind seethed. This new sultan was young, arrogant and headstrong. He made no attempt to hide his pederasty, and could be vicious. This was borne out when he began his first parade of state through Cairo. One of his sycophants whispered to him the Viceroy of Egypt, Amir Torontai, lay in wait to kill him. Hastily Khalil retreated back to al-Qal'ah.

He then sent messengers out to fetch Torontai. When the old amir, suspecting nothing, appeared in the Hall of Audience, Khalil barked the order, and his guards hacked him to pieces.

Khalil had the viceroy's home looted. Soldiers returned with a camel-train burdened by one million, six hundred thousand dinars of gold, much silver, jewelry, textiles and carpets, and leading a great herd of beautiful horses.

Days later Torontai's blind son came before the young sultan.

Stretching forth his hands like a beggar, his bald eyes searching impenetrable darkness, he pleaded, "Please, in the name of God, let us have something to eat." The family had been made so destitute it now starved. To his credit, Khalil allowed the family enough food to live on.

Khalil's first act as sultan was to send pigeons winging for Mecca. For religious purposes? Not hardly. He was summoning his lover back to the capital.

"Little redhead," read the note scribbled by Khalil, "it will be good to see you. Come back quickly."

Ibn al-Salous, a young Syrian, had started out as a merchant, coming to Cairo to advance himself. Sleek and portly, his red hair made him immediately attractive. He gained the attention of Prince Khalil who made him his favorite. But the Syrian's presence had enraged Qalaoon, and Ibn had to flee to Mecca, ostensibly for pilgrimage, in reality to stay alive. With the sultan's death, Khalil was free to flaunt openly his love for the Syrian.

As soon as Ibn al-Salous returned, the new sultan made him the sultanate's wazeer. This position placed him at the pinnacle of all administration throughout the realm. Traditionally, it was awarded only to one who had served the country for many years, and who had gained a reputation for wisdom as well as experience.

No wazeer had ever been so young or so powerful as Ibn al-Salous. Such power corrupted the young man and he treated all with contempt.

Rumors of parties full of roistering and depravity reached Karak, and Diyar shook his head. He had been through this all before with Baraka, the son of Baybars. That episode had nearly killed him, and he was almost relieved to be away from the capital.

Now came word Khalil wanted to continue the campaign against Acre, and by early spring, the whole sultanate was mobilizing. Diyar and his men were ordered north to the great fortress of Husn al-Akrad. The huge trebuchet named "The Victorious" was dismantled and distributed among a hundred wagons, and Diyar and his men's job was to protect part of the wagon train.

As soon as they left the confines of the Husn al-Akrad, heading out of the mountains for Damascus, snowstorms struck the army. Sodden wagons became heavier, and many of the oxen grew weak and died from the cold. Because of the foul weather and the ponderous oxen, the trip which would normally have taken eight days took twenty-eight. But by April when "The Victorious" finally arrived and was assembled under the walls of Acre, it joined the greatest artillery array ever collected.

And their foe was truly formidable.

The city was triangular with two sides protected by the sea. A high breakwater wall guarded the sea side of the city. And on the land side, not one but two huge walls curved around running from sea to sea. A wide sea-fed moat divided these, making the city an island. Nineteen tall towers reinforced the walls. And the city contained many individual castles, the castle of the Templars placed strategically at the south-west corner next to the sea.

When the tens of thousands of Muslim troops entered the plain east of the city, a pall of dust rose, masking the sun. The plain, nearly two leagues wide, was made up of plowed fields. These the invading troops and their animals soon picked clean and trampled to hard dirt.

Diyar and his men were part of the Hama army that took position along the north seashore. While Kareem set up camp, Diyar began pulling on his mail armor. His helmet and mail draping over his head and shoulders were fused together into one piece with only two oval eye-holes.

Mounting his horse, he motioned to Djanin and Karsuh to join him. "Let us see what they have."

The two mamluks eagerly sided him as he rode south, paralleling the walls. Out of bow range from the walls, engineers had erected the siege machines. Diyar had never seen so many, counting nearly a hundred.

Also cats, long sheds made of wood and covered with planks, iron and hides to deflect missiles and boiling oil from above, were being constructed. These would be pushed to the base of the walls protecting the sappers who would burrow into the ground to undermine the towers.

In front of the siege machines mamluks and halaqa sat astride their horses, bows in hand. Any Christian who dared show his head on the parapet could expect a cloud of arrows for his audacity.

One young mamluk, excited by his first combat, dashed forward and let fly an arrow at the parapets. But when he wheeled around, a crossbow bolt from the wall shot through his back, his saddle and into his horse. His mount careened sideways and fell. The young warrior tried to drag himself to safety but more bolts pinned him dead to the ground.

Diyar shook his head in disgust. Then he remembered his own rashness on his first campaign. *Experience will teach us--if we live long enough.*

The standards waving in the breeze atop the walls indicated the Military Orders that defended it. On the northern section, the redoubtable Templars' gonfalon fluttered, a red cross on a white field. South of the them flourished the Hospitaller banner, a white cross on a red field. They controlled the wall up to a huge tower, the New Tower. Next the Germanic Teutonic Order's black cross on a white field waved proudly.

South of the Teutonic Order the walls were manned by knights of the French, English, and Pisans. Finally the Venetian levies, the peasants who had provoked all the trouble, held the area just above the port itself.

In the city the populace, crazed with fear, rushed to the harbor and fought to board ships that would carry them to safety. Greedy ship captains, seeking to profit from their terror, bargained shrilly for the highest bids. Time was running out for the people of Acre,.

On the April 11, 1291, trumpets blared, drums thundered, cymbals crashed, and a war-cry erupted from the Muslims as the trebuchets unleashed boulders at Acre's walls. The sky darkened with arrows. Meanwhile "The Victorious," an equally formidable war machine, "The Furious," and scores of lesser trebuchet began pounding the towers.

Nor did the advent of night bring respite to the besieged Christians. Then the trebuchets were loaded with jars of Greek fire. Like great comets, the fiery concoction of naphtha, sulfur, and quick lime roared through the night with the blast of thunder. The huge flaming balls hit and exploded into a burning hell.

And below the clamor of war, a thousand engineers labored in silence, scooping out the underpinnings from the base of the towers.

Venetian ships attempted a counterattack against the Muslims along the north shore. Christians, protected by frames covered with buffalo-hides on these floating fortresses, shot arrows and manned ballistae. Thus the army from Hama found itself fighting on two fronts, the city and the sea.

After four days of ceaseless battle, Guillaume de Beaujeu, Grand Master of the Order, in he dark of night, led three hundred Templar knights and a party of English cavalrymen out the northern gate, the Porte St. Lazare, attempting to reach some of the trebuchets and set them afire. They were pounding through the Hama contingent, making for the siege machines, when they were hurled from their mounts. In the dark, their horses had become entangled in the Muslims' tent lines.

The screaming horses and the knights' curses brought the mamluks running from their mats. The knights struggled to clamber back into the saddles, but the warriors set upon them, hacking them down. One knight fell into a latrine trench and drowned in excrement.

The next morning, Al-Malik al-Muzaffar, Lord of Hama, had a number of Frankish heads attached to the necks of the captured horses, and presented them to the sultan as gifts.

Four nights later, the Hospitallers charged out from their section of wall through the Porte St. Antoine. But this time the Muslims were waiting for them. They lit torches and the Hospitallers were all struck down.

Diyar reclined on a rug against his saddle. Shaded by his tent awning, he watched as the trebuchets, with ponderous regularity, hurled great chunks of stone at the walls. Kareem had erected their tent slightly up the slope of a knoll, giving his master a fine view of the spectacle. It was 15th of May, the army had been besieging the great walls of Acre for a month.

The sultan's tent, larger, elaborately patterned with silk and embroidered with gold, stood far to his left near the center of the plain. Tents of his entourage clustered about it. From the beginning of the bivouac, Diyar had watched the amirs fawn over the young sultan, young amirs hoping for advancement, older amirs hoping to stay in favor, indeed, to stay alive.

He shook his head. It was enough to make a warrior resign. He had been considering resigning lately. He was wealthy enough. His marriage to the Lady Shajar and his growing businesses had brought him more wealth than he knew existed as a lad living in a yurt. So why go through all this discomfort of campaigning? He certainly did not enjoy it any longer. The exhilaration of the kill had long since departed.

Suddenly, near the Porte Saint Antoine, one of the towers groaned and, with a great rumble, its outer face collapsed into a mushrooming cloud of dust, the cross-bowmen on its high parapets hurtling down amid the rocky avalanche. Then another tower gave way, pulling down a section of the wall with it.

With a great roar of exultation, the Muslim ranks surged forward to clamber up the rubble to clash with the Christians.

Diyar found himself on his feet, his sword clutched in his fist, his whole being intent on the rift in the wall. He looked down at his sword. He did not even remember drawing it.

He relaxed. He now realized the thought of resigning was an illusion. He was a warrior. That was what he had been trained for, that was what he did best. The need for combat would leave him only when the life drained from his body.

Karsuh galloped up, eager to enter the fray. But Diyar squatted on his rug and watched the foot soldiers struggle up the wall's fallen face, bolts from the Christians' crossbows glancing off the boulders around them. It was not yet the time to enter the fight. There still lay the wide moat on the other side of the wall to span, and another ponderous wall to be breached before the battle could be met.

Unlike some ambitious amirs, he would not attempt to ascend to power over the corpses of his men. He remembered the advice of old Sudun Taz, "Fight as little as possible to win." Unless specifically ordered, he would keep his men out of harm's way.

Another tower cracked under the incessant pounding. When a tower or wall was breached, mantelets were lugged forward to protect the engineers as they used the wall's rubble to make a causeway across the moat.

The Christians' crossbow bolts could pass through a fully armored man—but they were slow to load. A mamluk could nearly empty his quiver by the time a Christian could load and loose a bolt. Also, Muslim arrows hit where their masters aimed.

And when a Christian fell there was no man to step up and replace him. No boats carried reinforcements into the city's harbor. But for every Muslim who fell, two more eagerly took his place. This ancient harbor-town, situated so strategically on the main military road along the coast, was the Crusaders' last great bastion in the Holy Land. When they were expelled from it, one of the two great enemies of the sultanate would be eradicated. Mamluk warriors, eager to make their mark, knew they would have fewer and fewer chances for fame and glory—and plunder.

The next day Diyar led his men up onto the outer wall, taking up residence in one of the towers. Then, after several days, the word was passed in the evening to all amirs: Enough causeways had been made across the moat, general assault on the inner wall in the morning.

That night the sultan massed the drums of the whole army along the walls and ordered all to beat together. The noise of the drums was deafening, terrible, horrible. The ground rumbled and the walls shook.

Throughout the night the thunderous clamor continued. From behind the walls the drum beats were pierced by the screams of terrified men driven mad from fear and the incessant din. Then, as a streak of light touched the eastern sky, the drums ceased and deadly silence fell on the walls, a silence as terrifying as the drums.

A mist hung over the camp. The gates of the outer walls, now in the hands of the Muslims, lay open. On the battlefield waited the jundiya, the Muslim foot soldiers, shouldering long ladders.

The sultan's trumpets blared an alert, and the drums beat an advance. The massive army, filling every foot of the plain, moved forward as one.

Diyar, watching from the parapet of his tower, turned to his men, and said quietly, "Time to go," and led the way down the tower's stone steps.

When the troops with the ladders reached the outer gates and the landfills across the moat, they let out a shout and broke into a run. Under a storm of arrows from the inner wall, they struggled to raise their ladders.

When men with a ladder passed by his tower, Diyar surged after them. As soon as they had propped up the long, willowy apparatus, he shouldered them aside, and began pulling himself up, his shield held above his head. And his men clambered up behind him.

Up and down the wall, wherever the engineers had filled in the moat, long lines of men waited to climb ladders, eager to get over the wall to loot the wealthy city. At the head of the ladders, defenders struggled to hurl down arrows, spears, rocks, bodies, anything which came to hand.

Diyar had nearly reached the parapet when a bucket helm peered down and a lance jabbed at him. Diyar's bow leapt to hand, and an arrow instantly followed. The helmet ducked back, and Diyar redoubled his effort up the ladder.

The Christian knight started to shove the ladder away with a crude pitchfork, but Diyar pulled his sword and chopped at its tongs. They splintered, and he crashed back against the wall. With another step, he leaped through the battlement's crenel.

Below him, he heard the ladder crack, but could not look down. The knight had sword in hand.

Mail armor covered the Frank from his helmet to his spurs.

Short and stocky, he looked wide as a door. His heavy sword slashed down.

Diyar parried it aside, and shouldered the man against the wall. Wedging his sword under the man's chin, kicked it sharply with his knee. The blade split the knight's armor and thrust up into his brain.

Diyar pushed him aside and glanced around. Nearby a bowman struggled to arm his crossbow, a padded tunic his only protection.

Diyar skipped across the intervening space, and buried his sword in the man's neck.

Behind the bowman, a sergeant with a crescent-headed ax turned on Diyar. He wore a skull-cap helmet and thigh-length mail. A scar running along the bone of his chin showed him to be a veteran. The sergeant approached, watching Diyar with steady eyes.

The man raised his ax and Diyar lunged to pierce his open face. Diyar saw the trap too late. The butt of the ax handle shot at his face.

He partially deflected it with his shield, and slashed at the man's exposed legs.

The sergeant leaped back, and with the advantage, hacked down for Diyar's exposed shoulder and back.

Diyar had no place to go but down. He fell to the floor of the parapet and twisted sideways. The ax slashed passed him, striking the inside of his shield.

On his side, Diyar jabbed upward into the man's exposed groin, his blade burrowing into the man's bowels.

The ax fell from the Christian's hands, and he slumped against the parapet wall. Holding his crotch, his eyes glazed toward death.

Diyar pushed to his feet. He shook his head. He had been lucky and knew it.

He looked around for another assailant. Although men flayed hand-to-hand all along the parapet, in the short section where he stood only corpses remained. Now, where were his men?

He peered over the wall. It was as he feared. The ladder had splintered, and they had fallen. Several lay sprawled at the base of the wall.

He shouted down to the remaining men. "Get to another ladder."

He turned back to the parapet. The few remaining defenders would soon be swept aside. Now to get into the city. That was were the prizes lay.

Nearby rose a tower, its door open—a stroke of good fortune. He held his shield above his head, he peeked in. No ambush. He ducked into the dimness, and ran down the stairs curving around to the tower's base and its main door.

He stepped into a lane and was assailed by the city's stench. Rotting corpses and piles of feces were heaped along the edges of the street. Farther down the lane, servants, scuttled for the harbor, sacks of loot over their shoulders.

He strode along until he came to a wall with an ornately carved gate. The house beyond rose tall and substantial, and the clear glass in the narrow windows bespoke of wealth. He pushed open the stout gate, noting he had seen its coat of arms before.

The neat courtyard stood in quiet contrast to the carnage raging on the walls but a few steps away. He entered the manor house and found the first floor deserted. But in the kitchen the fire under the spit still smoldered.

He crept up the stairs to the main hall, his sword held at the ready. He moved past the pantry and buttery, and peeked into the hall. Empty. Was there no one left alive?

He continued up the stairs. At the doorway to the master's bedroom he stopped dead. Across the room at an open window stood a woman, tall and beautiful, the light shimmering off her plaited blond hair.

She wore only a shimmering green gown, its neck deep and square, embroidered with gold. She was lovely, enticing.

He pulled off his mail hood and smoothed his long, blond hair, offering her a reassuring smile.

She watched him without moving, her eyes betraying nothing.

He stepped into the room.

Mistake!

Only at the last moment did he sense danger, and jerk his sword up. The descending sword glanced off his blade and struck his armored shoulder.

Automatically, he slashed back, decapitating the elderly maid servant holding the heavy sword in both hands. Her head bounced across the wooden floor, and her body fell like a sack of turnips.

With grim anger he turned back to the woman.

CHAPTER 30

In horror, she stared at the grisly head, its blood running along the cracks of the floor. Then her eyes sprang to him, and to his sword. She stepped back, felt the window sill and turned, seeking an escape. There was none—except the open window.

Diyar read her thoughts. No! Death was not going to save her.

He leaped and grabbed her arm, flinging her away from the window.

A great bed with ornately carved posts filled the center of the room. He raised his sword to her slim stomach and backed her to it. He shoved her onto it, sheathed his sword and unbuckled his weapons belt.

He pulled out his kindjal, knelt beside her, and rested the back edge on her neck. Terror rounded her eyes, and she jerked away from the cold steel.

He pulled up the hem of the dress. The white undergarment. was unfamiliar to him, somehow overlapping in back. But a flick of the blade and it fell open. He was lowering onto her—when he heard shouts from the great hall below.

With a growl of frustration, he sat up, clipped the woman on the chin with the pommel of his kindjal, and she passed out like a snuffed candle. He tied up his codpiece, grabbed his sword, and stalked down the stairs.

When he entered the hall, it was as he thought: several Syrian jundiya were rummaging around in a great trunk. They wore but thigh-length shirts and were barefoot and with no breeches. Their heads were covered by grimy turbans. They were as miserable looking as all Muslim foot soldiers, but they carried swords and bows, and they still had a few arrows left.

Silently he approached within swords-length, and in a voice that could carry a parade field, shouted, "Out, dog-turds. I have already claimed this property."

Startled, the men jerked around. But one, seeing no one with the Diyar, grasped his sword and snarled in garbled Turkish, "And who speaks boldly?"

An evil smile cut Diyar's lips. "I, Amir Diyar al-Mijiri al-Baybariya, I speak. Leave my house now, and live."

They heard the title of the Royal Mamluk and hesitated.

But Diyar gave them no chance to think. "NOW!" he roared, "And leave your arrows."

They hustled out, and he descended to the kitchen. He grabbed several burnt sticks from the fire, strode to the front gate, and scrawled his name and title on its wooden face over the coat of arms.

More Muslim troops hurried down the lane, seeking loot in the deserted houses, and he spied Kareem and a couple of his men.

They trotted up, and he first asked, "The men, how many made it?"

Djanin spoke up. "All but Karsuh."

"How bad is he?"

"His back was broken in the fall from the ladder. We had to leave him."

The pain of loss struck Diyar. Karsuh, a comrade since graduation, killed by a fall, what a waste.

Several more of the Diyar's ten and their sarrajuns arrived.

Diyar struggled to restrain his anger. "Now listen to me, I know you all have one thought in your heads: loot. But there will be plenty of time for that." He nodded to Kareem, "You and the other sarrajuns find a gate in the wall that is open and go get the horses and gear. Bring them here."

He turned to the rest of his men. "I want one of your sarrujun on this gate at all times. This is a fine house and I do now want to lose it. The rest of you can go looking for booty, but remember, it must be shared by all of us, and I will do the dividing. You can bring back your women here too, but no fighting. There are more women in this city than even you lot can bed, so if a mawla claims a maiden, let him have her. They are not worth getting killed for. Now go." He turned back to the house. "I have something to do."

The killing, rape and pillage continued for days. The Templar Knights retreated to their own castle and set up a defense, brave but hopeless. Muslim engineers began undermining their walls, and after ten days, the walls collapsed killing both friend and foe alike. The Templars were massacred to the last man.

Meanwhile, Diyar and his men lived well behind their own walls. Daily, as other warriors besieged the Templars, several of Diyar's men ventured forth on raids of forage.

The woman in the green dress was the lady of the house, and Diyar had met her husband. He was the stocky knight he had killed on the wall. Diyar ordered his body fetched down, and allowed her to bury it in the manor's small garden. Along side him, he placed the body of his friend and comrade-in-arms, Karsuh al-Nawruzi. He could see the lady did not approve, but he cared not.

One day, after the mid-day meal, as he sat at the long table, he saw her pass by the door on the way upstairs from the kitchen where she, under the auspices of Kareem, helped prepare their food. He called her in. She wore a simple gown of orange muslin, protected by green outer-sleeves.

Her name was Cythire, and speaking French, he said, "Lady, tell me where you are from."

She stood before him stony-faced. Indeed, since the dirt had covered her husband, she never again showed any emotion.

"The count and I were from neighboring manors in Normandy."

"Why did you come to our land?"

"The count was the third son and could not inherit. He came here, bought a house and land, and returned for me."

"You should not have come."

"We had nothing there."

"Now you have nothing here."

When the orders came to withdraw from Acre, Kareem, without telling his master, took the lady to the waterfront and sold her to a slaver. The slaver carried her to Damascus where she was bought by a Jewish gold merchant.

She had been married to the French knight for a number of years without producing a child and thought she was barren. But after spending time in the bed of the Muslim warrior, she found herself pregnant. She rasped raw her aristocratic fingers scrubbing floors for the gold merchant, grew heavier by the day, and vowed never to forget the name or forgive the man who had raped her and murdered her husband.

With the fall of Acre, the few Christian fortresses still on the Levanter surrendered to the Muslims, and for the first time in nearly two centuries of fighting, the only Crusaders remaining on Muslim soil, were prisoners, slaves or corpses.

That summer, 1291, after the sultan's army returned to al-Qalah, his perfidious wazeer, Ibn al-Salous, began a reign of terror among the sultanate's notables. Ibn bint al-Aaz, Chief Qadi of Cairo, was an old man widely respected. In a public sermon in his mosque, he expressed disgust at the young wazeer's mode of living.

Salous friends complained to the sultan and he ordered Ibn bint al-Aaz be paraded in shame. The Chief Qadi was the highest judge in the land. Twenty years before he had been Diyar's first teacher.

Diyar and Kareem, home on leave following the Acre campaign, were riding into the city on business, when they were horrified to see Diyar's old teacher, his clothes torn and dirty, being driven at lance point along the street by mounted soldiers.

A bolt of anger struck Diyar and he reached for his sword. "The sultan has gone too far this time," he growled.

Kareem leaned over. "Think, master. Only the sultan can change their orders. You can ask him, but it would be better to stay away from that evil court."

The old man staggered and fell, and was prodded to his feet.

Diyar shook his head. "I have no choice. This I must do for my old teacher," and he started for al-Qal'ah. He saw two other amirs of his old tibaq watching the spectacle, and paused. "I am off to the court to protest this outrage. Are you with me?"

With decisive nods they followed.

They gave their request for an audience to the Major Domo, then paced the anti-room, listening to the shouts of drunken revelry from the Great Hall. Finally they were called, and strode in through the crowd of sycophants.

They approached the throne, and Diyar observed Wazeer Ibn al-Salous sat on the sultan's right.

Diyar bowed. "O Most Noble King, may your reign be glorious. We apologize for interrupting court proceedings, but it has shocked and saddened us to see such a noble and righteous man as Qadi Ibn bint al-Aaz being driven through the streets on foot. With all respect, we protest against such treatment of a man who has been only the kindest and gentlest of teachers to us. We ask only that he be released to return to his duties."

The young sultan, clad in a gleaming robe of yellow silk, squinted at him for a long moment, then said, "It will be done."

But before they could leave, the Chief Qadi was led into the qa'at. Now the sultan called out in anger, "Allegations have been raised against you. What have you to say?"

No answer. Dirty and disheveled, the qadi was unable to raise his head or even to speak. Shame had broken his mind.

Irritably, the sultan motioned for him to be taken away.

Diyar's looked at Wazeer Salous who returned his gaze,

malevolence burning in his sullen eyes.

Outside the palace, Diyar hurried to Kareem who waited with the horses. "Go to the barracks. Tell the men to meet in my palace immediately. We leave for Karak this very night."

At home, he found Shajar in the harem playing with Ismail, and explained what had occurred. To her credit, she said, "Do not worry about us. If you think Karak will be safer you must go. Do you think Karak is far enough to be away from the clutches of the sultan?"

"No, but perhaps if I am away from the capital, he will not think of me."

But the look of hatred in the wazeer's eyes haunted him.

In Persia on March 1291, Arghoon, the Mongol Il-Khan, died and was succeeded by his brother, Kaikhatu, a drunkard addicted to sexual orgies. The Mongols selected him because, as a degenerate, he was unlikely to introduce reforms as his brother had.

In May, 1292, Sultan Khalil and Muslim army sacked the Mongol fortress of Qilaat al-Roum. His victory made him even more arrogant. At twenty-eight, he had degenerated into a depraved tyrant and began the purging of his father's most trusted amirs. The tension among the officer cadre was felt as far away as Karak.

"What do you think, master?" Kareem asked as they stood atop Karak's gate house. "It has been a year and a half. Perhaps he has forgotten your name."

"I doubt it."

Life with this young madman, he thought, *is a constant wait for the sword to fall.*

And indeed, one blustery fall afternoon, Diyar watched with a growing sense of dread as a contingent of the sultan's khasakiya trotted up the road. When it left, Diyar rode in its midst under arrest.

The line of condemned amirs marched into the Audience Hall and stood before the throne. A half dozen amirs of higher rank preceded Diyar. He knew them all, great generals, good men who had held positions of honor throughout the sultanate. But he felt no sympathy at all for one of the condemned: Sonkor al-Ashqar. The luck of the traitorous viceroy had finally ran out.

Khalil, slouching against a pillow, watched them enter. His eyes held an unreadable tension. Finally he said, "You men are accused of treason. What say you?" Then he waved a hand. "It does not matter."

Abruptly he sat up. "Bring me my bow."

A soldier strode up with bow and arrows encased in gold-inlaid quivers. "Strangle them with the bowstring," he ordered sharply.

The soldier hesitated. These men were great dignitaries. He knew he was not of sufficient rank to execute them.

"You heard me," Khalil screamed, "kill them, or you will die a thousand times more."

The soldier unhooked the bowstring and approached the first man, a white-bearded old amir and, as all watched in horror, wrapped the string around the man's neck and yanked it tight.

The old man did not struggle, and finally, after what seem an eternity, slumped to the marble floor. The young soldier stepped to the next man, repeated the execution—and moved on to the next.

Nearby lance-wielding guards stood at the ready, but they need not have worried. These amirs had been trained as warriors and knew their end might be violent. Stoically they awaited to die.

Sonkor al-Ashqar, to his credit, died with a sneer on his lips.

Sixth in line, just before Diyar, stood Husam al-Din Lajeen, also like Sonkor, a former Viceroy of Damascus. He took the bowstring without flinching. The soldier, now sweating from exertion, pulled the line tighter and tighter. But as Lajeen slid to the floor unconscious, the string snapped.

Immediately Amir Baidara, Viceroy of Egypt and one of the sultan's advisors, leaped forward. "Spare his life, O, Beneficent Ruler. Spare his life, and your name will be ever spoken of as the most merciful of rulers."

Khalil stared at the man on the floor. Salous, his wazeer, started to speak. But before he could, the sultan nodded abruptly. "Yes. I am merciful." He flicked his hand. "Take the rest away. They are pardoned for now." His voice, tinged with madness, rose. "You are all pardoned. Get out. Everybody out."

Diyar quickly grasped one of Lajeen's arms, Baidara the other, and together they hurried out to the horses. They lifted him up to a seat in front of one of Lajeen's mamluks who rode quickly out of al-Qal'ah to his house. Diyar leaped on his own horse and beat a hasty retreat back to Karak.

CHAPTER 31

January, 1293. Pigeons arrived at Karak. The sultan was on the march, and when he passed Karak, the fortress's garrison was ordered to join his army.

Throughout the year Diyar had been waiting for the arrival of arresting khasikiya, but they had not come.

"What is the sultan waiting for?" he grumbled to himself. He knew Ibn al-Salous was too vengeful to forget an affront. By now, the other two amirs who had, along with Diyar, protested their old qadi's shabby treatment had been arrested, tortured, nailed to camels, and paraded through the city. Finally and mercifully, they were executed and their property seized.

It was then that Diyar sent secret orders to Abd ar-Rahman. The manager was to take Diyar's treasure stored at his palace and split it, hiding half at his own house in Cairo, and the other half at Gouffre's in Alexandria. Lady Shajar was to be given an ample house allowance.

After a brief stay in Damascus, the sultan suddenly marched to Salamiya on the edge of the Syrian desert and arrested Mahanna ibn Isa ibn Mahanna, King of the Syrian Bedouins. Mahanna, son of the late Isa ibn Mahanna, Diyar's protector in the desert, had done nothing wrong and was taken completely by surprise. The treacherous sultan had struck again.

When the army returned Cairo again, Diyar received orders he was reassigned to the Citadel—the last place he wanted to be. His homecoming was bitter-sweet. He loved seeing Lady Shajar again. Motherhood had made her soft with deep breasts. Ismail was now twelve, approaching his father's height, and eager to learn the ways of a warrior. And around the harem crawled a round, little angel, Attala, Diyar's new daughter. It was a good family, which might be made bigger if only he could live a while longer.

The paranoia of the sultan was unbounded. Even several amirs chatting together might be seen as plotting. Then the khasikiya would arrive at their homes. Arrest, torture, and death followed.

But the sultan had reason to fear. Plotting among the ambitious amirs was widespread. In back rooms of hidden cafes, schemes were hatched, rejected, renewed.

Diyar stayed well out of it.

Then one day in the cool of winter, a khasikiya arrived at Diyar's palace with an invitation. "Because of your legendary prowess with the bow, you are requested to accompany The Most Noble King Khalil on a hunt."

A Royal Command: He had no choice but to go.

Later he shook his head and murmured to Kareem, "I try to keep as far away from the sultan as possible, and now he invites me to be a member of his hunting party. I do not know whether it is safer to be close to this man or far."

"No place in the realm is far enough away."

The sultan intended to take his hunting party across the Nile to shoot birds in the west delta region. Salous would be accompanying him plus a number of amirs. These included Amir Baidara, Viceroy of Egypt.

When the hunting party arrived across the river and the warriors led their mounts off the boats, Wazeer Salous, no hunter, remained on the royal galley and continued north with his entourage to Alexandria.

Diyar watched him go with relief. But after the party had been in the marshlands for several days, a messenger rode up from the wazeer carrying a letter of denunciation against Baidara, Viceroy of Egypt.

When the sultan, sitting on his portable throne in his pavilion, read the message, a scream of fury erupted from his throat. "Bring me the traitor Baidara. Call all the amirs to my tent now," and members of his bodyguard scurried off.

When the amirs rode up to the pavilion, they were stunned to see the viceroy being marched up at lance-point.

The sultan paced feverishly in front of his throne. He saw Baidara, and cried out, madness contorting his face. "You demon of treachery and deceit, you are the spawn of an Alexandian whore and a poxed camel. You should never enter into the presence of decent, God-worshiping men." Froth spewed from his lips. "When the Grand Wazeer returns, I will have you flogged before God and all the people."

The viceroy, the survivor of numberless battles, showed no emotion. "I assure you, O Most Noble King, my life's only desire is to serve God, and to serve you, and to be of some small use to the realm." Then, to the astonishment of all, he bowed, turned and left.

Shocked speechless by the viceroy's cool behavior, Khalil sagged into his chair and, after a moment, waved the assemblage away.

With the fall of evening, the warriors kept to their tents. But late in the night, Diyar heard a scratch on the wall of his tent and a whisper to meet at Baidara's pavilion.

Laying in the dark, Diyar thought long and hard. He had never joined in palace intrigues. But that was before this young lunatic had gained the throne. Then the memory of the day of the broken bow string came to him. He awakened Kareem and ordered him to saddle his horse, and began dressing.

The men squatted in a tight circle, the flickering light from a single-candled lamp mottling their tense faces. Next to Diyar sat Amir Husam al-Din Lajeen, a big man with red hair and cold, blue eyes. Outside, invisible in the darkness, their sarrajun stood watch.

Baidara spoke in low tones. "He must die, or we all will die."

Lajeen nodded grimly. "True, but how? The man is mad but no fool. He goes nowhere without half the khasikiya with him."

"True, but if an opportunity arises, all I ask is for your backing." He searched the eyes of each man. They all nodded, then slipped from the tent, men whose lives were now in jeopardy for even thinking treason.

But the days of the hunting expedition ran on with no opportunity for attack. Then, on the morning of the final day as the party began to strike camp, Diyar noticed something strange. The early morning sun shone through the rising dust of the sultan's Royal Bodyguard riding off with the supply train. But where was the sultan?

He called to Kareem and they rode to Baidara's tent. The viceroy appeared and Diyar leaned down and whispered. "The sultan's bodyguard left, but the sultan was not with it."

Interest sparked in the man's eyes. He glanced around. "This may be our chance." He gestured to several of his warriors. "Ride to Lajeen's tent and the other amirs who are with us. Tell them to meet us at the sultan's pavilion," and he, Diyar and Kareem rode to the sultan's tent. They had just arrived when servant carrying a load of linen came out.

Baidara smiled. "And where is our Most Noble King this morning."

From under the bundle, the little Egyptian extended a finger. "To the lake over that way. His Majesty heard there was a large number of birds, so he has taken a crossbow and gone to try his skill."

"Oh? And who was so fortunate as to accompany him?"

"Uh, just Amir Shikar, the Royal Huntsman who found the flock."

The viceroy nodded. "Thank you. Go on about your tasks."

He reined around and rode several paces away. He nodded to Diyar and Kareem. "Quickly, you two go find where they hunt. I will follow when the rest of the men arrive."

The men heard and obeyed.

When they approached the reed-bounded lake, they spied the Sultan and the Royal Huntsman watching a flock of geese lifting from the lake. A loaf of bread and a roasted chicken was spread between them. Immediately, Diyar and Kareem wheeled and galloped back.

They met the larger party of amirs, and Diyar spoke up. "It is as the servant said. But for Shikar, Khalil is alone.

When Shikar saw the men galloping towards them, he ran to his horse and mounted. But Baidara ignored him and galloped past, drawing his sword.

Khalil leaped to his feet but before he could pull his sword, the viceroy slashed down, chopping the man's arm, shattering the bone.

Another amir raced in Baidara's hoof prints. His blow smashed Khalil's shoulder. Lajeen came third, knocking the hapless man to the ground. Then all, all save one, leaped from their horses, chopping to death the young sultan

Still mounted, Diyar coolly watched the carnage.

Finally, with their blood-lust sated, the amirs left the carcass of the ruler of the great Mamluk Empire crumpled in the dust. It would remain there for two days before a local official found it, stuffed it in a bag, and carried it on camel back to the capital for burial.

Now calm, the men rode back to the sultan's pavilion. Baidara dismounted, walked to the throne and sat down. In one accord, the assembled amirs bowed their heads in fealty to their new sultan. Then they all headed back to the capital.

But one unspoken worry troubled them all: Would the other amirs accept Baidara as their sultan, or would the assassins end up like Khalil, their blood fertilizing the dust of the delta?

Kitbugha, a Mongol who had risen through the mamluk ranks to become an amir, was spending the morning shooting birds nearer the city with some of his brother Mongols, when he met a handful of Khalil's mamluks who had seen Baidara sitting on the Khalil's throne after the assassination. A shrewd look entered

Mongol's eyes.

He stood in his stirrups and called to his countrymen. "The sultan is dead. Now is our chance for power. Send to the city for more of our people, and we will meet Baidara and his men at the river. If they can take the throne from Khalil, we can take it from them."

Baidara and his party had not gone far when they met a group of Royal Mamluks out riding. Baidara raised his hand and reined up. "Greetings. We have great news. The degenerate pretender, Khalil, has been slain by us this very morning. You know his crimes. He has persecuted our fellow-warriors whose only crime was to faithfully follow our great sultan, Qalaoon. He has shown frivolity in handling the affairs of state, primarily appointing the fellow degenerate, Ibn al Salous, to the revered position of wazeer. And he murdered the highly respected Sonkor al-Ashqar."

Diyar rode to the shade of a tree, slid down, and made a point of inspecting its hoofs.

"Moreover," Baidara continued, "the man had no religion, drank wine in Ramadan, and held orgies with beardless boys."

The men nodded. All knew well Khalil's sins.

"So ride with us as we hail a new day, for God," Baidara raised a fist, "and the people." He urged his mount forward, and the Royal Mamluks joined the hunting party. If the former viceroy was to be the new sultan, they wanted to stay as close to him as possible.

Lajeen paused next to Diyar. "You seem less than impressed with our new leader."

Diyar did not look up. "I have heard speeches before."

The two and their sarrajun continued some distance behind the hunting party. The party was nearing the river when a large group could be seen approaching. It was Kitbugha, accompanied by over two thousand Mongols. As soon as he saw Baidara and his followers, he called out an order. At full charge his men let fly a swarm of arrows.

The mamluks fell, several shafts quivering in each. Then the

Mongols rode among them, completing the massacre with their swords.

Baidara's head was sliced from his body and mounted on a lance. The Mongols, spying Diyar, Lajeen and their sarrajun, spurred after them, and the men had to scatter and ride for their lives.

Galloping headlong, Diyar thought fast. *Could I make Alexandria? Gouffre might find a place for me to hide.* But he knew, with pigeons, an arrest warrant could be there before he was.

Can I reach the desert?

Ahead rolled the river. A fisherman's reed hut sat next to the shore, a narrow boat nearby.

He glanced back. The Mongols were coming fast. At the hut, Diyar skidded to a stop. A little brown man in a tattered loincloth came squinting out into the sun.

"Quickly, man," Diyar said, heading for the river, "I must get to the other side."

"Now, master?" but Diyar was already shoving the boat into the water.

The fisherman jumped in and paddled the boat, and Diyar held the mare's reins as she swam behind. They were nearly out of arrow range when the Mongols reined up at the water's edge. One warrior jumped to the ground, dropped to his back, and, bracing his bow with his feet, drew a long arrow as far back as he could. It sliced the water but a pace off the side of the mare.

"Break your back, boatman," growled Diyar, "or we die."

The little man redoubled his efforts.

While some of the warriors taunted and shook their fists at the boat, others set ablaze the hut. Sadly the fisherman looked away.

When they reached the other shore, Diyar tossed him several silver dirhems, enough to build a much finer hut, and continued his race across the delta.

MAMLUK

CHAPTER 32

When the Commander of the Fortress, Amir Sanjar al-Shujai, heard about Khalil's assassination, and the death of Baidara and his amirs, he ordered all boats on the western side of the Nile be brought to the city side. Kitbugha and his Mongols reached the river, eager to cross and take over the Citadel. But first they had to negotiated with Sanjar.

After much debate, the two men decided to rule the sultanate together, and installed Qalaoon's youngest son, Muhammad, all of eight years old, as sultan. The child was given the name al-Malik-al-Nasir, "Victorious King", Muhammad ibn Qalaoon.

Kitbugha took the position of Viceroy of Egypt, the second highest post in the realm, while Sanjar became the Wazeer. This was an administrative post normally held by an Egyptian or a Syrian, but he needed a position high enough to balance Kitbugha's power.

Immediately a number of amirs accused of being associates of Baidara were executed. They were nailed to planks, tied to the backs of camels and paraded through Cairo, preceded by the Baidara's head on a lance.

The procession was ordered to pass in front of the houses of the victims. When it reached the house of the Amir Altunbugha, his women slaves ran bareheaded into the streets with their children, weeping and beating themselves on the breasts and faces.

His pages tore their clothes, giving vent to lamentable cries. His wife ran to the roof to jump off and die with her husband, but her odalisques held her back. Still she continued to scream, "Would to God I could sacrifice myself for you."

Below, the crowd of onlookers sobbed with her.

Meanwhile, the young followers and slaves of Khalil blacked themselves and ran through the streets accompanied by professional weeping women.

When Khalil's lover, Ibn al Salous, heard of the death of sultan, the foolish young man returned to al-Qahirah and continued to strut the streets. But five days later, the khasikiya came for him. He was thrown into prison and only death ended his torture.

Diyar in Arab garb rode his weary mare down a narrow street in Damascus. Above him, all the low, flat roofs were piled high with hay bales. He approached the gate at the end of the street, and heard the discordant braying of camels. He rode through the gate, steering clear of mounds of manure, and entered the broad, open courtyard of Damascus's great camel market place.

Everywhere he looked, thousands of camels stood, while ancient Nubian herders, their black faces expressionless under strikingly white turbans, squatted quietly in the sun. Merchants huddled in corners arguing prices.

Some camels were tied by a rope from their muzzles to pegs in the ground. Some had their front legs hobbled, others their left front legs were trussed up. But even on three legs, a camel could move swiftly.

Diyar paused to find a merchant, when a large, hobbled camel nearby twisted and broke loose.

Pandemonium erupted.

The angry beast let out a deep-bass whinny that struck fear in the handlers. The three-legged monster careened through the herd, scattering merchants and buyers alike.

The rogue's handlers hitched up their flowing robes and set off in loud pursuit, brandishing their bamboo canes. A small boy bearing a tray of sweet water near them dove for cover.

The handlers closed in on the wild beast, lashing at it with their canes, trying to get it under control. But it ran down a couple of them and charged Diyar's mare.

Diyar held her quiet until the onrushing camel was nearly upon them. Then he turned her aside, whipped out his mace from his saddle, and smashed the camel's skull. It sprawled into the dust and did not move.

Sudden quiet descended over the court. Diyar took a number of dinars—twice what it had been worth—and dropped them onto the neck of the dead animal.

A Damascene merchant hurried over and retrieved the coins. "Now, how may I help you," he said in passable Turkish—he knew a rich mamluk when he saw one, regardless of how the man was dressed.

Diyar replied in Arabic, "I need two camels. A large male to carry supplies, and a dhalul, a racing camel, preferably a female, to ride."

The camel merchant almost rubbed his hands at the expectation of a fat fee. "I have just the ones," he said with a smile. "Please, follow me."

Diyar knew, as with horses, teeth were the best clue to a camel's age. He examined the canine teeth of a large male, two on both sides of its mouth, upper and lower, making eight, and despite the merchant's assurance it was three years old, adjudged it to be nearer five, but bought it anyway. A dhalul proved more difficult.

He rejected what the merchant tried to fob off. Then he spied what he wanted. It was being ridden by a passing Rueyli sheik. He rode after him and, to the sheik's delight, opened the bargaining.

Like most amirs, Diyar carried a full purse when he rode forth, and now the sheik lightened it by a goodly number of dinars. But Maha, the female, fawn-colored dhalul he bought, was well worth it.

She possessed a lion's head and great gazelle eyes, a long, ideal line along the back, and the high-swung, bell-line from the breastbone to the hind thighs. Her hips, neck and legs were slim, her hump small, but firm. No whips or spurs had ever touched her soft hair.

Diyar sold his horse and bought a shedad, a saddle of acacia wood and leather cushions, whose long rows of knotted tassels hung below Maha's belly and swung in rhythm with her gait.

Early the next morning Diyar joined a small trading caravan leaving Damascus heading east. After leaving the Syrian steppes, the caravan entered a dry, pebble-strewn desert. This was the Hamad, the North-Arabian uplands, a flat, hard desert with no breaks in its level monotony. Under a cloudless sky, a sheet of water ahead glistened in a depression of the desert—a mirage. Dry troughs filled with hot, glassy air and tricked the eye.

Soon the riders gave voice to rhythmic chants and yodeling that made the time and distance move easier. The Bedouin camel-songs were masculine, bold, and tuneful. The camels loved the diversion and walked easily to the songs' beat.

Maha's racing build gave her a pace which was even and long-striding. Her voice was soft and tender, a low gurgling or sobbing. But mostly she conversed by means of her speaking eyes or a gentle push with her nose against his shoulder or thigh. And at night he had a comfortable, sheltered bed in the curve of her warm body. Her satin skin never lost its luster.

After days in the desert, so vast the expanse, so monotonous the movement, Diyar lost his sense of progress.

Am I moving? The landscape seems never to change.

Then, from the edge of a steep escarpment, he saw spread before him, the Wadi Sirhan. Immensely wide, a medley of chalk-colored banks rose from lime rock, stony plains, salt marshes, sand dunes, grey shrubs.

At eventide the caravan dropped down to the wadi and had their evening meal: roasted camel calf, crisp bread-cakes, and fresh camel milk, ending with dates mixed with sour, sheep butter.

Throughout the night, the herders watered their animals at deep well-holes, wells as old as time. The creaking of the small wooden rollers as the dripping ropes were pulled up lulled him to sleep.

From the Hamad, the caravan entered the Bsayta, a perfectly level wasteland without water, without pasture, covered with a hail of black gravel, desolate.

Then came the Nufud, great waves of red sand, rising and falling evenly, stretched to infinity. Hills, red-flanked, rose to crests aflame in the sun. Gorges hid low shrubs and trees—tamarisk—with milk-white trunks and drooping green branches. These feathery twigs and grayish-green needles enticed Maha to pause, and she nibbled the young shoots with obvious delight.

At home in the Nufud, she carefully followed the tortuous slopes which, as a storm-tossed sea, ran from trough to crest past deep chasms. She would not be hurried. An undulation of sand, seemingly so harmless, could fall away into an abyss. Only the herd-instinct of the camels kept the small band of riders from being separated.

When the slopes became too steep, the riders had to lead the beasts, often stamping or scooping footholds in the dunes for steps.

They passed through tracks of a small herd of ibex, followed by those of a solitary panther. A troop of snow-white Ram gazelles, their dainty feet deep in the scarlet sand, also browsed on the drooping branches of the tamarisk, quenching their thirst on the dew that gathered on the leaves and flowers in the morning. A fox crept across the caravan's path. Ravens ascended from acacia bushes. Startled ostriches churned away in fright.

The sand-waves glowed deep red, then violet in the brief dusk, then night. In a sheltered gully, a fire of sticks flickered to life, its almost colorless flame burning without smoke. Over the glowing coals an iron baking sheet was spread, bread dough kneaded, and soon bread-cakes, dates, honey, and hard camel-cheese were served.

Throughout the night, pairs of sentinels scaled sand-hills and kept watch. On Diyar's turn he sat in wonder, mesmerized by the stillness of a desert under the unbroken, glimmering sky.

The blanket of night still lay over him, when a boy awoke him.

"Hurry. A storm approaches."

Diyar looked around. The night sky was purple with a silvery sheen, beautiful but eerie.

He had hardly dropped in the saddle when a gentle drizzle enveloped the train. The sun burst from the red horizon and a gleaming rainbow curved over the dunes. Far-distant thunder rumbled softly towards them. The clouds dropped, sweeping the dune-tops. Forked lightening flashed, and thunder shook the air, unleashing a heavy downpour. Under the lash of the rain, the hard sand sang, and the drenched camel's hair curled up. The riders dripped as if they had fallen into the sea.

With the deluge past, hot winds dried the riders and camels in minutes. But the wind increased, driving dense dust-clouds. Soon sand blasted the train with relentless fury, and the riders clutched their saddles to keep from being unseated.

The riders dismounted and, bent over and blinded by the fury of the storm, led their camels while holding the tail of camel in front. Hour after hour, day after day, the storm railed, hurtling clouds of swirling red sand at the tiny caravan. Visibility ceased beyond a pace. The men were wrapped tightly against the sand, and the heat-blast forced sweat from every pore. The bone-dry air cracked their skin.

Suffocated by day, the men were tormented by icy blasts at dusk that chilled their sweat-soggy robes, causing them to shake throughout the night. Diyar's fair hands and face soon chapped, and blood oozed through the fissures. And though he had water, his tongue ached from the fine sand which permeated everything. He struggled to breathe, panting in clouds of sand, and his parched eyes, palate and throat became inflamed.

One day, in the swirl of sand, the camel ahead of Diyar collapsed, and he fell over its rump. Too exhausted to move any farther, the beast was abandoned, its load distributed among the other weary animals.

Then a slave fainted, and had to be folded into a saddlebag. Another began vomiting, went mad, turned cold, and died. After another day, the slave in the saddlebag became delirious, and he too died, left in a shallow grave of sand.

Night, and Diyar slumped to his sheepskins like a man struck down. After hours of sleep of the dead, something brushed his face. Half awake, he fanned it away with annoyance. It came again. With irritation, he opened his eyes.

Persistently, Maha nuzzled his face, whimpering softly.

Diyar looked around to a land transformed. The sun, the wonderful sun, shown down on a world renewed. Scoured by the storm, the morning air was crystal-clear. Camels were afoot, saddles and loads in place. A driver, his robe fashioned like a sack, scattered fresh shoots for them. Life began again.

The next day, the train encountered a camp where the people welcomed the traders with open arms. The caravan's commander decided to rest the animals for a few days and allow them to pasture. In riding Maha out to the herds that searched the sparse pasture land, Diyar came upon a young herder, a bright, cheerful lad. The boy had the knack of clinging for hours on his camel's back, laying on his stomach over the hump as if it were a wooly pillow. It took Diyar some time to learn the trick, but learn it he did. And then it was time to move on.

After several days, the caravan entered the Harra. This high, flatland was exposed to frigid, northeast gales which froze water and milk solid. Flat blades of black and blue-grey flint covered the stark surface. Under the glare of the sun, the ground glittered unbearably, blinding the eyes. The camels, slipping over its brittle surface, disliked the plateau as much as the men.

The train stopped at Rueyshdat one evening, and was taking on water from the only running spring in the northern desert, when a large raiding party approached, war-mares tied to their camels. The men of the caravan gripped their swords. Though they carried travel permits from various clan chiefs, there were no guarantees of safety in the desert. With his khafakiya hiding his face, Diyar watched warily.

Soon the raiding party stopped, and its slaves began erecting tents. The leader of the party slid from his camel and into the saddle of his beautiful mare. Accompanied by several riders he approached the caravan. Though his face was hidden, there was something familiar about the way he sat his horse.

When the men neared, Diyar revealed his face.

Fuaz Shalan started, then leaped to the ground, and kissed Diyar on both cheeks. "My friend, it is the joy of a year in paradise to see your face again." Then he turned solemn. He stepped back, drew his dagger, and wedged its sharp tip into his left palm. Dipping his finger in the blood, he touched Diyar's forehead between his blond eyebrows, performing the old Bedouin "Nur-ed-Dam", the "Light of Blood".

Diyar pulled his kindjal and did the same to Fuaz. Thus the two became blood-brothers to the delight of all the watching raiders.

Now Diyar asked, "My friend, what brings you to such a unhappy place?"

"A ghazu—a raid—into the Hamad and the Wudian regions, against the Shammar Bedouins."

"Why do you set yourselves to kill the Shammar?"

Fuaz's head jerked back. "We do not want to kill anyone. We are thieves," he said with dignity. "We desire no harm to come to any of God's creatures."

"But what if someone gets killed?"

He shrugged. "It is God's will." The surrounding raiders nodded fatalistically.

"Besides, if we kill one of their men, we must pay, so many camels per man, more if he is a sharif, not that any of these dog-spawns are. No," he continued without rancor, "we only want to steal some of their herds."

"Why? Surely you have as many as you need."

"A man never has as many as he needs. Besides, it is only fair. They stole from us last spring."

The men murmured in assent, but one old warrior spoke up with a tooth-gapped grin, "Perhaps that is because we stole twice

as many from them in the winter," and the men bulged with
laughter.

CHAPTER 33

Diyar sat in the shade of his tent, smoothing an arrow shaft with a bone-handled khanjar, the knife he bought from a tribe member. A woman approached carrying dried camel chips for the fire. Divorced by a sheik who wanted a younger wife, the woman had simply taken her two children and returned to her brother's family. After living with Fuaz's clan for a few weeks, Diyar had asked for the woman, Duhiya, in marriage. Her brother had consented, and they had now been married for two years.

She dropped the camel chips outside the tent, then bent in. "Sire, Shiek Fuaz is coming."

At the sound of her voice, bells behind him tinkled softly. Diyar's great hawk, Mawia, its eyes shielded by a leather hood, shook its head nervously.

Diyar stepped outside to meet his friend.

"I have news," Fuaz said, stepping down from his mare. "We passed a caravan yesterday. Its leader said Kitbugha, the Mongol Viceroy of Egypt, had been disposed and was on the run, and a new sultan rules at Qalat al-Jabal, a nimrod named Lajeen."

Diyar could hardly believe it. He and Lajeen had barely escaped Kitbugha's arrows. Now Lajeen was sultan?

"But how did it happen?"

He shrugged. "I asked, but the trader had no more answers."

There was only one way for Diyar to find out. It was time to go home.

The white, winter sun hung in a sullen sky, and a bleak wind blew from off the Nile. Diyar approached his palace, and fat ravens squatting on the walls stirred and flapped away.

Where are the guards? They should be manning the walls. It does not augur well.

There had been other bad omens as he approached the capital. He was riding Maha and wearing the robes of a Rueyli Arab as disguise, and had skirted the city walls, heading for Fustat. On the dusty back road, human bones, picked clean by scavengers and the blowing sand, lay scattered in the ditches. To the Egyptians, both fastidious and superstitious, such leavings were unusual. What had happened to produce such behavior?

He neared his palace gate, and the anxiety was replaced by eagerness to see his family again. At the gate, from his saddle, he pulled the bell chain and waited for the call of the old bowwab.

Silence.

He pulled the chain again. In a moment, the tiny viewing door slid open, and a child's voice piped up, "Who is at the gate?"

The ends of his khafakiya covered Diyar's mouth as he replied, "I wish to speak to your master."

"He is too busy to speak to you."

Where was the lazy bowwab? Diyar was becoming irritated palavering with this child. After all, he was the master of this palace.

"Then get me the lady of the house?"

Now came a voice he did recognize. "There is no one here who wishes to speak to you. Be gone."

"Kareem, it is I. Open this gate and be quick about it."

A gasp, and the man cried, "O master, is it really you?" In a moment the gate swung open, and Kareem, tears starting in his eyes, ran out.

"O Master, it is you. Praise to God you are still alive," and he clutched Diyar's leg as he rode into the courtyard. Diyar slipped to the ground, and Kareem fell to his knees in joy and would have kissed his master's feet had not Diyar restrained him.

The weary traveler looked around expecting to see Lady Shajar—or Ismail, how tall he must be now, or little Attala.

No one, just several eunuchs slouching in a doorway.

But his quick eyes observed how unkempt the courtyard appeared. Where streams of water once laughed in the fountain, now only fetid liquid remained. The plants and shrubs bent brown, dead in the sun. Dust and sand heaped up in the corners.

He turned to Kareem. "What has happened here? Where is the lady of the house?"

The joy in Kareem's face wavered. Angrily he turned and called to the eunuchs. "Come quickly and unload the master's beasts and water them."

He took Diyar's arm and turned to the open door of the house. "Come inside, master, and let me get you a cold drink."

But Diyar pulled away. "Answer me, Kareem. What has happened here?"

The slave's face crumbled. "The plague, master. It took them all. The mistress, your son and little daughter. It took half the city."

Diyar froze, stunned. "Lady Shajar, my son, dead?

Kareem quickly took his arm and led him into shade of the house. He sat him on a divan.

Diyar, his mind no longer functioning, he did not notice as Kareem added a few drops from a vial into a goblet of sweetened juice.

When he awoke, a sadness, like a great, lowering cloud, descended over him. But he had to learn the details. He called for Kareem.

The sarrajun entered and sat on the rug before him. "It was that accursed Mongol, Kitbugha. He was the cause of all our problems. May God curse him to a thousand generations."

Wearily, Diyar leaned back and waited.

"At first, things were not too bad. Kitbugha and Sanjar ruled, with the boy, Malik-al-Nasir Muhammad, as sultan. But there can never be harmony with two rulers in one realm, and after a time, Kitbugha's men killed Sanjar. Amir Lajeen, who had been in hiding for less than a half a year, reappeared, and the sultan made him Viceroy."

Viceroy of Egypt, thought Diyar, the second highest ruler in the land? Lajeen who had lived through the broken bowstring? Lajeen the assassinator of Khalil? God must love him dearly for surely no man has ever led a more charmed life.

"My family," Diyar said quietly, "what about my wife and children."

Kareem bit his lip. "Yes, the mistress, the children. As I said, when the Mongol sat on the throne, God deserted us. The Nile failed to rise, not once but twice. So many people starved ditches were dug in the desert and the bodies dumped in without ceremony or mourners. Locusts, great clouds of them, rose out of the desert and devoured what little crops that still lived. People fought and died for the carcasses of dogs. And when the animals were gone, the people began to eat each other.

"I do not know if you heard, but in Persia, the degenerate Il-Khan Kaikhatu was assassinated by his cousin Ghazan who seized the throne."

Diyar shook his head.

Kareem continued. "To escape the new Il-Khan, many more Mongols came here with their families, debauchees all. Kitbugha, that Mongol dog, welcomed them with high honors. These heathen continued to imbibe kumiss, eat horse meat, but worse, refused to convert to Islam. That is when God sent the plague."

The plague, what mamluks feared the most. How could it be that they, bigger and stronger than the Egyptians, were always the first to die?

"So," Kareem was saying, "those who did not die of hunger, were killed by the plague. The mistress, so beautiful, the disease ate her beauty away in one day and she died the next, as did Ismail and little Attala." Again tears welled up in his eyes. "Why God did not claim me, I will never know. And your weavers...Lady Shajar spent much of her fortune trying to get food for them, but many died of starvation or the plague. I am afraid you have little of your fortune left."

But Diyar wanted to hear the end of the story. "And Kitbugha, what happened to him?"

Kareem nodded with satisfaction. "Ah, yes, he finally reaped the reward for his treachery. In the summer he took the army to Damascus. Many amirs there were arrested, tortured for stealing public funds, and replaced, so the amirs here knew no one was safe with him on the throne. When the army started back, many of the amirs met in Lajeen's tent and plotted against the Mongol. The next day, they surrounded the sultan's tent. Some of his bodyguard fought which gave him time to slip out the back. He mounted the duty horse and rode for his life with only four of his mawali escaping with him.

"Lajeen cut his way into Kitbugha's tent but missed him. When Lajeen rode back to his tent, all the other amirs walked beside his horse to show their loyalty.

"A few days later the great wise man, Ahmad al-Fazari, read through the whole of Buqhari's 'Traditions of the Prophet' in one sitting at the Great Umayyad Mosque in Damascus, and on the very same night it began to rain, and continued to do so for forty days and forty nights. The droughts and plagues were washed away. And thus, " he said in conclusion, "we rid ourselves of the affliction that had burdened our land. But not before a terrible toll had been paid."

He perked up. "But now, master, now that you are back, I know our fortunes will improve."

Diyar was not so sure. Lajeen was sultan, but how much trust could one put in a man so ruthless as to kill one sultan, and attempt to kill another?

"So, how rules the new sultan?"

Kareem hesitated. 'The people like him. When he mounted

the throne, he released a number of imprisoned amirs, including Baybars al-Jashnekeer. Kitbugha fled to Damascus, and Lajeen could have had him imprisoned. Instead he awarded him the governorship of the town of Salkhad.

"And he seems very pious. When he disappeared after killing Khalil, he hid in the ruined minaret of the mosque of Ibn Tulun. Now he has donated twenty thousand gold dinars to repair the mosque and to establish a number of religious schools. But..."

Diyar waited as his servant hesitated.

"But," Kareem continued slowly, "things have changed."

"How so?"

"When the amirs swore allegiance to him, they made him promise not to promote any of his own men, including his favorite, Mangu Timur, over the established amirs. But despite his promise, he made Mangu Timur viceroy. Then Mangu imprisoned the former viceroy, Amir Kara Sonkor and had Amir Kara's Egyptian secretary, Sharf-al-Din Yakoub flogged to death. Any amir who protested was banished to a distant post.

"It is Viceroy Mangu Timur who rules. We hardly ever see the sultan. He fasts and prays all the time, and has banned gambling, expensive clothes and gold embroidery. The people love him for his piety, but more and more he becomes a recluse in his own palace." He sighed. "And once again, the sultanate is tossed as a ship in a storm. No one knows what will be the outcome."

The sarrajun fell silent, and Diyar said, "One more question—where is my family buried?"

"Oh, yes, I chose a nice spot inside the walls where the morning sun first hits. Come, I will show you."

The tiny mausoleum stood cozened in the shadow of the walls. Kareem opened the doors, then discretely withdrew.

Diyar stepped into cool, stark room. The larger bier was flanked by two smaller ones, and his eyes smarted with tears as he was struck again by the anguish of loss.

Sweet Shajar, so soft, so yielding, but with such dignity, what a wife should be.

Unbidden, the memories came, crushing his heart. He could not stay in the sad, little crypt, and returned to his divan.

The thought of his first home, the steppes, so green so fertile came to him. How unlike this parched, plague-wracked land they were.

Perhaps I will return, escape this sadness. I will build her a proper mausoleum, something more fitting our love, then return to the land of my father.

Consumed by sorrow, exhausted by grief, he leaned back.

Perhaps tomorrow.

But the next morning a pair of khasikiya waited in the courtyard, a warrant for his appearance at al-Qal'ah in hand.

CHAPTER 34

He stood at the entrance of the sultan's private iwan as the Major Domo carried in his warrant. It was an audience chamber Qalaoon had built, high-ceilinged and cool. High on the walls, in a band of blue topaz encircling the room, the sayings of the Prophet were scripted in gold.

After a moment, the Major Domo gestured for him to enter. At one end of the hall, a white silk divan spread beneath a sculpted marble canopy. On the divan, also in ascetic white silk, sat al-Malik-al-Mansoor Lajeen al-Mansoori, sultan of Egypt and Syria, leaning forward over a large copy of the Koran on a stand.

Diyar approached, and Lajeen stood and came to meet him. The two men of the steppes were much alike, tall, fair. Diyar's blond hair was blanching to white at the edges, while Lajeen's red hair faded to grey.

Diyar started to bow, but Lajeen took his hand. "My old friend," he said earnestly, "how good it is to see you again. You have not changed."

"Nor you, Malana."

But Diyar lied. Lajeen's eyes, once cold and calculating, now glowed with the intense fire of a fanatic.

Did the months of isolation hiding in the minaret unbalanced him? The failed bowstring execution, the assassinations, had they created a religious madman?

Diyar continued. "All I have heard since my return is how the people love their sultan, how grateful and triumphant was the parade after your recovery from your polo accident."

"Yes," he said in solemn tones. "It was a manifestation of God's love for me and the people. It humbled me. I prayed the night out in gratitude."

He motioned to a nearby amir. "But, now, I have something for you. This is my new Assistant Commander-in-Chief."

Diyar observed the second highest ranking amir in the army. The man was half his age. The general casually handed Diyar a scroll as the sultan intoned, "In honor of your dedication to your sultan, I hereby advance you to the ranking of Amir al-Tablkhana. I hope you will always remain as loyal to me as you are now."

He nodded to the Major Domo. The man clapped his hands, and a clerk hurried in. With the clerk came a slave bearing a robe of honor. The clerk made a note on a scroll, and the slave stepped forward with the robe.

Diyar took a deep breath. What irony. One day he was hiding in the desert, the next he was an Amir of Forty. "Thank you, Malana. I pledge I will be loyal to you as long as either of us live."

The ascetic sultan eyed him bleakly. No one knew better than he the peril of rule. "Good. Your first assignment will be to escort Muhammad, the son of Qalaoon, to the fortress at Karak." He turned back to his divan.

The audience over, the Major Domo indicated for Diyar to follow him out. Instead he spoke up. "I have but one request, Malana?"

The sultan did not look back. "Yes?"

"If possible, I would like to be assigned as many of my former men as possible."

The sultan sat and turned to his book. "It will be done," he said without looking up.

Diyar, heading for the door, glanced back at the ruler of the empire. Baybars spent every day while in the Citadel on the practice field with his mamluks, honing their skills, while this hermit laid about shuffling the pages of his religious books. Once again the security of the empire was threatened, not from without but from within.

Diyar's new recruits were a motley lot, and he ordered his few veterans to work to beat them into shape.

When he and his men formed up an escort detail for Muhammad and his mother, Diyar observed the former sultan for the first time. The boy, eleven, small and frail, limped from a lame foot, a birth defect. His mother, a handsome woman, was a Kipchak. The boy rode a fine mare, she in a silken traveling litter atop a near-white camel.

Diyar could understand the prince's timidity. After a sultan dies, his sons grow up never knowing when the vagaries of politics might send a guard detail to the harem to escort them to the executioner. The recent loss of Diyar's son made him sympathetic to the lad, and as they rode, he entertained him with stories, anecdotes about the Arabs, the Ababdeh, the Nubians, the Cilicians, those people at the edges of the realm. Diyar found the boy possessed a quick intelligence, and when they played chess in the evening, a worthy opponent.

One morning, before the camp had risen, the two rode out on a hunt. At the top of a rocky knoll, Diyar spotted a wolf, and they gave chase, dodging in and out of the boulders. The boy was not a good horseman, but enthusiastic, happy to be free of the confines of stone walls.

They drove the beast out into open range and he was tiring. They closed in on him, but as the prince dropped his lance for the kill, Diyar gently eased the prince away.

"Why did you break it off?" the boy said panting. "We had him."

"True, sire, we had him. So we did not need his death to show we had won."

They trotted back to camp, and a glance showed Diyar Muhammad was thinking about his words. And when the escort procession arrived in Karak came to an end, he was sorry to say goodbye to the banished prince.

He returned to Cairo to learn the new Viceroy, Mangu Timur, had reduced the shares of land allotted to the amirs and halaqa. Some of the wealthier amirs refused to accept the new deeds of land, and resigned their commissions. This wrangling made the Viceroy look bad, and he angrily issued an order that all who complained would be flogged and imprisoned.

Wisely, Diyar kept quiet, concentrating instead on making his forty the best warriors in the sultanate. But he felt the growing tension among the cadre. Who next was to be tortured and executed?

Diyar, several of his men and their sarrajun cantered down a dark, narrow lane in a remote section of the city. They rode through the gate in front of a great, low building, and a fat, Egyptian merchant stepped out from the doorway bowing.

"Come, O Great Amir, my wares are the finest in the land." Despite the sultan's edict that the populace should dress modestly, the Egyptian wore fine silks, lustrous shoes, and an expansive turban.

Diyar and the men dismounted. Inside a large, tiled hall, the man led them to divans, then motioned to one of his men, who herded out a score of girls, several little older than children.

The slaver stepped up to the first girl and with a flourish, whipped off her woolen gown. "Have you ever seen such a beauty at such an insignificant price."

She stood totally nude. Her black tresses, braided into enormous plaits, were saturated with butter which streamed down her shoulders and breasts, making her shimmer in the wan light.

"Here, girl," he called out, shoving the girl's elbow, "pass in front of the esteemed amir, allow him to see your lovely, round breasts, your shapely loins." His eyes watched Diyar's. "Is she not a beauty, amir? That belly will drop many fine slaves, a man with your sharp eye can tell."

The girl showed no shame but covered her mouth and giggled.

She took a few steps in front of the men and returned. And as she caught the eyes of the other girls, they all burst into nervous laughter.

The slave merchant tugged her hand away from her face, and thrust his thumb into her mouth. "Come, great amir, see for yourself. She is healthy and strong, with a bite like a mule."

Diyar glanced at Kareem who immediately took charge. "First, we need older women. Ones to cook and clean. There will be time for these later."

Diyar saw the look in his men's eyes and added, "True. But, after we have an adequate household staff, we may want to pick several maids as serving girls. This one in particular."

And so, Diyar took up the duties of ruling a palace again. He sent for Abd ar-Rahman and Gouffre to find what state his businesses were in and, using monies from his newly acquired emirate, reestablished his trade connections, commenced again his looms and copy shops.

But mornings were spent on the practice field with his men.

There had been a time when an amir had to wait his turn before drilling his cavalry. Now one could loose an arrow across the hippodrome and not hit a rider. Since the sultan reduced the number of fiefs dedicated to the men, they felt little incentive to practice.

One day Kareem raced onto the field with news. "Master, have you heard? Mangu Timur sent soldiers to Syria to arrest some of the most notable amirs there, including Amir Qipchak, the Viceroy of Damascus. He wanted to appoint more of the sultan's favorites in their stead. They must have been warned because, can you believe it, they rode off and joined Il-Khan Ghazan, the King of the Mongols!"

Mamluk amirs deserting their sultan to fight for the hated Mongols? Was this the end of the sultanate?

He quickly assembled the men and returned to his palace. Until this latest ill-wind blew over, it was best to pull in their heads and remain behind closed gates.

But other amirs did not pull in their heads. Plotting increased. Then one day in December, 1298, the sultan fasted all day. But at sunset, he broke the fast and called the Chief Qadi in for chess. When he sat down to the chess table, he removed his sword and laid it next to him.

The Amir Kurji, a friend of the sultan, entered, and soon the Fortress's Duty Officer for that night, Amir Nougai Karmouni. "Is our lord, the sultan, going to say the evening prayer?" Kurji asked.

"Ah yes, I will do so," the sultan replied, and rose from the chess table.

While Lajeen knelt in prayer, Nougai moved the sultan's sword out of his reach. Instantly, Kurji whipped out his sword and struck, chopping deeply into the sultan's shoulder.

The sultan struggled to reach his sword but, finding it gone, the big man leaped on Kurji and wrestled him to the floor. Nougai drew his sword and slashed the sultan's back. The force of the blow knocked him off of Kurji, and Kurji's men, who had been stationed outside the sultan's chamber, charged in and hacked the hapless sultan to pieces.

News of the murder soon rang out in the night, and people lit torches and ran out into the streets in confusion. Amirs called on Mangu Timur, the sultan's favorite, and persuaded him to go up to the Citadel. Perhaps, they suggested, he might be voted to become the next sultan. But once he had entered the walls of the Fortress, the rebellious amirs cut him down too.

Several of Kurji's men arrived at Diyar's palace with the news, concluding, "And the Amir Kurji wants all the amirs to come to al-Qal'ah now. A new sultan must be chosen. Come alone," and they galloped off to take their message to other amirs.

Come alone? Not if I can avoid it.

With Kareem and several of his veterans, he rode into al-Qal'ah. But in the courtyard in front of the Hall of Audience, tabardariya barred their way, and Diyar had to continue without his men.

In the hall Kurji and Amir Taghji, the man who had actually planned the assassination, stood before the milling amirs. Diyar, with his new title, was announced by the Major Domo in a loud voice to be heard over the confused muttering of the men: "Amir Arda'in Diyar al-Mijiri al-Baybariya."

Kurji stood at the steps leading up to the throne. Seeing Diyar, he strode over, his dark eyes intense with self-importance. "Amir Diyar, the sultan Lajeen appointed you amir arda'in. But now where do your loyalties lie?"

Diyar had survived enough coups to know how to answer. "I will serve faithfully any man the amirs choose."

Kurji spun and returned to stand beneath the throne. His voice rang out. "Men of God, we have rid ourselves of a weak leader and his hated viceroy. Now we must choose a new sultan." He turned to Taghji. "And nowhere in the realm is there a more qualified man than Amir Taghji. Who will join me now in pledging allegiance to Amir Taghji, the natural choice as sultan? I, of course, put myself forth for the post of Viceroy of Egypt. Who is with us?" he concluded, his voice rising, his fist in the air.

To Kurji's amazement, the amirs shuffled, silent and uncertain. Diyar saw the ambition in their eyes. They were searching for ways to advance themselves in the confusion. And despite the urging of both Taghji and Kurji, the meeting broke up without a decision.

A decision still had not been made a few days later when the army, returning from campaigning in Cilicia, camped in Bilbeis, a half a league north-east of the capital. It was led by the Commander-in-Chief, Amir Bektash al-Fakhri, an old general with many years of honorable service. A simple soldier, Bektash was devoted to duty and had never taken part in the many power-struggles which had ripped the capital.

The amirs broke off their debating and rode out to meet Bektash. Taghji, still aspiring to become sultan, rode in front. But when Bektash heard Taghji had arranged the sultan's murder, he let out a roar of rage. One of his officers charged Taghji and split his head apart with his sword. More of Bektash's staff chopped down Kurji, putting a quick end to the two men's dreams of glory.

Then old Bektash, refusing the amirs' entreaty to become their sultan, led the army into al-Qahirah, dismissed them, and adjourned to his home. But the quarreling continued, first one amir and then another vying for power. Now only chaos reigned.

Finally, as senior amirs continued to govern the empire, it was agreed, in order to avoid civil war, to recall the young Malik-al-Nasir Muhammad from Karak. Diyar volunteered his forty for the escort duty and, as he had shown no preferences for any of the factions, was judged to be a safe enough choice.

CHAPTER 35

When Diyar met Prince Muhammad, now thirteen, he found him little changed physically. But he observed a canniness, a cleverness in the boy's eyes. He wondered if he could still beat him at chess—or if he should.

When he saw Diyar, Muhammad called out happily, "Amir, it is wonderful to see you again. Somehow, we have both survived another year."

"May God be praised," Diyar intoned honestly.

Several days later when they approached the walls of the capital, they saw a mob milling about. Diyar took no chances.

"Djanin," he barked to his second-in-command, "I want three squads leading us, one squad following. Let no one approach."

But when the crowd saw the boy, cheers erupted. The people carried flags, and welcome banners streamed over the entrance of the great Gate of Conquests. Inside the gate, bands struck up, creating a cacophony of elation. Banners and crowds lined the entire length of Main Avenue, spilling out the south wall through the gate Bab Zuwaylah.

Once again enthroned in the Hall of Audience, Malik-al-Nasir Muhammad received the oaths of loyalty of the amirs and notables. But Diyar knew, watching the boy-sultan nod to each passing amir, being underage, he had no executive power. And after the ceremonies, Amir Salar, a Mongol, was made regent, and he and Baybars al-Jashnekeer issued orders as if they ruled jointly.

Months past and news leaked out of al-Qal'ah the young monarch was little more than a prisoner of the two ambitious amirs. Though eager to learn how the government functioned, he was ignored. And to keep him from garnering influence, he was given but a pittance for an allowance.

Meanwhile, Salar and Baybars al-Jashnekeer constantly wrangled over the governing of the sultanate. And with the sultanate weakened, dispatches arrived reporting the Mongols were mobilizing. The Il Khan was going to take advantage of the chaos.

War.

Preparations began at once. The prices of horses, camels, weapons and supplies soared. The troops asked Salar and Baybars al-Jashnekeer for a grant to buy their equipment, but the rulers refused, and the army's morale plummeted.

In the Fall of 1299, the army, led by the two amirs with the young sultan in tow, struck out for Damascus. One of the night-stops was at Gaza. The servants were bustling about erecting tents and starting the cooking fires, when a cry of attack rang out, and the evening sun caught the flash of a sword.

An Uwairat Mongol charged Baybars, his sword on high. He wounded the amir, but his blow glanced down and cut the throat of Baybars' horse, killing it. Instantly the amir's bodyguards hacked down the Mongol, but confusion reigned as the khasikiya whipped out their swords and cast about for more assassins.

Now the Uwairats launched an attack on the young sultan's tents, but his mamluks mounted and charged to meet them. They enveloped the Mongols, slashing away, and the rebels fell to the dust in a spray of blood. Surrounded, the remaining Mongols threw down their swords.

But who was behind the rebellion?

"The young sultan," shouted an amir. "Perhaps he planned it." But when the armor-clad amirs burst into the boy's quarters, blood dripping from their swords, the terrified youth gave a simple display of his innocence—he burst into tears.

Outside, a scream rang out from one of Baybars al-Jashnekeer's supporters, "It had to be Salar who wanted to kill the amir," and immediately the two factions squared off at swords' lengths. They were about to charge, when an old amir galloped between them. "Wait, brothers," he cried. "If you want to know who started the rebellion, ask those who started it, ask the heathen Mongols."

A murmur of assent rose from both sides, ropes were found and a group of the Mongols were stretched out in the dirt and beaten until one nodded he would speak.

"The plot was all ours, the Uwairat's," he said in broken Turkish. "Kitbugha brought us into your city, he let us fight with you. Then Lajeen threw him out and put our leaders in chains. We wanted Kitbugha back as sultan. Things were better for us with him."

With a growl, the mamluks fell upon the Uwairats, strangling scores of them on the spot. Then the mamluks rode through the army searching for hiding Mongols, creating more chaos. After four days of confusion, the troops dragged on, their spirits flagging.

A few nights later, as the camp lay sleeping, the horses began quivering nervously and the camels growled with suspicion. Then, with a spiky blaze of lightning and an explosion of thunder that bolted the horses, the heavens opened, and a deluge collapsed on the hapless troops. In the midst of the downpour, a flash flood roared through the camp, rolling up men, horses, camels, and baggage in a wall of water. In the inky darkness, the troops staggered about in blind confusion, pummeled by water, mud, debris, dead and dying animals.

Dawn brought a scene of devastation.

Servants struggled knee deep in mud to find their animals and supplies. Several passed by Diyar's camp dragging a dead camel calf. Exhausted and benumbed, the troops' minds were reduced to only thoughts of fire and dry clothes.

Diyar, mustering his troops, found several had lost everything, horses, supplies and supply camels. He commandeered the horses of their sarrajun, and had the men ride double until they arrived in Damascus and could purchase more mounts.

The army pulled itself together once again and limped on. Then the sky blackened and within moments, the troops were immersed in a stinking, whirring cloud of locusts. The insects caught in the men's eyes, in their nostrils, suffocating them.

Horses bolted, mad with fear. They careened into troops and animals, screaming and kicking at anything that got near, causing pandemonium.

In a panic, the army charged up the road to escape the plaguing insects. Finally free, they were even more exhausted, even more dispirited.

Kareem, usually ready to turn a cheerful face to his master, now muttered, "This campaign is cursed by God and man, sire. Only evil can come of it."

Silently, Diyar agreed.

Soon after the troops straggled into Damascus, refugees from Hims poured through the gates spreading the word the Mongols were coming. Now, whenever the panic-stricken people of Damascus saw a mamluk, they cried out, "You will never defeat the Mongols. They will kill us all."

"For this," Diyar muttered to Djanin, "we ought to leave these people for the Mongols."

His friend nodded. "They deserve worse."

On the 15th of December 1299, with the sultan at its head, the army snaked out of Damascus for Hims. Arab scouts reported the Mongols waited east near Salamiya. At Hims, the men were allowed to rest for three days, but the inactivity did little to revive morale. Then, with the morning sun glowing dully in a cold, glazed sky, the army donned armor, hefted lances, and rode out, the boy-sultan leading them.

At mid-morning, Mongol scouts were spotted ahead,

watching. Messengers from the sultan's advisors dashed through the army with orders. One pounded by Diyar and shouted, "Down lances, use only swords or maces."

Diyar stared at Djanin in disbelief. "We are to make a charge without lances? What can the idiots up there be thinking?"

A bewildered head shake from his lieutenant was the man's only reply. They handed their lances back to the supply servants and drew out swords. They were soldiers. They would do as they were told, but neither had much hope of living through the day.

The army continued to advance until, at Majma al Murooj— "the Meeting of Pastures"—they formed into battle lines. On the right flank rode the Bedouins and the contingents from the cities of Aleppo and Hama. The old campaigner, Amir Bektash, led the mamluk left. With him, rode Akoosh, the "Lion-Killer", and his men.

Suddenly, Baybars al-Jashnekeer was taken ill, and the troops watched as he was ignominiously toted from the battlefield on a litter. That left the regent, Amir Salar, in the center, commanding the whole army.

The Mongols deployed. Their ranks stretched across the dusty plain until out of sight.

Silence fell over the Muslim line. A mare scraped at the ground, impatient for battle.

With the sultan looking on, Salar rode out in front of the troops. "Warriors of God," he cried, "we, the chosen instruments of God, come here today to do His will and to rid the earth of the heathen. Fight well, and the gates of Heavenly Paradise will open wide for you."

Other amirs, following his lead, fronted their troops with words of religious inspiration, some so eloquent as to bring tears to the eyes of their men.

Diyar turned and looked over his men. Their faces, like his, but for the eye holes, were completely covered by mail. Their mighfar, helmets with plume, sat firmly on the mail. They were the men of a wealthy amir and over their armor they wore beautiful silk robes, glistening in the sun.

They waited to see what he might say, but he remained silent, his eyes more eloquent than words: *Do your best.*

The speeches over, it was time for battle. A khasikiya messenger raced back to Diyar. "The Amir Salar orders you appear in front of him immediately," the lad called breathlessly.

"Now what?" Diyar grouched to Djanin. "The men are ready to fight. Why delay?" But he followed the courier up to the front of the ranks.

When their horses stood abreast, Diyar said, "Yes, Sire?"

Salar, his swarthy countenance betraying his Mongolian lineage, leaned close. "You and your men have the solemn task of protecting the sultan. Take him back to the mound there and guard him with your life." His voice dropped. "No matter what happens, he is not to join in a charge—or a retreat." The politician's eyes emphasized these last words. "Now go," he said louder, and pulled on his helmet.

Diyar returned and gathered his men. When he approached the sultan, he said, "Come, Lord, I think you will be able to see better from back here."

Seeing Diyar, the lad's eyes lit up, and he fell in beside him, his mamluks intermingling with Diyar's forty.

Now Salar signaled, and five hundred riders galloped to the front. They carried tubes with buckets of Greek fire. With a shout, the artificers lit the Greek fire. But the fires sputtered out, and the men had to beat a hasty retreat.

Diyar shook his head with disgust. These new weapons would never replace the lance, sword or bow.

The Mongols remained motionless. Their lamellar armor shining like mirrors in the sun, fell to their boot tops. Their mounts, buff-colored Persians, were thoroughbreds, indefatigable.

Now, Il-Khan Ghazan turned to one of his generals. A signal was given, trumpets blared, and ten thousand Mongols on foot streamed out of the ranks of the cavalry, and took up position in front of the army. Instead of the light, composite bow of the mounted warriors, they carried long bows, reaching high above their heads.

At the command, they launched a vast barrage of arrows that blackened the sky. The barrage easily carried the wide distance between the two armies, arcing down mostly into the Bedouins and contingents from Aleppo and Hama on the mamluk right. Horses and men screamed to the ground, mortally wounded. So many horses fell that confusion spread among the troops on the right, and they broke and fell back.

Old Bektash, on the mamluk left, did not hesitate. He bellowed for a charge, and his troops obeyed instantly. They swooped into the Mongol right, screaming and hacking their way into the more numerous Mongols.

Struck by such a berserk attack, the Mongol right buckled and spun to flee in panic. Chased by the frenzied Muslims, they galloped screaming from the battlefield.

Diyar, watching from his vantage point, observed Ghazan turn and wave for a general retreat. But then Amir Qipchak, the former Viceroy of Damascus, now among the Il-Khan's retinue, raced up to him, screaming encouragement.

Reassured, the Il-Khan waved to his generals for a counterattack. He urged his horse forward leading the vanguard.

Salar saw the avalanche of Mongols descending on him and he panicked. He wheeled his horse around, screaming at his bodyguard to let him through. And when the remaining Tower Mamluks saw the frantic retreat of their master, they too bolted.

The retreating army churned away, billows of dust boiling up behind them, obscuring the knoll where Diyar, the sultan and his men stood. The Mongols, blinded by their intensity to catch the fleeing Muslims, pounded past without seeing them.

With the troops roaring by, Diyar knew he had to calm the sultan. He grabbed the reins of the boy's horse. "Do not worry, sire," he shouted. "We will prevail. We always have."

Sultan Malik-al-Nasir Muhammad burst into tears. "O Lord! Let me not be the means of bringing disaster to the Muslims."

Diyar twisted around and signaled his men not to move. The

Mongol long-bowmen, now mounted, were the last to speed after the routed mamluks. Diyar watched, targeted the last archer to ride past, and whipping out his bow, let fly. The archer fell to the ground, an arrow in his neck.

He called Kareem. "Fetch that man's bow."

When the dust cleared, Diyar took a head count. Only his veterans remained. Fatalism had rendered them fearless. They were certain this was to be their final battle.

Diyar released sultan's reins. "Come, sire, we must go."

Fearfully he boy cast about. "But where, the heathen are everywhere. They are surely on all the roads."

"We will not go by the roads."

Muhammad's eyes transversed the wide plain. "But we will get lost."

"We will travel by the stars."

"But without water, we will die as surely as by a heathen's arrow."

"I have friends among the Rueyli Arab tribe. They have given me permission to use their wells. Come, we must get away from this evil place as quickly as possible."

When night approached, the Mongol riders were spread wide afield, chopping down any Muslim they overtook. Ghazan, not wanting to lose control of his troops in the dark, sent out couriers to muster them. By now, the panicked Muslims were racing by Hims, and by the 26th of December, they had reached Damascus. But no sooner had they gained the safety of the city walls, when a cry rang out. The Mongols were right behind them. Now the terrified Muslim troops threw away arms, equipment and baggage, and fled down the coastal plain of Palestine.

The people of Damascus, catching the infection of fear, abandoned their homes and shops, and ran wildly through the city, fighting like wild beasts to get out the gates. Outside, they scattered over the open country, or headed for the mountains. Convicts, abandoned in the city, broke out of the prisons and began looting.

When the country people and mountain tribes encountered the city-dwellers and the fleeing soldiers, vulnerable without weapons, they robbed them without mercy.

In the city, on the morning of the 29th of December, the few men who remained, gathered together and chose two leaders to go and beg mercy of the approaching Il-Khan. They were the Chief Qadi, Muhammad ibn Jumaa, and the Sheik al Islam, Ahmad ibn Taimiya. The two met the Il-Khan two days north of Damascus at Nebk. The Il-Khan slowed his horse, and the Syrians hastily dismounted from their camels and kissed the ground before him.

He paused only long enough to hear their plea. He was only there to destroy the mamluks, and promised no civilians would be hurt. Then he rode on.

But when he reached the walls of the city and had set up camp, he sent troops sweeping south to the countryside around Karak and Jerusalem where they killed and looted without mercy.

Meanwhile, in Damascus, Sanjar al-Mansoori, often called Arjuwash, the mamluk commander of the city's citadel, locked the fortress's gates and refused to surrender to the Mongols. Even when Ghazan called up the traitor Amir Qipchak, the former Viceroy of the city, to give the order, the man would not relent.

The Il-Khan had a decree read out from the roof of the great Umayyad Mosque stating his intentions were only honorable, then had handfuls of gold and silver thrown to the crowd. But still Arjuwash kept the citadel's gates closed.

This enraged the Mongols, and soon the wails of looted men and raped women could be heard throughout the city. And nearly ten thousand citizens were herded together and led off to become slaves.

The city was world famous for the beauty of its mosques and colleges. The Mongols stripped them of their lamps and carpets, then turned them into flaming infernos. Whores and prostitutes were rounded up and driven to the Umayyad Mosque, perhaps the most spectacular mosque in the world. There the Mongols sated their drunken lusts on them, many of the girls dying from the warriors rapacity.

Ibn Taimiya rode to Ghazan's camp to protest, but was not given an audience. The Il-Khan was too drunk to talk. Later, during a sober moment, Ghazan, weary of Arjuwash's obduracy, called for siege machines to be constructed outside the citadel's walls. But the indomitable amir sent out a raiding party and destroyed them as they were being constructed.

Now the Mongols ran amok. People were grabbed on the street and flogged and murdered. Greater and greater amounts of tribute were demanded of the city, and finally three million, six hundred thousand dirhems were paid. More than twenty thousand pack animals, horses and camels, were commandeered to carry off the city's loot, and after a month, Ghazan and his army rode away. The troops of a rival Mongol faction had invaded their territory, and they had to return to defend it.

The Il-Khan left the traitor Qipchak in charge of the city with the title of Governor of Syria. A fellow deserter, the Amir Bektimur, became the Governor of Aleppo, and Ghazan left twenty-four thousand Mongol warriors to help them keep control.

CHAPTER 36

Staying well inland, Diyar's party picked their way over rocky hills and dried lake beds, and on the 7th of January 1300, wearily entered the gates of Qal'at al-Jabal. Day after day, more soldiers staggered in by ones and twos. In all his days as a Royal Mamluk, Diyar had never seen troops in such terrible condition. Dispirited, many wounded, they limped in on any mount they could find, horse, camel, even burros. Many had lost their weapons and armor, trading them for food and water, or discarding them in their panic-filled flight. Some staggered in naked and on foot, stripped and robbed by country-folk.

Immediately the amirs began rebuilding the army, its weaponry, its morale. The clang of hammers once again reverberated from armorers' shops as new armor and weapons took shape. Warriors scoured the countryside for mounts, and the price of horses tripled. Even the poor horses that turned the water-wheels were impressed as chargers.

The amirs, Diyar included, dug into their own treasuries to rebuild their units. This time he recruited as many of the older veterans as he could find, half of his forty being Bahri Mamluks.

When news reached Cairo that Ghazan had returned to Persia, the young sultan, al-Nasir Muhammad, wrote to Qipchak, Bektimur and the other deserters, calling upon them to leave

Damascus and return to the capital and submit to the sultan's rule. Without hesitation, they all abandoned their posts and set out for al-Qal'ah. With their leaders gone, the Mongols in Damascus hastened to join up with their main army now in Aleppo.

The gallant Amir Arjuwash, who had held the citadel of Damascus against the Mongol army, assumed control of the city. The first order he gave was for the Great Mosque to be cleaned out and services of gratitude held.

Spring came and Salar and Baybars al-Jashnekeer set out with the army to reclaim Syria. Muhammad accompanied them with Diyar and his forty, who had become his permanent bodyguard. A column of swift warriors were sent on ahead and surprised the Mongol garrison at Aleppo. All caught were instantly slaughtered.

In Damascus, anyone who had collaborated with the Mongols was tortured and killed. Local tribes who had plundered the fugitives were made to return the loot.

The Druse of Lebanon, a secret religious sect, had plundered many of the fleeing Muslim soldiers. A column of mamluks rode out to confront them, but the Druse retreated to the mountains. There, with thousands of archers hidden in precipitous passes, they delayed the column with deadly ambushes. But they could not hold out forever, and finally a peace was concluded and part of the loot returned.

That fall, intelligence reports flew to the capital stating that Ghazan intended to attack Syria once again. In preparation for the campaign, extra-heavy taxes were imposed on the city folk, and farmers had their crops confiscated.

Resentment among the populace boiled into anger. Diyar, riding into town to inspect his businesses, was set upon by an angry shop keeper. "Yesterday you ran away from the enemy, now today you want to rob us. You are brave enough against civilians, but your courage fails against the Mongols."

Diyar was shocked. As a Royal Mamluk, and especially an amir, he had never witnessed such disrespect. In his entire career as a soldier, he had never run from an enemy. But he said nothing, and rode on. He knew the reasons behind the citizen's taunting.

The man was underpaid, overtaxed, and afraid—more than enough reasons for hostility.

Once again the hapless citizens of Aleppo and Hama abandoned their homes to the oncoming Mongols and plodded south to Damascus. This time, Ghazan entrusted the command of the Mongol army to Kutlugh Shah, who advanced by forced marches to occupy as much territory as possible before the mamluk army arrived.

When the Mongol army approached Damascus, it sent out scouts to observe the city. Many of the city folk, spying the scouts, fled in fear. Throughout the night, prayer vigils were held in the city's mosques, and the next morning, the scouts had disappeared.

The mamluk army left Cairo and arrived at Shaqhab, a days ride south of Damascus. They made camp below a rocky ridge near the main road.

Kutlugh Shah and the Mongols took up a position along the ridge above them. Although the Mongols occupied the strategically superior position, the mamluks controlled a geographical feature of great importance: a stream of cool water that ran through their ranks.

In the center of the Muslim army stood the young sultan with Diyar and his men as bodyguard.

The Muslims were still taking up their battle positions, when Kutlugh Shah, who commanded at least fifty thousand men, led a charge of ten thousand down the hill against the mamluk right wing.

Through a hailstorm of arrows they raced. When they reached the mamluk line, they struck a wall of lances, broke through, and fell on the Muslims with sword and mace. But the mamluks held and then beat them back, and the Mongols retreated up the ridge.

The sultan's Commander-in-Chief called for a quick casualty count and found that a thousand mamluks had been killed, including six senior amirs.

Now the Mongols attacked the center ranks, where Salar and the Tower Mamluks waited. As the screaming warriors galloped into range, the mamluks unleashed a hail of arrows. Waves of horses, shrieking in pain, fell forward into the dust. But on surged the Mongols, through the lances, into the thick of the army, hacking and slashing.

The mamluks fought back, sometimes having two and three horses slaughtered under them. The Mongols withdrew, regrouped and attacked again.

Diyar, guarding the young sultan deep in the center ranks, itched to get into the fray. He pulled from his saddle the Mongol's long bow he had retrieved at the disastrous Battle of Hims, stood in his stirrups and fired into the Mongols' ranks, aiming for officers. A cheer rang out from the sultan's bodyguard when a Mongol rolled from the saddle with one of their leader's long arrows jutting from his armor.

The mamluks appeared to be weakening but the day was drawing to a close and Kutlugh Shah led his men back up to the ridge. He looked back to seem many of the rear ranks of the Muslims retreating, he felt confident he had carried the day.

Throughout the night the mamluk drums boomed, calling the stragglers back to the fold. The amirs rode through their ranks, reorganizing and encouraging their men. And when dawn broke over the rugged landscape, and Kutlugh Shah strutted out the door of his tent, he saw to his rage the entire mamluk army stood in perfect battle array, each commander standing proudly before his unit.

Now the whole of the Mongol army poured down the ridge. While the rest of the mamluk army stood fast, the Royal Mamluks trotted forth to meet them, leaned into a gallop, and slammed into the Mongol center.

All morning the battle raged. When Diyar spotted a weaknesses in the Mongol's attack, he grimaced with frustration. How he wanted to be up there.

Suddenly the young sultan, no longer able to resist, dashed past him, his sword flashing in the sun. "I must fight. They need my help."

"Come back, sire," Diyar cried, and kicked his mount after him, the bodyguard close on his horse's heels.

MAMLUK

A Mongol commander, seeing the charging young sultan immaculate in his white-silk robe, shouted to his troops, and they cut through the mamluk line to get to the boy. If the mamluks' leader could be killed, perhaps so too could their spirit.

Diyar and his men caught up with the sultan, but the Mongols hurled themselves into his unit, overwhelming it. Diyar, surrounded and hacking away on both sides with a sharpened mace, fought savagely to protect the sultan. He fell the Mongol on his right, and attempted to ride off the one on his left by wheeling his horse into him.

But when he whirled back to the sultan, a blow struck his back. He leaned away, but the man was behind his left shoulder. The next blow crashed against the back of his skull. A familiar pain shot through his brain, terrible in its promise, and he slumped forward semiconscious.

A looped rope snaked out, pinning his arms. He was wrenched from the saddle, and crashed to the ground.

A hiss in his ears, then, as awareness dawned, the roar of battle crescendoed over him. He opened his eyes. Pain racked his head, forcing bile into his throat. Horses surrounded him, rearing and stamping. In a daze, he slowly cast around for his mace, but it had disappeared in the dust. He tried to sit up, but the rope yanked him back.

The Mongols were fighting their way out of the melee. Another blow whirled down, knocking his helmet away, and smashing him flat. Another lasso dropped around his neck, and the two Mongols, galloped up the slope, dragging him behind.

Mamluk arrows plummeted down all around them. One of the riders dragging Diyar careened away, an arrow protruding from his back. But the other rode on, hauling him over the rocky ground.

He passed out, strangled by the ever-tightening noose.

An ear-ringing slap woke him, followed by another, and another. A vicious kick to his side cracked once-fractured ribs.

He fought for breath and struggled to sit up but found thongs bound his hands and feet, thongs wet with his blood. Stripped of his armor and clothes, he lay naked and dirty in the dust. He rolled to his knees, and the young Mongol warrior slapped him down again.

The man, panting from his exertion, started to kick him again, when a voice stopped him. An older warrior, sitting in the shade of his horse, waved at him to stop.

Diyar squinted using the one eye which had not been kicked shut. He did not know the language, but he understood the words. "Save your strength, boy," the old man must be saying. "You are going to need it."

The young man grunted with frustration, moved away a pace, and dropped wearily into his mount's shadow, balefully eyeing his prisoner.

Diyar glanced around. All about him on the ridge top, men sat or lay, many with blood staining their armor. Their helmets were off, and sweat coursed down their faces. They heaved with exertion. The heads of their horses hung in exhaustion. Nearby, two screaming warriors fought over the last few drops from a water bag.

Then it came to him. *They are dying of thirst*, he thought with a glimmer of hope.

The sun beat down on them, and the Mongols stared with frenzied eyes at the cool stream below that flowed through their enemy's ranks. Diyar knew from experience nothing creates a greater thirst than hand-to-hand combat. And if these men did not get water soon, they would perish. He kept his head down and waited.

Night. No moon. Along the ridge, a few safety fires fought the darkness, but by the middle of the night, these were neglected. The spent soldiers snored uneasily, too weary even to keep watch.

Diyar steeled himself to the shredding of his skin, and scraped the thongs binding his wrists over a sharp rock. Finally they broke and as if in sleep, he rolled over, reaching for the thongs around his ankles.

He freed his feet, rose to a crouch, and stole to the edge of the ridge and over. He started to run down the slope, but pain shot through his side where the fractured ribs floated, and he sprawled headlong into the rocky soil.

He pulled to his feet, wedged his arm in his side and, holding it with the other hand, hobbled on.

Near the bottom of the hill, a cautious call met him. He answered with his name, and in moments a torch flared, and a horseman galloped out. As he was jerked up behind the rider, he could not keep from crying out in anguish. But the man did not pause as he sped back to the safety of his lines.

The pain in his side made breathing a torture, but he croaked out an order, "Take me to the Commanders' tent, and be quick."

As soon as he called out his name to the sentries guarding the big, stripped tent, Muhammad bolted out. He peered up into Diyar's face, his eyes pleading. "Are you all right, my friend? I was so worried. If you had been killed because of my recklessness, I would have never forgiven myself. How did you ever escape?" He took off his qaba and wrapped it around Diyar's naked shoulders.

He saw that Diyar could not stand erect. "You are hurt." He turned to a guard. "Bring the Royal Surgeon immediately," and the man leapt on his horse and set out at a gallop.

Salar, Baybars al-Jashnekeer, and several Amirs of a Thousand also came to the tent's doorway. To their questions, he raised a weary hand. "It is not important how I got away, the important thing is, the Mongols are dying. Without water, they perish. I doubt if they will survive another day if they do not gain the stream."

"He is right," spoke up Salar. "We must keep them from the stream."

Many of the amirs nodded in agreement, determined to hold.

But Diyar spoke up. "No, sire. Only one thing possesses their mind: the stream. Let them gain it, and as they drink, they will make perfect targets."

Old Bektash nodded. "He is right. It is a good plan."

Now all the amirs assented. Couriers dashed out to alert the troops to line up behind the stream.

As the nascent sun tinged the ridge, the alarm rang out. The great army of the Mongols were charging down the hill en masse, their all-consuming thirst spurring them on. Pell-mell they hurled themselves into the water, men and horses trampling each other, all with but one thought: to drink.

Now the mamluks fell upon them, hacking and slashing. In moments, the stream ran crimson with blood. Those Mongols that could scattered, pursued by the triumphant Muslims. The war was won.

So exhausted and dispirited were many of the Mongols, they simply dropped their weapons, sat down and silently awaited to be killed. They even allowed country-folk to pick up their weapons and kill them. Thus, the great majority of Mongols were killed, not in the battle, but in the flight. Less than a tenth of them reached home.

When reports arrived at his palace in Persia of the magnitude of the catastrophe, Il-Khan Ghazan was struck dumb. And when Kutlugh Shah staggered into his court, the enraged Il-Khan scourged him with abuse, then ordered his execution.

The Il-Khan's advisors pleaded for him to be merciful, and Ghazan temporized. Still, he ordered everyone in the great audience hall to pass by the defeated general and spit in his face.

Ramadan, the month when Muslims fast during the day but can eat after sundown, had just begun at the beginning of the battle. For the rest of the month, the sultan remained in Damascus, fasting days, but spending each evening in joyful festivities. In his jubilation, he did not forget Diyar. He gave him a fine apartment in the Piebald castle where he could mend his broken ribs. And soon servants arrived with not only a new robe of honor in his favorite color, the color of his unit, deep blue, but a beautifully crafted suit of armor to replace the one lost at the battle.

On the 23rd of May 1303, the sultan, with Diyar leading his honor guard, left the jubilant city enroute to Cairo.

In contrast, Ghazan never recovered from the shame of the disaster. He brooded about it for months, and finally died. Too soft, perhaps, to be a powerful warlord, he was the first Il-Khan to attempt to justly govern Persia.

Not long after, on July 21st, word reached Cairo, Oljaitu had become Il-Khan, and the ever-nervous population wondered what kind of foe he would be.

CHAPTER 37

Four years after the Battle of Shaqhab, on March 10, 1308, Sultan Al-Nasir Muhammad, now twenty-three, departed Cairo, apparently on a pilgrimage to Mecca. A number of amirs accompanied him, their bands playing stoutly.

Vast crowds turned out, weeping and calling down blessings on his head as he and his entourage passed through the city, for the Egyptians had taken the young man to their hearts. They knew that, although the land was growing richer by the day, Salar and Baybars al-Jashnekeer kept the young sultan penniless.

When the procession reached the fortress of Karak, the sultan called the amirs to its audience chamber. "I have decided to renounce the title of Sultan."

A murmur of surprise rolled over the assemblage and he continued. "I intend to remain here at peace at Karak where I spent many happy days as a child. Therefore..." and he motioned for a qadi carrying a silver tray with a scroll on it, "...I am sending this document of abdication to the regents in Cairo."

He turned to Diyar standing at the left of his throne with the commander of the garrison, "Would you see they get this?"

Muhammad stood. "And, since I am no longer your sultan, would you see this throne is taken away," and he limped through the shocked amirs and out of the room.

When it was learned at Qalat al-Jabal Muhammad had

abdicated, a power struggle immediately broke out between Salar and Baybars al-Jashnekeer. Baybars proved victorious, and one of his first acts was to appoint Malik-al-Nasir Muhammad governor of Karak. In turn, Muhammad requested Diyar be made his deputy. But Baybars al-Jashnekeer opposed the idea.

Diyar sat with Muhammad in the great hall of Karak's fortress. The prince handed him the message. "He orders you and your men back to the capital. He will allow me to stay here, but without power or influence. What are you going to do?"

"I am a Royal Mamluk and must follow orders." Then a twinkle glinted in his eyes. "But the order does not say when to return."

A hint of a smile played across Muhammad's thin lips. They understood each other. Both knew Baybars al-Jashnekeer was not the cleverest of men. They would just have to wait and see what he would do next.

Soon another message arrived, demanding Karak's fortress commander seize all of Muhammad's money and horses, and to disarm his mamluks.

"It is clear," Diyar said to Muhammad, "he fears you will try to regain the throne. Now, it is my turn to ask you. What will you do?"

"As a loyal subject of the sultan, I too will comply with his wishes—at least partially." He smiled. He was beginning to enjoy the game. But it was a game that could only end in someone's death.

A camel train soon snaked out of the fortress carrying part of the ex-sultan's wealth, horses and troops, but Diyar and his forty remained.

No sooner had Baybars inspected Muhammad's possessions, than he sent a message demanding Muhammad's entire holdings be transported immediately.

Diyar received a summons to come to Muhammad's apartment where the ex-sultan motioned for him to join him on his silk couch. He then waved his hand, and the room emptied of his entourage. It was the first time since the two hunted together that Diyar was alone with the young man.

Muhammad's eyes burned with a quiet intensity. "My friend, would you remain loyal to me if I attempted to once again ascend to the throne?"

He did not hesitate. "I pledge my allegiance to you, Malik-al-Nasir, and we will prevail, if it be God's will."

Muhammad nodded. "Good. I want you to return to the capital—travel in secret—and contact all amirs who you are absolutely certain would be sympathetic to our cause. I am also sending out couriers, men whom I believe to be loyal, to the governors of the other provinces, to probe their affiliations. If they, too, are loyal, it will make my ascension easier. Now go and, if God wills it, we will succeed."

When, dressed as Arabs, Diyar and Kareem slipped into Cairo, they found the city astir with unrest. They paused at a sweet meats cart and while Diyar kept his blue eyes shaded by his khafakiya, Kareem said to the vendor, "What is amiss? The whole city seems to be buzzing."

"Oh," the little Egyptian moaned, "it is a calamity. The blessed Nile has refused to rise." He dropped his voice. "It is this new sultan, Baybars al-Jashnekeer. God is against his disposing of our beloved Malik-al-Nasir, would that he would return."

Diyar and Kareem's eyes met. This calamity—the lack of inundation—though ruinous for the populace, could prove providential for them.

For the next few days the two darted from one sympathetic faction to another, and soon several hundred mamluks and their sarrajun had slipped out of the capital and joined al-Nasir in Karak. Meanwhile al-Nasir was receiving declarations of loyalty from the governors of Aleppo, Hama, Safad and Jerusalem. When the Viceroy of Damascus hesitated, saying, "Good people of Damascus! You have no sultan but Malik-al-Muzaffar Baybars al-Jashnekeer," the amirs and judges shouted him down.

"No! No!" they cried. "We have no sultan but Malik-al-Nasir Muhammad," and sent word of their loyalty to Muhammad at Karak.

Soon a courier informed Diyar that Muhammad wanted him back at Karak, so he and Kareem pounded the road north again. There they found him preparing to leave.

"We will ride north to Damascus," he told Diyar. "Many mawali have joined us and we should meet more there."

By the time they approached the city, so many amirs, each with his band and banners, had come out and linked up with them, Muhammad's entourage had become a triumphal procession. They entered the city to find royal colors decorating the streets, and carpets spread before the feet of their horses.

The Viceroy of Damascus waited to meet him. Though dressed in a ceremonial robe, he carried his grave winding sheet under his arm. He had backed Baybars al-Jashnekeer, and now stood ready to die for his loyalty. But al-Nasir greeted him graciously, forgave him, and before all, reconfirmed him as the city's viceroy.

Now Malik-al-Nasir's procession turned south to Cairo. As it neared, officers and men of the city deserted their posts and rode out to join it.

Baybars al-Jashnekeer and Salar, seeing resistance to the popular young monarch was hopeless, abandoned all opposition. While Salar remained in the capital preparing a huge banquet in honor of Muhammad's return, Baybars, accompanied by all his mamluks, went to meet him.

Diyar stood near al-Nasir in front of his royal tent when Baybars rode up at the head of his army. In front of the young man, Baybars jumped from his horse and knelt.

"O, Malik-al-Nasir, may your reign be glorious. I pledge you my complete and total loyalty. May you use me in anyway you see fit in the service God." Then he looked up to hear his fate.

All watched to see what the new sultan's first action would be.

Muhammad observed him quietly for a moment. "Baybars al-Jashnekeer," he said in a high, thin voice, "I want to thank you for your pledge of loyalty, and I am inclined to treat you leniently." Then his voice hardened. "But I can not forgive, nor forget, the poor treatment you showed my mother and myself, the many times while I was growing to a man we asked for better food and clothing, and the many times you refused. For myself, it mattered little, but for the sultana of the great al-Malik-al-Mansoor Qalaoon, such treatment was unforgivable," and he waved his hand for Baybars to get from his sight.

Baybars al-Jashnekeer, shamed in front of all the amirs and men, mounted stone-faced and, followed by only two servants, rode to the back edges of the congregation. That night he was quietly strangled in his tent.

So, for the third time, al-Malik-al-Nasir Muhammad became sultan of Egypt and Syria. Salar was first given the post of Governor of the small town of Shobek, south of Karak, but later al-Nasir had second thoughts. He did not want the Mongol and his men to desert to the Il-Khan, so he persuaded him to return to the capital. There he was imprisoned and executed.

Salar had gone from the lowest of circumstances to the highest only to fall to the depths again. He had been taken as a prisoner by Qalaoon in the wars against the Mongols. The sultan had taken a fancy to him and advanced him until he rose to become the Viceroy of Egypt.

When al-Nasir's officers went to confiscate Salar's property, they found many millions of gold dinars, and incalculable wealth in jewels, art treasures, textiles, horses, camels and slaves.

The executions of Salar and Baybars al-Jashnekeer shot fear into many of the amirs' hearts, especially those who had pledged loyalty to them when they ruled. And rightfully so. In one day, the new sultan had thirty amirs arrested. After a lifetime of captivity in one fortress or another, the young sultan had learned what it took to keep the ambitious amirs in line: fear.

But the sultan could also be generous to his favorites. He sent for Diyar.

The last time Diyar had been the Citadel's private apartments of the sultan, the ascetic, Lajeen, had sat on the white, silk, divan. Now, Muhammad strode to meet him.

"Come, my friend, it is time to reward the faithful. You have saved my life more than once. Now it is my turn to repay you. I want you to become my Royal Taster."

The Royal Taster! Though the office was ceremonial, it was one of close intimacy with the ruler. It not only meant he stood next to the sultan at banquets, or sat, as commanded, but it meant he could speak to him at any time, offer his opinions, influence him, without being asked. It was a post of high honor and carried with it the promotion to Amir Muqaddam, or Muqaddam Alf— Amir of a Hundred.

Diyar paused.

Al-Nasir's quick eyes saw the hesitation and smiled. "What? You do not want the office? You hurt me, my friend."

"Malana, You know I would not do that for any office. Still, I had hoped..."

"I know," al-Nasir interrupted pleasantly. "You had hoped for the position of Commander-in-Chief."

"Yes, Lord. From there I could influence the training of the corps of cadets."

"We have talked about this before. I realize you do not approve of the way I would reward the young cadets when they first arrive in the tibaqs, how I award them with robe, armor and horse at the beginning of their training instead of at its completion like you were. But you see, these poor lads, when they receive such a wealth of gifts, it makes them instantly loyal. And I am more interested in their loyalty than their training."

Diyar saw there could be no compromising with the sultan, so he said, "Sire, if you are truly sincere about rewarding me, may I be given the Governorship of Karak. Like you, I spent many happy days there."

Surprised, the sultan paused. "You mean you would want to be sent away from the capital? I do not understand."

"I think it is an important post, one of the last fortresses before the capital, and deserves a strong defense. I would like that honor." *And besides*, he thought, *that way I can train my men the way I want, without interference.*

The sultan nodded. "Yes, I can see why you would want the post." Though Diyar stood nearly a head taller, the sultan clapped him on the shoulder. "And you shall have it. But do not be surprised if I send for you now and again. I like to see the faces of my friends around me. I have had little opportunity in the past."

So Diyar al-Mijiri al-Baybariya, 56, became Governor of Karak and the surrounding countryside. When he had graduated to become a Royal Mamluk, his fief brought him about thirteen hundred dinars a year, as an amir ashara, over nine thousand dinars, as an amir al-tablaqhana, over thirty-six thousand, and now as a amir of hundred, and Viceroy of Karak, he made several times more than that. His fiefs in the Egyptian countryside included ten villages, his businesses and trading brought him far more.

After taking over the governor's palace, Diyar contacted Mijir al-Din, his first owner. Now in his seventies, the old slaver still had agents combing the steppes for hardy, young boys and girls who wanted better lives. Soon there arrived bright, young slaves ready and willing to be trained—Diyar's way.

Meanwhile, he made sure he received reports on the activities of his new master, Sultan Muhammad. For his new palace in Qal'at al-Jabal, Muhammad razed the pavilions of Qalaoon and the first sultan Baybars, and erected a new pavilion whose design was borrowed from the fabulous Qasr al-Ablaq, the Striped Palace in Damascus. This palace, actually pavilions of huge proportions linked by covered passageways, contained one enormous reception hall with a high, vaulted ceiling—with two more lofty halls, three stories high, above it!

To grace the main iwan, al-Nasir had 32 colossal columns of Aswan red granite removed from some forgotten Pharaonic temple, and hauled up to al-Qal'ah. Above these columns curved black-and-yellow stone arches.

If al-Nasir was feared by the amirs, he was loved by the people. In captivity, he had spent much thought on how to improve the realm, and now began promoting public works, improving roads, irrigation systems and public buildings.

He took a strong interest in how the administration of the government ran, diligently checking accounts and maintaining files and records. He started traveling throughout the sultanate to investigate how it was being governed by the provincial governors, often stopping at Karak, where he and Diyar had long discussions on how to improve the well-being and prosperity of their subjects.

As the Muhammad acquired new mamluks, he made it a point to know each by name and their histories. He possessed a deep affection for fine horses, and ordered a huge stud farm built where he housed three thousand pampered mares, keeping a stud-book on each.

Also, perhaps because of his humiliating confinement, he showed a sincere consideration for the people he dealt with daily: the officials, the soldiers, even the grooms and stable boys, the men who looked after his hawks, the cooks and servants of the palace.

Unlike the excesses shown by some of the sultans, he soon displayed an almost puritanical fanaticism about his morals. He always spoke using the proper etiquette—indeed, it was his politeness as a lad which first attracted Diyar to him—and he was never heard to swear or use a deprecating word.

In a court which was growing more pronounced in its gorgeous display, he maintained restraint in his dress, never wearing silk, jewels or gold, but a simple cotton tunic.

In strict Islamic practice, he vehemently opposed the imbibing of alcohol, and any amir found doing so was instantly banished from the court. Equally strict in his sexual morals, he had all brothels in the city closed, again exiling any who was found guilty of improprieties.

On the other hand, he loved beautiful things around him, including odalisques, whom he adorned with pearls, gold bangles and gold sandals, and insisted they have silks for their clothes and beds.

In Karak, Diyar's life settled into a comfortable pattern of tending the needs of his people, training his mamluks, and playing polo with his officers. One evening, as he relaxed with a book in his apartments in the Governor's palace, Kareem entered with a decanter of sweetened orange juice. He fussed about the divan until finally Diyar laid down the book with a sigh. "What?"

"Master, I am troubled."

"So I see. What is it?"

"You have a large harem, but no one in it. Gorucu, 'go-betweens', appear at our gate, sent by other amirs who have beautiful daughters. But you ignore them. You should speak to these old women when they call."

He shook his head. "I went through that once. I will not do it again."

"But, Master, think of the women. Remember what it says in our beloved Koran: 'The good wife has a chance of eternal happiness only if it is her husband's will. The fortunate fair, who has given pleasure to her master, will have the privilege of appearing before him in paradise. Like the crescent moon, she will preserve all her youth and beauty until the end of time.' Now, Master, would you keep some willing, young ray-of-the-moon from eternal paradise?"

"It is also written, when wives enter the front gate, peace flees out the back. Now give me peace. It is unseemly for you to be speaking to your master of such things."

Kareem had been in too many battles with his master to be cowed. "But you do not even call for an odalisque. I worry about you."

Diyar picked up his book. "Worry not. My life is quiet, and if it is God's will the sultan lives long, it is without threat. I want to keep it that way."

The superstitious Arab glanced at his master, comfortably reading, and suppressed a shiver. Life had shown him whenever one is least expecting, the worst happens.

CHAPTER 38

The elderly man striding into Diyar's audience hall looked like a wealthy, Arab merchant. He wore silk robes and soft, red boots. Merchant he was, but hardly Arab. The gleaming, blue turban topping his head indicated that he was a Christian.

Gouffre, Comte de Perros-Guirec, nearly eighty but still upright and strong, bowed in greeting. "O great amir, how good it is to see you again. All I have is yours," which was almost true.

"It is good to see you again, old friend," Diyar said. "Come, we will go where we can speak more intimately."

In an airy, high-ceilinged room, where soft light filtered through several tiers of latticed windows onto warm, cream-colored walls, the two reposed on an alcoved divan.

"When you said you had information you could only relay in person," Diyar continued, "I knew it had to be important. What is this information?"

Pensive, Gouffre fell silent, and Diyar waited patiently. Finally, the old count said, "First, I must tell you something about myself. You are the first person I have told this to, though there may be some record of it still in al-Qal'at. When you met me in prison, a document of death awaited me in the prison governor's office. It had sat there since my capture. At that time, Amir Aibek, when he became sultan, sent his agents to talk to me. They said, if I did not want die, I would have to become his eyes in prison. I thought my people would some day return and rescue me so, to keep alive, I passed on bits of information to the prison commander. They were in code, and were supposed to be forwarded on to the sultan's office in al-Qal'at. I do not know if they were, but every month, I received a small allowance. With this money, I not only kept alive, but created a network of friends throughout the prison. When some of these men were released, they occasionally gave me information which I passed on.

"After you had me released, and our business started to grow, I remained in contact with a number of these men. These friends have helped me in anticipating problems as well as opportunities in our business. Now one of my sources has informed me someone of influence has approached the 'Old Man of the Mountains' and has paid for your assassination."

Assassination! What every man of power in the sultanate feared.

Nothing in Diyar's face betrayed his thoughts. "Do you know who has paid for my death, or when it is to occur?"

"I am sorry, sire, this is all the information I have so far. Usually, as you know, an attack is by only one man. But if he who is to be murdered is high enough placed, there may be more than one assassin. This is all I have to tell you, except, for friendship's sake, please be careful."

After the count left Diyar sat quietly. Somewhere a hidden blade awaited him. No bodyguard was strong enough to protect a man at all times from a killer. Unless he stayed locked behind his walls and never went out, he would be at risk.

Diyar led the small procession out from the governor's palace. The late spring sun glanced off of their silk tunics. Below the city, the valley running to Yam Hamelah—the Dead Sea—was a green carpet of grain. On Diyar's left rode his Master of Horse. Their sarrajun followed, Kareem behind Diyar.

Unlike many amirs who never rode among the people without an ostentatious show of soldiers, Diyar preferred to be accompanied by just a squad of mamluks, two leading with the amirs' banners. The streets of the fortress town were narrow, and a large contingency of riders shouldering aside the merchants and shoppers would be disruptive and resented.

As viceroy, Diyar held sway over his own court, a smaller version of the court of Cairo. But unlike many viceroys who reveled in court pomp and showy ceremony, he preferred to spend as much time as he could each day on the exercise field. Afternoons were often abandoned to rough matches of polo.

The procession made its way to the stables. Located inside the city's lower walls, these great, long tunnels of stalls followed the walls as they rolled over the uneven ground. The fortress of Karak could house several thousand men, which in time of war would triple with halaqa.

At the stables, pages ran out to hold their horses. The Stable Master hurried out, and Diyar slid down and said, "I would like to inspect the mares which arrived from Sheik Ibn al-Hazas."

"Yes, sire. They are midway down on the left, stalls twenty-one through thirty-one."

Diyar approached the stable opening when he was struck by a sense of foreboding. He paused, then turned to the Master of Horse, "Get the mares documents." And to the Stable Master, "And you bring the tack book so we can become acquainted with them."

To Kareem and the Amir's sarrajun, he said. "See about getting us cool drink. The rest of you wait here."

Alone, he entered the dimly lit building. Other than a stable hand mucking out a stall, only horses moved in the stable. Diyar passed the youth without a glance, walked several steps, then spun, whipping out his sword. The stable hand was right behind him, a dagger in his hand. Diyar plunged his sword deep into the youth's stomach.

The young man slipped to the floor, but Diyar left his sword in his belly. He did not want him to die just yet. He bent over him. "Who sent you?"

Hatred twisted the youth's handsome features. He tried to spit at the face above him, but was too weak, and the spittle dribbled off his cheek. A spasm of pain shook him and he grimaced, tears trickling from the corners of his eyes. "I came so close," he whispered.

A look of disgust came over the older man's face. "You have no worries now. Paradise is your destination."

"But I wanted revenge, revenge for what you did to my mother."

"And who was your mother?"

A sneer tugged the man's mouth. "You probably do not remember, you have raped so many."

"True, but tell me, you have little time left, who was she?"

Kareem entered the end of the stable, cup in hand. When he saw Diyar on his knees with his sword buried in the bowels of a floored man, he dropped the cup and his sword leaped to hand. He called over his shoulder, "Amir, more swords," and continued in, cautiously searching the stalls as he came.

The young man's voice dropped to a whisper. "It was Acre… the Countess Cythire… I am the result of your unholy union." He tried to smile. "Congratulations, old man, you have just killed your own son."

The youth's face twisted with pain. He tore the sword from his stomach. The blade shredded his palms, but he did not feel it. His last breath rasped from his throat, and he relaxed into death.

More men pounded up. Diyar stood, retrieved his sword, wiping it off on the dead man's shirt. "Search him," he said to Kareem, "and bring his blade." He turned to the Stable Master. "And I want to know how this man came to you."

Once again in sunlight, he said to his Master of Horse, "I will not be riding today. I have work to do."

Kareem strode up. "He had nothing, sire."

"I thought not."

"There is one thing, sire."

"Yes?"

"The blade..." He handed it Diyar. "Your name is inscribed on it."

Diyar hefted the tapered weapon. "Hm. Good balance." He tucked it into his belt. "Since it was for me and has my name on it, I will keep it." He shot Kareem a steely look. "Come, you have some questions to answer about this whole matter."

MAMLUK

CHAPTER 39

Diyar, followed by Kareem and an amir of forty and his men, passed through the great South Gate of Damascus. He sent a pair of mamluks riding to the office of the city's viceroy. As a visiting governor, protocol required he inform the bureau of his presence. Then he led the way to the Umayyad Mosque, passing through its south gate to the coppersmith bazaar, thence to a small palace nearby.

When the bowwab had opened the palace gate, a stocky, young man, dark and handsome, strode out to greet them. He wore a long shirt and qaba of fine, white, Indian muslin. His turban, according to regulations, was yellow indicating he was a Jew.

He bowed effusively. "O Great Amir! Welcome, welcome, and a thousand times welcome. We are honored to have this visit. Please come in out of the sun and refresh yourself. Your visit must be long or I shall feel great sorrow."

Diyar and his men dismounted and entered the coolness of his high-ceilinged rooms. They sat on divans while Diyar's men spread out along the wall. Servants hurried in with juices.

"Thank you, Ibn al-Ibrahim, but I want to be on the road back to Karak as soon as possible. Did you find anything out for me?"

Ibn al-Ibrahim was Diyar's trade representative in Damascus. Much of the oriental trade which moved up the Red Sea, either water-born, or on land through Mecca, flowed through Damascus, and Diyar took advantage of it. But competition in the beautiful city was fierce, and he needed someone with a shrewd eye and quick wit. Ibn al-Ibrahim was such a man.

As a boy, Ibn had started as a clerk in a stall selling fine copperware, tried to expand, but was blocked because he lacked influential patronage. The amirs he approached thought him too young, too brash.

Not Diyar. He gave Ibn al-Ibrahim all the backing he needed to start a truly international trading house. His instructions were simple: "Be cunning, be clever. but if you cheat me, I will kill you."

Al-Ibrahim leaned forward and spoke confidentially. "I did, master. The woman you seek died nearly two years ago. She labored for many years for a gold merchant who died about the same time. Though he was a son of Israel, I am ashamed to say he was less than a pleasant person, wasting his money on wine and whores. Though at one time rich, he left his poor widow nothing. She now subsists as a 'bundle woman', one who sells cheap trinkets to harems. Perhaps it is God's retribution, because rumor has it she is a woman of evil temper and complaining ways. I am afraid the woman you seek could not have had a very pleasant life, but perhaps now she has found peace."

Diyar finished his drink and stood. "Take me to this 'bundle-woman'."

"But, Lord," the merchant protested, "It is unseemly one of your great importance should go to her room. I will simply send for her."

"No. I want to see where the dead woman lived."

Ibn al-Ibrahim on a quick-footed burro whose soft hair was nearly as white as the Jew's muslin, led the way. Diyar and his men followed ducking projecting meshrebiyehs.

At a tiny walkway between a row of stalls and a high wall, Ibn al-Ibrahim slid off his burro. "The old woman's place is down here."

Diyar glanced at the amir in charge of his bodyguard, and the man quickly motioned for a pair of warriors to lead the way. The powerful warriors had to twist sideways down the narrow walk. Ibn al-Ibrahim and Diyar followed, engulfed by the stench of boiling onions and stale urine.

At an open doorway, al-Ibrahim called out, and presently a stooped crone draped in black appeared.

"Old woman," he said, "a great amir, Rukn al-din Diyar al-Mijiri al-Baybariya, the Viceroy of Karak, has deigned to call on you. Will you invite us in?"

Confusion and fear leaked into her rheumy eyes, and she backed in, bowing even lower. "Great sirs, I have little to offer you. When my husband was alive, ours was the finest gold shop in Damascus, but now I have nothing. Perhaps a cup of cool water to sooth your throats on a dusty day. My daughter is just getting it." She cast around. "Now where is that lazy girl?" she said querulously. "Just when one needs her she is always gone. I know she will be back soon. Perhaps…"

Her voice trailed off, then she reached for a shabby bundle in the corner. "Perhaps, while we wait, a few pretty baubles for the lovely ones in your harem, O great Amir?"

Ibn al-Ibrahim spoke up. "We have not come to buy anything. We seek information about the Frankish woman who your husband purchased as a slave many years ago."

Fearfully, the woman raised a hand. "I know nothing about her before she came here. Besides, she died…" she tried to think "…uh, some time ago. A whining tone entered her voice. "My husband died, and then, so did she, just when I needed her. Then my son deserted me, and I was left alone."

Diyar spoke for the first time, his voice ominous. "Your son, old woman? Was he not the son of the Frankish woman?"

The old woman's toothless mouth quivered. "Oh…yes…It is just that I thought of him as my own."

"Your own? Did you not treat him in the same manner you treated his mother—like a slave?"

The woman began to whimper. "But, O Great Amir, we broke

no law. The offspring of a slave is the owners' property. He was the one who broke the law by running away." Her voice hardened. "And you can be sure, when he is caught, he will be punished."

"He has been punished enough. He is dead."

A crash in the doorway snatched their attention. A tall, slim girl in brown rags stood frozen, the shards of a water jug at her feet. "Aaron dead," she whispered, then slowly folded to the floor in a faint.

Kareem, stepped in from the walkway, bent over and, dipping a handkerchief in the spilled water, laid the cool cloth across her forehead. The girl's face, fine-boned with dark, hollow eyes, was exquisite. He glanced up at his master with a wondering look. Who was this lovely creature?

The old woman skittered over and kicked the girl in the leg. "I-e-e, look what you have done. You broke the jug." She tried to kick the fallen figure again, but Kareem fended her off. Still she cried, "Get up, you lazy wench. We have important guests. They need refreshments."

Ibn al-Ibrahim spoke for all of them. "Who is this girl?"

"She is my daughter, and a lazier girl there never was."

It took but a glance to see this lovely creature could never be the woman's offspring. Diyar stepped in front of her. "The truth, whose child is this?"

The woman shrank back. "O Great Amir, God saw fit not to give me children." Bitterness tainted her voice. "She is the child of my husband and the Frankish slave, and she is as lazy and worthless as her mother."

The girl's eyes fluttered open, soft grey, under brown lashes. She looked up at Kareem. "Aaron?" she whispered. "Dead?"

He nodded, and tears filled her eyes.

"Aaron was her brother," the old woman said with disgust. "They and their mother always had their heads together trying to find ways to get out of work. In those times, we lived in a fine house, but my husband got sick and we lost it all." Her hand waved feebly. "Now we live in this hole, not fit for rats."

She started at the girl again, hand raised. "Now get up and find our guests some water."

Diyar gestured and Ibn al-Ibrahim quickly stopped the woman. "We need no water, thank you," the merchant said, then looked to the viceroy for instructions.

He nodded toward a battered, hardwood chest, and Kareem helped the girl to be seated. To Ibn al-Ibrahim, he said, "Bring the smaller box in my saddle bags."

The man hurried out, and the room fell silent.

The room, a storage room at the back of a boarded stall, was little bigger than arms-length. Its only piece of furniture was the chest. A rolled mat lay in the corner.

The tiny room was overwhelmed by the viceroy's presence. Over his white silk shirt and trousers, he wore a robe of yellow satin fringed with beaver, then an outer robe of red satin embroidered with gold thread and trimmed with miniver. His large, white turban was wrapped around a skull-cap of gold brocade. His gold weapons-belt, a personal gift from the sultan, glowed in the dim light. Its wide gold buckle was studded with rubies, emeralds and pearls. Sunlight from the narrow door glinted off the jeweled handle of his sword. Beside it the plain-handled dagger seemed out of place.

Still confused, the old woman once again reached for the dirty bundle of trinkets. "Perhaps now, O Great Amir, you would like to see my wares, perfect for the beauties of your harem."

Diyar, his arms folded, stared silently out the doorway.

In a moment, Ibn al-Ibrahim returned with a small, bronze chest. Diyar turned to the woman. "Old woman, I want to buy your slave."

Again fear shook the woman. "But, sire, she is all I have. I am old and sick. Without her I would surely die." Then craftiness entered her eyes. "How much?"

"I will not bargain with you." He nodded to Ibn al-Ibrahim. "Open it."

The chest's lid was raised to display a cache of gold coins.

"Here are five hundred gold dinars, enough to buy a dozen serving girls and to live long. Take the coins before I change my mind."

The chest was thrust upon the woman who staggered under its weight.

He turned to Ibn al-Ibrahim "I leave the details to you. Record the sale and send me her papers." He glanced at the girl. "Have her bathed and clothed and delivered to my palace in Karak. Kareem will stay back with some men as her escort."

He reached for the money bag attached to his belt under his tunic, but Ibn al-Ibrahim raised his hand with a smile. "Please allow me the honor to take care of this matter as a gift to a much-appreciated patron."

Diyar strode out, and Ibn al-Ibrahim helped the girl to her feet. "What is your name, child?"

She seemed unable to grasp what was happening. "Sarah, sire."

"Sarah, on this day, fortune has smiled on you." He marveled at her beauty. "Who would have thought in this hovel such a jewel would be found."

"But, sire...Aaron, my brother?"

"Ah, your brother. Worry no more about that. All will be explained to you in time." But he wondered, *Could I sleep soundly next to a girl whose mother I had raped, whose brother I had killed?*

The thought made him shudder.

CHAPTER 40

She entered his chamber with her eyes down, a girl little older than the two odalisques who accompanied her. A waistcoat of white silk, solid with pearls and fringed with gold thread, encircled her slim waist. Rose damask pantaloons brocaded with silver flowers revealed the subtle curves of her slim legs. Her long-sleeved caftan of white damask hung to the floor. A girdle the width of a hand and encrusted with diamonds, molded her shape perfectly. Her tarhah, a long scarf of silvery gauze trimmed with gold thread, hung from her head down her back. Tiny white boots, embroidered with gold, encased her feet.

He stared at her for a long time, then said, "Look at me, girl."

Her eyes flicked up.

Grey eyes! Under black lashes and brows. What a marvel.

Her eyes watched him unwaveringly. Finally he decided, and turned to Kareem. "Go to the mosque and fetch a qadi. I will marry the girl."

To the girl, he said, "Come up here. I want to tell you about your brother."

A chair was brought and she sat, her eyes still down.

"When your brother buried your mother, so great was his hate for me, he escaped Damascus and ran into the mountains. He was captured by Ismaili assassins and trained to obey their master. He had only one dream, to kill me. And one day he got his chance. Alas, his zeal was greater than his skill. Only after I had killed him, did I learn he was my son. I am sorry it ended as it did, but it could end no other way. Hate is the most harmful thing one can do to oneself. It is slow death. I only speeded the process."

They were married and the next year, she gave him a son, and the next year, a daughter was born on which the amir, now in his late fifties, doted. He named the boy Muctader, and the girl Shajar, after his first wife.

Karak was considered by the Muslim court in Cairo as being primarily a Christian city. Consequently, many of the more repressive Islamic laws were not enforced. This suited well its viceroy. And his wife, after becoming adjusted to her position and the power she possessed, began quietly attending the Christian basilica. Not long after, Sarah began calling her daughter Angelica, and Diyar did not protest.

In 1313, Diyar quietly celebrated his sixtieth birthday. Several years later, Oljaitu, the Il-Khan of Persia, died and was succeeded by his son Abu Said. Devoutly Muslim, the Mongol throne had finally been assimilated into the Persian culture and posed little threat to the powerful Mamluk Sultanate.

When Diyar approached seventy, the sultan ordered the invasion of the Christian Armenian Kingdom of Cilicia and its port city of Ayas, an economic rival to Alexandria.

Diyar called Muctader to his library. The cream-colored walls where circled by bookcases, the largest private library in the realm. After a servant left juice on a small table in front of their divan, Diyar turned to his son, now twelve.

"The sultan has ordered war against Cilicia. As this may be the last opportunity..." he did not add, whether because of his, Diyar's, advancing age, or because there simply were no more enemies to attack, "...I have decided to take you with me. Have your servants prepare your gear."

He watched to see if the order would stir excitement in the lad, and was not disappointed when it did not. He had long before decided Muctader would become a merchant, not a soldier. But before he did, he wanted him to see the horrors of war.

And see them he did, the blood, the death, the pillage and rape, and Diyar was inwardly pleased that the terrible sights disgusted the boy.

After Ayas had been razed, and Oshin, the Armenian King killed, Diyar asked the sultan for permission to visit his homeland on the banks of the Volga, that is, if Aibek, the great Khan of the Golden Horde would allow him passage on his land.

The sultan agreed, and Diyar, after sending a casket of gold to the Khan's ambassador in Trapezunt on the Black Sea, received travel permits, and he and Muctader and a bodyguard of twenty headed north. From Trapezunt, they sailed to Rostov, then boarded a barge up the Don River, cut across land to the Volga, there boarding another barge to cruise up that river.

Days cooled, and with the sea of grass that rolled away from the river, a haunting sense of memory, like the remembrance of an old dream, came upon Diyar. Had he really once lived in this lush, green land? At each village, he inquired about his clan, but none had heard of it. The great Mongol empire had swallowed it up.

Then, after a few days, he spied the palisades where his family had pitched their winter camp, and suppressing excitement, ordered the barge be put into shore.

He pointed to the cliffs and turned to Muctader. "When I was even younger than you, I used to climb...."

But the boy's attention was fixed on several polers who were playing dice in the bottom of the barge. "You know, father," the boy said without looking up, "when they are trying to get their numbers, with good odds, their winnings would be higher if they would increase their bets."

Diyar bit his lip and turned to disembark.

The mamluks led their horses down the gangplank, and a Mongol captain in charge of a patrol of Kipchaks rode up and demanded to see some kind of documentation. Diyar showed him, but it was obvious the Mongol could not read. The stolid soldier sent a rider flying for instructions, then withdrew and watched Diyar and his men with suspicion.

Diyar began to speak about the rigors of life as a nomad but soon saw his son listened with only mild interest. Life in a yurt of skins was beyond the grasp of a lad who grew up in the confines of a palace harem. Resignedly Diyar returned to the barge and ordered the captain to head back downstream.

Not long after their arrival back in Karak, Kareem died. He had over-exerted himself accompanying his master on the Armenian campaign. Diyar had protested his undertaking the journey—the old sarrajun sat a horse only with pain—but Kareem had insisted. He was not about to allow the back of his master be protected by anyone else.

Diyar had a small mausoleum built for him at Karak. He made inquiries to ascertain if Kareem had provided his four wives with an inheritance, and learned the canny servant had made numerous investments and was quite wealthy.

In May, 1332, Sultan Muhammad's eldest son, Anook, was married to the daughter of the Amir Bektimur al-Saqi. On the wedding night, the honored guests rode through the gate to Qal'at al-Jabal and up the Sultan's Road. After passing through several more gates they entered a large courtyard where five hundred mamluks wearing long white robes and turbans of green and black were drawn up in rank. Then another gate and the guests moved into a larger court where a thousand more warriors stood dressed in even more gaudy finery.

When the first Baybars became sultan, the country was poor, the mamluks shabbily garbed. Since then, throughout the Near East all trade competition was overcome, and all trade from the Far East, the silks, gems, spices, so dearly desired by Medieval Europe, passed through the sultanate. Sultan Muhammad and his amirs controlled the trade and their palaces became the most lavish and luxurious in the world.

Strict protocol was followed, and Diyar, being highly placed in the Empire's hierarchy, was, along with his men, among the first to pay his respects to the sultan. Before they reached the sultan's pavilion, they halted before seven successive curtains.

The men were given tall, lit candles. The curtain was drawn aside, and they bowed and kissed the ground. This continued until at last they came to face the sultan. He sat on a high dais, covered with fine carpets and shaded by a tent of rare and costly silks and decorated with gems. Once again Diyar and his men kissed the floor in front of his throne, then continued on.

After his amirs had passed in line, al-Nasir moved into his private quarters, where the amirs' wives presented themselves, kissing the floor and offering wedding gifts.

Then came the celebration. Every dancer and musician in Cairo had been summoned to Qal'at al-Jabal, and the rest of the night passed in music and dancing, until the time came to escort the bride, in a formal procession, to the bridal chamber.

The next day, the sultan held an immense reception where robes of honor were awarded to all the amirs, civil officials and qadi. More gifts were sent in to the wives. Twenty thousand animals were slaughtered for public feasting: sheep, cattle, chickens, and, because of the special occasion, horses. Nine hundred tons of sweets and sweet drinks were consumed by the city's populace.

When the festivities were over, knowing the sultan to be in a jubilant mood, Diyar requested a private audience. To enter the sultan's recently completed palace complex, he had to pass through a seemingly endless succession of halls and courtyards. The marble-tiled gardens contained sweet-smelling pomegranate and orange trees, with pools of cool water and splashing fountains. The palace apartments were ablaze with ceilings inlaid in gold and azure—patterns of colored glass shining high in vaulted walls. He crossed costly rugs spread upon mosaic-patterned floors, and the air quivered with the sweet warbling of singing birds, their golden cages suspended between each massive column.

When he was ushered into al-Nasir's private pavilion, he approached and bowed. "O Victorious King, live forever. With your permission I would like to use this auspicious occasion to ask a favor."

The sultan nodded benignly, and Diyar continued.

"Sire, I have served you long and loyally, but now I believe it time for a younger man to undertake the responsibility. So, with your permission, I wish to take this opportunity to resign my post as Viceroy of Karak."

Again al-Nasir nodded. "I will grant your request on one condition, you return here and allow me to build you a pleasure palace where we can meet and talk as the mood takes us."

"You give me great honor, Malana."

It was a wise move on the part of the canny sultan. Diyar's power and wealth had grown to the point where the sultan wanted him close so his movements could be monitored.

When Diyar and his men finally returned to Karak, laden with gifts and robes from a grateful sultan, Sarah requested an audience with him. In his private chamber she approached, eyes down.

"Grace be to you, my lord, and peace from God our Father," she said formally. "With your permission, I would speak with you."

In all the years they had been married, she had remained an enigma to him, and this was the first time she had ever initiated a conversation with him.

"Speak your heart, my wife."

"I fear a move to the capital. The people there have little affection for Christians. With your permission, I will not go."

"What will you do?"

"With your permission, I would like to travel to be with my mother's people. I have written letters to the Baron de Brissac, my uncle, and he has invited me to come live with him. With your permission, I will take Angelica and go there."

Diyar knew his wife's plans. She had used Count Gouffre's eldest son, Andre, to contact relatives in Normandy. Andre had done as asked, but kept Diyar posted about her actions. He dared not do otherwise.

But the loss of Angelica gave him pause. She had grown nearly as beautiful as her mother, and though she had had many offers of marriage, she never accepted any of them, nor did Diyar insist she do so. The offers had all come from amirs for their sons. They had been Muslims, she a Christian, and though this gulf had often been bridged by conversion for convenience sake, her faith was too deep for such hypocrisy.

Now he saw her accompanying her mother, though painful for him, was the best possible solution for her.

"The departure of you and Angelica will leave me with a heavy heart. Still, you have my permission to go. And I make you a guarantee, you will go in a manner befitting the daughter of a famous countess, and the wife of an amir of the great al-Malik-al-Nasir Muhammad."

If he could not have Angelica near his side in the waning years of his life, he would make sure she had the wherewithal to attract some worthy husband.

He turned the task of transporting Sara and Angelica to Andre, who split their treasure—the chests of gold, the many bolts of silk, and precious art works, including many Christian artifacts stolen during the numerous pillaging of the Frankish states, and the ten, perfectly matched, chestnut-colored Arabian pure-bred horses—into three Venetian freighters, with a half-dozen caravels sailing as protection against pirates.

Diyar sent a hundred of his finest men, carrying his banner and all dressed in matching blue silk robes, as protection.

Muctader also went along. There was a plan behind Diyar's sending such a treasure, and in such an ostentatious way. Weeks later, when the ships landed in Le Havre, a trading office was set up with Muctader representing Diyar's company. Diyar knew, when the Norman's saw the beautiful goods that his wife brought back from the Levant, many would want the same, and he wanted to be the merchant that provided them. But he never saw his family again.

MAMLUK

CHAPTER 41

Diyar's pleasure palace overlooked the sultan's polo ground. Often, after the sultan had played a chukker or two, he would join Diyar on his balcony for a cool drink.

In 1340, an Egyptian Christian finance clerk called Neshu won the acclaim of the sultan, and was placed in charge of revenue collection, the fattest plum of the sultanate's bureaucracy.

Neshu was a Copt, a bone-thin Ethiopian. Now he made a great show of converting to Islam. Soon he began conducting secret inquiries into the wealth of every amir or merchant. When he located a rich man, he would accuse the man of acquiring his money by dishonest means. He would then strip the victim of his wealth and turn it over to the sultan. With delight, the sultan watched his revenues' rapid increase.

Neshu's two brothers and his brother-in-law also received important positions. Any official opposing Neshu was accused of speculation, forbidden under Islamic law. He would then be tried before a bribed jury, sentenced, and his fortune forfeited.

Confident of the sultan's support, Neshu's outrages increased. Daily, some rich man was arrested and flogged until he handed over five or ten thousand dinars, money allegedly owed to the treasury.

Neshu grew so bold as to demand money from the amirs. And if an amir opposed him, he accused him of being a secret alcoholic, and the puritanical sultan would immediately exile the officer to some minor post on the frontier. The amirs lived in fear, knowing that any complaint against Neshu would mean their banishment, or worse, the poisoning by one of the larcenous official's assassins.

Neshu employed a band of old women, invisible in crowds, who skulked the city, spying and carrying out his orders of assassination with poison.

The sultan seemed in the dark about Neshu's evil methods. But perhaps not. He never had any great love for the amirs, and his sons had even greater disdain for them. The princes spurned the company of mamluks, and prowled the city in company of the lowest riffraff and the filthiest whores.

One day, as Diyar rode down from his palace enroute to the polo grounds, a great pain shot through his skull, and he fell, rolling in the dust. Quickly, his guards riding with him bore him back to the palace.

Through the pain he tried to smile. "I have not fallen from a horse since the old wolf laughed at me."

His guards thought him delirious.

Word streaked through the capital: "The old warrior is dying," and soon several amirs called to bring condolences.

He scoffed. "I am fine, my friends. I eat. I sleep. At my age, I can ask for no more," but his speech was slurred and his eyes leaked.

Then, after a moments hesitation, Bushtak, an old comrade, stepped forward. "O Amir, you are in a unique position to help us. You have shown great courage on the battlefield, show it once more for your khushdashiya. Would you undertake the mission of speaking to the sultan about his tax official's nefarious ways?"

Diyar nodded solemnly. "I would be honored. And if it is God's will, he will listen to reason."

"Thank you, but beware. Neshu's eyes are everywhere, and his finger of death can point at anyone."

When the sultan heard his old friend was bedridden, he came

to visit. As he entered the palace gates, and the word spread throughout the household of his arrival, an old woman with a glass on a tray hastened to Diyar's divan.

"Come, O great amir, the sultan is here. Quickly, this is from your physician. It is to relieve your pain."

Weakly he pushed her away. "The physician? That old fraud. He has never relieved anyone of anything but the weight of a purse."

But she would not be put off. "Quickly, sire. Drink your medicine so you will be able to speak with the sultan."

"All right," he said grumpily. "Give it to me and go."

She watched as he upended the vial, then slipped from the room.

Suddenly a spasm of pain stabbed him in his stomach, and he knew something was terribly wrong. He tried to rise, but his legs would not move, and he fell back. Then he knew. He had been poisoned.

He wanted to call for a servant, but his breath caught. Weariness and hopelessness overcame him. All he wanted to do was close his eyes and sleep.

His head jerked up. He had to stay alive just a few moments longer. It was his duty. He had one last mission.

His eyes slid to the doorway.

Where is he? Where is the sultan? I must speak to him before it was too late.

The effort to raise his head forced sweat to bead on his brow, but his face paled to gray.

He tried to focus on the doorway but could not move his head.

Will he never come?

The sultan, chatting with one of his officials, finally entered. He saw the sick man's ashen face twisted with pain, and a gasp escaped his throat.

He ran to his side. "O great amir, let me get you something. I will call for my physician," and he started to turn to a servant.

Diyar clutched at his sleeve. "Malana," he said, his voice little more than an a breath, "warning! Neshu is cheating you, stealing from you, but worse...,"

He gasped heavily several times. His eyes fluttered close, and his voice grew even fainter.

Al-Nasir leaned closer.

"...worse, sire, he destroys your subjects loyalty...." He fell back, and the room grew dim.

Distraught, the sultan shook his shoulders. "Live, O great amir," he cried. "Be it God's will you live."

But Diyar did not move. The last thing he heard was a voice in the distance, "O dear friend, forgive me. I sent the assassin to Karak. A wicked advisor whispered you were disloyal, as if you could be. Please, do not die without giving me your forgiveness."

But Diyar was gone.

Seeing this great man who had been such a fearless defender of his realm, his pale cheeks now wet with tears, the sultan could not keep from sobbing too.

Now he was truly alarmed. Diyar al-Mijiri had never lied to him. What he said at the moment of his death had to be true.

He twisted around and screamed, "Arrest the traitor Neshu. Arrest him now. I want him in chains in my iwan before I get back. Search his house. He claims to live in poverty. Let us see if he speaks the truth."

Fifteen thousand dinars of gold were found at the tax collector's home, as were ropes of pearls, jewels, gold and silver artifacts and antiques, silk tapestries embroidered with gold, rare china dinner services, and articles of luxury. Great quantities of food were found stored: two hundred jars of fish, quantities of cheese. Also much bacon and four hundred jars of wine—so much for his pious claims at being a devout Muslim. Four hundred suits of clothing not yet worn, women's dresses, costly textiles, the list went on and on.

The house of his brother-in-law was also ransacked and found to contain valuables worth some twenty-five thousand dinars.

When Neshu and his brothers were marched in, and their

goods laid before al-Nasir, the sultan felt the deep bite of shame. So many times he had defended the tax collector in front of the amirs, and here was the proof of the man's guilt.

He stood and roared, "May God damn all Copts. I want him and all his relatives tortured to their last breath. These traitors claimed to have served me faithfully for eight years. Would their pain could last as long."

When the people of the city learned of the arrest and death of the corrupt official and his gang, so great was their relief, they closed all the shops, decorated the streets, and spent a week in a mad revelry.

At an appropriate time following the celebration, a solemn procession commemorating the life of Amir Muqaddam Rukn al-Din Diyar al-Mijiri al-Baybariya, Viceroy of Karak, moved through the city. The sultan ordered a great mausoleum built for his friend and faithful subject, and it can still be seen on the outskirts of Cairo, although it is now claimed by tour guides to have been built for a famous caliph.

The End

ABOUT THE AUTHOR

PAUL BRANDIS has served tours in the U. S. Navy, and Marine Corps. He earned degrees in Art History and Philosophy, and taught Art History, and Drawing and Painting at a college in Washington State. He is a widower with two children and three beautiful granddaughters. He lives in a condo overlooking Puget Sound and drives a dark-red Jaguar coupe named RADIANT that is so fast it's spooky.

www.ingramcontent.com/pod-product-compliance
Lightning Source LLC
Chambersburg PA
CBHW071041250626
47159CB00002B/324